Previously published Worldwide Suspense titles by
JANE ISAAC

THE TRUTH WILL OUT
A DEATHLY SILENCE
BEFORE IT'S TOO LATE
BENEATH THE ASHES

THE LIES WITHIN

JANE ISAAC

W❂RLDWIDE

TORONTO • NEW YORK • LONDON
AMSTERDAM • PARIS • SYDNEY • HAMBURG
STOCKHOLM • ATHENS • TOKYO • MILAN
MADRID • WARSAW • BUDAPEST • AUCKLAND

W🌐RLDWIDE™

Recycling programs
for this product may
not exist in your area.

ISBN-13: 978-1-335-91084-4

The Lies Within

First published in 2017 by Legend Press Ltd.
This edition published in 2021.

Copyright © 2017 by Jane Isaac

This edition published by arrangement with Harlequin Books S.A.

For questions and comments about the quality of this book,
please contact us at CustomerService@Harlequin.com.

Harlequin Enterprises ULC
22 Adelaide St. West, 40th Floor
Toronto, Ontario M5H 4E3, Canada
www.ReaderService.com

Printed in U.S.A.

THE LIES WITHIN

To Colin Williams
The best storyteller I know

PART ONE

PROLOGUE

August 2016-Criminal Court 3, Leicester Crown Court

THE BARRISTER TILTS his head back. "Members of the jury, I turn your attention to Grace Daniels, the woman who stands before you this afternoon."

The eyes of the courtroom descend upon Grace. She searches for a gap in the sea of faces, desperately trying to maintain her composure while avoiding the anxious gaze of her youngest daughter, Lydia, seated next to the rest of her family in the public gallery. Right now she wants nothing more than to be swaddled in the comfort of their support. But even the shortest of glances will induce fresh tears to her eyes. And she can't allow that to happen. Not now.

The barrister, James Sheldon, a tall, slender man with curls of thick brown hair that tumble out of the back of his wig, pauses for the briefest of moments. "During the course of this trial you will hear accounts from friends, family, neighbours and employers about her good character and nature. She is a mother, sister-in-law, daughter and grandmother. A woman who works and contributes to the fabric of society. But you are not here to consider her character. You are here to examine the facts." His words hang in the air as he moves down the line, pulling the eyes of every juror with him.

Grace notices Lydia turn away and risks a fleeting

glance. When her girls were young she'd impressed upon them the importance of being honest. "You have nothing to worry about if you've done nothing wrong," she would say. What would Lydia make of that today? She's sixteen now, although her blue eyes bulge with the same trepidation they held on her first day at school.

Grace flicks her gaze to the jury. Seven women and five men. On the face of it, they seem a reasonable mix. Earlier that morning, several of them faltered over their words as they were sworn in. It was strange to think that they could possibly feel more nervous than she. The woman on the end wore a dark jumper overlaid with a colourful vintage scarf. Sheets of hair were tucked behind her ears, her expression kind and comforting.

Sheldon is concluding the prosecution opening with the assured confidence of a man skilled in his art. In spite of the curled wig, the black gown that flaps behind him as he moves, his gestures are convincingly subtle. A simple touch. A gentle, considered turn. No sweeping theatrics. Not a moment's hesitation in his voice.

Grace looks across at the profile of Eleanor Talbot-Deane, her defence barrister, through the glass screen that separates her from the courtroom. Eleanor is as still as stone. His words haven't fazed her, yet Grace feels her hands start to tremble and squeezes them together.

"Over the next few days the Crown will produce compelling evidence to support the fact that this woman meticulously planned a cold-blooded murder."

Grace recoils, aware of Lydia's eyes boring into the side of her face. They'd talked about this moment several times. Together. With her solicitor. With her barrister. As a family. But no amount of talking could prepare her for the real prospect of losing her mother to the confines of prison walls. No child should ever have to watch a parent on trial.

"You will hear evidence that places her at the scene, witnesses who heard her plan the murder," Sheldon continues. "Plan how to kill a woman who considered herself a friend."

A head on the jury turns. The woman with the vintage scarf. Grace imagines she is just like her, with a job and a family; a small dog that sits beside her on the sofa while she watches *MasterChef* on television. But there is no familiarity in her expression, no sorority. Just cold, hard shock.

Grace's throat constricts. Even though she has been briefed on how to react: what to say, what not to say. Even though she has been dragged through hours of police questioning, nothing can truly prepare her for the exhausting fatigue that exudes from the intensity of hanging on to every word, every tiny detail, still trying to find a hole in the evidence mounting against her. And this is only the beginning of a trial that is scheduled to run for days.

"Be under no illusions by her smart clothes, her kind face, her eloquent manner. Do not form judgements. I implore you to keep a clear mind and consider the evidence in front of you. And that evidence alone. This woman is guilty of murder. And by the time this trial has finished, you will be in no doubt that she should go to prison for life."

CHAPTER ONE

10 months earlier

DETECTIVE INSPECTOR WILL JACKMAN watched the brown fluid ooze into the Styrofoam cup. It was surprising how quickly he'd developed a taste for this excuse for coffee when it was all that was available. The iridescent lights buzzed and flickered as he made his way back down the corridor.

It was darker in his office, a single desk lamp providing the only light in the small area. A nest of photos stared back at him as he sat and sipped his drink. Jackman had seen many shocking images over the years: bodies gouged with gunshot wounds, stab victims left in a pool of their own blood, dismembered body parts after car accidents. Every one of them stayed with him, but none more so than the living. The bright eyes of these young women had screamed of youth, opportunity, vitality. Until they were brutally assaulted.

He moved the photos aside and instead stared into the faces of the victims after the attack. Seventeen-year-old Eugenie Trentwood's long hair was the only resemblance she bore to the original photo. Her right eye was swollen to twice the size; a gash in her temple resembled a puckered pair of lips. Almost immediately, detectives linked the case with the unsolved attack on Shelley Barnstaple, nine years earlier. Just a year older than Eugenie at the time of the incident, the swelling around Shelley's crown was so severe it gave the appearance of an odd-shaped head. Dark smudges sat beneath her eyes. Both women had been attacked on their way home from a night out, within a mile of each other in Leicester's Oadby district.

He dug out the map, slowly ran his finger along each of their routes on the nights of the incidents. Eugenie had been walking down a side alley, almost home. Shelley had taken a shortcut across waste ground. Both had a ligature thrown around their neck. They awoke later to find themselves on the ground. They'd been sexually assaulted. Eugenie's stilettos had disappeared. Shelley's necklace stolen. Neither saw anything.

Jackman sat back in his chair. He'd protested fiercely when Superintendent Janus had called him into her office, a few weeks earlier, and told him she was assigning him to special projects. "The force are rewriting their public protection policy. I'd like you to be the regional lead on adult sexual offences." She'd dressed it up as a developmental move, temporarily promoting him to Chief Inspector, seconding him to region to visit neighbouring forces and review outstanding cases with a view to looking for links and streamlining methods of working. "It'll be a good opportunity to see how other serious crime teams work, to network with other senior investigating officers," she had said, peering up at him from beneath her heavy fringe. Jackman could see the merit of review teams: a fresh pair of eyes, a new approach when all previous leads had dried up. But the prospect of several weeks being confined to a desk, picking through the bones of someone else's investigation with a view to overhauling working practises just left him numb.

He switched back to the photos. Bruising and indentation on their necks indicated the presence of a ligature. Both women had been taken to within an inch of their life, and yet they hadn't been killed. Whoever had done this had wanted them to live with the enduring terror.

In spite of an army of CSIs dispatched to comb both scenes, they'd recovered nothing of any significance. Stranger attacks were relatively rare. Most people were assaulted by someone they knew, someone close to them. Yet officers hadn't found anything in either of the girls' backgrounds to indicate a stalker or somebody acting out of the ordinary and, apart from the fact that they were both of slight build with long curly hair, nothing to indicate why the assailant had picked those two, or to explain the time lapse in between.

Speculation about a serial offender grew in the media as confidence in the police waned. He looked back at the fresh-faced photo of Eugenie. Seventeen years old. Her family claimed she was a diligent student with an ambition to become a lawyer. This time last year she would have been studying for her GCSEs.

But endless hours of interviewing officers, trawling through bank records, phone logs and rereading witness statements had yielded nothing new. Even after visiting the victims and their families, hopeful faces staring across at him, imploring some new evidence that might put an end to their terror, Jackman was no closer to finding a motive, let alone a suspect. And he had nothing to help him write the first part of his tedious policy report.

He glanced across at the pile of boxes on the desk

opposite. The word "archive" made him flinch. It suggested a pile of historical documents, or old bank records, not statements, phone records or items of bloody clothing belonging to real people. These women were somebody's sister, somebody's daughter. Victims of real crimes left unsolved. The investigation was code-named Operation Ascott. Files would be kept open, fresh appeals put out for information, but the evidence of those crimes that had cast a shadow over their lives and of those around them was destined to be bundled up and shut away in the confines of a dark box.

The window rattled in the light breeze. Jackman checked his watch. Almost midnight. Not for the first time, he cursed the roadworks on the Coventry roundabout. He knew there would be cars almost at a standstill, even at this late hour. The subsequent tailbacks and delays on his commute from Stratford this past week had forced him to check into a hotel nearby. Although, right now, he was hardly in a rush to get to the bland hotel room.

The sound of his mobile buzzing at this late hour startled him. He fished it out of his pocket.

"Sir, this is Inspector Peters, Leicester control room. The body of a woman has been found in rural Leicestershire. Our duty SIO is handling a drugs-related kidnapping in the east of the city. You're listed as reserve."

Jackman grabbed his pen. "What do we know?"

"A cyclist discovered the body on his ride home from work at 23.18 hours and called it in. The CID nightshift are escorting him back to the station to make a statement. The victim is naked, thought to be late teens. Looks like she's been strangled. Nothing to indicate her ID." He relayed the address.

"No other witnesses?" Jackman asked, jotting down the details.

"Not, as yet. Uniform have cordoned off the area. CID have called in CSI and a pathologist. DS Wilson is at the scene. She'll fill you in." Jackman stood, dislodging a pile of papers on the corner of his desk in his haste.

"One other thing."

He watched the papers splash to the floor. "Yes?"

"The body shows signs of sexual assault."

LEICESTER LANE WAS a quiet country road flanked by trees on one side and a ditch that ran practically its full length on the other. Bare fields unrolled into the open countryside beyond.

Jackman parked up at the end of a line of cars. Under the obliging light of a full moon, he could see a huddle of CSIs further up the road, skirting around a temporary lamp.

The blue and white police tape flapped in the breeze as he climbed out of the car and opened the boot. He was struggling with the zipper on his holdall when he heard a voice behind him. "You must be our SIO." He whisked around, just as the woman pulled back her hood and proffered her hand. "Sergeant Dee Wilson." Her words sent a spray of white air out into the night.

"Will Jackman." He shook her hand.

Her white teeth gleamed against her dark skin as she smiled back up at him. "Have the control room filled you in?"

"Pretty much." Jackman relayed the scant details. "Anything else I should know?" He retrieved some coveralls from the bag and started pulling them on.

"I don't think so. There's not much to go on at the moment."

Jackman was bent down, snapping on his overshoes when he felt another presence nearby.

"Sergeant Wilson!"

He followed the voice and stood back to see a heavy-set man in a dark jacket approach. Raven hair was gelled back from an inquisitive face.

Wilson turned. "Well, well. Artie Black, *Leicester Herald*'s finest. Caught a whiff of this one quickly, didn't you? You'd better keep out of our way, otherwise you'll be in line for the next sniffer dog intake." The journalist gave a fake chortle. "Can't tell you anything at the moment, Artie," Wilson added.

"Come on, now. You must have something?" The journalist pointed at Jackman. "Who's this?"

"This is DCI Jackman," Wilson said. "You're wasting your time, Artie. He won't tell you anything either."

Artie reached out a hand, which Jackman reluctantly shook. The handshake was firm, eager. Jackman withdrew to find a business card in his palm. "Give me a shout as soon as you've got something," Artie said. "I'm sure we can work together on this."

Jackman shook his head and shoved the card into his pocket as Artie disappeared into the shadows. He fleetingly wondered how much time the journalist spent skulking around, watching, waiting for the next scoop. It was pitiful.

Tiny stars peeked out of the inky blue sky above. Jackman scanned the surrounding area. It was remote and unlit. "I understand the informant was a cyclist?" he said as they started to walk towards the other officers.

Wilson nodded. "He's back at the station, giving a statement."

"What was he doing cycling down here in the middle of the night?"

"This road links the back end of Market Harborough with Airfield Business Park. Mostly warehouses and factory units. Many of their workers are on shift patterns. We'll check it out, of course, but I'm guessing he was on a late shift."

"Anything on the victim?"

Wilson shook her head. They'd reached the edge of the tape now and she turned her attention to the officer guarding the cordon, exchanging pleasantries as they paused to sign the incident log.

They drew closer to the light. A CSI was moving around, photographing the body from all angles. A woman in blue coveralls was crouched down in the ditch examining the body.

"Morning, Celeste," Wilson said as they approached. "This is DCI Jackman, our SIO."

The pathologist stood, stretched her shoulders back and beamed. "I know Will Jackman," she said, a rich French accent coating her words. She snapped off a glove, pushed away the wisps of dark hair escaping from her hood and shook his hand, then looked towards Wilson. "We worked together…goodness, it must be ten years ago now, when I was training."

"Good to see you again, Celeste," Jackman said. "How're you doing?"

"Okay, thanks. Nothing a couple more hours of sleep couldn't cure. How are your lovely family?"

Jackman hesitated for a second before he replied. "Fine, thanks." He lowered his eyes to the victim. She was petite, her face ornate, almost doll-like, even with her glassy eyes hung open. Brown hair was swept back and coiffed into a twist making the dark ring that encircled her neck all the more prominent.

Celeste inhaled a long breath before she spoke. "Looking at the welt around her neck and the enlarged tongue I'm pretty sure the cause of death was strangulation. Bruising on the inner thighs indicates possible sexual interference." She pulled off her other glove, scratched the side of her face. "Rigor is just starting to set in. I'd estimate time of death within the last 4-5 hours. Looking at the environment and the state of the body, I'd say she was attacked elsewhere. She looks too clean to have been killed here, but I'll be more sure when I get her back to the lab."

Jackman crouched down. The blueish tinge on the victim's torso made her look cold and exposed. He felt an urge to cover her over. "Any signs of a struggle?"

"Some sporadic grazes and bruising on her forearms. Could be defensive. Not enough to suggest she put up much of a fight though."

"Possibly someone she knew then?"

"Maybe. I'll know more when I get a better look at her."

As Jackman stood he noticed a CSI wandering towards them holding an evidence bag out at an odd angle. A single piece of jewellery slipped about in the bottom. "Not sure if this is relevant, but we found it in the hedge up the way." Jackman followed his gaze to a line of hawthorn hedging. It couldn't have been more than ten yards from the body.

Jackman thanked the CSI, took the bag and peered in closer. "Looks like an earring of some sort." He pulled out his torch and shone it on the contents. It was silver, inlaid with what appeared to be blue, white and black circles of glass. There was a tiny chip in the side, but it didn't look weathered. It hadn't been there long.

"It's an evil eye," Wilson said. "They were all over the place when I went on holiday to Turkey last year. Supposed to protect you against bad luck."

Jackman looked back at the victim. Her ears were bare. "Why remove her clothes, yet leave something like this nearby?"

Wilson shrugged. "Maybe it slipped out, or they dropped it?"

Jackman glanced around him at the rough scrub. "After taking the trouble to strip her, bring her out here?" He turned to Celeste. "What do you think they used to strangle her with?"

"The marks are distinct, fairly straight and deep," Celeste said. "Some kind of strapping, I'd say."

"Dee, has anyone checked for missing person reports?"

Wilson snapped a nod. "Already done, sir."

"Good. Get them to check the National Missing Persons' Database too, will you? And ask someone to compile a list of all known sex offenders in the area. We could do with checking their movements yesterday evening."

Wilson walked away, pressing her mobile phone to her ear. Jackman stared out into the darkness. It seemed a strange place to leave a body, especially with the promise of traffic, albeit a slow stream, running through from the nearby industrial estate.

Shoes squeaked on the tarmac behind him. Wilson pocketed her phone as she rejoined him. The whites of her eyes looked oddly eerie in the darkness. "Done.

The list should be ready by the time we get back to headquarters."

The mention of headquarters reminded Jackman he wasn't on home territory. Unlike his home force of Warwickshire, Leicestershire preferred their incident rooms to run out of their head office and had designated suites for them. He wouldn't get away with calling in favours and setting up a room in a nearby station here. He took another look at the surrounding countryside. A quick scan of the map earlier showed the small market town to be on the edge of the Leicestershire border, almost twenty miles from the Enderby-based headquarters.

"Okay, take the cordon out wider and make sure it's guarded," Jackman said. "We don't want any more visiting reporters. And get a tent erected over her, please."

CHAPTER TWO

THE FIRST THING Jackman heard as he entered the incident room was the shrill sound of phones ringing in unison in the background. He immediately thought of Artie Black back at the crime scene. It didn't take long for the vultures to descend.

A single photograph of the victim sat beside a map of the area on the board at the front.

Officers in plain clothes gathered around the board as they entered. Wilson moved to the front, briefing them on their findings so far. "ID is our current priority," she said. "Who does the earring belong to? Let's get the victim's photograph circulated to neighbouring forces, and keep trawling through the Missing Persons' Database."

She looked across at Jackman. "Some of you will have met DCI Jackman, who's been with us reviewing our sexual offences cases over the past couple of weeks. We're very fortunate to still have his assistance as SIO at the moment. He came out to the scene with me tonight."

Jackman stepped forward and turned to address the array of faces in front of him. "Thank you everyone, for coming in at short notice. I really appreciate your input. Please speak up if you have any thoughts at all, however insignificant you may think they are. Sometimes the smallest point can lead us in the right direction." He smiled as he continued. "Most of us haven't worked together before, so please raise your hand when you wish to speak and introduce yourself." He turned to the map again, pointed at the single marker indicating the crime scene. "Okay, the pathologist is pretty sure that the victim was killed elsewhere and moved to this point. Why there? We need to check all routes leading to Leicester Lane for police cameras and scrutinise the CCTV footage for vehicles heading in that direction. Who interviewed the informant?"

A hand rose at the back of the room. A female officer wearing a stretched white shirt, that looked like it could probably have done with a damn good iron, and dark hair pulled back into a high ponytail spoke up, "DC Emma Parsons." A brief smile flickered across her face. "I interviewed the informant. A Ray Shields. He'd just finished a ten-hour shift at Carlson's Distribution Centre and was cycling home to Main Street, Great Bowden in Market Harborough when he noticed the body at the side of the road. He says he thought the local kids had been messing about at first, leaving a shop mannequin with her hair all tied up in the ditch. When he dismounted and saw it was a body, he called the police."

"Thanks, Emma. What are your initial thoughts?"

"He was shaken, understandably so. We contacted his workplace. His account checks out, they have a clocking-in system and CCTV. He lives with his wife. There's no police record or intelligence on him. We took his clothes for forensic examination, just in case."

"Thanks. Let's run all the usual background checks on him, bank accounts, phone and so on, to make sure that he's not linked to the victim in any way."

The officer looked up from her notes and nodded as Jackman continued. "We'll need to contact the key holders for the units at the nearby industrial estate. Get details of who was working and when they finished. Did they employ security firms that visited the site at night and might have passed through Leicester Lane?" He paused for a moment. "Is there any news on that list of registered sex offenders in the area?"

"We've gathered it together." Jackman followed the Scottish accent to a grey-haired bear of a man with his shirt-sleeves rolled up at the back of the room. "It'll take a while to work our way through it. Is there any chance our victim could be linked to Operation Ascott?"

"And you are?"

"Stuart McDonald, sir."

"Thank you, Stuart." Jackman thought back to the body. "It's difficult to say at this stage. The victim's profile fits with the other girls: female, late teens, sexually assaulted, ligature marks around her neck. No suggestion she was beaten though. The pathologist reckons she was strangled with a strap or belt. But if it is linked they've changed their approach. She wasn't merely assaulted. She was killed and stripped naked. Initial thoughts are they moved the body afterwards. Why?"

"Maybe something went wrong?"

"It's possible. The autopsy is scheduled for this morning. They'll run the usual toxicology tests. The scene has been secured. We'll get a POLSA search team out at first light to examine the surrounding area and see what else comes up. Let's focus on missing persons and see if we can identify the victim. We'll get a press appeal out for any sightings, so brace yourselves for more phone calls. Thank you, everyone."

Wilson sidled across as the officers dispersed to their desks. "Do you have somebody on call in your press office?" Jackman asked her. "We could do with putting an appeal out for witness sightings as soon as possible—late night dog walkers, people that were in the area to come forward. The press have already got hold of this. Let's give them something to report before they have a chance to start poking about themselves."

Wilson nodded. "I'll get hold of someone."

"Thanks."

Jackman wandered down the corridor to his office and dumped his coat over the back of the chair. The pile of papers were still scattered haphazardly on the floor. He bent down to gather them up and pulled out the photo of Eugenie Trentwood taken after her attack. Her face looked pale, sallow. He stood and replaced the case notes and photos in a wire tray on the corner of his desk, settling down to outline their findings, something that would form the basis of a structure for an investigation. He was vaguely aware of a mug of coffee pushed under his nose, phones ringing in the background, officers passing in the corridor, the sound of keys tapping through the open door.

By the time Wilson put her head around the doorframe, he was watching the footage of the informant's interview on his laptop. Ray Shields was a thin man with pinched features, swamped by the dark jogging suit he'd changed into to replace his cycling clothes. His voice held the edge of a stutter as he diligently answered the questions. Jackman watched his body language, looked for signs of latent guilt. But all he saw was a terrified middle-aged man, haunted by the images he'd witnessed earlier that evening. Images that would no doubt revisit his thoughts on many occasions in the upcoming days, weeks and months ahead.

"Sir, I think there's something you should see," Wilson said.

The excitement in her voice caught Jackman's attention. He followed her down the corridor and into the incident room. Officers were searching through filing cabinets, watching footage, talking into phone receivers.

Wilson moved over to DC McDonald in the corner, who was working his screen with his mouse, and beckoned Jackman to join them. "CSIs found a student discount card in the hedging, about fifty yards from where the earring was found," she said. "It belongs to a student named Jo Lamborne, from The University of Nottingham."

"We're thinking the card belongs to the victim?"

"It's a photo ID card. We're just getting it enlarged."

McDonald tapped a few more keys and sat back. "There."

The head of a young woman filled the computer screen. Her face was stretched into a wide smile; corkscrew curls rested on her shoulders. Her brown eyes sparkled and at this angle she appeared to be staring back at them. It was slightly disconcerting. Seconds later, the photo was reduced to make room for the image of the victim to fit alongside. Jackman switched from one to the other. The curls were missing, the hair twisted gently back behind her head, but the resemblance was striking.

"Do we know what she was doing in Leicestershire?" Jackman asked.

McDonald clicked a few more keys. The photos were replaced with a page of broken text. He paused a few seconds, and then highlighted a couple of lines close to the middle of the screen. "Jo Lamborne, on the voters' register at 102 Arden Way, Market Harborough. Also registered there are Grace and Philip Daniels. And there's a minor living at the same address, a Lydia Lamborne."

"Different names," Wilson said.

McDonald scrolled down. "Grace was previously known as Lamborne. Looks like she changed her name, remarried maybe."

"Are any of them known to us?" Jackman asked.

"No, not that I can see."

Jackman turned to the rest of the room. "Okay, it looks like we might have identified the victim as a Jo Lamborne, a student from The University of Nottingham, possibly home visiting friends or relatives. Let's see what we can find out about her. What was she studying at Nottingham? Does she have a boyfriend? Who are her friends, acquaintances, family? Who did she go out with tonight? Keep it low-key at the moment. Sergeant Wilson and I will head out to see the family. We don't want any details of the victim getting out before she's been formally identified."

Jackman thanked the room and followed Wilson across to the board at the front. She stretched a hand up towards the top of the map, pointing out 102 Arden Way, Market Harborough, then followed it down to a marker near the bottom, indicating the crime scene. "The address is only a couple of miles from where the victim was found," she said. "Everything is pretty close in Market Harborough, it's such a compact little market town."

"Morning!" Jackman followed the eyes of the room

to Detective Superintendent Taylor who beamed as he entered. "Thanks for putting in the extra hours," he said. He weaved through the desks with the agility of a man far younger than his years and smiled at Wilson as he reached them. "Hi, Dee. How's it going?"

"Good, thanks, sir. We've just got a potential ID on the body."

"Excellent. Keep me posted," he said and abruptly faced Jackman. "Could I have a word?"

Jackman followed the superintendent down the corridor, past the office he had been using this past two weeks, until they reached the door before the lift. Cool air rushed out of the room as Taylor opened it and switched on the light. It looked like a meeting room of sorts, with a round table in the middle, a couple of cushioned chairs surrounding. Taylor undid his jacket and sat, indicating for Jackman to do the same. The light glistened through the thinning grey hairs around his crown.

He settled back into his chair. "Why don't you bring me up to speed?"

Jackman checked his watch. Almost 6am. He was impressed to see Taylor in the office so early, although not surprised. In the short time he'd been seconded to Leicester HQ he'd had several dealings with Taylor who managed the Homicide and Major Incident Team. Taylor was a trained detective himself, showed a personal interest in the cases under his watch and knew each of his staff by first name. Jackman sighed inwardly. With talk of direct entrant inspectors, that kind of old school, hands-on experience was likely to be on the decline. He laid out their progress so far.

"Nothing from the press appeal yet?" Taylor asked as Jackman finished up.

"Not yet, but it's still early. The radio has promised to put out hourly bulletins, asking for anyone that passed through the area last night, or close by, to contact us, and the *Herald* have already put our appeal on their web page. I've made a start on a policy log, outlining the current strategies and priorities."

"Very thorough. We appreciate your help." He leant forward. "If you let me have your notes, we'll take it from here."

Jackman took a breath, held it a moment before he answered. "I'd like to be Senior Investigating Officer on this one."

Taylor stared at him. Frowned slightly. "You're seconded to region. I should bring in another SIO."

"There are possible links with Operation Ascott. I'll work with Wilson. If it's the same perpetrator, I'll spot the links."

"I'm not sure."

"We have a live time situation here. If you bring somebody else in there'll be a delay at a crucial part of the investigation."

A muscle flexed in Taylor's jaw. "What are the possible links with Op Ascott?"

"A woman attacked, sexually assaulted, late teens. Ligature marks around her neck."

"Is that it?"

"Do you need any more?"

"She could have been attacked by a boyfriend."

"It's possible," Jackman said. "The first two women were attacked in relatively quiet, isolated areas. This one is different. They took the trouble to drive her out to a rural area. Moving the body was risky."

"So, we don't think it's the same offender?"

"It's a different approach, but that doesn't necessarily mean it's not the same person. Maybe it's not connected. Or maybe it is and they are changing the way they work, growing in confidence, adapting." He mentioned the presence of the journalist in Leicester Lane that morning.

"Artie Black. He's just a pain in the arse."

"Whatever we think right now, these are high profile cases that remain unsolved. The attacker is still out there. The press are bound to make links. We need to act fast, reassure the public." Taylor walked across to the window, rested his hands on his hips and stared out into the night, deep in thought. "Look at it from the public's point of view," Jackman continued. "You are pulling out all the stops, assigning the regional lead on adult sexual offences to the case. Shows initiative, positive action."

Taylor rubbed his chin and turned back. His face brightened a little at the last words. It never ceased to amaze Jackman how sometimes you had to massage an ego in order to sell a decision. He also knew that Taylor was due to retire in a few weeks. He'd heard talk in the office, they were planning his retirement party. No detective, especially one with a record as decorated as his, would want to leave under the shadow of such a high profile investigation, still ongoing. "I'll speak to your Super and the Assistant Chief Constable. But I'm not making any promises."

A door clicked open behind them. Wilson's face appeared around the doorframe. "We really need to go, sir."

Jackman switched back to Taylor. "Do you mind?"

Taylor stood. "Okay, continue as you are for now. I'll see what I can do. But keep your phone with you."

CHAPTER THREE

GRACE WAS UNPACKING the dishwasher when the door-bell rang. It was almost 7am and darkness still clung to the windows outside, holding onto the final minutes of night. Her head felt woolly from the evening before, but nothing, it seemed, not even a hangover, would prevent her habitual early rising.

Lucky, her Jack Russell, started barking almost immediately. She hushed the dog and shut her in the kitchen, rushing out to answer before they rang the bell again.

Phil was already at the door by the time Grace reached the hallway. His eyes met hers for long enough to pull a face. They weren't expecting visitors. He opened the door to reveal a tall man with a mop of dark hair, a solid stance and striking green eyes. The black woman next to him was smaller, but almost as stocky. Her mouth formed a thin smile. She looked past Phil towards Grace. "Mrs Daniels?"

Grace didn't answer, switching her gaze from one to the other. "Has something happened?"

"I'm Detective Sergeant Wilson and this is Acting Detective Chief Inspector Jackman. Are you Mrs Grace Daniels?" Grace nodded slowly, taking in the plain clothes and ID badges in their hands. "May we come in?"

An icy chill slid down Grace's back, rooting her to the spot.

"Grace?" Phil touched the edge of her elbow.

"Sorry." She moved aside.

They made a play of wiping their feet as they entered. Lucky gave a few excited barks as Phil guided them into the front room and invited them to sit.

"Mrs Daniels, would you join us?" the female detective called back.

Grace was still standing in the hall, slowly closing the door. Spurred on to move by the detective's request she followed them in, moved across to the other sofa and sat down.

"Is your daughter Jo Lamborne?" Wilson asked.

Grace gave a single nod.

"Can you tell me where she is right now?"

"What?" Grace replied, barely able to trust her own hearing.

"A body has been discovered. I'm sorry to say, we believe it is possibly your daughter, Jo."

Grace's throat constricted. "No, she's upstairs. In her bedroom. Asleep, no doubt." She glanced at Phil. "We were at my niece's wedding reception last night. She came home after us."

"Have you seen her this morning?"

Silence saturated the room. Grace looked from one detective to another, jumped up and ran towards the stairs, ignoring the voices calling out after her. The short journey to Jo's room was laboured, like wading through water. Finally she reached the door, pushed it open. And then gasped. The curtains were undrawn, the bed made.

Grace opened the wardrobe, leaving the doors to

bang shut as she ducked to look underneath the bed. Desperation wrenched every ounce of energy from her limbs. She was so sure Jo had come in late. After they'd all gone to bed.

She collapsed on the edge of the bed as Phil joined her, covering her face. The shrill pitch that escaped her pierced the air.

Phil rushed to her side and enveloped her in his arms.

The sound of a door snapping open followed. Lydia appeared, her fair hair messy and unkempt. A sleep crease ran the length of her cheek. She blinked wide. "What's happened? Mum?"

Phil stood, reached out a protective arm, but she shrugged it away. "What's going on?"

"Something's happened to Jo," he said.

"What do you mean?"

Grace raised her eyes, opened her mouth to speak and closed it again.

Another face at the doorway. Detective Wilson. "I'm sorry but I need to ask you all to come downstairs."

Lydia looked from one to another, confounded, but said nothing.

Grace's world blurred as she descended the stairs. Family photos traced her route. The girls when they were young on the beach, bridesmaids in blue silk dresses at her friend's wedding, with Lucky as a puppy. The images swirled in front of her eyes, merging together. Jo. Her Jo.

Before Grace realised it she was back in the front room, sandwiched between Phil and Lydia. Lucky gave a bark from the kitchen. The nausea waned, but her head was swimming. Now it was Detective Jackman that sat forward and folded his hands, empathy etched on his face.

Phil turned to him. "Can you tell us what's happened?"

"We still have to establish that," Jackman said gently. "But we are treating her death as suspicious."

"You mean murder?" Lydia's voice splintered. Her hand flew to her face. Grace reached out, pulled her close, animal instincts taking over as she protected her young.

"I'm afraid so."

Grace pressed her eyes together, for the first time aware of the salty tears stinging her cheeks. "Where?"

"A body was found in Leicester Lane, just before midnight. By a man cycling home from work."

A gasp from Lydia. It subsided into sobs. She buried her head in her mother's shoulder.

Grace sat very still, uncomfortably aware of the detective's eyes darting about, taking in the photos of her daughters at various stages of growth that littered the walls; the framed picture of her parents above the dining room table at the far end; the toddler photos of their granddaughter on the mantel above the wood burner.

"When did you last see Jo?" he asked eventually.

"Last night," Phil said. "We were at our…" he hesitated, looked across at Grace. She wasn't their niece, she was Grace's. Grace's niece from her first marriage, just like the girls. But that didn't seem important now. "…niece's wedding reception at The Three Swans on the High Street. We left just before half ten, came home. Jo stayed on, planned to make a night of it in town."

"Was she with anyone when you left?" Jackman said.

"Chloe." Grace's voice whispered the ailing words out. "Phil's daughter from his first marriage."

"And you're sure of the time?"

She nodded. "Lydia wanted to go with them, but she's only fifteen."

"Have you spoken with Chloe since?"

Phil sat forward. "She texted me this morning. Her daughter, Meggy, was up early."

"So she's home?"

He nodded.

Wilson returned, carrying a tray of mugs. Grace watched as her assured movement passed them around. She had gone into her kitchen. Found mugs, coffee, sugar. Hushed her dog. How many times had she done this in other people's homes? The voices continued around her. She was aware of the inspector asking more questions, "Do you know of anyone who might want to hurt Jo? Has she upset anyone recently?" Phil kept shaking his head.

Grace could feel herself trembling, unable to control the shaking. She lifted her head. The clock on the mantel stared back at her. Almost a quarter past seven. She felt a pull to get up, move the clock hand back, wipe away events of the last twenty minutes as if it had never happened.

Lydia's breathing regulated. She lifted her head, cut through the detective's words. "How did she die?"

He paused for a second, his eyes mournful. "We believe she was strangled."

Lydia slumped as she began to cry again. Grace clung to her, aware that the questions continued, yet they sounded a long way off. The pain was suffocating, pressing down on her chest, crushing out the air.

Then, out of the depths of the hearing well, she

picked out a line: "We will need somebody to formally identify the body."

And there it was, a lifeline. Maybe it wasn't Jo. Maybe they'd made a mistake. But Wilson was gazing at a photograph in the alcove of Jo at her school prom, in the black gothic dress she'd insisted on wearing. As Grace met her eyes, she guessed her thoughts. "Your daughter's student card was found at the scene. I'm very sorry."

Desperation bubbled beneath Grace's skin. She wanted to scream, shout, accuse them of making a mistake; ask if they had a family, children, if they had any idea of how she felt. Instead, a single thought rushed into her head. She stood.

"Grace?" It was Phil. His skin was like paper, tinged with grey. He'd held it together, answered the detective's questions, yet his face had aged years in the last half an hour.

"I have to go to her room." She was almost at the door when a hand shot out and caught her forearm.

"I'm sorry, I'm going to have to ask you not to go in there." Wilson let go almost immediately. "Not for a while."

"W-what?"

"We have to get it searched, forensically. I'm sorry."

"I don't understand," Grace replied.

"We'll need to look at everything, to piece together what happened."

The words were light, shallow. They didn't penetrate the surface. Her daughter was dead, yet she couldn't go to the one place where she would feel close to her, breathe in her sweet aroma, look at the everyday objects that captured so many memories.

"We'll need a list of her friends, family, people who were at the reception last night," Jackman said. His voice softened. "Is there someone we can call? To help you."

Grace turned to Phil. "We should call Chloe."

"I'm afraid we'll need to speak with her first," Jackman said. Grace glared at the detective. "She was the last person seen with Jo," he added. "We will need to be there when you tell her. We can take you with us?"

"I'll go," Phil said.

"No."

"Please, Grace. Stay here. With Lydia."

Minutes later, Grace stood at the window and watched the car pull off the drive. Out of the corner of her eye, she could see Lydia in the armchair beside her, still dressed in her tartan brush-cotton pyjamas, eyes entranced in space. Mugs clunked together as Wilson carried them into the kitchen. A bitter chill rushed through her. Jo was gone. Her baby. The anguish was too unbearable to contemplate.

"We'll need her mobile phone number."

Grace raised her eyes to face the detective. She hadn't heard her come back in from the kitchen. For a moment her voice was mute.

"She did have a mobile phone?"

CHAPTER FOUR

JACKMAN STOOD NEXT to Phil as he rapped on the front door of the modern semi-detached home. Daylight was creeping in on the horizon, the sun's rays promising a bright winter's day to melt the covering of light frost that veiled the surroundings.

A child shrieked with laughter in the distance. Phil knocked again, harder this time.

The door was pulled open by a pale-faced young woman in jeans and a black jumper. Messy dark hair rested on her shoulders. Her smile fell as soon as she caught their sombre faces. She eyed Jackman suspiciously, turned to Phil. "Dad. What's happened?"

At that moment a toddler pushed through her legs. "Pap!" She flung herself at Phil's knees.

"Hello, Pumpkin," Phil said, hoisting her onto his hip. His face slackened as he looked up. "Can we come in, Chloe?"

She stood aside for them to enter.

"Meggy, would you go and wake Daddy?" Chloe said. "Ask him to put the kettle on for our guests?" She was fighting to keep her voice even. "I'm sure Pap and his friend would like a drink."

Meggy wriggled to get down and raced off towards the back of the bungalow. Chloe guided them into the front room and closed the door. "What's going on?" she asked.

Jackman flashed his badge and introduced himself. "Would you mind sitting down?"

She looked across at Phil. "Is it Grace?"

Phil shook his head. "I'm afraid it's Jo. Something has happened. They think she's been killed."

Chloe pressed her hand to her chest and tumbled back onto the edge of the sofa.

Phil moved to sit next to her, grabbing hold of her free hand.

"I don't understand. When, where?"

Phil looked across at Jackman. "A body was found in Leicester Lane early this morning," Jackman said. "We have reason to believe it was Jo. We are treating her death as suspicious."

Chloe gasped. Her eyes brimmed with tears. "How?"

"I'm sorry?"

"How did she die?"

"We believe she'd been strangled."

Chloe covered her face with her hands, shook her head, almost to dismiss the bad thoughts, and wept.

"I'm so very sorry," Jackman said. The words were empty, inadequate, and he knew that. He gave her a moment before he continued. "Do you feel up to answering some questions? It would really help us."

The door burst open. A short man with a matt of dark hair and a beard entered carrying a tray, followed by Meggy who was walking very slowly and carrying a bowl of sugar lumps in her hands. The man opened his mouth to speak, but as soon as he saw Chloe he planted down the tray next to the bowl and retreated, pulling the toddler out with him. The last thing they heard was her sharp wail. "Want to see Paps…" It sliced through the room, although Chloe appeared oblivious.

Jackman heaped two teaspoons of sugar into a mug and passed it to Chloe. "Drink this. It'll help with the shock."

Jackman glanced at the photo on the hearth. It was the toddler, a larger version of the one he'd seen at the Daniels' home earlier. Phil had been helpful in the car on the way over, giving him a brief outline of their family, sharing that both Grace and he were widows who'd remarried just under four years ago. He was ten years older than Grace, Chloe was his daughter by his first marriage, and Lydia and Jo were Grace's. But they were all treated the same. "One big happy family," he'd said, his voice cracking as he'd choked the words out.

"Can you confirm where you were last night?" Jackman asked when she'd had a chance to drink some of the tea and calmed slightly.

She looked at him blankly. "At my cousin's wedding reception at The Three Swans."

"When did you last see Jo?"

She dabbed her eyes and swallowed before she answered. "Around twenty to eleven. Matt had taken Meggy home. Jo and I were going to head down to The Angel for last orders."

"Just the two of you?"

Chloe nodded. "But as soon as I hit the air, I didn't feel well. I'd overdone the wine. She waited with me outside the hotel until a taxi arrived. Waved me off. That was the last time I saw her." Her bottom lip quivered. Phil put his arm around her shoulders, handed her a folded tissue from his pocket.

"Did you come straight home?"

Chloe nodded. "Matt was still watching the end of *Match of the Day* when I arrived back."

"Do you know where Jo was planning to go after you left her?"

"Still down to The Angel, I think. She said she'd meet up with some friends."

"Did she say who?"

She closed her eyes, shook her head. "I shouldn't have gone. I should have stayed with her."

"It's not your fault, love," Phil said.

"I'm so sorry," Jackman said. "I know this is difficult, but do you know of anyone who might want to hurt Jo?"

"No."

"Would you be able to give me a list of her friends, a boyfriend, family, work colleagues?" he asked gently. "I've asked Grace too, but the more people we speak to, the more chance we have of finding out what happened. I'll also need her mobile number."

She nodded, turned to her dad. "How's Grace? And Lydia?"

Phil hesitated. "They're as well as can be expected, love."

"What was Jo wearing last night?" Jackman asked.

She looked up at him, puzzled. "Her lilac bridesmaid dress. Same as me and Lydia."

"Did she have any earrings in?"

"Yes, just plain gold studs. We all wore the same."

"Are you sure?"

"I don't get it?" Her face contorted. "If it was her, you'd have known that…"

"We just have to check the details."

She buried herself in her father's chest, muffling the wails that followed.

Jackman looked away unobtrusively, gathering his thoughts. The earring wasn't weathered enough to have been in the hedgerow long. If it didn't belong to Jo, who did it belong to? His mind raced. Why strip the victim naked, yet leave her details nearby? It was almost as if the killer wanted them to know who she was.

CHAPTER FIVE

JACKMAN TAPPED HIS pen twice against the picture on the board. The hollow sound reverberated around the room. "Jo Lamborne. Nineteen. Undergraduate studying sociology at The University of Nottingham. Came home earlier this week to attend her cousin's wedding at The Three Swans Hotel in Market Harborough yesterday."

The room fell silent as twelve pairs of eyes focused on the photos of the young woman before them.

"Anything from the press appeal yet?" Jackman asked.

"Plenty of calls coming through," Wilson said. "Nothing significant yet. We're prioritising at the moment to anyone who actually knew her or saw her yesterday."

Jackman nodded his thanks and turned to the room. "Let's get the hotel rota for Thursday and work through it," he said. "A guest list is on its way from the family. It was a small wedding, around thirty people attending, so we'll start with those. We also need to follow Jo's movements last night from when she left the hotel. Who was the last person to see her? How was her mood? She told her sister that she was going to The Angel to meet friends. Check with the pub, see if anyone remembers her arriving. Who did she meet? Was she seen talking to anyone on the way?"

"Surely someone must have seen her in Market Harborough," Wilson said, "especially in a lilac bridesmaid dress?"

"You'd think so. We've asked the press to focus on the dress and the matching shoes. It's possible they may have been dumped somewhere. Let's check the town cameras to see if she features there. Check for vehicles coming through too, see if anyone picked her up. I want another team focused on victimology," he continued. "What company does she keep? Who has she spent time with recently? Let's look at her life in Nottingham and try to build up a picture of her movements during the past few weeks. Emma Parsons will be spending time with the family, obtaining an account of their movements so that we can cross reference for consistency, feeding back information as and when she gleans it. We haven't located the victim's phone, but we have her mobile number so we can apply for her call records."

His eyes scanned the room and rested on McDonald. "See if you can get the techies to pull her social media records. We know she was on Facebook, so we'll need to appeal for witnesses there. What about Twitter, or Instagram? Let's see if there are any new followers or abnormal activity." McDonald nodded and made some notes on his pad. "Wilson and I will get down to the morgue and see what the pathologist says."

Jackman thanked them all and returned to his office. By the time he had shut down his computer and collected his jacket, Wilson was at the back door of the station, waiting for him. A thought occurred to him as she battled with her overcoat. "See if you can get hold of your friend in the press office, will you?" he said. "I'd like to do a live appeal this evening."

PAIN. A SCREAMING VOICE, trapped inside, suppressing every sense. Jo was gone. The world was empty. The raw reality was suffocating. Incomprehensible. Unbearable. Grace wanted to scream, but her body let her down. All she could do, all she was capable of, was to sit staring into nothingness.

Hushed voices filtered through from the kitchen. Phil's dulcet tones. Whispers of doctors and sedation.

Pictures of Jo flashed through her mind. The little girl with the unruly curls that people stopped in the street to admire. The same curls that blighted her as a teenager. The straight talking toddler with the open heart who became intensely private in her later years. Going to university and living away from home had given her the sense of independence and identity she'd sought so rigorously. She was just starting to thrive, a butterfly emerging from its chrysalis, spreading its wings...

Lydia moaned, shifted position and slipped back into her slumber. Grace held her close. Chloe had come and sat with Lydia when they'd had to go out earlier. Consoling each other with their tears. By the time they arrived back and Chloe returned home to Meggy, Lydia was exhausted and fell asleep with Lucky by her side.

Grace shuddered. As soon as they'd arrived in the morgue car park, she realised it was a mistake. Wanted to turn back. But at the same time something compelled her to stay. The desperate need to see her girl.

On television programmes, when people identified their loved ones they stroked their faces, touched their lips, kissed their foreheads. But any thoughts that she might touch Jo, embrace her even, were soon dashed when Phil and she were guided into a viewing area with a clear screen that separated them from the room beyond. A thick aroma of bleach pervaded the air.

She'd moved towards the screen, within touching distance of the gurney on the other side when the sheet was pulled back. Jo's hair was still tucked into the pleat from the night before, her face still touched with make-up, although pale and tinged blue. No curls. The last image she would see of her daughter would be without those beautiful curls.

A spear of raw anguish had risen from the pit of her stomach. But her reaction surprised her. She didn't scream or wail. Phil's hand pressed on her shoulder, his face contorted in grief. Yet Grace was numb.

Grace pushed her aching back into the sofa cushions. How could Jo be gone? Only yesterday she was seated right here in this spot, chuckling over not being able to get up early enough to help with the wedding arrangements.

The wedding. It seemed a lifetime ago.

The moments following the screened room were jumbled and mingled together, like clothes tumbling in a dryer. The sound of a chair leg as it was dragged across the floor was followed by a weight on her shoulder, gently easing her down into it. Consoling words from Phil. Eventually being led back through to another room and asked a stream of questions. Sitting in a muted trance as Phil replied to the detectives. Soothing, soft voices. Kind faces staring at her, sympathising, trying to make it as easy as possible.

Despair clawed at her insides and she welcomed it. She wanted to feel the pain. Because it was all she had left of Jo.

CHAPTER SIX

"I HATE THIS PLACE," Wilson said. She stared through the window into the laboratory as she pulled on her overshoes.

Jackman gave a wry smile. "It's a morgue. You're not supposed to enjoy it."

"It's all those drains." She pulled a face. "I've never been squeamish, but the sight of them makes my toes curl."

"Better keep your eyes up then," Jackman said. He opened the door and entered the pathology lab. Immediately a sterile smell filled his nose. Spotlights bounced off the stainless steel surfaces. His eyes flicked over the drains and rested on Celeste who was bent over a metal gurney in the middle. A CSI in a white suit was moving around the body, photographing places of interest.

"Morning again, Celeste."

Celeste sent a draft of cool air towards them as she moved back and exchanged pleasantries. The mortuary always felt cold, even in the height of summer. The victim looked lily-white, the welt around her neck darker under the fluorescent lighting. "We've done the preliminaries, hands and fingernails," Celeste said. "Apart from a little bruising and grazing on her forearms, nothing there to suggest she put up much of a fight, so I'd suggest she knew her attacker. There's bruising on her inner thighs and some internal tissue damage. No obvious sign of semen, but we've taken swabs, just in case."

"So, we're thinking a sexual motive?" Jackman said. "How does it compare to the attacks on Operation Ascott?"

Celeste paused a moment. "I didn't examine those women. I'll need to take a look at their files. As far as I'm aware, the first was raped, the second assaulted while unconscious?" She looked across at Jackman who nodded. "This victim has tearing and bruising to the vaginal wall, possibly from some kind of a blunt object."

Jackman felt Wilson flinch beside him.

"Obviously we'll need to run toxicology tests to see what was in her system at the time." Celeste moved around to the side of the table and examined the head. "No sign of any grass or mud in her hair, so I'm pretty sure she was killed first and dumped at the scene."

"Why remove her clothes?" Wilson asked.

Celeste looked up at her. "No idea. Maybe there was something on them. Or maybe the killer wanted to keep them."

Wilson's mobile phone rang and she excused herself. The lab door clicked shut behind her. Jackman looked back at the victim. Nineteen years old. Barely a year younger than his own daughter, Celia, although she looked small, young for her age. His gaze fell on her feet, the toenails painted a bright red. The nail varnish looked freshly applied and yet she'd lost her life in the past twenty-four hours since she'd painted them. He imagined her applying her make-up, drying her hair, painting her nails, getting ready for the wedding. Where did she go after she left her sister last night? Who did she speak to?

"There is one other thing I would like you to see," Celeste said. She pulled a light from the side, shone it over the victim's thighs. It highlighted sporadic white lines like tiny worms.

Jackman looked closer. "Old scars?"

Celeste nodded. "They're quite old, more than a few years I'd say. And not deep. They only show up under the UV lamp."

"What are you thinking?"

Celeste switched off the lamp and looked across at him. "We occasionally see this in people who have experienced emotional distress. Sometimes on the wrists too and in other areas. The thigh area is popular because it can be covered."

"You're saying she cut herself?"

"I'm saying those cuts appeared over a period of time. But they were never deep enough to cause a visible scar."

The door swung back and hit the wall as Wilson re-entered. "They've pulled her phone records," she said. "Just working through them now."

"Good."

"And you've a message from a Superintendent Janus in Warwickshire. Wants to speak to you urgently."

Jackman nodded and left Wilson to finish up with Celeste who was preparing to make a Y-shaped incision from each shoulder, and down to the bottom of the victim's abdomen. He stepped out of the lab and checked his phone. Two missed calls from Janus. He took a deep breath and dialled back.

"Will?" She didn't attempt to hide the irritation in her voice.

"Hello, ma'am."

"I've had Leicestershire's Chief Constable on the

phone this morning. I understand you want to be SIO on a new case?"

"It's a fresh murder investigation. Early examination shows signs of a sexual assault."

"You were sent to region to look at working practises, Will, not get involved in a new case."

Jackman closed his eyes and pinched the bridge of his nose with his thumb and forefinger. He'd worked with Janus for long enough to know that she liked her own way and from the moment he'd expressed an interest in taking over the case that morning, he'd been expecting this call. "And I am," he said, "but this is potentially a serial offender. I've got the background knowledge of the other cases."

"I placed you on project work, Will, while you are recuperating from an injury. This is a good opportunity for you. I don't want you out there in the field until you are fit."

Jackman instinctively stretched out his left arm. The skin was still tight from the burn, an injury he'd gained on his last case. "I'm fine. The doctor signed me off four weeks ago. Working this case with Leicester Homicide Team will give me a greater insight into their work live-time. It'll help with my report."

She breathed out a long sigh. "Well, it seems I have no choice since both Chief Constables are behind you. Make sure you take it easy, and use your team. I don't want you taking any risks."

"Of course."

"And let me remind you, we have a regional deadline of the end of January for this policy report. I don't want that date missed."

CHAPTER SEVEN

GRACE FELT A hand brush her cheek and blinked to focus at the broken numbers of the carriage clock on the mantel. It was 2pm.

"Can I get you anything?" She looked up to find Phil's face, etched with concern, bearing down on her. She shook her head and retrieved her arm from beneath Lydia who wriggled and turned to face the back of the sofa. Moments later, her breathing relaxed into a steady rhythm once more.

Grace surveyed her longingly.

Phil offered a sad smile. "Best place for her right now."

A chorus of words in the kitchen grabbed her attention. She craned her neck towards the door, trying to catch what was being said but it was too muffled.

Lucky followed Grace through to the kitchen, dancing around her feet as if something was about to happen. Grace ignored her, eyes glued to DC Emma Parsons who ended the call abruptly. Too abruptly. "Can I get you something to eat?" the detective asked.

Grace shook her head.

"Why don't we all sit down?" She guided Grace towards a chair, pulled out another for Phil and sat opposite them. Lucky slunk over to her basket and curled up, already bored of the conversation.

"I realise this is difficult for you, but I do need to ask some more questions. We need your help to catch whoever did this, and the sooner we move forward the better. Do you think you'd be up to answering some questions now?"

Grace slumped inwardly. She watched the detective retrieve her bag. Right now she wanted to wrap herself in her misery and grief. Speak to no one. "Call me Emma," she had said when she arrived earlier and took over from the other detective. But it felt too informal, too invasive. She could only think of her as Detective Parsons.

"Has Jo ever been to Turkey?"

Grace shook her head. "Why?"

The detective pulled a photograph out of her bag and handed it to Grace. It was an earring, enlarged to show the detail. "We found this earring near Jo's body. It has been identified as an evil eye, readily available in countries like Turkey. It may be unrelated, but I just need to check if you've seen it before?"

"No, never." Grace passed the photo to Phil who shook his head, baffled.

"We are working on the contacts you've given us, but we will need to put out a press appeal this evening and share Jo's details," Parsons continued. "Do you have any photos from yesterday, of Jo in her bridesmaid dress?"

Phil bristled. "Is that really necessary?"

"I'm afraid so. It'll give people a focus, help us to track Jo's movements last night. A photo is much better than a description."

The words cut through Grace. People: family, friends, strangers, hotel staff. Extended family, even those people they only saw every few years at weddings and funerals. The most intimate details of Jo's life were about to be chewed over by everyone. No longer would she be remembered as the chubby-faced child in primary school, or the colourful teen who was always dyeing her hair. The seriousness of this event would erase those memories and sit at the forefront of their mind. Daisy, her niece, was the daughter of her first husband, Jamie's, only brother. The family had emigrated to New Zealand when Daisy was in her early teens, yet she'd flown back for an English wedding to make it extra special, with her family around her. She pictured Daisy being interviewed by the police and shuddered. Every year when she celebrated her own wedding anniversary, Daisy would be reminded of the day Jo had been murdered. The thought sickened her.

Phil was about to speak, but Grace placed a weary hand on his forearm. "It's okay." She retrieved her phone from the kitchen side, handed it to Phil. She wasn't ready to look at photos of her daughter from just the day before, all dressed in her finery.

"How was Jo's mood on Saturday?" Parsons asked gently.

Grace swallowed, struggling to see the relevance of the question. "Good. She was happy. We all were. It was a family celebration."

"Did you see her talking to anyone?"

"Of course. There were lots of people there. I…"

"Arguing with anyone?"

The interruption caught her by surprise. She fidgeted. "No. Why would she?"

Parsons shook her head, gave a kind smile to dismiss the question. "Did she have much to drink?"

"We were all drinking. But she wasn't drunk if that's what you're implying?"

"My job isn't to imply. It's to establish the facts." So

gentle. Controlled. Direct with just the right measure of warmth. "Did you see her talking to anyone, apart from friends and family that had been invited to the event?"

"No, but then I wasn't watching her every move." Grace stared back at the detective. Her dark hair was pulled back into a ponytail exposing a face that showed signs of prettiness but had sagged with age. She wondered if she had children of her own. Daughters, maybe.

Parsons tilted her head to the side. "Has she spoken to you about a boyfriend, or girlfriend?"

"What?"

"Was she seeing anyone?"

"No. She's been single for a while. She didn't want to be tied into a relationship when she was going away to university."

"Are you sure?"

"Yes. No." Grace swiped a hand over her forehead. "Jo is…was…quite secretive. If she was seeing someone at university, in Nottingham, she didn't mention it."

"I will need a list of all her previous partners so that we can eliminate them from our enquiries. There is one other thing I need to ask you." Parsons paused. "The pathologist found some old scars on Jo's thighs. Do you know anything about those?"

Grace's heart pitted into the depths of her stomach. Were they to have no secrets? She closed her eyes. When she opened them the detective was looking directly at her. "Jo took it bad when her father died. She struggled. It was a while before any of us knew she was hurting herself." She looked away. "And managed to help her."

The sound of the pen scratching against the paper as the detective made notes caught Grace. Anger rose inside her. Questions, intrusion. Violating Jo's life. All their lives.

"What actually happened?"

"I'm sorry?"

"To Jo."

"Her body was found…"

"I already know where her body," Grace shrunk back as the word *body* made her recoil, "was found. I want to know what state she was in. What happened to her?"

The detective looked back at her a moment, as if she wasn't really sure how much to say.

Phil cleared his throat. "Maybe this isn't the time."

Grace shook her head. "No, Phil. She's my daughter." She turned back to the detective. "I want to know. I need to know. Everything."

CHAPTER EIGHT

JACKMAN TUCKED HIS car into the last space available on the High Street, turned his collar up and wandered down to the hotel. The clouds had moved in after lunch, blocking any trace of the earlier sun and making for a dreary afternoon. Shoppers scurried past with pinched faces and hunched shoulders. A woman was battling a buggy against the wind, the sleeping baby inside oblivious of the inclement weather.

He paused outside The Three Swans and looked up at the white cottage-style frontage set directly onto the pavement. The former sixteenth century coaching inn was quaint in appearance with a black wooden door sandwiched between double windows edged in black. An ornate hanging sign above creaked in the wind. A knot of people were collected in the small bar area which looked invitingly cosy under the low lighting. Jackman walked past the entrance and down an open archway at the side, just wide enough to take a small car, towards the back of the hotel.

The smell of fine dining tickled his senses as he passed through a patio area, although he couldn't imagine many people eating outside today. He kept walking until he reached a sprawling car park at the rear with access out onto the street beyond. He stood a moment, watching a couple of cars whizz past, followed by a van and a motorcyclist. It appeared to be a residential area, the streets opposite lined with old terraced houses. He was just making a mental note to check the maps for any council CCTV cameras on the route, and also organise some house-to-house enquiries in case anyone had seen two people arguing out back, when he felt a presence nearby.

Artie Black's face widened into a smile. "Good afternoon, Detective Chief Inspector."

Jackman nodded a distracted greeting. "What brings you here?" he asked.

"I noticed the police presence and wondered whether it was linked to your inquiry. It seems I was right."

Jackman ignored his answer and inhaled a deep breath before he pointed to the road opposite. "Where does that lead to?"

"That's Fairfield Road," Artie said. "It's a through route. Leads back towards the High Street if you turn right, out towards East Farndon and Lutterworth if you go left."

"Busy?"

"Depends what time of day."

Jackman gave a thoughtful nod.

Artie scratched his temple. "So, any thoughts I can pass forward? As I said before, I'm sure we can work together on this one."

Jackman knew that journalists could be a real hindrance when they latched onto a case, especially if they opted to take on their own covert investigation. "I'm holding a press conference in the Harborough Theatre at 6pm," he said. "Why don't you come along?"

Artie's eyes shone. He gave a quick nod. "Right. See you there."

Jackman waited for him to reach his car before he

made his way towards the back of the hotel. It looked as though the original old building had been extended several times over the years and was now an eclectic mix of ancient and modern. A plethora of doors and windows lined the route.

Wilson was just stepping out of a side entrance as he reached the end of the patio area. She smiled up at him. "Ah, hello. You found us okay then?"

He nodded and looked across at the young man with a slick of dark hair and sideburns to match who'd followed her outside. His well-cut black suit screamed of ambition. "Neil Sanders," he said with a nod. "Hotel Manager. It goes without saying that we'll do anything to help."

"We've got a room inside the hotel," Wilson said. She pointed back through the main entrance. "We've started interviewing the staff on duty last night."

Jackman thanked them both. He glanced up at a winding metal fire escape that led down from the back of the old building. "How many doors and exits does the hotel have all together?"

Sanders looked as if he'd been caught off guard. He quickly recovered himself. "I'm not completely sure. We've had a number of extensions. I can get some maps of the layout sent over to you?"

"That would be helpful, thanks. How many rooms do you have?"

"We have fifty-nine in total, although as you can see they are quite spread out in several different buildings. And we have one restaurant upstairs and a bistro downstairs." He pointed across to an inside area behind the patio. "There's also a bar area at the front and several functions rooms. The wedding yesterday was held in a suite on the first floor at the front of the hotel." He indicated for them to follow him. They made their way inside, climbed the staircase and followed Sanders into a room with a high-corniced ceiling and sash windows overlooking the road. A rectangular table ran the length of the far wall, beneath the windows.

"It's quite compact for a wedding reception," Wilson said.

"We have several rooms," Sanders said with the air of a salesman. "People tend to like this one for smaller functions. I think it's the traditional features. We usually set up a mini-bar in the room next door."

They followed him down the corridor and into a smaller room, with a makeshift bar in the corner. A door at the far end led to the metal fire escape Jackman had noticed earlier. "Is that accessible?" he asked.

Sanders nodded. "Health and safety. You know how it is."

They moved back out to the top of the main stairs. "Where does that lead to?" Jackman said, pointing at the long corridor that led in the opposite direction from the function room.

"To the restaurant." Sanders smiled, clearly enjoying himself as they followed him past the toilets, down a narrow corridor and through another door. The room here opened out into an airy space and was surprisingly modern. Sharp tables were decorated with fanned yellow napkins and lit candles ready for the evening sitting. A waiter was moving around the tables putting out wine glasses that sparkled in the candlelight.

Jackman's eyes rested on another staircase at the far end just as he heard a voice behind him, "Mr Sanders?"

He followed the voice to a woman in a red trouser suit. "You're needed in reception."

Sanders turned to Jackman and Wilson. "Would you excuse me for a moment?"

Wilson watched him go and scanned the restaurant. "Lovely venue for a wedding."

Jackman took another look at the staircase. "A nightmare for us though."

"What do you mean?"

"All the doors. With so many entrances, exits and fire escapes, there's no way we can ever account for all the comings and goings last night. It wouldn't be difficult to come in and see someone, arrange to meet later and not be seen." He chewed the side of his mouth. "Check what cameras they've got, will you? They might have some in the yard area, where the patio is, or out front. We could see if our victim features on any of them."

She snapped a nod. "Come on. There's someone you should meet."

He followed her down the stairs and into the front bar area. The earlier crowd had dispersed. Apart from a business man hunched over a laptop in the corner, they had the room to themselves. A young woman in a crisp white shirt and matching black waistcoat and trousers was hanging a fresh bottle of whisky behind the bar. She clicked the bottle into place and smiled at Wilson as they approached. "Can I get you anything?"

"No, thank you," Wilson said and turned to Jackman. "This is Sophie Jennings, sir. She was working the bar last night."

Jackman introduced himself and gave her a kind smile. "I realise you've had a huge shock, but anything you can tell us will really help piece together what happened. Did you speak with Jo last night?"

The woman nodded. In spite of the touch of make-up that covered her smooth complexion, her face looked drawn. "I can't believe it's happened."

"Can you tell me what you saw?"

"Not much really." Sophie's voice trembled slightly. "The other detective's already asked."

Jackman pulled over a couple of bar stools for himself and Wilson and sat down. "I realise this is difficult," he said. "What time did you start work yesterday?"

"Two o'clock. I wasn't due in until four, but one of the other girls phoned in sick so they called me in early."

"Was the hotel busy?"

"I only cover the bar area down here. We weren't busy, early on. A few people called in. The wedding party arrived just after three."

Jackman took in the surroundings as he let the words sink in. The ornate bar faced the door, offering a perfect view of the street out front through the windows either side. "Would you recognise the girl that was killed?" He spoke the words slowly, careful not to release any more information than was absolutely necessary.

Sophie nodded. "She was a bridesmaid. Jo, they called her. She'd been popping in and out all evening for a sneaky cigarette. We chatted a bit." A half-smile lit up her face. "She was funny, made me laugh. I let her keep her ciggies behind the counter because she didn't have a pocket."

Jackman smiled. He guessed Sophie was similar in age to their victim. "Did she have anyone with her?"

Sophie shook her head. "She usually came down on her own."

"When was the last time you saw her?"

"Just after ten thirty, I think. I remember it because she got her bracelet caught on her earring while she was pulling on her coat. I helped her free it up while her sister was in the ladies. We giggled about it."

"What happened next?"

"Her sister, Chloe, joined her. They stood outside for a while. I was busy serving other customers, but I do remember Chloe holding her head. She looked poorly. I thought about going out at one point, but I couldn't leave the bar. The next time I looked in that direction she'd gone." Tears welled in her eyes. "It's so awful. I keep thinking, what if I was the last person to see her?"

"What time was that?"

"I'm not sure. They were only outside for about ten minutes, I think."

"Did you see who came and went around that time?"

"No, it was busy, and we were short-staffed."

"What about earlier when she came down for a cigarette. Did she talk to anyone in the bar, or outside?"

"Not that I remember."

"Strange that she came down here," Jackman said. "She could easily have used the fire escape upstairs."

"Her family didn't like her smoking. I had to help her smuggle the ciggies back into her bag when her sister wasn't looking."

"What time did you finish?"

"It must have been about half two before I got out of here."

Jackman scanned the view of the street again. "When did you find out she'd been attacked?" he asked gently.

"This morning. I heard it on the radio. Didn't make the connection at first. Then I got a text from Tim, he works the early shift. He told me the police were here and one of the bridesmaids from the wedding party yesterday had been killed."

Jackman thanked Sophie and stepped out into the High Street with Wilson. He looked out at the line of shops opposite and tried to imagine what they would have looked like, bathed in darkness the night before. "How well lit is this stretch at night?" he asked.

"It's not too bad, being the main drag," Wilson said. "And it wasn't particularly late either."

CHAPTER NINE

GRACE HAULED HERSELF UP, wavering as she reached standing. Phil put an arm out to support her, but she shook it away and moved towards the door.

"Grace. Where are you going?" Phil's face was pained. The details of Jo's attack had been vivid.

"Jo's room."

Parsons' head shot up. "I'm sorry, Grace, I have to ask you not to go…"

"I'm not going to go *in* there," Grace shouted, the pithiness in her voice rising with every word. The police interest was starting to feel like a rat, tunnelling its way through her family life, tarnishing everything in sight.

She felt Phil's heavy footsteps behind her as she reached the stairs. "Grace…"

"Please. Leave me alone." She turned, closing her eyes to block out the hurt in his face. "I just need some time."

He nodded. Reached out and stroked the side of her arm, then made his way back to the kitchen.

Grace waited for him to go before she continued up to the top, hovering a moment at Jo's door. She breathed in deeply, hoping for a scent of her daughter, but there was nothing. None of the pots and perfumes, the candles and burners that decorated Jo's room. Those smells that all mixed together to create a sweet musky fragrance every time she'd popped her head around the door. She leaned her shoulder against the wall, slid down onto the top step.

The detective's words pummelled her. "Signs of sexual interference…" She squeezed her eyes shut. For a moment she couldn't breathe. No. Not her Jo. Please. The thought of her baby going through an attack was too unbearable. Grace knew that. Knew exactly how it felt. Because it had happened to her.

She was eighteen. Barely a year younger than Jo. His hands pawing at her, tugging at her hair, forcing himself inside her.

She could still remember the day it happened. It was the day after her eighteenth birthday. Having taken her out for a family meal on the night of her birthday, her parents reluctantly agreed to let her go out with the girls.

It wasn't her first time out alone. But it was the first time they didn't insist on picking her up. All those years of her parents watching, waiting, collecting her were over. She was eighteen. She could finally do it her own way.

Her friends, Susi and Kath, came round to get ready at her house. They'd played music, dressed to the sounds of Take That and REM. Grace wore her new dress, the long black one that clung to her figure that she'd bought with her birthday money. On her way out, her mother had pressed a ten pound note into her hand. "That's your taxi money," she'd said. "Keep it separate and don't forget."

The nightclub was heaving with bodies pressed in against each other. A kaleidoscope of flashing lights lit the silvery darkness; loud music blared, the bass vibrating in her chest. She spotted her friend Jenna beside the bar and gave her a wave. Drinks were expensive. Before Grace knew it she'd spent her wages from her part time job at the newsagents and the tenner was all she had left. She ran the tips of her fingers across it in her pocket. But she didn't forget her mother's words.

At the end of the evening she'd walked out with Susi and Kath. The cool air sent them into an alcohol-induced giggle. Susi stopped and lit up. "You getting a cab, Grace?"

Grace pushed her hand into her side pocket. The money was missing. She searched her handbag. She must have dropped it. "Err…yeah."

"We'll walk you to the taxi rank."

"There's no need."

"My mum would never forgive me if I didn't. She made me promise to look out for you. She went on about it so much that I'd get a cab with you myself if I didn't live at the opposite end of town." Susi took a drag on her cigarette and passed it across to Kath. As they moved away from the club, the fresh night air slapped Grace in the face. Suddenly she felt alert. Afraid. The prospect of walking home alone didn't seem so appealing. Susi stubbed out her cigarette on the pavement. As she did so, the contents of her upturned handbag fell to the ground. Lipsticks, a hairbrush and a packet of chewing gum all rattled as they hit the ground. A few coins circled the pavement.

"Is that all you have left?" Kath asked Susi.

"Looks like it!"

They both giggled again as they scrabbled about, picking it all up. "Well, it's more than I have."

"Did you see where Jenna went?" Grace asked as

they reached the taxi rank. Jenna lived down the road from her. They could walk back together.

But her idea was dashed in the next line. "Off with Mark. Won't see her until the morning now." The girls both hugged Grace.

"Let us know when you get home," Susi said.

"Sure." Grace was stood behind a couple holding hands.

She watched them totter away in their heels. Maybe walking home wouldn't be so bad. She'd be back in no time if she hurried. Buoyed up, she waited until the girls had disappeared around the corner and then walked back through the High Street and took a left into Bowden Lane. It was well lit. She could hear her heels clicking as they tapped the pavement. This wasn't so bad. She turned the next corner and the next. She was coming towards the edge of the town now. The street-lights were less frequent.

Grace was only minutes from home when it happened. She remembered seeing the motorcyclist pulling up. He climbed off, was wrestling with his helmet as she passed. She'd smiled weakly at him, not wishing to look frightened, and took the shortcut past the garages. It was darker down there, only a few of the streetlights remained.

A push from behind. She teetered forward, just steadying herself when she was slammed up against the wall. White spots flashed in front of her eyes as she was pulled around. His mouth was on her. Thick beer-filled breath. She turned her face, tried to scream but he grabbed her chin, forced it back.

She could still remember the smell of him, menthol mixed with beer. The world swirled. Fear engulfed her.

Sat on the stairs, Grace couldn't help but wonder if Jo had felt the same terror, the same excruciating pain. She dropped her head, covered her face with her hands and wept.

CHAPTER TEN

THE DAMP NIGHT air nipped at Jackman's skin as he stepped out of The Angel hotel, wiping away the blanket of weariness that clung to him from the lack of sleep the night before. The first seventy-two hours after any serious crime were critical and, aware that he was on foreign territory, he'd decided to move hotels from Enderby to Market Harborough to familiarise himself with the market town and the many routes that snaked through its centre.

A light drizzle started as he walked, peppering his shoulders. He turned up his collar, cast intermittent glances into the lit windows of the upmarket boutiques that lined his route. The Three Swans bar was crowded as he wandered past, the people of Harborough enjoying a drink on a Friday evening. He moved on past coffee houses and heaving restaurants. Alice would love it here, he thought to himself. A buzzing town amidst a scenic backdrop. He could almost see his wife's pale blue eyes dancing with that familiar sense of adventure. But almost as quickly as it arrived, the image melted away, replaced with that of a thin hunched woman with glassy eyes, staring into the distance. Alice would never explore anything again. He sunk his hands into the depths of his pockets and trudged forward. In the square, he passed a cluster of wooden huts and a sign advertising a German Market.

His mind floated back to the press conference earlier that evening. Seated beside Taylor, facing a sea of journalists, flashes of photographers punctuating their appeal. The day had been frustrating, interviews at the hotels and investigations into Jo's background providing little new to share. Two enlarged photos adorned the screen beside them: a formal one of the victim in her bridesmaid dress posing for a photo with her sister, and another of her sitting at a table at The Three Swans, raising a wine glass to the camera, her mouth pulled into a wide grin.

Predictively, there were questions about links to Operation Ascott, speculation that the murder was connected to the attacks on the other girls. They'd played them down. Murmurs of discontent had spread around the room. The hacks weren't going to let this one lie. Artie Black sat at the front, pressing home the similarities.

Taylor had stood. His imposing presence shutting down the room as he talked about the extra officers he had drafted in to work around the clock to track down the killer. It was clear that the people of Harborough respected him, despite general confidence in the police investigation on Operation Ascott waning. He'd pressed forward, appealing for the media and the police to unite, focus on this case, work together to catch the killer of a vulnerable girl. So unlike Jackman's own superintendent in Stratford who hated press conferences, the one area that exposed the weak link in her armour. By the time they'd finished the press were placated. For the moment. Jackman gave the usual advice in these situations, asking local people to be sensible and wary of their own safety. Girls to go out in pairs, stick to lit areas and take registered cabs after dark. Although as they left, Artie Black shot him a look that left him under no illusion. He wasn't likely to be quiet for long.

But in spite of all this, and phones ringing off the hook in the incident room, they were still no closer to a firm lead.

Jackman checked his watch. It was almost twenty-four hours since the initial call had come through. The informant was a local man, yet they'd found no connection between him and the victim, no reason to suggest he was involved.

As he crossed the road and walked through the back streets he thought about the team of officers he'd sent up to Nottingham earlier, rummaging through Jo's room, speaking to her friends and tutors. He hoped they'd come up with something soon.

By the time Jackman was heading back up to The Three Swans, almost an hour had passed. He paused, swiped a hand through his wet hair, causing a shower of droplets to fall to the pavement as he glanced across at the ancient Grammar School. The old stone was fresh, clean. Recently renovated. This was a manicured town, the centre pretty, well maintained and steeped in history with a river running through the centre. In some ways it reminded him of a smaller version of his home town of Stratford-upon-Avon. There were a few hotels, although its Midlands setting didn't really lend itself to the droves of tourists they received in Warwickshire. The number of restaurants, tea shops and coffee houses suggested a sense of local community. The crime figures were standard: the usual burglary, criminal damage, domestic violence. But serious crime, murders and sexual attacks, were in the minority by percentage of population compared to larger towns and cities.

A young couple exited their car and rushed past him into the pub, the girl squealing as she covered her hair with her handbag. The rain had picked up, falling in sheets from an angry sky. Jackman hovered outside the pub for some time, water dripping off his chin as he glanced across at the intersection opposite. This is where Jo had stood last night, only an hour or so earlier. Before she met her end. Where had she gone afterwards? Her sister said she was meeting friends in The Angel, yet enquiries there and subsequent checks of their CCTV suggested she'd never arrived. Did she change her mind? Take another route? He'd checked the map. The roads opposite led in the general direction of her mother's home, although they ran in and out of each other and there were a number of different routes she could have taken. Mostly residential too, which meant little chance of cameras.

His hair was saturated again now, his shoulders damp where the rain had penetrated his jacket. He turned and walked slowly back towards his room at The Angel. Hopefully tomorrow would bring something new.

CHAPTER ELEVEN

THERE'S SOMETHING SINISTER about lies. They curl and fold, tie themselves around in knots so that in the end they become a tangled ball of wool and you can't find the end. Grace had wanted to tell someone, all those years ago. But how could she? Her mother had trusted her, given her the taxi fare herself. She wasn't sure how she'd made it home that night. Vague memories of scrabbling around for her shoes on the concrete slipped in and out of the shadows of her mind.

The following morning her mother came into her bedroom, sat on the edge of her bed and asked how the night out had gone. Grace remembered pulling the bedclothes over her head, shutting out the world. At the time her mother mistook the gesture for a hangover. She even laughed as she left the room, returned with paracetamol and water and left her to sleep it off.

But Grace withdrew, frightened, a child in an adult's world. It hurt to sit down and move around for several days afterwards. She feigned a stomach upset so that she didn't have to go out. What if he was still out there? What if he knew who she was and came looking?

She ignored her friends' calls over the ensuing days. When Susi and Kath came looking, they were so sympathetic that she almost told them. Almost. But she couldn't. They'd taken her to the taxi rank, thought she was safe. They would be wracked with guilt and there was a chance they'd tell her mother, alert the police. She couldn't go through with it.

As the weeks passed it became a dirty secret. Buried deep. Grace desperately tried to put it all behind her and push forward. It was summertime. She'd finished her A levels, taken extra hours at the newsagents over the holidays. She started to venture out in the evenings with friends, but insisted on driving. Her parents seemed pleased. At least it meant she wasn't drinking.

But the empty feeling in the pit of her stomach remained. She didn't want to go anywhere alone and even in company felt queasy and weak. When they sent her home early from work, she suddenly realised that her period was late.

And now, with her beautiful daughter gone, there was a pounding inside Grace's skull as she lay there in the darkness, the old memories filtering through her mind. Burning eyes searched for the illuminated digits on the bedside clock. It was 2.07am. The damp pillow clung to her cheek. Phil's heavy mass emitted slow breaths beside her, the only sound that broke the silence of the room. She released her fingers from his grip, slipped out of bed. She needed something for the pain. Now.

Her limbs felt soft and rubbery as she navigated the stairs. In the kitchen, Lucky raised a weary head from her basket, but didn't bother to climb out when Grace switched on a light. By the time she had searched through the cupboard, popped two of the strong painkillers that Phil had been prescribed for a back injury last year, and downed a pint glass of water, Lucky had emerged and was stood by the back door, looking up at her expectantly.

The cold night air reached in as she opened the door, working its way underneath her nightshirt, filling every corner of emptiness. It was chillingly sharp, almost cutting into her flesh.

The pregnancy, all those years ago, had cast the attack into a whole new light. As time passed, how could she tell anyone that she'd maintained a front for so long? She was pushed deeper into a well of despair. Booked into an independent clinic in Leicester where they confirmed her darkest fear.

Grace remembered leaving the clinic that day in a daze, stopping at a café in the city for a coffee. She sat at a table on her own in the corner. The room was busy, but it paled into insignificance as the reality of her situation crowded her mind.

She was eighteen, single and pregnant.

No more university. No more freedom.

It's not that she was a virgin. But Jamie and she had broken up recently, much to her mum's displeasure. Jamie was their neighbour, two years older than her, who'd recently trained as a plasterer. They'd been pushed together since children. As they had grown up, his infectious personality and quick wit made him a great friend. In his late teens he'd thickened out and she'd watched the other girls drool over him. But to Grace, he was almost the brother she'd never had. When they became adventurous in their teenage years, she was underwhelmed. Maybe sex wasn't what it was cracked up to be. Until her friends talked in giggled whispers of their own experiences and she began to realise that she feigned the excitement her peers claimed to enjoy. Something was missing. Days before her eighteenth birthday, Grace was starting to feel suffocated and ended the relationship. She wanted out. To explore the real world. To fall in love.

Being adopted and an only child, Grace hankered for a large family herself. Although her parents fostered and there were always children coming and going, there was no constant. She wanted a family of her own one day, siblings that would grow together, be company for each other. But not then. Not like that.

She considered a termination. The idea of raising her attacker's child repulsed her. But somehow, she was already starting to feel different, protective over the new life growing inside her. And it wasn't the child's fault. The dilemma bore down on her. She didn't sleep and barely ate. Finally, the thought of her parents' disappointment crushed her resolve. She called the clinic and arranged a termination for a week later.

The Saturday before the appointment, Susi persuaded her to go out into town. When they arrived at the club, Jamie was at the end of the bar and she sat next to him, reluctant to join her friends twirling around the dance floor. Kath had offered to drive and, given the chance of alcohol to numb the pain, Grace had polished off several vodka and cokes before the clock hit ten. Jamie chatted away, edging closer as she laughed at his ridiculous jokes. She later remembered him kissing her. He'd walked her home that night and the following morning she could still feel the warmth of his arm around her shoulder.

He called her the next day, took her out for a walk. Within a few days they'd picked up the remnants of their relationship. Jamie wasn't her idea of a life partner. As much as she tried, there were no thrills, no excitement, no butterflies in the stomach. But he was kind, a great friend and he adored her. And, in the midst of the fog, he became her safe haven.

The following week she called the clinic and cancelled the appointment.

When Jo was born, he never questioned her dark hair, her olive skin, in spite of the fact that they were all fair. They joked she was a family throwback, from generations past.

Grace wasn't sure how long she stood there in the cold. Time stood still. Her clogged mind stared out into the silvery moonlight. A siren in the distance caught her attention. Lucky was back in and tucked up in her basket before she became aware of her senses and closed the door.

She switched off the light and slowly walked up the stairs. At the top, Grace's gaze rested on Jo's door. She paused. Hovering for just a split second, she gave in to the sense of longing beckoning her and entered, closing the door behind her.

Grace brushed past the dark curtains, trailed her fingertips along the top of Jo's dressing table. Feathered fairy lights were wound around the pictures on the far wall. The girls shared this room when they were little and had pleaded for those lights. They hadn't worked in years, yet Jo refused to part with them. Her eyes rested on a framed photo of Jo and Lucky on the bedside table. Jo loved animals. She'd plagued her parents for a dog for months until they'd finally given in and rescued Lucky.

Grace planted herself down on the edge of the bed, her eyes taking in every poster, every ornament. This room was Jo. The little girl who believed in fairies, who danced around the garden in long dresses and wellingtons and loved to sing. The teenager with the odd fashion sense, the sharp wit and dry sense of humour.

The cold hand of grief engulfed Grace once more. She could smell the sweet aroma of Jo's perfume as she laid back on the bed. The scent was at its strongest on the pillow. Grace pulled it down and hugged it, inhaling deeply, until a wave of fatigue washed over her and she fell into a deep sleep.

CHAPTER TWELVE

JACKMAN ARRIVED AT the incident room before seven the next morning. After a restless night he'd woken early, turning the case over and over in his mind, examining the different scenarios that the victim could have faced in her final hours. In the end he rose, drove into the office and sat at a desk in the main incident room, outlining their priorities for the day. He was aware of people trickling in, calling greetings and removing jackets. Phones rang in the distance. A mug of coffee was placed in front of him. It wasn't until he felt a presence beside him and looked up to see Jenny, one of the support staff, that he realised daylight had reached in and spread throughout the room, extinguishing the shadows.

"I'm guessing I have your seat?" he said.

She nodded. "If you want me to move elsewhere…"

"Of course not." He smiled, gathered his papers together and moved over to the map on the far wall, marking the possible routes the victim could have taken from The Three Swans the night she died.

"Sir, you need to see this." He followed the voice across the room to where Wilson was standing behind McDonald, hands on her hips.

As soon as he reached their desk, McDonald clicked a button on his computer. An image of The Three Swans faced them. A blurred figure rushed past. Then nothing. Jackman looked across at Wilson, but she raised a hand.

A young woman slowly came into view. Her hand was cupped in front of her face. She removed it to reveal a lit cigarette, took a drag and dropped her hand, rocking from side to side as if trying to keep warm. McDonald zoomed in. A jacket was slung over her shoulders but he glimpsed a lilac dress beneath. Her hair was tied back. It was Jo.

Jackman leant into the screen. She looked easy, relaxed. A couple passed by, hand in hand. A black BMW cruised down the road, a hand casually draped out of the window. She rolled her eyes at them, looked away. They disappeared. For a few more seconds she stood there, puffing at her cigarette.

"Is that it?" Jackman asked.

"Wait." Wilson tilted her head back to the screen.

All of sudden, Jackman saw Jo look up and smile. She waved her hand, stubbed out the cigarette and crossed the road, disappearing from view.

"Play it again," Wilson said.

The footage restarted. They watched the victim go through the same routine.

"Can we get any cameras from the other side of the road?" Jackman asked.

Wilson shook her head. "We've already checked. So far this seems the only place she's featuring on any kind of town centre footage."

"She didn't walk that far then?" Jackman said.

"Either she didn't walk that far, or there weren't cameras on her route. Market Harborough's a small town. A main drag and then it pretty quickly turns residential."

"What about friends, family, hotel staff?"

"We're still interviewing, but so far the last person to come forward and claim to have seen her is her sister."

"See if you can enhance the image and trace the BMW. Looks like they'd slowed to speak to her. They might have seen who she went to meet," Jackman said. He thought about Celeste's comments at the scene, "Nothing to suggest she'd put up much of a fight." So far all the evidence suggested she knew her attacker. "Any news on the movements of known sex offenders in the vicinity?"

She shook her head. "Again we're still working through the list, but it's not leading us anywhere at the moment. There's only a handful that don't have a sub-stantiated alibi and we can't link any of them with the victim at present. We've also had the preliminary fo-rensic report through, but there's little in it."

"No footprints at the scene?"

"The vegetation was broken around the area, but no clear prints."

"Okay, what about our guys in Nottingham?"

"They've searched her room at the college, and are now interviewing her friends and tutors. They did find some medication in her room. Citalopram. It's an anti-depressant. Might be significant."

Jackman frowned. The marks on Jo's thighs pushed to the forefront of his mind. "Get Parsons to check with the family, see if they know anything about them. And find out which surgery she's registered with. Anything else?"

"The search team found her phone in the field, only about twenty yards from her body."

"Really? Did they find anything else?"

She shook her head.

"It's odd to find an earring, a student card and her

phone, all nearby. Scattered around. Almost as if they'd been placed deliberately."

"They wanted us to find them," Wilson said, guessing his thoughts. "But why?"

"The phone and student card are personal items. They wanted us to be able to identify her quickly."

Nobody spoke for a while.

"The techies have pulled some interesting stuff off her phone," Wilson said eventually. "Mostly standard texts to friends, it seems. But there is one number…" She crossed the room, pulled a sheet of paper from her desk. "Looks like she got to know this guy really well."

She passed him the paper and he ran his eyes down the messages, resting his gaze on three highlighted lines, all sent within the past two weeks:

The house is empty. Undress to impress.

I can still taste you.

Be here in ten. We're gonna play a game.

The contact was saved as FWB.

"Who's FWB?" Jackman asked.

"No idea. Sounds a bit clandestine to me."

"Can we trace them?"

"Their phone isn't registered. I've got our team up in Nottingham asking her friends and acquaintances if she was seeing anyone."

"Okay, thanks." He tapped the sheet twice with his forefinger before he passed it back to her. "Pull all the records you can get for that number. See if any of the numbers correspond with numbers on Jo's phone. It might be that someone else in her contacts can identify them."

"Will do. There is one other thing you need to know. According to one of her tutors she's been catching the train back to Market Harborough every Wednesday lunchtime for several weeks. Apparently she had a routine appointment in the afternoon. Was back in college the next morning."

"Get Parsons to check with the family," he said. "See if they can shed any light."

Jackman's phone rang as he moved back down the corridor to his room. He hated being stuck down there, away from his team. If the room hadn't been packed so tight, with the extra bodies Taylor had drafted in, he'd have been minded to take a desk in the corner so that he was nearby. But the reality was that there simply wasn't the space right now.

"Chief Inspector." Celeste's thick French accent was accentuated over the phone line.

"Morning, Celeste," Jackman said. "What have you got for me?"

"Toxicology results are back," she said. "They show a reasonable level of alcohol, nothing excessive. No evidence of Rohypnol, or a similar date drug."

That stifled another line of enquiry.

"I've read through the other cases in Operation Ascott," she continued. "The ligature marks on all three women are positioned on the mid-section of the neck, fairly consistent with some kind of strapping. Compression of carotid arteries restricts the oxygen supply to the brain, rendering most people unconsciousness within 10-15 seconds. But asphyxiation is very imprecise."

"Are you saying they could be linked and the attacker went too far with the third victim?"

"Partial strangulation is a risky business. I had a case last year of auto-erotic asphyxiation. The deceased, a middle-aged man, deliberately created a noose to temporarily compress the carotid arteries in his neck to make him lightheaded during orgasm. He got his timing wrong. A couple of seconds is all it can take."

"But you do think they're linked?"

"Well, I'd like to look into it more before I could be sure. The first woman was brutally raped. At the examination they found evidence of semen, but haven't been able to find a DNA match. There was some tearing on the right side of the vaginal passage on the second woman. No semen, or pubic hairs. No semen or hairs with our current victim too, although her vaginal passage bears tissue damage in the same place."

"So he used a condom with the second two?"

Celeste was quiet a moment. "I don't think so."

"What do you mean?"

"The injuries on the second two are more consistent with a blunt instrument, inserted at an angle. No evidence of bleeding on our current victim, so the damage was probably done post mortem."

Jackman thanked Celeste and ended the call. He'd reached his room now. He lowered himself into his chair, hung his head back. He was aware of the lack of forensic evidence in the second case. Police at the time had speculated that the attacker had possibly been disturbed and ran from the scene before he was able to finish the attack. But, although Jo's body was moved, there was nothing to suggest that her attacker had been disturbed. "A blunt instrument…inserted post mortem." The words ran through him. Jo's body had been undressed and moved. But why?

CHAPTER THIRTEEN

A TUGGING AT her arm heaved her back from the deep depths of the ocean. Grace turned away. It was warm below, a heavy weight anchoring her down. But the tugging was strong. Too strong to resist. Such was the depth of her slumber, it took a moment to focus. Phil was crouched next to her, filling her line of vision.

"You okay, love?"

Grace blinked several times. Her eyes felt heavy. She looked past him, around the room. Jo's crumpled denims were pooled on a chair in the corner. She'd never learnt to fold her clothes.

Phil reached forward. Encased her in a long hard hug. Grace didn't respond, a rag doll, her limbs lifeless. "Goodness, you're as cold as ice," he said. She'd fallen asleep on top of Jo's bed with only her cotton nightshirt covering her. But Grace didn't feel cold. This morning she didn't feel anything at all.

"I thought you were downstairs when I woke up and you were gone," he said, pulling back. "It's almost eight thirty." Grace hadn't slept past seven in years. Somewhere in the back of her mind she knew this. Although it didn't seem relevant anymore.

"I made you some tea." He gently placed an arm around her, pulled her forward and held the mug to her lips. Reluctantly she let go of the pillow she was still clutching, took a sip. It tasted odd. In all their time together Phil had never managed to make tea the way she liked it. Always too much milk. She took another sip, pushed it away.

"Lydia…" Her voice croaked.

"I've checked on her. She's still asleep."

He put the mug on the bedside table and disappeared a moment, returning with a robe and slippers. "Let's get you out of here before *you know who* arrives, eh?"

Strong arms lifted her forward, twisting her around so that her legs hung off the edge of the bed. Carefully he lifted each arm, placing them into the robe, one after the other, heaving her to standing as he tied the cord with the deftness of a parent dressing a toddler. Next he sat her down, pulled the slippers over her feet. Grace hated cold feet and was always moaning at the kids for not wearing their slippers. Today she sat there, feeling the odd tug, shift, side movement as he worked.

Even as he placed his hand in the small of her back, guided her out of the room and down the stairs, Grace still didn't utter another word. In the kitchen, he sat her down at the table and let Lucky in from the garden who came to greet her like a long lost friend. Grace instinctively stroked the dog's head, blinked again. Her mind was a fug. And that's when she heard it. The babble of conversation. Voices in the background.

She frowned, disorientated for a moment before turning towards the radio. "Detectives have identified the woman found dead on Thursday night, just outside the Leicestershire town of Market Harborough, as a Jo Lamborne…" Phil dashed forward. A loud click. The kitchen was immersed in silence.

Suddenly the mist lifted. Grace was snapped back into the present. The world in which her daughter had been murdered. The phone rang. Phil moved into the front room, closed the door behind him. Seconds later he returned. She looked up at him expectantly, but he shook his head. "Wrong number," he said. But something about his expression wasn't right.

"Who was it?"

"Nobody."

"Phil?" Grace could hear her own voice rising. This wasn't the time for secrets.

Phil's face folded. "It was a journalist."

Grace was flabbergasted. "How did they get our number?"

He shook his head, clearly dumbfounded.

The phone rang again. Grace turned her head towards the hallway. "The answerphone can get it," he said.

"Why?" But as soon as the word left Grace's mouth, she knew the answer to her question. A story, a quote, even a photograph would be top news at the moment. Hadn't they suffered enough? It was torturous. Grace placed her elbows on the table, dropped her head into her hands. "Oh, Phil. When is this going to end?"

Phil exhaled a ragged sigh. "It will. When they catch him. In the meantime, we don't answer the phone. I'll tell Chloe to text me if she needs me."

A movement upstairs. Lydia was awake.

The sound of the doorbell. Lucky barked and rushed off to the hallway, closely followed by Phil. Grace recognised DC Emma Parsons' voice as she greeted him. A rush of cold air followed the detective into the kitchen.

"Any news?" Phil asked as he followed her through.

Parsons shook her head and gave Grace a gentle smile. "How are you feeling today?"

Grace blinked, looked away.

"I do have some more questions, if you feel up to it?" Parsons said.

A floorboard creaked above them. "I have to go to Lydia," she said. And with that she marched out of the kitchen and up the stairs.

JACKMAN WANDERED BACK into the incident room later that afternoon. Officers pored over desks, stared at computer screens; some had phones glued to their ears, others were tapping away at keys. He halted beside McDonald's desk. "Any news on the BMW?"

"Not yet," McDonald replied. "I've done some work on the footage, but we still can't decipher the number plate. It doesn't seem to have been picked up on any of the police cameras, coming in or out of Harborough either, probably turned off into one of the side roads." He sighed. "There's so many of them."

"Check the town centre residences and businesses for any private camera footage on that route. Might be clearer. And contact the press office to put out an appeal for the car. The driver or passengers could well have seen whoever it was that was waiting for the victim." Jackman looked around, addressed the room. "Anything else?" Heads shook in unison.

He turned as Wilson rushed in, holding her phone high as if it was a winning lottery ticket.

"Good news," Wilson said. "We've traced FWB. The texting friend."

Jackman felt a frisson of excitement. "Who is he?"

"Name's Anthony Kendall. A fellow student at Nottingham, studying psychology. He's on his way down to talk to us now."

CHAPTER FOURTEEN

GRACE TOOK ONE last look at Lydia before she shut the door to her bedroom and made her way downstairs. Lydia's friend had visited to comfort her. Perhaps it would take her mind off things for a while.

At the bottom of the stairs she could hear voices coming from the kitchen and veered off into the front room. It was quiet in there. She sat on the small sofa, rested her head back and looked up at the ceiling. Her eyes ached, her head felt heavy, but sleep danced on the edge of her vision, refusing to come forward and sweep her away.

It wasn't long before the door pushed open. Detective Parsons appeared, a cup of tea in hand. "Heard you coming downstairs," she said. "Thought you might like one of these."

Grace stared at her suspiciously, but when she didn't follow it up with any more questions, she relaxed slightly, took a sip. It tasted good, not like the weak excuses for tea that Phil made.

They sat there for a while. The detective passed comment on the weather, although Grace wasn't really listening. Phil came through, sat beside Grace and gave her an awkward smile.

Eventually the detective eased forward. "Could you tell me more about the problems Jo suffered in her teens?"

Grace shook her head. "I'd rather not talk about it. It's something we put behind us. Years ago."

"I'm afraid I do need to ask some more questions about it."

"Why?"

"It's essential for us to get to know the real Jo, so that we can put together a picture of her life, old and new. It's possible that an event somewhere might trigger something fresh."

Grace drew a long, defeated breath before she spoke. "Most people didn't really know Jo," she said. "They saw the confident girl that made everyone laugh, singing at karaoke, not afraid to share her opinions with the world. But she was quite fragile underneath." She rubbed her forehead. "She took her father's death badly in her early teens. Became withdrawn and quiet. We all rallied around, supporting each other. But Jo's always been stubborn. She keeps things inside." She hesitated a moment. "Like the scars on her legs…"

Parsons nodded, encouraging her to continue.

"She kept them covered up. I walked in on her in the shower one day, noticed them by accident. Turns out she'd been cutting herself for months." Tears pricked Grace's eyelids. "It was so difficult. She refused to admit anything was wrong. Said she felt suffocated, by all of us. Only agreed to get help if we backed off and let her do it her own way." Grace swiped a tear from her cheek. "It took a while, but medication and counselling really made a difference. That was years ago and she's been fine, all through her A levels. We've put it behind us."

"We found some Citalopram in her room." Parsons voice was barely a whisper.

Grace felt as though she'd been plunged into cold water. "What?"

"It's an antidepressant."

"I know what it is," Grace snapped. She was struggling to breathe. "But it wasn't necessarily Jo's. She shared the room with another student."

"It was found amongst her belongings." The detective's face softened. "I'm sorry, but I have to ask you if…"

"No. *If* Jo was back on antidepressants, I didn't know."

Grace was still for a moment. Searching through her memories. Trying to recall moments, indications that Jo had relapsed. But there were none.

"There's something else I need to ask you," Parsons said. "It's been reported that she has been coming back to Market Harborough on a Wednesday afternoon for an appointment."

"What do you mean?"

"It's been confirmed by two sources at Nottingham, although they don't know why. Do you know anything about that? Apparently she was getting a train on a Wednesday lunchtime, returning so as to be back in class the next morning."

"No, I don't know anything about it." Grace shot Phil a look. He shook his head too, mystified.

"Perhaps your other daughter, or Chloe might be able to help?"

"No." Grace shook her head firmly. "I will not have you talking to Lydia. I'll speak to her. And Chloe. But I very much doubt either of them knew anything. Like I said, Jo didn't always like to share."

"I'm sorry. I know this is difficult for you. But is there anything else you haven't told us? Maybe an old relationship, or something that has gone wrong in Jo's life, or the family in general?"

Grace swallowed. She grappled with her thoughts, wondering if she should share the details of her own attack. But what good would it do? She had no idea who'd attacked her all those years ago. What relevance could it possibly have now? She sat tall, shook her head. "We keep getting calls from reporters," she said, changing the subject.

"Yes. Your husband has spoken to me about that. We'll be dealing directly with the press. They shouldn't be contacting you. If you receive any more calls, please let me know and I'll take it further."

ANTHONY KENDALL LOOKED up as Jackman and Wilson entered the room. He was of average build, with light brown hair swept back to hide a thinning patch around the crown and striking hazel eyes that followed their every movement.

Jackman mustered a kind smile and introduced them both. "Thank you for coming down from Nottingham to see us today," he said.

"Anything I can do to help. Still can't believe it, to be honest."

Jackman sat on the sofa opposite, Wilson beside him. He'd reserved one of the softer rooms they usually kept for vulnerable witnesses to interview Anthony, expecting a nervous young student, and was surprised when a mature man had arrived at reception. "Can I get you a glass of water, or a coffee?"

"No, thank you."

"When did you find out about Jo?" Jackman asked when they'd settled themselves down.

"Friday evening. We were in the student bar. Everyone was talking about it."

"It must have been quite a shock."

"You can say that again." He shook his head.

"How long have you known Jo?"

"We both joined university at the end of September. Became friends soon after."

Jackman eased back into his seat. "You're a mature student?"

"Yes."

"Studying?"

"Psychology."

"May I ask what you did before?"

"I've been in sales for most of my working life. A couple of years ago I decided I needed a change."

"Where did you live before?"

"I've always lived in Nottingham. Was fortunate to get a place at the local uni."

Wilson's pen scratched the pad as she made her notes. "How long have you been seeing Jo?" Jackman asked.

"We weren't…seeing each other as such. We just got together sometimes."

"What do you mean?"

"Well, she wasn't my girlfriend or anything like that."

Wilson clicked the end of her pen twice. "Can you remember when you first spoke to her?"

"I'd seen her in the student union bar a few times, chatting, drinking. She used to complain about the music they played. One evening she brought in some of her own. Biffy Clyro, I think it was. I congratulated her on her music taste and we got talking. Must have been," he stroked his chin, "a week or so after we started."

"About four weeks ago then?" Jackman said.

He gave a slow nod.

"How often did you see her?"

Anthony rubbed the back of his neck. "Maybe a couple of times a week."

"But she was just a friend?"

"Kind of."

Wilson looked up from her notes. "Do you have a girlfriend, Anthony?" she asked.

He shook his head. "Happily single."

Jackman surveyed him a moment. His demin jacket and scarf seemed a feeble attempt at student attire. A far cry from the sales world he was previously used to, Jackman imagined. "So she wasn't your girlfriend. She was your 'kind of' friend?" Jackman said.

"Yes."

Nobody spoke for a minute. Anthony shifted in his seat.

Jackman retrieved a paper from the file on the table beside him and passed it across to Anthony. "Do you recognise these text messages?" Anthony glanced at the paper and dragged a flat hand down the front of his face, leaving it to rest on his chin. "Did you send them?" Jackman added.

He nodded.

"It seems you had quite an intimate relationship for a friend."

"Look, she was a good laugh. We met up some times. Had sex. Neither of us wanted more than that."

Jackman pointed to one of the text messages. "What do you mean by 'a game'?"

Anthony's hand dropped to his lap. "She was a bit… adventurous. Liked to do things differently. You know."

Jackman shook his head. Celeste's comments about

auto-erotic asphyxiation skipped into his mind. "Have you ever put anything around Jo's neck?"

"What? No!"

"Or your own?"

"What is this?"

Jackman ignored the question. "How old are you, Mr Kendall?"

"I don't see that's relevant." The silence lingered. "Thirty-six," he said eventually.

"And Jo was…" He made a play of consulting his notes. "Nineteen. So you met up with a nineteen-year-old for occasional sex?"

"Nothing illegal about that."

"So why do you feel uncomfortable about it?"

Anthony looked down. It was a moment before he met Jackman's gaze. "Well she's dead, isn't she? Doesn't feel right talking about her like that now."

Jackman softened his tone. "Did Jo talk to you much when you were together?"

"A little." He shrugged a single shoulder. "Sometimes not at all. Depended on her mood really."

"What did you talk about?"

"Nothing much. Uni stuff."

"Did she ever seem upset? Mention someone that might be angry with her, want to hurt her?"

"No."

"What about at university. Was she popular?"

Anthony gave a half-hearted nod. "She always seemed to have friends around her."

Jackman sighed inwardly. He'd read through the statements from her friends at Nottingham. They spent time together, knew about her family. But none of them claimed to be close confidantes. Her friends in Market

Harborough had also been interviewed. Even her best friend from secondary school didn't appear to know much more about her. It seemed she kept herself to herself. What was it about this girl that made her so mysterious? "When was the last time you saw her?" he asked.

"Last Saturday. She came over at lunchtime. Stayed about an hour." His bottom lip quivered as he looked away. "When she left, I remember I said, 'Catch you later'. And she said, 'Maybe'."

"What do you think she meant by that?"

"Nothing. She was always like that when we parted. Aloof. Used to make me laugh." He raised his eyes, met Jackman's gaze. "But now I can't get it out of my head."

"And you didn't see her again?"

He shook his head. "We only got together if one of us texted. She'd told me she was coming home on Tuesday for a family wedding. I didn't really expect to hear anything from her for a while."

"Anthony, can you tell me what were you doing last Thursday evening?"

Anthony's eyes widened. "Am I a suspect?"

"I didn't say that. But you knew Jo, were close to her. We need to eliminate you from our enquiries."

Anthony looked from one detective to another. "I was playing football early evening, then went out drinking with the lads, then to a club. We didn't get home until the early hours."

"Thank you. We'll need the names of the people you were with. Have you ever visited Market Harborough before?" Jackman said. "Perhaps to see Jo's parents?"

"Not to see her parents. I did take Jo there once though. She had an appointment. They'd cut out some trains midday, urgent work on the line, and she asked me to drive her. I think I was one of her few friends with a car."

"When was this?"

"Two weeks ago. On the Wednesday. I remember exactly because I missed my lecture in the afternoon and had to borrow the notes from someone."

"What did she come back for?"

"I don't know. She wouldn't tell me anything about it. I was only allowed to drop her at the station. Jo could be like that sometimes."

"Like what?"

"Secretive. If she didn't want to tell you something there was no way of getting it out of her."

"Where did you pick her up from on that Wednesday?"

"I didn't. She got the train back."

"So you just drove down to Market Harborough and straight back up to Nottingham?"

He gave a single nod. "It's not that far. She insisted on giving me her train fare for petrol."

The droning sound of a lorry filled the room as it passed outside. Anthony studied his feet.

"Do you have other girls you meet for sex?"

"I don't see that's relevant."

"Anthony, where were you on the nights of the 24th of April 2015, and the 28th of April 2006?"

"What? I have no idea. I'd have to check. Why?"

"Two other girls were attacked and strangled, but not killed."

"And you think it was me?"

"I didn't say that. But once again, we do need to eliminate you from our enquiries."

Anthony looked stunned. His face drawn with the sudden realisation of it all.

"Sergeant Wilson will take the details. Please also give her your contact number and address in case we need to speak to you again." Jackman made for the door, rested his hand on the handle and turned as another thought occurred to him. "One other thing. What does FWB stand for?"

Anthony coughed. It was a moment before he answered. "Friend with benefits." His eyes watered. "Jo thought it was funny."

LATER THAT EVENING, Jackman glanced at the clock at the bottom of his computer screen. It was now almost forty-eight hours since Jo's body had been found. Something about Anthony Kendall bothered him. Over the course of his career, Jackman had interviewed endless victims, suspects and witnesses. Some were nervous of law enforcement, some overconfident, others aggressive. Yet most of the time their story explained how they presented. Kendall had no previous police record and colleagues in Nottingham claimed to have no intelligence on file for him. He could account for his movements when Jo was attacked. He'd come forward voluntarily, as soon as he heard they wanted to speak to Jo's associates, and offered to be interviewed. But he'd seemed edgy in interview. Was Anthony generally nervous of the police, grief stricken at the loss of Jo, a friend he claimed to barely know, or was there something else going on that he wasn't talking about?

CHAPTER FIFTEEN

BEWARE OF FEELING too happy, of smiling inwardly and being thankful for all you have in the world. Because that's when it all tends to go wrong. These thoughts plagued Grace as she blinked into the darkness.

After hours of tossing and turning like an abandoned boat at sea, she'd left her bed and padded downstairs. She wasn't sure how long she'd sat there on the sofa. The mug she cradled was stone cold. The room was shrouded in darkness, although this didn't seem to make much difference; days morphed into night as sleep eluded her.

Grace sat back, her mind slipping in and out of memories. Lydia playing the flute at the last concert of primary school. The smile that shone on Jo's face as she stood in the kitchen and waved an envelope containing her A level results. The girls in their bridesmaid dresses on her wedding day to Phil.

An image of their father, Jamie, filled her mind. She could still remember the day he told her he was going to die. She was in the kitchen ironing, listening to Billy Connolly on *Desert Island Discs*. The patio doors were open, the kitchen full of the aroma of sweet peas that wafted in from the garden.

She heard the front door bang, the click of the handle as it was forced up several times before the key turned. Jamie had never been light-handed.

Moments later his face appeared in the doorway. "Cup of tea?"

No greeting, but then he rarely passed greetings. 'Hellos and goodbyes are for people you don't see very often,' he used to say. 'We have no need for either.'

Grace had nodded. "If you're making." Her usual response. She didn't notice the sadness in his face that day, lost in the ironing as he placed the mugs on the table. It wasn't until he reached across and took the iron from her hand that she looked up.

"Come over here. We need to talk."

Within moments of them sitting down, her world changed. He had cancer. It was terminal. She recalled the shock, tears and disbelief that manifested itself in the questions she fired at him. But resistance was futile. For months he'd been through tests, keeping it all to himself until he was absolutely sure that all the avenues had been exhausted.

Less than two months later he passed away, quietly, with his family around him.

After she lost Jamie, Grace resolved herself to a life alone. He may not have been her true love, but they had navigated the ebb and flow of life together for so many years that their lives had become entwined. He was a kind and considerate father, a generous husband. Always made time for the children when they were young, even after a long day at work, supported her as she studied for her English Literature degree and rallied around to help in the home.

The months after Jamie's death had been difficult, not only emotionally but also financially. Their mortgage was paid off, but Jamie was self-employed and had made no provision for life insurance. Grace went back to work full time, had to be extra careful with money to ensure the girls didn't miss out.

She could never have imagined that a chance meeting, six months afterwards, would eventually lead to marriage. When she stepped into the supermarket that Saturday morning and someone grabbed her bag, the man that came to her aid turned out to be the manager. After the police were called and the robber apprehended, he offered her a milky tea in his office. Dinner followed. More dates. Her girls choosing her clothes, arranging her hair. Only a year after their father's death, Phil proposed. She remembered the girls were apprehensive at first. But his easy-going nature won them round in the end. It seemed her girls, mature beyond their years, were far more concerned with her future happiness than she was.

After the wedding and subsequent sale of Phil's house, all those months of scrimping and saving were behind her. She reduced her hours at the library, focused on renovating the house. Spent more time with her girls, indulged in her love of cooking and planning meals for her family. Rather unexpectedly, her life had turned around.

But she would give it all up, right now, to turn back the clock and have her girl back.

She recalled those first difficult months after Jamie died. Even though they'd had some time to prepare, to face the idea of losing him, it didn't seem to make the loss any easier to bear. The gaping hole he left behind sat as a permanent void in the midst of family life. But they had pieced together the fragments, found a path through the grief. And gradually, they realised they were able to share the memories of him with smiles instead of tears.

A pang of guilt made her flinch. She hadn't seen how the grief had penetrated Jo, ripping her apart, limb by limb until the knife had wedged itself in so deep it was difficult to remove. Their GP recommended medication and therapy. Two years of support groups improved things. Jo adored Phil. The last few years had been easier. They'd put her struggles behind them, or so she'd thought.

How could she not have known that her daughter was back on antidepressants? She thought of Jo's beautiful olive skin, marked by the scars of her teenage years. What kind of mother misses the signs twice?

The guilt grew, gnawing away at her. What else didn't she know?

The fabric of their lives was being torn apart again. But this wasn't a tear that Grace could stitch together or even a hole that could be patched up. No, this was a slash right through the middle. And right now she had no idea how to even start piecing together the threads to mend it.

Her head jerked forward. Cold tea spilled into her lap, merging with the tears that dripped from her chin as she wept.

CHAPTER SIXTEEN

"ANTHONY KENDALL. No previous record. Not known to us. We know he had rather a clandestine relationship with Jo Lamborne. They texted, met up for sex. He said she liked to do things differently." Jackman paused a moment. Quiet fell upon their morning briefing as the word *differently* hung in the air. "We know he was in Nottingham at the time of her murder. That doesn't mean he wasn't involved in some way. We haven't found anything that suggested Jo Lamborne, Shelley Barnstaple and Eugenie Trentwood knew each other. If the cases are linked, there has to be something, somewhere." He took a deep breath, slowly exhaled. "Anthony Kendall is a mature student of average build—seems to keep himself fit. He fits the profile. Is he our link? Has he crossed paths with the other victims? Does he have other women he regularly meets for sex? Is he part of a group that targets girls for sex?" A phone rang in the background. "Pull his phone records, examine his social media and speak to previous work colleagues. He said he's only visited Leicestershire a couple of times. Let's make sure he's telling the truth there."

Jackman scanned the room until he found McDonald, perched on the edge of a desk that was bowing slightly. "Any news on the BMW?"

McDonald nodded. "It's not good. We finally managed to enhance the number plate. Traced it back to a businesswoman from Northampton who was away in Manchester all week, with her car. The plates had been cloned. I'm trawling through reports of stolen cars at the moment to see if we can identify it."

"Okay, thanks."

Jackman reached down to gather his notes when the sound of a receiver being replaced at the back of the room caught his attention. He looked up as Wilson stood and gave him a startled glance. "You're not going to believe this, sir. A man walked into Wigston Station this morning and said he wants to confess to the attack on Shelley Barnstaple."

A SHRILL SCREAM shot through the darkness. Grace jolted forward in bed. It was coming from the ground floor. The pitch so familiar, it almost rang inside her. She jumped up and made for the stairs. Stumbled at the top, grabbing the banister to save herself. The screaming grew louder. She pushed forward, missed a step. Faltered...

Grace woke with a start. Her heart was racing. Her body drenched in a cold sweat. She was in Jo's room, the duvet curled around her legs from the night before. A dream. It was only a dream.

Instinctively she reached across, pulled a handful of tissues out of the box beside her, wiped the sweat from the back of her neck and shoulders. Footsteps shuffled across the tiles in the kitchen below. A cupboard door closed. The whirr of the kettle as it heated up. Grace raised her head to view Jo's clock on the bedside table. It was 7.15am. She tossed the tissues towards the bin in the corner, sighed when they missed and rested back into the pillow. Phil's sister, Geraldine, or Ged as she preferred to be called, was coming over from Spain today. Her flight wasn't due in until late afternoon but Phil's careful nature wouldn't allow him to settle until he'd collected her. His day would be consumed with watching the internet for plane delays, mapping his route to the airport around the roadworks on the M1, making sure that he timed it all right.

This was the earliest flight Ged had been able to book without paying an extortionate fee. Phil and Ged were close. Ten years older than him, she divorced young and gave her life to a career at the Home Office, travelling the world. It was no surprise that she chose to settle in Spain when she'd retired, two years earlier. She'd busied herself with buying up cheap apartments, renovating and reselling them to supplement her pension. They'd been out to see her several times, stayed in half-completed apartments with swimming pools and basked in the sunshine. Ged had embraced Grace and her girls as soon as her brother announced their engagement. With no children of her own, Phil's family were her family. Grace usually looked forward to her visits, they all did. Ged was great company. Although this time it wouldn't quite be the same.

Grace glanced idly around the room. An old cobweb in the corner fluttered in the breeze of the open window. She watched it awhile, until she became aware of mumblings from the radio below. The mention of Jo's name caught her attention. She craned her neck towards the voices. It was turned down, she had to strain to listen, but she could just about make out the local news report. The press were talking about Jo in the same breath as the other two girls that had been attacked in Oadby. Was it the same offender?

The thought that Jo had possibly been attacked by the same person repulsed her. Her eyes burned with the fresh assault of tears. The dream rushed back into her mind. It was Jo, screaming, calling for her. And she wasn't there when she needed her most.

CHAPTER SEVENTEEN

OLIVER TURNER WAS a thickset man with grey stubble covering his chin and a road map of broken veins tracing his cheeks. He pushed his fringe out of his eyes and leant an elbow on the empty chair beside him. "Shelley Barnstaple went out with my late brother, Ken. He died of leukaemia almost ten years ago." He cleared his throat. "She worked at The Windmill pub in Oadby behind the bar. Had done for years. Ken and I used to drink in there on a Friday night." He snorted, shook his head. "He had a fling with her. It broke up his marriage. Thirty years younger than him she was, and he was pretty chuffed to pull her. They'd been seeing each other about a year when he died. She was always working late, flirting with the locals. There were rumours it was more than that, but none of it seemed to bother Ken. He was almost proud of the fact that other men found her attractive. Like my wife and I, neither of them had children. Only each other."

He paused for a moment, lost in thought, before he continued. "My brother took sick very quickly. He was diagnosed and died within a week. It was a huge shock to everyone at the time. We all felt sorry for Shelley. Rallied around. Essie made stews, lasagne, took them around to her home."

Wilson looked up from her notes. "Essie?"

"Sorry, my wife. Her name was Vanessa, but everyone called her Essie." Oliver turned back to Jackman. "A week later, the day after my brother's funeral, Shelley was back behind the bar, same as usual. I didn't judge her. I know everyone copes differently with grief, but there was no…" he grimaced, "sadness in her. If you didn't know, you'd say she'd been away for a couple of weeks on holiday. I continued to drink in there on a Friday night, but moved to sit in the lounge. Too many memories of my brother in the bar area. And I couldn't bear to watch her laughing and joking with the customers, flaunting herself. It didn't seem right. Shelley was cold with me, didn't answer Essie's calls after the funeral. We'd never been close, but she seemed to be cutting us off, erasing every memory she had of my brother.

"Then Essie told me Shelley had been seen getting cosy with John, one of the barflies, in the car park. Well, more than cosy. I couldn't believe it, my brother hadn't been dead a month. I was furious, wanted to go down there, teach them both a lesson. I'd worked with John on a factory refit the year before and he'd always been a dirty sod. No principles. But Essie wouldn't let me go. She said it was just a malicious rumour." His eyes softened. "Essie always saw the best in everyone.

"The following Friday I left the pub early. Essie had caught a bug in the week and I didn't want to leave her too long. She had a bad heart, was vulnerable to illness. And I saw Shelley, out by the bins, worse this time. Her skirt was hitched up to her thighs, him pumping into her." His nostrils flared at the memory. "But it wasn't John. It was another of the guys. Tim, I think they called him. I could hear her, that cackle of a laugh. It went through me. It was all I could do to stop myself going over there and beating them both to a pulp. But I had to think of Essie. All the way home, the image stayed with me. How dare she soil my dead brother's memory? He thought the world of her.

"I stopped going to that pub. Stayed in with Essie on a Friday night. But she was always in bed by ten and I was restless. It was the end of the week. Sometimes I'd go out for a late walk. If I passed The Windmill I'd often see Shelley, finishing her shift. Sometimes on her own, sometimes she was with someone. Usually I'd hear that distinctive cackle before I even set eyes on her. She never saw me, I stayed back in the shadows. If she was on her own I followed her home. That's when the idea came to me. I wanted to do something. To frighten her. Stop her from making a fool of herself, for degrading my brother's memory. I didn't intend to hurt her." He shook his head.

"Tell me about the night of the 28th of April 2006," Jackman said.

Oliver drew a ragged breath. "I went for a walk, hung around the pub, waited for her to leave. She was later than usual. I was about to change my mind when she wobbled out, clearly drunk, a man I didn't recognise with her. She turned and snogged him, before he walked off in the opposite direction. I was angry. More than angry. I'd never felt fury like it. I remember pulling my belt out of the stays, snapping it together. She looked around. I thought she'd seen me, but she turned away and started towards her home."

"And you followed her?"

Oliver nodded. His eyes were sad. A defeated look on his face. "I waited until she reached the waste ground at the bottom of her road and flung the belt around her neck." He covered his face with his hands a moment. "I don't know, it all happened so quickly after that." He looked up. "I'd researched for hours on how to strangle someone without actually killing them—just pull at the ligature until they go limp. But she fought like a cat. I remember punching her, watching her fall to the ground."

Wilson looked up. "What happened then?"

He choked a swallow. In that moment his large form seemed to reduce to a third of its actual size. "I was in a rage, I didn't know what I was doing. One moment she was on the ground, the next I was zipping up my trousers, brushing off my knees."

"You raped her?"

"Yes." His face turned ashen.

Jackman squared his hands on the table between them. "Did the police speak to you at the time?"

Oliver nodded. "They spoke to everyone who knew her. Essie said I was at home. She thought I was. Had left me in the armchair when she went up to bed. But it was in the news. I was convinced the detectives would eventually find out. I dreaded the phone ringing, dreaded every knock at the door. And as the days and weeks passed, when it didn't come, I thought I'd feel relieved." He shook his head. "But I didn't. It ate away at me. And I couldn't confess, dredge it all back up. It would have broken Essie, especially with her bad heart. She didn't deserve any of this."

Jackman's eyes rested on the gold chain in an evidence bag, sat on the table between them. "Why did you keep her necklace?"

Turner followed his gaze. "I don't know really. I don't even remember pulling it off her neck. It wasn't until

I got home that I found it in my pocket, when I put my clothes through the washer. It was a present from my brother. I remember when he showed it to me. I guess I didn't think she deserved it. But it didn't seem right to throw it away. I hid it in with my spanners down the shed."

"Why come forward now?" Jackman asked.

Oliver reached for the cup to his side. His hand trembled as he took a sip. "Essie died earlier this year. I wanted to come then. I planned to, after the funeral, when I'd laid her to rest."

"And where were you on Friday the 24th April 2015?"

Oliver met Jackman's gaze. "I know what you're thinking, but it wasn't me. The 24th of April was the date we buried Essie. I was at her wake when the second girl was attacked. Didn't hear about it until the next day. But it scared the living daylights out of me. The timing, the similarities. It was almost as if somebody knew, was making me pay… I watched the news reports again and again, turned it over and over in my mind."

"Why now?" Jackman said.

"The other girl, the teenager that was killed. I saw it on the news and thought I ought to come forward, to clear any link with Shelley's case."

"So you've grown a conscience?" Wilson said.

"Look, I don't know who attacked the other two girls, but it certainly wasn't me."

CHAPTER EIGHTEEN

"His story seems to check out," Wilson said. They were seated in a small meeting room, on a conference call with Taylor. "We're getting it all confirmed but the 24th of April was the date of his wife's funeral. There are bound to be witnesses. And initial enquiries confirm that last Thursday he was at The Red Lion. Apparently he's been going there since his wife died. Landlord put him in a taxi at 12.30am, drunk."

"Where does that leave us?" Taylor said.

"If his confession stands we'll get a DNA match with the semen found on Shelley Barnstaple and we can charge him with her attack," Jackman said. He thought of Artie Black and his unrelenting interest in the case. "The papers are bound to latch onto this one. We've arrested Oliver Turner on suspicion of all three attacks to give us time to confirm whether or not his alibis play out. Let's keep him in custody and keep it to ourselves for the moment, until we know what we're dealing with. I want to check out his movements before we make any statements."

Wilson scrunched her face, causing tiny lines to appear down each side of her nose. "I can't believe he got away with it," she said. "Stranger rape is so uncommon. It was before my time, but it would have been allocated high priority. They would have pulled out all the stops."

"It was almost ten years ago," Jackman said. "We

weren't obsessed with cameras like we are now, very few people had CCTV. A residential area. No witnesses…"

"Okay," Taylor interjected. "Get the DNA pushed through. I don't care how much it costs. I don't want this lingering for any longer than necessary. How about the others?"

Wilson caught Jackman's eye. "If they're not connected, then someone's definitely done their homework," she said.

"What about the guy from Nottingham? Anthony Kendall?"

"We're still looking into his background," Jackman said. "At the moment, nothing suggests he's involved, but we're keeping an open mind."

"Okay, keep me updated on all developments." The phone line crackled as he ended the call.

It was a moment before Jackman spoke. "Get somebody to look into Oliver Turner's background," he said almost to himself. "He's given himself a motive for Shelley's attack. Does he have an association with the other girls? We'll need to seize his computer and his phone, and get his house locked down and guarded until we've had a chance to give it a thorough search. Make sure they're discreet though, will you? I don't want to draw any undue attention. And see if there's any association between Turner and Kendall."

Wilson looked up from her notes. "What are you thinking?"

"It's a long shot." He recalled Celeste's comments about the similarities and differences between the attacks. "But we can't rule out the fact that they might have been working together, or even as part of a group."

GRACE WAS STANDING by the kitchen window when the sound of the doorbell caught her attention. She turned her head as Parsons answered. The door rattled as it opened. Parsons greeted the caller with recognition in her voice. Lydia looked up from her magazine and stretched her arms back as her mother leant towards the door, listening intently. "Is that Auntie Ged?" Lydia said, her words muffled by a yawn.

Grace flicked her eyes to the clock. She walked over and brushed the hair out of Lydia's face. "I don't think so, darling. Her flight wasn't due in until after two. I doubt she'll be here for at least another half an hour."

Grace was surprised to see the chief inspector enter the room, followed by Parsons. A shot of adrenalin rushed through her. His presence meant news.

They all walked into the front room. He sat on the edge of the sofa, clasped his hands together.

"How are you, Grace?" he said.

"Okay," Grace managed to squeeze out through bated breath.

Jackman nodded soberly. "I wonder if I could ask you a couple more questions?"

Grace's breath faltered. For a brief moment she'd thought he'd come to tell her they'd made an arrest.

"Has Jo ever mentioned the names Oliver Turner or Anthony Kendall to you?"

Grace shook her head.

"Think hard, please," Jackman said. "It might be important."

Grace sat quietly, digging into the depths of her memory. "I don't think so. Why?"

The detective's face was impassive. "They're just lines of enquiry we're investigating. Has Jo ever been associated with The Windmill pub, or had any friends in Oadby?"

"Not that she mentioned."

"Okay, thank you."

"You haven't caught him then?"

"We are working on several leads, but no charge has been made yet." He inched forward. "We have some camera footage of Jo standing outside The Three Swans, after her sister left on Thursday night. It shows her waving at somebody, crossing the road towards them. Do you know who that might be?"

Grace shrugged. "Could be someone from the wedding. I really don't know." The news report from earlier that morning played on her mind. She met his gaze. "Can I ask you a question, Inspector?"

"Of course."

"Do you think the person that attacked Jo also attacked those other two girls, in Oadby?"

"Again, it's a line of enquiry we are looking at. We can't be sure at the moment."

"But the similarities…" Her voice broke.

"I understand your concern," Jackman replied.

"But you still don't know?"

"Not at this precise moment, no." His words were soft, quiet. He placed his hand in his pocket and pulled out a card. "I'm so sorry," he said. "I know this is difficult. But we are doing everything we can. If you think of anything, or have any questions, please give me a call. That's my direct number."

Grace couldn't move. Her throat constricted. Lydia reached out and took the card.

A car door slammed on the driveway. The sound of the front door opening followed. Phil's face appeared around the door, his eyes immediately widening as they rested on Jackman. "What's happened?"

Grace looked up at him. "Nothing, love," she said. "Absolutely nothing."

CHAPTER NINETEEN

JACKMAN GLANCED OUT of the open shed door and into the garden beyond. The early morning clouds had thickened, bringing with them the threat of rain and casting a murky sheen on the surrounding area. He pressed a switch. The light bulb flickered a couple of times before illuminating the room. He pushed the door to a cabinet shut, peered up at the ceiling beams, then crouched beside a workbench. Apart from an array of old cobwebs masking the windows, Oliver Turner's shed was possibly the most ordered he'd been in. He wasn't really sure what he was looking for, but the fact that Oliver claimed to have kept Shelley's necklace in his toolbox felt significant, almost as if he wished to bury his secrets down there, away from the house.

He rubbed his hand along the workbench, the wood tugging at the rubber of his glove, before he switched off the light. His mobile rang as he shut the door behind him. "Wilson" flashed up on the screen.

"I've been in touch with the doctors' surgery this morning," Wilson said. "It seems Jo Lamborne's own GP is away in Cyprus until next week. They've accessed the medical records and confirmed her prescription, but couldn't see anything in her notes to confirm a weekly medical appointment. Want me to go out and visit, see if I can speak to one of the other doctors there?"

"No, if there's nothing in her notes, it's unlikely

they'll be able to tell you anything. We'll leave it until her own GP's back. She may have discussed things with her that aren't on file. What about Oliver Turner's alibis?"

"We are working our way through his late wife's friends and family. It seems he's been rather a loner since his brother died. We just need to account for all his movements during her wake, in case he dropped out for a bit."

"And last Thursday?"

"Landlord's confirmed he was in The Red Lion from 9pm until the early hours. It was his birthday. Apparently he drunk the best part of a bottle of whisky and made quite a nuisance of himself."

"Okay, anything else?"

"Forensics have discovered a tiny spot of blood on the earring found at the crime scene, barely visible to the eye but they've managed to extract the DNA. It doesn't match Jo."

"Excellent. Get it checked with Oliver's, will you?"

Jackman ended the call and glanced up at the back of Oliver's house. The CSI team were clambering around inside. So far, no amount of searching had uncovered anything to link him with the two other girls.

GRACE SAT AT the kitchen table in her pyjamas, a white towelling bath robe hanging off the edge of her shoulders, a tepid cup of tea in her hand. She could hear Phil and Ged in the front room, the floorboards above creaking as Lydia moved around upstairs. A food magazine sat open in front of her, although she'd barely looked at it for the last twenty minutes she'd sat there. Lucky scampered over and placed a paw on her calf. She bent down and stroked the dog's head.

Dinner with Ged had been a sober affair last night, a takeaway from the nearby Chinese. Poor Phil. He'd chosen crispy duck and pancakes, Grace's favourite, in an attempt to encourage her to eat, no doubt, but she could only manage to nibble the edge of one of them. They talked in half-sentences about his sister's flight and her house in Spain. Danced around the incident with Jo. It was clear that Ged wanted to hear all the details. Grace understood this, although not wishing to hear them relayed again she'd excused herself and gone to bed.

Today, Ged had risen early, gone shopping for eggs and bacon and cooked them all a breakfast. It was good to have Ged here, to care for the family, allow her to escape into her own world. She hadn't even passed comment when she'd found Grace sleeping in Jo's room this morning.

Lucky curled around her ankles. Grace watched her a moment, admiring her ability to instantly fall into a deep sleep, then scanned the kitchen, her eyes eventually resting on the laptop on the corner of the table. She pulled it towards her, opened it, logged onto the internet and gasped.

It was all over the news.

Of course it would be. She had to check herself. But the stark reality of it made her breath catch in her throat. Grace read through the reports, one by one, fresh tears itching her face as they sloped down her cheekbones. There was heavy speculation about a connection with the other attacks. The press talked about clumsy police work, a failure to link the investigations. Grace was both drawn to and appalled by what she read. She recalled the short-lived elation she'd felt yesterday when she'd seen the detective, only to be scuppered by more questions.

The detective's attempt at reassurance had fallen on deaf ears. She liked the DCI. He seemed a nice man. He'd come out to see her himself, tried to answer her questions, given her his personal card. The newspaper articles said he was a senior officer, brought in especially as a regional lead. Yet they were no closer to catching Jo's killer. He'd asked more questions, talked about lines of enquiry. She dragged a hand through her hair as she tried to remember the two names he'd mentioned: Oliver Turner and… She wracked her brains.

Grace didn't hear Ged appear. Wasn't aware of her presence until she felt a hand on her arm. "Oh, Grace." Ged closed the laptop before her eyes. "Don't torture yourself." Before she had time to protest, Ged had pulled out the chair and sat beside her sister-in-law, wrapping her arms around her. "What a bloody awful thing to have happened," Ged continued, rubbing Grace's back tenderly. "She was such a lovely girl. I can't believe she's gone."

The clocks stopped as they wept softly together. Phil came through and passed them tissues. Finally Grace drew back and took a deep breath. "I want to do something to help," she said feebly.

"Of course you do," Ged said, pressing her hand on Grace's. "It's only natural you'd want to do that. You were her mother."

"The papers are linking it to the other attacks in Oadby."

"I know, love," Ged said. "But we have to leave the case to the police now. We'll help as much as we can."

"I think we can do more." Grace flipped open the laptop. "If we only…"

"Don't," Phil said quietly, putting his hand over hers. The computer light switched off as the lid closed. "Don't read the news reports."

"But they've raised all sorts of issues. There's one reporter, he's…"

"Phil's right," Ged said. Her face slackened as fresh tears swelled in her eyes. "Don't do it, Grace. It'll only mess with your head."

TAYLOR STEEPLED HIS fingers as Jackman updated him later that afternoon. "The techies are going through their social media accounts, checking for any association between Oliver Turner, Anthony Kendall and any of the girls. Nothing's cropped up yet."

"What about Oliver and the other girls?"

"Eugenie Trentwood claims she's never met him. We've spoken to Jo's family. If he was acquainted with Jo, they didn't know."

"Where does that leave us?"

"We're still waiting for the DNA on Oliver before we charge him with the first attack, but his alibis for the other two attacks seem to stand."

Taylor dug the heels of his hands into his eyes. "There has to be something."

Jackman relayed Celeste's concerns over the differences. "There is one other possibility we haven't considered," Jackman said. "It could be a copycat. Somebody who saw the press attention linked to the first attack and sought the media attention."

"Nine years later? That's a stretch."

Jackman shrugged a single shoulder. "So would the

same attacker surfacing after nine years, only to strike again after another six months. I've got my team checking through prison records to see if there are any other cases with a similar MO, just in case the dates coincide with a release, but it's turned up nothing so far."

Taylor rested his head back. "This is all I need."

"We're still trying to trace the BMW that drove through and spoke to Jo on the night of her murder."

"The one that was stolen?"

Jackman nodded. "We know Jo approached somebody on the other side of the road. It might have been the last person she spoke to, or could have been her attacker. They haven't come forward, but somebody in that car might have seen them. I've repeated an appeal for them both."

Taylor sighed as he stood. "Okay, get an extension to hold Oliver Turner for a bit longer. I don't want any charges being made public until we are absolutely sure."

He brushed past Wilson on his way out, giving a brief nod before he disappeared.

"He doesn't look well," she said.

"Stress of impending retirement, I guess."

She huffed. "I wouldn't mind finishing on his pension." She brandished a piece of paper in front of him. "Message from the press office. Artie Black wants a chat. Only with you, apparently." She raised a brow and dropped the slip of paper onto Jackman's desk.

CHAPTER TWENTY

JACKMAN TURNED HIS collar up as he walked across the garden centre car park the following morning. Artie Black stood and tilted his head as Jackman approached the café at the far corner, indicating for Jackman to join him at the table by the window.

"Interesting choice of places," Artie said and sat down, opening the buttons on his jacket to reveal an open-necked plaid shirt.

Jackman slid into the chair opposite. From the moment he'd received the message from Wilson, he'd done some digging. Artie had been lead crime reporter for the *Leicester Herald* for almost fifteen years and was well known for his moralistic claims of serving the people of Leicestershire with his investigative reporting. Wilson had suggested the café at Sapcote Garden Centre for their meeting as it was close to the motorway, but away from the prying eyes of Leicester City or Market Harborough town where Artie might be recognised. The last thing Jackman wanted was to feed his ego.

This wasn't the first time Jackman had been plagued by annoying journalists. The relationship with the press was always shifting and moving in a high profile investigation. Reporters were under pressure to seek gripping news stories. The police used them as a tool to feed updates to the public, appeal for information, and only shared what was absolutely necessary to drive an investigation forward. But Jackman was also acutely aware that he was in a new town where nobody knew him and he needed to keep the media on side. For now.

Jackman checked his watch, ordered an espresso. He didn't want to give Artie any indication that this was going to be a long meeting.

Artie clasped his hands on the table in front. "How's the case going?"

"We are working on several lines of enquiry," Jackman said.

"Anything I can help with?"

The waitress arrived, placed the espresso on the table between them. "You said on the phone you have some information for me?" Jackman asked as the waitress retreated.

A smile tickled the edge of Artie's lips. He didn't miss the fact that Jackman had ignored his earlier question. This was a game to him and he was clearly enjoying himself. "I've been contacted by a man who was near The Three Swans last night. Saw the victim standing outside shortly after 10.30pm. She was alone. But there was somebody else on the other side of the street watching her."

"Then I need to speak to him," Jackman said.

"I'm afraid that's not possible."

"Why not?"

"For ethical reasons. I can't reveal my source."

Jackman raised his brows. "He might have been involved."

"He wasn't."

"Then he has nothing to worry about coming forward."

"I'm trying to help here, Inspector. I don't have to give you more details."

"You're not going to pull the journalistic privilege card on me, surely? This is a murder investigation. Everything is open to scrutiny."

"Look, he's a public figure, an associate of mine. Doesn't want to be identified for personal reasons. But I do have a description." Artie pulled a piece of paper out of his pocket and unfolded it. "Average height and build, baggy denims, black hoody pulled down over their face."

Jackman had to stop himself from rolling his eyes at the scant information. The description probably applied to half of the town's teenage population. "Male or female?"

"His thoughts are male, but he only caught a quick glance, from the rear. Couldn't be sure."

"Did they speak to anyone?"

Artie shook his head.

"Where?"

"What?"

"Where was your informant, and where was the other person he saw standing?"

"The person he saw was on the other side of the street, outside Joules clothing store."

"What were they doing?"

"Nothing. Just standing."

"And your man was…"

"I'm not prepared to say."

"So your man saw someone—we don't know if they are male or female—in a black hoody and denims on the other side of the road."

"That's about the sum of it. Do you want me to put an appeal out?" Artie said.

"No. If we need a public appeal, we'll organise a press release."

"I was rather hoping we could work together on this."

"And I was rather hoping the witness would come forward and work with us to provide a better description."

Artie scowled.

"Look," Jackman tipped the espresso back, pushed his cup away. It scraped across the laminate table top. "I'm not here to broker deals. I want details of your informant."

"It's tricky. He's a public figure. Out without his wife's knowledge, shall we say? He doesn't want this to get out."

Jackman surveyed him a moment. "Why are you helping him?"

"He's an old friend."

"Is that it?"

"I'm sorry?"

"Is that the only reason you wanted to see me?"

Artie stared at him, said nothing.

"Look, if I have to get a court order to make you disclose your witness, I will. But know this. If this investigation is hampered by your withholding information, I'll make sure both the public and your editors are made fully aware."

Artie appeared unfazed, but when he spoke there was a conciliatory note in his voice. "Inspector. We want the same things. Maybe we could print a piece to gain more details, offer my source anonymity?"

"You know I can't give any guarantees."

Jackman watched him take a sip of coffee. "Any news on the others?" Artie asked as he placed the mug back down on the table. "The other cases," Artie repeated. "Linked to this one."

"We haven't made a direct connection between the murder and the other attacks," Jackman said.

"No, but you haven't denied it. Both women were the same age as the victim. All had strapping of some kind placed around their necks, all—"

"I'm familiar with the cases," Jackman interrupted.

"Then you'll be aware of the similarities. Let's be honest here, Inspector. You can deny it all you like, but the evidence points to a single attacker."

Jackman stood. They hadn't shared Oliver Turner's arrest with the world yet. It would be interesting to see how the press spun that one. But he needed to be careful what he said here. The last thing he wanted was to be quoted out of context. "At this stage we are keeping an open mind, examining all possibilities," he said. And with that he turned and left the café.

CHAPTER TWENTY-ONE

THE HUM OF the vacuum cleaner woke Grace. Almost as soon as she'd arrived, Ged had fallen into the rhythm of cooking the meals, cleaning the house and looking after the family. A clone of her brother, she found it difficult to sit down, constantly on the go. Grace crawled out of the shadows to sit around the table and attempt to eat, then disappeared directly afterwards. Back upstairs. Back to Jo.

She turned her head to the side. The scent in Jo's bed was waning, replaced by a faint mustiness. She'd resisted having the sheets washed, much to Ged's disdain, but the aroma of Jo's shampoo and perfume was fading. Grace uncoiled her body and shifted position, sinking into the slight dip in the mattress. She imagined Jo's body laying there, her dark curls sprawled across the pillow, and nestled in further.

Grace closed her eyes. Part of her wanted to sleep, seek some respite from the pain of the void. But another part of her resisted it fervently. In sleep she was at the mercy of her subconscious. And the nightmares were haunting.

The vacuum cleaner stopped. She could hear the detective was downstairs with Phil. She was beginning to become accustomed to the whispers, to conversations ending suddenly as she walked in, of laptops being snapped shut. They were trying to protect her, she knew that. And right now she didn't care, numbed in her world with Jo.

The door pushed open and Lydia appeared.

Grace sat up, forced a smile. "Hello, darling. How are you doing?"

Lydia buried her eyes in the carpet. "Okay."

Grace patted the duvet for her to sit and stroked her daughter's back, just like she had when she was little. "Do you want to chat?"

Lydia shook her head. "I keep getting messages on my Facebook page," she said eventually. "People saying sorry for Jo. They're on your page too." She bit her lip. "I don't know what to say to them."

Grace had ignored all the phone calls, the messages and shut the world out. It hadn't occurred to her that others might not wish to. "Would you like to answer them?"

Lydia gave a small nod.

"Okay. How about posting a general message rather than going through them all individually? Thanking everyone for their messages and something about how we all appreciate their thoughts and wishes."

"They're on Jo's page too. Loads of them."

Grace baulked inwardly. The very thought of looking at Jo's own page, where she shared the highs and lows of her life, made her sad. She pulled herself together, desperate not to show her youngest daughter her feelings. "You could post the message on all our timelines if you want. Would that be okay?"

"Could you write it down?"

"Of course."

Lydia disappeared and returned with a lined piece of paper and a pen. The corner was ripped, as if she'd torn it out of an exercise book. Grace fought to keep her hand even as she wrote out the sentiment and handed it over.

Lydia's bottom lip quivered.

"What is it?"

"I want to go back to school." As soon as the words left her mouth, the tears followed. "I'm sorry."

Grace embraced her daughter. "Don't be." She brushed her hair out of her eyes, kissed the side of her forehead.

"I thought you'd be angry."

"Why? Because you want to go back to school?"

Lydia sniffed in acknowledgement.

"Of course I'm not."

"It's just…"

"What?"

"I can't sleep in the daytime like you. And I can't stop thinking about everything. It makes me feel worse."

"Sweetheart, we all cope with grief in different ways. If you think it's easier for you to go back to school, then that's the right thing for you."

"You're not angry?"

"Of course not. Look at Ged and Phil. They can't sit down."

Lydia managed a thin smile.

"Do you want me to speak to any of your teachers?"

Lydia shook her head. "I just want to go back. I'll sort it all out then."

Grace sunk back into the pillows after Lydia had left. Facebook. Her girls shared their lives on there, from what they were eating, to places they visited and nights out. She remembered once having to speak to Lydia because she'd told the world they were going to Fuerteventura on holiday "next weekend." People left little thought to advertising that their houses would be left empty. A calling card to the nearest burglar. They followed everyone they met too. An idea pushed in. The names the detective had mentioned: Anthony Kendall and Oliver Turner. She remembered both names now. Maybe she should check Jo's friendship list, see if there was any connection there.

"THE TECHIES HAVE spent days trawling through Oliver Turner's computer," Jackman said. "He was a big gambler it seems, but no record of any social media accounts where he may have contacted the other girls. No violent pornography and no emails to link him to either Anthony Kendall or the victims."

It was Wednesday evening. Taylor had called in for an impromptu meeting and they sat under the cover of lamplight, mulling over the most recent details. Jackman rubbed his forehead as he continued. "We've spoken to some of his associates. Seems he imploded after his wife died. He doesn't have any other family. Apart from occasional visits to his local pub, where he sat on his own, he didn't mix. We are waiting for forensics, of course, but there was nothing else of significance found in his house search.

"He had Shelley Barnstaple's necklace, he had motive and he's confessed to her attack. But his DNA doesn't match the blood sample on the earring and there doesn't seem to be anything else to link him to the other attacks."

Taylor looked weary. The desperation to find some resolution, to put this case behind him before he retired, his final swansong, showed in his sallow face. "What about the others?"

"The links are stronger between Eugenie and Jo. The marks on their necks, the sexual interference, they're almost identical. We've checked locally and nationally but can't find any further attacks with similar hallmarks."

"So we are treating Shelley's attack as a separate case?"

"It certainly looks that way."

"Put a statement out to the press, confirming Oliver Turner's charge on the first attack. Say enquiries are ongoing."

"Are you sure you don't want to do a press conference? They know you. Might appease them a bit."

Taylor whipped back to face Jackman. "I'm not going into a room with those pen boys right now. They'll tear us apart."

Wilson walked into the room waving a piece of paper in her hand. "Artie Black's given up his witness source."

Taylor checked his watch. "Just before the court order." He sighed. "Talk about timing."

"What news?" Jackman said.

"It's Quentin Doherty."

"The Northamptonshire cricketer? No wonder he wanted to keep that under wraps."

"I've just spoken to Quentin on the phone. He was able to confirm the description we were given."

"Is that it?"

"Yes. He's coming in to make a statement tomorrow. We'll carry out the normal checks, but it looks like we're barking up the wrong tree there."

CHAPTER TWENTY-TWO

THE YOUNG WOMAN slammed the car door, tapped her nail twice on the window and beamed. The car pulled away slowly, the woman inside giving her a weary wave, before it accelerated up the High Street. Soon all she could see was the dull glow of the rear lights.

She stepped back and lent on the cold mortar, scrabbling with the contents of her bag. Moments later, she pulled out a cigarette, cupped her hand around the lighter and took a long drag, resting her head back on the wall behind her as she blew puffballs of smoke out into the night. A couple on the opposite side of the road caught her eye as they strolled along. A group of women climbing into a car nearby filled the air with their incessant chattering. It was a buoyant Thursday evening in Market Harborough.

A car full of lads with windows wound down passed by, the staccato beat of their music momentarily filling the air. It whipped up a gust of wind that made her pull her jacket tighter around her shoulders. Bridesmaid dresses weren't designed with minus temperatures in mind.

She took another drag and savoured it a moment until something in the distance caught her attention. She squinted, smiled, raised her hand to wave. The half-smoked cigarette was dropped. There was a fluidity to her movements as she crossed the road.

Jackman watched the purple silk of the woman's dress disappear from view. A hive of activity followed as a group nearby started talking. A man checked the settings on his camera. He watched Superintendent Taylor speak to the cameraman, his face tense.

To stage a reconstruction only a week after a murder was a risky decision. In spite of the strong presence of officers in Harborough over the past week, speaking to patrons in pubs in the evenings and appealing for any sightings, they hadn't uncovered any fresh leads. The charge of Oliver Turner had gone some way to appease the media, but still raised urgent questions about the other attack, as well as the recent murder. The press were still talking about links. Taylor was determined to pull out all the stops. A specially trained team had been drafted in to recruit good likenesses to their victim and witnesses, record accurate footage to be sent out to local news teams and be posted on social media in the hopes of jogging someone's memory. But the truth of the matter was that the leads were drying up and this served as another reminder to the press, public and families that they were running out of ideas.

Jackman watched Taylor turn, speak to the camera and make another desperate appeal for witnesses before he crossed the road and headed back to his car.

CHAPTER TWENTY-THREE

"You're on your last packet of tea bags," Ged announced.

Grace looked up from her position on the kitchen floor. Meggy was sat beside her playing with the pots she'd taken out of the cupboard, making pretend meals for everyone. "I'm sure Phil will pick some up."

"You're almost out of cheese too, and eggs," Ged added, glancing through the fridge as she replaced the milk. "In fact you could probably do with a good top up."

Grace hauled herself up and joined Chloe who was seated at the table, fiddling with her phone.

"I could do the shopping if you like?" Ged asked.

"If you like," Grace said wearily. Ged had been with them almost a week and, while Grace was grateful for everything she'd done, her presence and energy were starting to grind her down.

"Good, that's settled then. I'll go and switch the computer on." Grace exchanged a glance with Chloe as Ged continued. "I can't face going to the supermarket. I don't know how my brother does it, day in, day out. I'll set you up online. They'll deliver tomorrow." She bustled out of the room.

"She likes to be busy, doesn't she?" Chloe said and pulled a mock grin.

Meggy climbed up onto her grandma's lap, leaving the pots and pans scattered across the floor. Grace passed her a baby cup and she guzzled down the juice inside. After a moment, she stopped and wriggled around to face her grandma. Warm sticky breath blew in bursts into Grace's eyes making her blink. "Granny," she said, "Mummy said Auntie Jo's gone away to heaven."

Grace looked into her wide, innocent eyes and nodded.

"Are you sad?" asked Meggy.

"We're all sad, because we'll miss her."

She picked at a button on her grandmother's cardigan. "What's heaven like?"

Grace forced a smile. "It's beautiful. She'll have lots of friends there and be able to eat chocolate every day."

"I want to see her."

A lump formed in Grace's throat, preventing her from answering. She looked at Chloe and could see her eyes watering. Meggy climbed down from her lap and toddled back to the pans, oblivious to the misery around her.

The day before, in what had taken less than a minute, Grace had watched a replay of the last moments of her daughter's life. A tsunami of grief had washed over her as she'd turned off the TV. The actress was a good likeness. There was a confidence to her movements, very similar to Jo. But it wasn't Jo. It wasn't her at all.

Grace had listened to Ged's advice and hadn't checked the news reports since last Monday. But a week later the police were no closer to catching the killer.

Chloe lowered her voice. "Have you thought about arranging the funeral?"

Grace looked across at her. "Not yet."

"Sorry," Chloe said. "I just thought it might help. You know, a beautiful service, her favourite songs, some of her friends to speak. It would be personal. Might help to put her to rest."

"That sounds nice."

Chloe's face brightened. "Why don't we think of a few things now, to start you off?"

Grace nodded and rose with a glimmer of vigour, pulling a pen and paper out of a nearby drawer. "Where should we hold it?" she asked as she returned to the table.

Chloe thought for a minute. "Somewhere peaceful."

"I could ask the vicar of Great Bowden?"

Chloe nodded. "I'd like to say a few words, if that's okay?"

"She'd love that," Grace replied, and made a note of Chloe's name. "I'll ask Lydia too. What about other friends?"

They worked through several names and Grace noted them with a question mark, intending to contact them individually. She drew a line underneath, looked up and felt her face stretch into a smile for the first time in days. "Thanks, Chloe. I'll speak with Emma, the detective who has been looking after us. See if she can help with some dates."

IT WAS LATE afternoon before the detective arrived. Grace ignored the look of surprise on Emma Parsons' face when she met her at the door, before she'd even pressed the bell, and invited her through into the kitchen.

"Any news?" she asked brightly.

"From the reconstruction?" Parsons shook her head. "Not just yet. But it's still early days. We've lots of calls to work through."

Grace flicked the switch on the kettle and started preparing the mugs for tea.

"So, how have you been, Grace?" Parsons asked, her head inclined.

"Okay, thanks. Lydia has gone back to school."

"How is she doing?"

"Better, I think. Sugar?"

"One, thank you. Is your sister-in-law still with you?"

"Yes, she's just taken Lucky for a walk with Phil."

Steam rose out of the mugs as Grace placed them on the kitchen table. "There's something I want to talk to you about actually," she said. "I need to check with you when Jo can come back to us." Suddenly she sounded like a child's mother arranging a playdate and swallowed, fighting to keep her voice even. "I'd like to arrange a service."

The detective hesitated before she spoke. "Of course, I'll check. But the investigation is still live and usually we need to keep the deceased in case of further forensic examination."

Grace's face fell. "What do you mean?"

"It's likely to be a while before we'll be able to release her to be buried."

The disappointment rained down on Grace. Each new setback pounding into her skin like hailstones. "How long's a while?"

"Weeks. Maybe longer. It's difficult to say at this moment." Her tone softened. "It doesn't stop you organising a service of remembrance though. I think that's a lovely idea. Especially if it helps."

Grace looked up. "This isn't about helping me, or anyone else for that matter. It's about Jo." Grace placed the mugs on the table and stirred her tea, tapping the spoon excessively on the side of the mug as the anger festered inside her. "I want her back."

"I'm afraid it's not that easy."

"She's not a piece of meat to be pulled apart, used as evidence in some inquiry." The tremor in Grace's voice only served to exacerbate her anger. "She deserves some dignity."

The back door clicked open to reveal Phil and Ged, their cheeks pink from the cold wind. "What's going on?" Phil asked, seeing the look on Grace's face.

Lucky pushed through the gaps in his ankles to greet them at the table, but Grace ignored her. She ignored all of them. A headache throbbed at her temple. Everything was spinning, spiralling out of control. The table rocked as she shoved it forward and marched out of the room.

CHAPTER TWENTY-FOUR

GED STROKED THE back of Grace's head. "I wish I could stay longer."

It was Saturday and, almost a week after she'd arrived, it was time for Ged to go home. With a heavy heart, Grace released herself from her embrace. "You've done enough. And you have your apartment on the market. You need to be back in Spain."

Ged took Grace's hands in hers, held on to them a moment before she spoke. "Call me, if you need anything, you hear? I'm only a short flight away."

"I will."

"Are you sure you won't come to the airport?"

Grace shook her head. "I'm better here." She rubbed her sister-in-law's arm fondly. "Thanks so much for looking after us."

Phil pecked Grace on the cheek and picked up his sister's suitcase. Ged gave Lydia one last hug and walked out of the door after him.

Grace and Lydia were stood watching Phil lift the case into the boot when Grace heard Ged speak in a low voice. "Look after her, Phil. I'm worried about her. She seems to have lost a stone in a week." Lydia was checking her phone beside her mother, oblivious, but Grace heard every word of the exchange. When did people start talking about her as though she wasn't even there?

The car pulled off the drive. Grace instinctively

lifted her hand to wave but stopped herself and closed the door. As Lydia retreated to her room to finish her homework, the anger inside Grace intensified. It made her feel weak, out of control. Is that how they saw her?

She placed her hands on her forehead. It would have been easy to drop off the tightrope this past week, fall into the abyss with only her own thoughts for company. Everyone rallied around, dealing with grief in their own way. But Grace couldn't resort to cleaning, cooking and housework. It seemed wrong somehow. Too normal. She knew that Phil was worried about her sleeping in Jo's room. Had heard him say to Ged that he found it unnatural. The fact that she'd parked herself in Jo's room didn't seem to bother Lydia, who came to see her mother when she came in from school, called in to say goodnight when she went to bed. But Phil responded awkwardly and rattled around the house, desperately trying to carry on. Grace could see the helplessness in his face. He couldn't solve the problem and was at a loss to know what to do. He craved his old routine, some kind of reality from their former lives to cling on to.

With Ged now gone Grace felt an ache in her belly as she realised just how much she would miss her.

The detective's words on Friday were still raw in her mind. They wouldn't be releasing Jo any time soon. The thought of all those people pulling Jo around, examining every inch of her made her rile with anger and shame. Even after suffering an awful death, Jo was still subject to humiliation.

Grace drew a breath. Oliver Turner and Anthony Kendall. The names rang out in her head. She cast a furtive glance at the laptop and waited for Lydia to settle upstairs. When she could hear the soft beat of her music, she opened it up and searched the news, flicking through the latest report, and then googled Oliver Turner. Several links came up: one to a blog, the Facebook profile of a man in Texas; an obituary for someone that died in 2012. Grace replaced the search with Anthony Kendall. A string of entries littered the screen. She clicked on one of a man searching his genealogy; another was a Facebook profile, this time of somebody in America. How would she even know if she found the right one?

She switched to Facebook, entered Jo's account. A group photo filled the screen. It looked like it had been taken in the parklands at The University of Nottingham's campus. They were sitting on the grass, leaning in for the photo, arms slung around each other. Jo was centre stage, a huge grin on her face. Grace peered in closer. She didn't recognise the people in the photo. They must be other students, friends she hadn't yet met.

She searched Jo's friend listing. Oliver Turner didn't appear, but Anthony Kendall came up. His profile picture was of a garden gnome. She clicked on his name and waited for the screen to change, but a message appeared across the front of the screen. Anthony's privacy levels were high. She had to be friends with him to see his profile.

Grace switched back to the main page. A pang shot through her chest as she reached what seemed a never-ending list of condolence messages. *Goodnight, Jo. We'll love you forever... Darling Jo, taken from us too early.* She skipped past the other messages, scrolled down to early October.

Jo had posted almost daily. There was a picture of a sunset, a note saying she missed Lucky. Grace paused over a photo of a group of women, all raising glasses to the camera; another where Jo looked like she was on a night out. Further down was a joke about a couple, the dog taking up all the room on the bed. Underneath was the caption, *Priorities, Anthony.* She clicked on the name and the same Anthony Kendall's profile came up, with the same privacy message. Further down was a post to another name she didn't recognise, *Don't mention to Anthony about the happy hour change at Sack's Bar...he's bound to want to join us.* A winking face next to it. Was he a boyfriend in Nottingham? Grace closed the laptop. In some ways it was comforting to think that her daughter had found someone special in Nottingham. But why didn't Jo tell her about it? And why did the police want to question him?

ON SUNDAY EVENING, Erik swivelled around Jackman's legs as he thanked his neighbour and guided the dog back to his own house. "Come on, mate," he said, cuffing the dog's head as he pushed open the back door.

Erik bolted inside, his paws slipping on the kitchen tiles in his haste. Jackman smiled. He'd missed Erik over the last few days, his wide Labrador smile, his excitement and lust for life. He followed the dog into the front room and flung open the French doors. The cool night air rushed in, immediately freshening up the stale aroma of a room that hadn't been used in days.

The sound of the phone ringing pulled Jackman into the hallway. He leant down and picked up his mail as he answered.

"Don't you answer your mobile?"

Jackman smiled at the sound of his daughter's voice. He laid the post on the table and fished his mobile out of his pocket with his free hand. The screen showed three missed calls from Celia, two voicemail messages. "I was driving," he said.

"And you didn't think to use the hands-free? Come on, Dad, it's about time you started using it, don't you think?"

"Did you phone for a reason, or just to whinge at me for not checking my phone?"

A hint of humour cut into her voice. "Actually, I phoned to wish you a happy birthday. Or maybe you forgot? I'm guessing you worked through it?"

Jackman leant up against the cold plaster of the hall-way. It wasn't that he'd forgotten it was his birthday, it just didn't seem important these days. An irrelevance in the whole scheme of things. "Thanks."

"Did you get my card?"

"Yes." He stretched out the word, furiously sorting through the pile of post until he uncovered a silver envelope marked with her handwriting.

"You haven't opened it."

"Give me a chance, I only got home from Leicestershire ten minutes ago. I've just collected Erik."

"Aw, bet he missed you?"

Erik padded in from the garden and cocked his head comically, almost as if he knew they were talking about him. "He's fine. Angie's been looking after him."

Celia laughed. "Spoiling him rotten more like. You home for good now?"

"No, I'm back in Leicestershire tomorrow. Got a case on."

"Ah." Her voice dropped an octave. "Sorry I couldn't come home for your birthday, Dad."

He watched the dog scamper back into the front

room. "We discussed this. You have an exam tomorrow, it's no problem. I wouldn't have been around much anyway."

"Well, I'll be back soon and we'll have a good celebration then, make up for it."

"Sure."

"How's Mum?"

Jackman swallowed. "The same, darling."

"Okay. Give her my love when you see her."

They said their goodbyes and Jackman ended the call. He was looking forward to seeing Celia. Although she was now in her third year at Southampton University studying marine biology, he'd never quite got used to the house without her presence.

Erik had now rejoined him. "Shall we go for a run?" Jackman said. The words whipped the dog into a frenzy. He leapt into the air and his whole body waggled in unison as Jackman raced up the stairs and got changed. By the time he was ready, Erik was waiting by the back door, his tail bashing the side of a kitchen cupboard.

Jackman jogged across the Shipston Road, through the underpass and crossed into the recreational ground, welcoming the fresh night air that rushed into his lungs. His muscles were taut after a week behind a desk and it felt good to stretch them out properly. A light covering of rain had fallen earlier, sparkling along the hedgerow. It was good to be back in Stratford-upon-Avon, on home turf, running around his beloved park. Bright stars dotted the inky blue sky above, illuminating his path. The field beyond was empty. The only sound to be heard was the occasional car passing on the road nearby.

After two laps of the field, he moved towards the canal. Moonlight flickered on the swirls of water that gently lapped against the sides. It was calming, in spite of the chill in the air. Eventually he slowed, sat on the grass and enjoyed the vista. Erik slumped beside him and he rested back, using the dog as a pillow.

Eugenie Trentwood's face drifted into his mind. She'd sat on the sofa beside her mother when he'd visited last week, her lank hair parted like curtains to reveal sunken cheeks and patches of indigo under her eyes. He thought of the photos on her file, the pictures of her before the attack they'd used to appeal for witnesses. Statements from friends and family described her as a strong, fun-loving, bubbly girl. She'd been brave to come forward to do a press appeal and identify herself. But as the weeks after her attack turned into months, and no promise of an arrest was forthcoming, she'd retreated into the shadows, a shell of her former self. And his visit had done nothing to change that.

It had been almost ten days since the murder and every day that now passed made it more difficult to gather the evidence required to secure a conviction. Witness memories were less clear, evidence was degraded by the elements, suspects had potential chances to clean up and cover their tracks.

Quentin Doherty, the cricketer, had given his statement but Wilson had been right in her assumption. All he could do was to confirm the description they already had of someone in a hoody. He claimed he hadn't really taken much notice. Jackman couldn't help but wonder if Artie already knew this and, if so, why he hadn't given him up earlier.

His team had worked their way through the staff at the hotel, and friends and family, all to no avail. Detectives in Nottingham had searched Jo's room, her personal possessions, interviewed friends and tutors, yet hadn't dug up anything interesting on her life there.

Anthony Kendall's frightened face at the interview slipped into his mind. None of Jo's friends or family knew why she travelled back to Market Harborough every Wednesday.

He thought about Oliver Turner. His admission to the first attack could explain the inconsistencies between the three incidents. But it also confirmed their fears of a link between the other two cases. Did another attacker copy his methods? Was Celeste right? Was asphyxiation so imprecise that they killed Jo by accident? But why move her body, and why leave items nearby to enable them to identify her so easily?

His mind was racing with all the unanswered questions. But right now one question screamed out at him, louder than the others. If they did have a serial attacker on their hands, when was he going to strike next?

CHAPTER TWENTY-FIVE

THE FOLLOWING MORNING, Jackman glanced around the hospital waiting area. A nurse rushed past, followed by a porter, the wheels of his empty trolley rattling across the floor. He checked his watch. He'd lost count of the number of times he'd sat in hospital waiting areas over the last year. A pungent heat filled his nose from the bodies crowded into the small room, their coats damp from the persistent rain that clattered the windows nearby. A woman walked in, her young son hanging off her hip, fast asleep. Jackman stood and offered her his seat, which she took, nodding at him gratefully.

The air in the corridor was only marginally fresher. His phone trilled and he moved far enough away to take the call without annoying the nearby patients, but near enough not to miss his name if it was called.

"Morning, sir," Wilson said.

"Morning. What news?"

"Possible new lead. Leicester CID have been running an operation on auto-crime. Last night they arrested a guy who claims to have been in the car that drove past our victim on the night of the murder."

"The stolen BMW?"

"That's the one. Reckons he saw the witness on the other side of the road."

"Really. Can he give a description?"

"So he says. But he wants immunity from prosecution for the car thefts."

Jackman scoffed. "Get down there and interview him, will you? I'll be back as soon as I can."

Wilson rang off, just as a nurse called Jackman's name from the end of the corridor.

Jackman held up his hand. "Dr Wheeler is ready for you now," she said, and led him through to a small office.

The doctor looked up as Jackman entered, pushed the glasses further up the bridge of his nose and indicated for Jackman to sit on one of the plastic chairs opposite. He opened a file and leafed through the pages before he spoke. "Mr Jackman, you requested that we carry out a review of your wife's condition." He turned another page. "We know that the car accident, just over a year ago, damaged the basilar arteries in her neck, leaving her in a state of total locked-in syndrome." Jackman's heart dipped at the medical phrase. It had been rattled off so many times, yet nobody put it in real terms. His wife was like a caged animal, able to think, feel pain, be aware of everything that was going on around her, yet completely unable to move or communicate.

"An MRI shows up the damage to her brain stems, but no other neurological damage is highlighted, confirming the diagnosis," the doctor continued. "We've assessed Alice, carried out all the usual tests. As you are aware, some patients with this syndrome are able to communicate through eye movements and blinking. Others through sniffing. It is also true that many early signs of recovery start in these areas. But I'm sorry to say that we haven't noted any progress with Alice's condition since her last assessment, six months ago."

Jackman sat forward. "I don't understand. The staff at Broom Hills Nursing Home have reported instances of Alice winking, almost to indicate agreement, when they've asked questions. That's what prompted us to request these tests."

The doctor nodded. "I've read the notes. But they suggest her winking is intermittent, it only happens occasionally. And they cannot get her to repeat the process when prompted. It is possible that it's coincidental."

Jackman sighed. Many a time, over the past twelve months, both him and Celia had seen a blink or an eye movement they'd mistaken for communication. He recalled their initial elation, only to be disappointed when it didn't happen again. But this time it was different. The staff at Broom Hills were specially trained, not family. "Three different staff have noticed something. Surely that can't be a coincidence?"

"It's common, in cases such as these, for people to mistake what they see. I'm sorry. If Alice had shown any indication of recognition it would have presented in our results and we could have taken it further. But, for the moment, we have to wait. Try not to be despondent. We have had instances of patients showing signs of recovery a year or more after the event. Sometimes all they need is time."

"What do you mean you could have taken it further?" Jackman asked.

"More intensive testing with more stimuli. Recording brain activity. But this kind of testing is expensive and there is nothing to suggest…"

"I want them done. I'll pay for it privately if I have to."

"That's your choice, Mr Jackman. We will, of course, send you the details. It'll take a while to schedule in at any case. But I must caution. Until it is proven through our tests, I cannot record it as a change or significant way forward."

Jackman thanked the doctor, made his way out of the office, retrieved his phone and scrolled down until he found Celia's number. He was about to press dial when something stopped him. Celia wasn't aware of the Broom Hills' notes. He'd been hoping to surprise her. But the doctor's caution caught him. If the further tests found nothing, her hopes for an improvement in her mother's condition would be dashed. Again. He slipped the phone back into his pocket. No, for the moment, he would keep this news to himself.

GRACE CLOSED THE door behind Chloe and leant back on the cold wood, listening to her footsteps trudge down the path. The house was now screamingly empty. Even Lucky was quiet, curled up in a tight ball in her basket in the kitchen.

Grace went through the motions of loading the dishwasher and glanced around the kitchen. Thanks to Ged's visit, every inch of the cooker gleamed in the sunlight that seeped through the window. The ironing basket was empty for the first time in months. She idly chewed the side of her mouth. Her phone buzzed. It was a message from Phil, *Hope you're okay. Call me if you need anything.*

She tossed the phone aside, considered switching on the television and almost instantly changed her mind, instead deciding to take a shower. She moved back upstairs, taking her time under the hot spray, allowing the water to pour down over her.

Wrapped in a bathrobe, wet hair clumped around her

shoulders, Grace padded back down to the kitchen and flicked the switch on the kettle. Lucky raised her head for a brief moment and lowered it again. The rhythmic sound of passing cars hummed outside.

A thought seized her. She looked across at her computer languishing on the side, the edge of a magazine poking from beneath it. Right now the urge to do something to help Jo, to work towards finally putting her to rest was all consuming.

She logged on to the local news and immediately faced an article about the council failing to stick to their collection timetable for waste bins. She clicked back. A report on a burglary in Leicester flashed up. She clicked more keys, switched sites. There was nothing more on Jo's murder since the news report she'd read on Saturday. Surely Jo wasn't becoming old news already?

The reality of it winded her. How could the press move on so idly? She needed to do something, anything to put it back in peoples' minds, to get them to focus.

Grace flicked back through the pages until she found the news report from Saturday and read the byline: *Artie Black, Lead Crime Reporter.* She checked the other reports she'd read. Most of them were written by him. She had to do something. But she couldn't do it alone. She stared at the phone. Maybe it was time to enlist some help.

CHAPTER TWENTY-SIX

JACKMAN FINISHED HIS COFFEE, lay the empty mug on the side and stroked his wife's hair. He'd broken his journey back to Leicestershire, compelled to see her after his meeting with the doctor that morning. Alice was settled in an easy chair beside her bed. Blue straps that secured her peeped out from underneath hands that were neatly folded in her lap. Too neatly. He wondered how long they'd sat in that position. Instinctively he untangled her hands, gave them a rub and placed them on her knees.

He fell into conversation about his week, the investigation, walking her through the streets of Market Harborough. Over the months he'd grown accustomed to Alice's silence, had learnt to fill in the gaps himself, but today the doctor's words pressed on him. He narrowed his eyes as he spoke, watching her carefully, trying to gauge some sort of reaction. "Celia phoned yesterday. She'll be home in December. We could come here, spend Christmas Day with you. You'd like that, wouldn't you?"

He rambled on, desperately trying to touch a nerve, force a reaction. But no matter how hard he tried, he couldn't elicit any kind of response. The rise and fall of Bach battled with the hum of the electric bed in the background. Alice was betrayed by a body that wouldn't obey her commands. The very idea filled him with sadness. Sadness and unrelenting guilt.

In his mind he could still see her before the accident. The vibrant Dane with the sharp wit and quirky sense of humour, singing as she moved around the house and marched over the fields with the ever-keen Erik. Although that person bore little resemblance to who was sat before him today. She'd lost weight this past year, more than she could afford. Her cardigan hung off her narrow shoulders. The beautiful white-blonde hair that he'd always been able to spot in a crowd was now thin and lank.

The consultant's earlier words gnawed at him. Jackman had read all the literature, listened to all the advice. He knew the chances were slim, especially the longer the situation prevailed, but a part of him still clung on to the hope of some kind of recovery for Alice. He couldn't give up. He wouldn't. The thought of her sat here, like this, for the rest of her days was unbearable.

The image of Alice's head wedged against the roof of their Ford Focus, a single line of blood trickling from her ear, flickered in and out of his mind and served as a constant reminder, exacerbating the guilt that trailed him like a shadow. Alice would never have been on the road that night if it wasn't for him.

Christine, one of the day nurses, smiled at Jackman as she entered the room with a vase of roses, the petals delicately in the process of unfurling from their bud. "Look, Alice," she said in her merry Irish accent. "Yellow roses. Your favourite. Aren't we being spoilt today now?"

Jackman smiled. Christine was one of his favourite carers at Broom Hills. She built up an affinity with each person, spent time with families to learn about their patient's likes and dislikes, hobbies and interests.

He suspected it was her who'd put on Alice's beloved Bach for her to listen to in the background.

Christine shuffled forward and busied herself with adjusting Alice's cushion, pulling her into a more upright position. "There, that's better," she said before turning to Jackman. "Are you staying long today?"

"Just a flying visit. Got to get back to work."

She gave a single nod. Another thing he liked about Christine: She didn't judge.

"Ah, well they're putting *Mamma Mia* on in the front room later," she said. "That'll be nice, won't it, Alice?" She didn't blink when Alice didn't answer, instead moving around the room, tidying, smoothing the bedclothes. "Well, I'll see you in a bit then." She nodded at Jackman and left the room.

Jackman gathered his keys, gave his wife a hug and was just about to make a move when he heard someone in the corridor. A Geordie accent. He turned to the entrance as the owner of the accent filled the doorway, a chubby toddler straddled across her waist.

"Hey! I didn't know you were coming today," Annie Davies said. She unfolded her free arm, pulling him into a hug. The toddler squealed as he was squashed between them.

Jackman grinned as he stepped back and touched the little boy's sausage finger. "You've grown, mister," he said. The toddler stared back at him, wide eyed. "It's good to see you, Annie."

"You too. Don't see much of you now that you're a high flying regional leader."

Jackman laughed. After working with DS Annie Davies for almost ten years on the Warwickshire homicide team, he'd grown accustomed to her quick wit. "It's only temporary."

She passed the toddler to him and moved across to Alice. "Just thought we'd come and see you, darling," she said, bending down and kissing Alice's forehead. "It's been ages."

The gesture was personal, touching. It was easy to forget how friendly the two women had been before the accident. Flashbacks sparked in his mind. Images of summer BBQs. Sitting on the patio in their garden, the two women giggling, empty glasses of Pimms scattered around them. The memories made him smile. Davies was always great company, and spoke with a raw honesty that he admired.

"So, how are things at Leicester?" Davies asked.

"Busy. Working on a homicide." The boy wriggled in his arms and he placed him down on floor.

"So I hear. The Super was furious."

"Nothing new there then."

Davies winked. "It's only because she knows she's lost you for a while. What's your new team like?"

"Seem like a good bunch."

"Anyone I know?"

"Celeste is their pathologist."

"I remember her. Intense. We had a great laugh at a hen night for one of the civvies when she was here. She drank a yard of ale. Always wondered how she fitted all that beer into such a tiny frame." She gave a false flick of her hair. "Bet your DS isn't as sassy as her Warwickshire counterpart."

Jackman pictured Dee Wilson and rolled his eyes amusingly.

"So. Come on. Spill the beans. Any top totty at Leicester I should know about?"

Jackman frowned, looked across at his wife.

"What? Alice won't mind. In fact, if I'm not mistaken, she's thinking the same thing." Davies gave Alice's arm a gentle nudge and chuckled.

Jackman looked down at the toddler. "Is he walking yet?" he said, keen to change the subject.

"Nope. Lazy devil, aren't you, darling?" She leant across, ruffled his hair. "Just like your daddy." She met Jackman's gaze. "John didn't walk until he was almost two. According to his mother, he's ran everywhere ever since."

They both laughed. John was a triathlete and one of the fittest people Jackman knew.

"Are you still on cold case?"

Davies gave a mock yawn. "I must have royally pissed Janus off because she's put me on a fraud, based at Leamington."

"Not holding your interest?"

"What do you think? It's like walking through glue ploughing through all that paperwork. Not like working a real inquiry. I can barely remember what that's like."

Jackman checked his watch. "Which reminds me, I'd better get back to it. I'll give you a shout if I need some help."

"Make sure you do that. Don't be a stranger."

Jackman rested his hand on Davies' shoulder before he kissed his wife's cheek. As soon as he was out of the door his phone found signal and he called Wilson. She answered on the second ring.

Jackman didn't waste time with pleasantries. "Any news on the new witness?"

"Not much. He's part of an ongoing project concentrating on car crime. Steals cars to order and sells them on. Most of them go abroad. They've got him marked for at least four thefts so far, but reckon he's part of a much bigger investigation. He couldn't give us any more than we already have, hoody and dark jeans. Wouldn't give details of anyone else in the car either."

"Is that it?"

"Not completely. He did say it was a woman in the hoody."

Jackman stopped in his tracks. "How can he be so sure?"

"Well, using his words, 'She had a fair pair of tits on her.'"

The exchange played on Jackman's mind as he drove back to Leicestershire later that morning. The woman in the hoody on the other side of the road was potentially the last person to see Jo alive. Why hadn't she come forward? He made a note to put out another press appeal. They needed to trace her, and fast.

CHAPTER TWENTY-SEVEN

GRACE WATCHED ARTIE BLACK scribble a few more notes on the pad balanced precariously on his knee. It had taken a couple of days for her to muster the courage to call the newspaper. She'd wondered if she should speak to Phil first, but there never seemed to be the right moment.

Finally, yesterday afternoon, she'd dialled the news desk and was surprised when Artie Black called her back himself within the hour, arranging an appointment for the following day.

Doubt set in early. She almost cancelled. If it wasn't for the desperate loyalty to Jo fighting inside her, compelling her to do something to move the case forward, she would have made that call. But as soon as Lydia had left for school, she'd showered and got dressed properly. For the first time in weeks.

The journalist was a bear of a man, with chunky features and an easy smile. Fresh doubts crept in as she brought the coffee through to the front room to find him standing beside the fireplace, examining their family photos. Perhaps she should have arranged to meet him somewhere neutral. But as soon as they started talking he relieved her fears. He had a pleasant manner about him, a gentle unassuming nature. He explained how he'd reported on the other attacks, the police investigation, reiterated how he felt a personal piece might help to bring in fresh leads. His sense of conviction was heartening and Grace started to rest easier.

"Could you run through the evening's events with me again, Mrs Daniels?" he asked.

Grace nodded and explained the little she knew, finishing up with the last time she saw Jo.

"And she'd only just come back from Nottingham for the wedding?"

"Yes, she'd been up in Nottingham about 6 weeks, studying sociology. She'd planned to return at the weekend."

"Do you have any contact details at the university? Friends, tutors?"

Grace held his gaze a moment, suddenly baffled.

"It's okay. I just wondered about her associations there. Do you have a photo you'd be happy for us to use, to illustrate the piece?"

Grace opened the top drawer of the dresser and lifted out the photo she'd printed earlier. "That's lovely," he said as she handed it across. "But I was rather thinking of a family group? This one has already been used in the police appeals. One of all the family might jog a memory. We are trying to raise the profile, after all. If you could email it to me?" He gave another reassuring smile.

"Oh." Grace pulled out her phone, started to scroll through the images.

"Take your time," Artie said. "It needs to be a photo you're comfortable with." He stood. "Could I use your toilet?"

Grace nodded and gave him directions. She bit her lip, worked her way through the images on her phone as he left the room. It seemed the wedding was the first time since she'd got this phone where they'd taken group pictures. Finding a suitable one proved more of a challenge than she'd anticipated. The first family shot was missing Lydia. Another showed Chloe's eyes closed. Finally she found one of the girls about to leave the house for the church. Phil wasn't in the photograph, probably taking it at the time, and Meggy was missing, but it was the best of a bad bunch. She'd just pressed the button to email it to the journalist when he came back into the room.

He smiled. "You have a lovely house."

"Thank you. I've sent you another photo. Let me know if it's suitable."

"Great." He finished the last drops of coffee and placed his mug back on the coaster.

Grace couldn't help wondering how many other families he'd visited during the course of his career as a crime reporter, how many other desperate people's mugs he'd drunk out of.

The telephone calls they received after Jo died dripped into her mind. She glanced at Artie Black. Was that reassuring smile genuine? He'd been gentle and courteous throughout their interview. No, he certainly didn't seem like the kind of journalist that would sensationalise a story to gain a few extra readers. She pushed the idea aside.

"Well, I think I have everything. I'll put together a piece for the weekly newsprint. Should be out tomorrow."

Grace watched him slide his pen into the inside pocket of his jacket. "You really think it will help? The police investigation, I mean?"

"I often find a personal piece focuses the mind,"

he said. "Somebody out there knows who killed your daughter. This could just be the prompt they need to come forward."

CHAPTER TWENTY-EIGHT

JACKMAN CLOSED THE door behind him. "Thank you for seeing me this morning, Doctor Aston."

She stood, sleek and tall in a brown trouser suit, shook his hand and indicated for him to take the chair nearby. "I'm happy to help," she said. "It's a tragedy."

The chair scraped across the floor as Jackman moved it slightly closer and they both settled into their seats. "How long have you been Jo Lamborne's GP?" he asked.

The doctor folded her hands in her lap. "For about the last ten years. The Lamborne family joined us when we set the practice up."

"And you've been here since the beginning?"

"Yes. I'm one of the partners."

"So you treated Jo through her teenage years?"

She nodded.

"Did Jo have any health problems that required treatment recently?"

"Inspector, you do realise I'm bound by an oath of confidentiality?"

"I realise that. And we will be applying for her medical records formally. But this is a murder inquiry. Anything you can do to help us find who did this, and quickly, would be appreciated."

She paused for the shortest of seconds, before she turned to the side and tapped some keys on the computer. "She came to see me last March. I diagnosed depression and prescribed Citalopram, which she's been taking ever since. Three months ago we increased the dosage."

"Had she been treated for depression in the past?"

"When she was fourteen she lost her father. There was some evidence of self-harming. She was treated with antidepressants and a course of therapy."

"And she became well?"

"It took about two years before she was weaned off the medication."

"No other health complaints?"

Doctor Aston tapped away at the keyboard. Jackman craned his neck, but the sun was streaming through the window, bouncing off the screen, obscuring his view from this angle.

"Apart from a course of antibiotics in February last year to treat an ear infection, nothing else to speak of."

"Why do you think the depression has returned now?"

"It's difficult to say. Could be any number of things, or maybe just a chemical imbalance in the brain, something that needs adjustment."

"She didn't talk about anything else in her life that might be a trigger?"

"Not to me."

"She hadn't shared this with her family. Why do you think that was?"

"It's hard to say. Maybe she didn't want to worry anyone, preferred to deal with it herself."

"We've been trying to track down her movements over the past few weeks and discovered that she came back to Market Harborough every Wednesday afternoon from Nottingham. Do you know anything about that?"

She turned to the computer, clicked a few more keys and frowned. For a moment she was deep in thought. "I did recommend a group therapy session. It's possible it could be that."

"You don't keep a record?"

She stared at the screen. "I thought I'd put it in her notes." She clicked a few more keys. "I don't keep records of her sessions. That's down to the therapist. They just contact me if they think there's a problem or her medication might need tweaking."

"Can we speak to the therapist?"

The doctor turned to face Jackman. "I'll contact her. Put her in touch with you. But be aware she's also bound by confidentiality rules regarding her other patients. She'll only be able to talk to you about Jo."

"Anything you can do to help."

LESS THAN FORTY minutes later, Jackman had just pulled into a parking space at Leicester Headquarters when his mobile rang again.

"Chief Inspector Jackman?"

"Yes."

"My name is Karen Wakefield. I've been contacted by Doctor Aston. I understand you wanted to talk to me about one of the support groups I run?"

Jackman cut the engine. "Yes, thanks for calling back so promptly. I'm investigating the murder of Jo Lamborne and trying to build up a profile of her life. I wondered if you, or any of your group could help?"

"What are you looking for?"

"Any information on Jo really. We know she travelled from Nottingham to Market Harborough to attend a meeting every Wednesday afternoon. I assume that was with you?"

Karen cleared her throat. "I run a support group for people with mental health issues on a Wednesday afternoon in Market Harborough Health Centre. It's a voluntary group, numbers vary from six to nine people. Jo attended around six sessions before…" she broke off. "We were all devastated to hear what happened to her."

"Why did she come to you?"

"Jo had a breakdown in her teens and still suffered from anxiety issues. Outwardly she appeared confident, but beneath the surface she struggled with change. She came to talk through her issues."

"Did she forge friendships with any particular members, see them outside of the group?"

"Not that I'm aware of. She wasn't with us for long."

"Would any of your members be prepared to speak to us? Even the smallest detail about her life can help in an investigation like this. I could arrange for them to be interviewed by an officer out of the Leicester area, in confidence, if that helps?"

The line was quiet a moment. "I'm sure Doctor Aston will already have made you aware, I can't give you any contact details. But I can raise the issue with the group. It's possible some of them might be comfortable talking to you, especially if the officer isn't local."

Jackman thanked her, ended the call and immediately searched the contact details of his phone as the seed of an idea planted itself in his mind.

Davies answered on the second ring. "Twice in one day. I am honoured."

Jackman chuckled. "I've something I think you might be able to help me with."

"I see, might have known it would be about work. What are you after?"

Jackman gave her a short overview of the case and explained about the support group and his phone conversation with Karen Wakefield. "I'm looking for someone out of area to interview any of the members who come forward. We don't have reason to believe any of them are suspects, so just the normal background interview to see if Jo saw any of them outside of the sessions, ask if they knew her personally or anything about her life. What do you think?"

"Sounds like a good idea. At least it would get me away from the dreaded spreadsheets."

"Great. I'll be in touch."

CHAPTER TWENTY-NINE

LYDIA AND PHIL were gathered around the kitchen table when Grace walked in with Lucky the following afternoon. They looked up as she opened the back door. The dog rushed in to greet them, her little tail whipping against the chair legs.

"You're both home early," Grace said. The fresh air had made her feel brighter and fresher than she had in days. Almost immediately she noticed their grave expressions. "Has something happened? Is it Jo?"

Phil nodded to a chair opposite him at the table. "Come and sit down, love."

Grace shook off her coat and hung it on the back of the chair. "What is all this about?" Her eyes rested on the newspaper between them. She unfolded it. On the front was the photograph she'd given the journalist. *Family Consumed in Grief* read the headline.

Grace lowered herself into her seat. "I'm just trying to do something to appeal for help."

"Don't you think you should have spoken to us first?" Lydia said.

"I didn't think you would mind," Grace said. "We all want to catch Jo's killer, don't we?"

"Have you read the article, Grace?" Phil asked.

"Not yet." She looked past him towards the front door. "They only produce a paper copy once a week. I assume it's just arrived." Grace felt their eyes boring into her. "What is it?" She looked at the print. The article was a page long. The journalist opened with brief information about the crime. He went on to talk about the possible links with other cases. Eventually he talked about the family and how the prolonged police investigation was impacting on their grief. She flicked through the next paragraph. One sentence stood out: *Jo was the glue that held the family together.*

Grace gasped. "I didn't say that!" She read on about how Jo's bedroom had been turned into a shrine as the family failed to accept the loss. She recalled the journalist's open manner, his concerned expression. She'd thought he really cared, when all he was really trying to do was to dish the dirt. The words blurred as tears swelled in her eyes. There was an open appeal at the end. The main reason for the article, to appeal to readers, encourage someone to come forward. Yet all he'd done was to pick through the embers of Jo's life and create something akin to a gossip column. "We have to complain to someone," she said quietly. "I didn't say those things."

Phil rubbed his lips together before he answered. "He hasn't quoted you."

"That doesn't matter. Surely?"

Phil gave a conciliatory shrug. "We can complain if you want, but I doubt anything will come of it."

"What he's said is wrong…"

"He's just played with the truth, put his own spin on it. That's what journalists do. They're not the police. Their agenda is different."

"But he said he wanted to help."

"How could you do this, Mum?" Lydia shook her head.

"I wanted to do something constructive. You have to understand that."

"And you didn't think to ask us first? Me, Chloe… Before you slap a photograph of us across the newspaper and share what you think we feel!"

"What do you mean? You miss her, don't you?"

"It's not about that. Do you know how difficult it was to go back to school last week? People don't know what to say to you. They stare. Whisper in corners. Stop talking as you walk into a room. Even the teachers were weird for the first couple of days. Things were just starting to get back to normal. And now you do this." Lydia poked the paper. "How could you?"

Grace reached out, about to say how sorry she was, that she'd done it with the best possible intentions, for all of them, but it was too late. Lydia pulled her hand away. "You talk about her as if she's still here. You even sleep in her bed. It's like you're obsessed!" Lydia left the room. The sound of a door slamming rang through the house.

Tears trickled down Grace's face. "I just wanted to do something to help. I didn't mean…" The words caught in her throat.

Phil moved around to her side of the table and crouched down beside her. "I know." His face was inches from hers. "You've been under so much pressure."

"I should go and speak to her."

"Might be best to leave her for now. Give her time to cool down."

Her eyes were stinging as she closed them momentarily. "What about Chloe, Meggy? Have they seen it?"

Phil nodded. "It was Chloe that told me about it. She phoned me at work."

"Was she upset?"

His face darkened slightly, betraying his thoughts, but when he spoke his voice was even. "She was shocked more than anything. Because she didn't know. But she's worried about you. We all are." Grace buried her face in Phil's shoulder. "I could ask Ged to come back, if you like? Just for a while."

The offer was tempting. It would be a comfort to have her sister-in-law back, someone close to her, to talk to. Someone that seemed to understand. But Ged was needed elsewhere. "It wouldn't be fair."

"We've been talking, Lydia, Chloe and I. And we think you need some help. To get you through this."

Grace thought about her trips to the surgery after Jamie died. The small room with the sofa and the fake flowers, the box of tissues on the table. The long silences as Kathryn, her therapist, waited for her to speak. She'd been through grief before, knew she had to work her way through, find the path. But this was different. They hadn't caught the person who'd attacked Jo. How could she possibly rest, navigate a route through the fog when there were so many unanswered questions? It was like an open wound that kept weeping and no amount of grief counselling was going to heal it.

But one look at Phil's face told her that she needed to give a concession. He'd been kind, smoothed over the newspaper article, hadn't been angry that she'd invited a journalist into their home to talk about private family matters when he had every right to be. She thought about Lydia's comment, accusing her of being obsessed.

Was this right? Was she neglecting her family? She eased back, met Phil's gaze. "I just need some time."

"You'll make an appointment with the doctor?"

She pressed her lips together. "I'll think about it."

CHAPTER THIRTY

JACKMAN SQUEEZED THROUGH the bodies until he reached the bar. The staff were busy, moving down the line, switching from one waved note to another. He sat on a nearby stool and glanced around the area. He'd lost count of how many retirement celebrations he'd been to over the years, both in Warwickshire, in the Met and in the Marines beforehand. Usually these were places where he saw familiar faces, met colleagues he'd worked with, caught up with old friends. But due to the short time he'd worked in Leicestershire, there were very few people here he could claim acquaintance with.

His eyes rested on a sheet of blonde hair beside the door. It glistened under the lights and swished as the petite woman shook her head back. At the sound of her laugh he turned away, towards the bar. Quickly.

"Good turnout for Taylor, isn't it?" Wilson said, nudging his elbow.

Jackman nodded. "Not surprising though. Do you know anything about his replacement?"

"She joins us next week. Can't remember her name, but she's here somewhere." Wilson made a play of looking around, before her own name was called from the other side of the room. She made her apologies and disappeared into the throng.

Vowing to stay for one drink, he waved his note at the bartender who now faced him. "Mineral water, please."

"I recognise that voice." Jackman felt the weight of her gaze on his back. It was the blonde woman. He turned to face Carmela Hanson, Head of Regional Training, and tried to look composed as he smiled a greeting. They'd spent some time together, earlier in the year, when she'd helped him prepare for a promotion board. But their friendship had ended awkwardly when he hadn't attended the interview.

"It's good to see you, Will." She surprised him by leaning forward, planting a kiss on his cheek. "How is that bouncy dog of yours?"

Jackman's mouth twitched as he looked back at her. Carmela's smile was infectious. "Oh, you know, a handful. What are you doing here?"

"I was just thinking the same," she said. "This is off home turf for you." She raised her wine glass to her lips.

Jackman was just about to answer when Taylor appeared at his side and cut in. "Meet your new superintendent," he said, tucking a protective arm around Carmela's shoulder. Jackman's stomach dipped as he looked from one to the other.

"So, this is the SIO you've been telling me about," Carmela said. "Will and I already know each other."

"Good!" Taylor clapped Jackman's arm. "I'm sorry I haven't been able to wrap this case up with you, but I'm sure you'll find Carmela very supportive. She's promised to make it a priority."

"I certainly will," she replied.

Jackman stared at them both. It wasn't often he was stumped for words. Instead, he raised his glass. "A toast to good working relationships, old and new."

CHAPTER THIRTY-ONE

GRACE STARED OUT of the windscreen at the sea of cars that clogged the supermarket car park. This was Phil's work. The staff knew her as the manager's wife from social evenings and events they'd attended together. Some of them were even guests at their wedding. She'd always loved coming here, chatting to people on the way around, passing the time of day.

Not today though. Her stomach churned. This was her first outing since they'd lost Jo, apart from the odd walk with Lucky, and the thought of people flocking towards her with their sorry eyes made her suddenly want to leave. But she needed to do this. To show her family that she could function. That they mattered too.

Phil cut the engine and released his seatbelt. "I'll just get us a trolley."

The car door slammed shut behind him. Grace summoned all of her energy in order to gather her bag and walk the short distance across the car park towards the entrance where Phil was waiting. He was talking to David, the trolley gatherer who turned and smiled as she approached. "Good to see you, Grace," he said, and moved away to help an elderly lady load her shopping into her car.

Grace took the trolley from Phil and crossed the threshold. She immediately spotted the familiar faces of Steve and Ruth re-stocking the grocery section. They smiled, gave a simple greeting. Ruth winked. No head tilts, no pained faces. Phil had obviously prepared them for her visit and she was grateful for his tact. They moved up and down the aisles. At the deli counter, Sharon touched her wrist and said, "It's good to see you."

Grace felt her shoulders slacken and immersed herself in the familiar routine, asking Phil to reach up to the high shelves, taking time to browse the shop's different offers. Grace had always loved to cook and was rarely happier than when she was in the kitchen, creating some new dish for everyone to try. To her, the supermarket was like a sweet shop to a child, and she savoured the experience, cruising up and down the aisles, selecting just the right fruit and vegetables, picking out new ingredients to try.

Phil's constant presence at her side though was starting to irritate her. Food shopping was something she'd always done alone and she enjoyed the time to herself. She sent him off to select some wine and started to peruse the baking section. She would make bread. Both Lydia and Phil loved her homemade loaves and the delicious smell that wafted through the house. It seemed months since she had made one. She was reading the back of a packet of organic strong bread flour when she heard her name. A figure loomed in front of her.

"I thought it was you!"

Grace stared at the woman, desperately collecting her thoughts. She was dressed in denims. An open shirt hung over a fitted white t-shirt. No supermarket uniform, not one of Phil's staff then unless it was her day off. But there was something about her that looked vaguely familiar.

"Faye. Faye Campbell," the woman said, pressing her hand to her chest.

A hazy recollection of the name filtered into Grace's mind, although she couldn't place her.

"Goodness, it's been years." Faye's blue eyes lit up as she smiled. Soft wrinkles marked an attractive face. Wisps of hair escaped from a messy ponytail and somehow looked demure as they decorated her cheekbones. Grace suddenly felt drab.

The light smile on Faye's face faded, replaced by a wistful sadness. "I was sorry to hear about Jo."

Grace's chest tightened. This was the conversation she'd dreaded. "Thank you," she managed to whisper.

"It must be so hard."

Grace said nothing. She wasn't ready for this. She glanced down the aisle for an escape route, but Faye's trolley was pulled in front of her at an inadvertent angle. It would have been rude to push around it.

Faye had pulled her bag open, was rummaging through for something. She pulled out a pen, scribbled a number on a piece of paper and passed it over. "Look, if you ever want to talk or just fancy a break—"

"Everything all right?"

Grace hadn't noticed Phil sidle up beside her. Her gaze passed from him to Faye and back again. "This is…"

"Faye Campbell." The woman smiled, stepped forward and shook Phil's hand, before moving her trolley away. "Give me a call, Grace. I've just moved back into the area. Be great to catch up." She turned the corner and was gone.

"Who was that?" Phil asked, only half interested as he smiled at a passing member of staff.

The paper slipped out of her hand and drifted to the floor as Grace placed the packet of flour she was still clutching in the trolley. "Oh, just an old friend." She pushed the exchange out of her mind and moved forward to finish her shopping.

JACKMAN'S PHONE BUZZED as he walked down the corridor. It was a text from Celia. He ached to give Celia the news about her mother's further tests, but with no evidence of an improvement it wouldn't be fair to raise her hopes. Not yet. He rounded the corner and immediately saw Carmela Hanson step forward and press the button on the lifts. For a split second he contemplated passing her, taking the stairs as normal, but she'd already seen him. She caught his eye and smiled. Best to get the awkwardness out of the way. They'd be working together soon enough.

He returned her smile as he approached the lifts and waited.

"How are you?" she said.

"Good, thanks. First day?"

"Sort of. Taylor doesn't officially finish until Wednesday. I take over on Thursday morning. We're doing a handover. I'm coming in for meetings and briefings beforehand. This morning it was to meet the chief constable's team."

"Sounds fascinating."

"You could say that. I'll give you a shout on Thursday morning, if that's okay? I'll also need a briefing on Operation Ascott."

He nodded. They gazed at the lift dial a moment. "I looked for you after the speeches the other night," Carmela said. "Was hoping we could catch up."

"I left early. Had to head back to Stratford."

"Ah, I see. How's your arm?"

Jackman resisted the temptation to stretch out the taut skin on his upper arm. "Good, thank you."

The lift hovered on the floor above. He stared at the button, willing it to move.

Carmela turned to face him. "You know, I could never understand why you didn't return my texts in the summer."

Jackman's mouth formed a thin line. He remembered their last meet vividly. It was a wet Saturday morning. He'd been both surprised and touched that she'd driven the forty-five minute journey from her home in Banbury to Stratford on her day off to deliver some last minute preparation notes for his interview board. He could still picture her, standing just inside the back entrance of Stratford station. Raindrops dripping from her umbrella. An awkward moment had followed as his colleagues had burst through the door and crashed their conversation. They'd parted. He couldn't deny he enjoyed her company. Their working relationship morphed into a friendship. But when colleagues joked about a possible relationship, he had to put a stop to it. She'd texted him several times after she left Warwickshire. Sweet, friendly texts that he didn't respond to. "I wasn't sure what to say," he said. "I didn't make the interview board."

Finally, the lift pinged, the doors flung open and they both entered.

"You going down?" she asked.

He nodded.

The aroma of her perfume filled the small area as the doors swung shut again and the lift juddered into action.

The doors opened at the next floor. They both looked out, but the area was bare. Carmela pressed the button, twice.

The lift rocked as they descended. Jackman could feel her eyes on him. He gave a half-smile. She held his gaze. He forced himself to look away. An image of Alice filled his mind. Her small frame in the chair beside her bed at Broom Hills. Jackman blinked and focused on the numbers, highlighted in turn as they moved down the floors.

The lift creaked to a stop. The doors flung open. "See you on Thursday," she said. There was a glint in her eye as she stepped out. A smile tickled her lips.

Jackman walked out of the back door to the station and gulped a mouthful of fresh air. There was a good reason why he hadn't returned her texts. And right now, he couldn't imagine how in the hell he was going to be able to work with her.

CHAPTER THIRTY-TWO

A LINE OF sunshine blinded Grace as she woke later that day. She blinked several times, rubbed the back of her neck as she sat forward. Lucky, curled up on the floor beside the sofa, raised her head. Grace recalled coming home, Phil making himself a cheese and ham sandwich for lunch. She must have fallen asleep on the sofa. The sound of voices in the distance caught her attention. Grace jumped up, glanced out of the window. Phil was stood beside her car, a dripping sponge in his hand, talking to their neighbour, Beryl.

She moved back, not wishing to be seen. The last thing she wanted was to engage in their conversation. She checked the clock on the mantel. Lydia would be home from school in a couple of hours. Perhaps she should get started on that bread.

In the kitchen she started to pull her ingredients from the cupboards. The scales clicked and clattered as she weighed everything out in turn and placed them in a bowl. It wasn't long before the dough had been kneaded and was proving.

Grace was drying her hands, wondering what to do next when she saw the laptop plugged in on the edge of the table. The blue light indicated it was fully charged. Instinctively she flicked back the lid. She popped back into the front room, took another look out of the window. The neighbour had disappeared. Both cars glistened in the afternoon sunlight. Phil's head was tucked underneath the bonnet of his Volvo, examining something. He was always tinkering with the cars. She glanced back at the clock. Lydia would be at least another hour.

She dashed back to the kitchen, logged on and opened Jo's Facebook page. The same group photo greeted her. Her eyes lingered on Jo's wide grin, exposing her perfect white teeth, before she scrolled down. There hadn't been any new messages since she'd looked last week.

A thought struck her. The girls had persuaded her to open her own Facebook page, mainly so that they could share family stuff. She'd been reluctant at first, but eventually enjoyed the experience, especially when Jo showed her how to look up former acquaintances and she'd managed to trace some old school friends. It was fun and slightly addictive to check in and find out how everybody was doing. Although she'd rarely looked at it these past few weeks.

She forced herself to scroll through her friends' posts, interlaced with condolence messages about Jo. Time passed slowly as she browsed. She broke off, placed the bread in the oven. When she returned, an entry, some way down, caught her eye.

I'm so sorry to hear of your loss. Children are precious. Thinking of you and your family at this sad time. Faye x

Grace reread the message. It was similar to so many of the others on the page, but for some reason it intrigued her. Was this the Faye she'd met in the supermarket the other day? She'd implied she was an old friend. Grace peered in closer. The headshot looked younger, but it sported the same wispy blonde hair. She couldn't be sure. She clicked on the picture to Faye's profile. There weren't many updates. A few pictures of clifftops and scenery, probably from a holiday, and a couple of a black and white cat. Grace flicked back to the top. And then she saw it. Former pupil at Welland Park. Perhaps she *was* an old school friend. Her age was forty, three years older.

Grace eased back in her chair, satisfied she'd at least made the connection. The smell of the bread was starting to fill the room and for the first time in days she actually felt hungry. But something about the name, Faye Campbell, didn't sound familiar. Was that the surname the woman in the supermarket used? She jumped up, grabbed her handbag, pulled out her purse and a packet of tissues as she searched for the scrap of paper Faye had given to her with her details on it. When she had no luck, she moved out to the coat rack in the hallway and checked her pockets. But apart from a few dog biscuits, it was empty. Grace was just cursing herself for losing it when the front door pushed open and Lydia appeared.

"Oh, hello," she said to her mother. "What are you doing out here?"

CHAPTER THIRTY-THREE

CARMELA WAS DRESSED in a dark trouser suit with a black and white spotted scarf arranged elegantly around her neck. But the formal appearance wasn't the only difference Jackman noticed when he entered her office that morning. There was a sharpness to her that he'd not witnessed before as she welcomed him in and invited him to take a seat. None of the teasing smile, or sparkle in her eye from the lift.

He rested back in his chair. Maybe this wasn't going to be as tricky as he'd imagined.

She collected a day book and pen from her desk and moved over to join him, pulling out the chair nearby and angling it so that they faced each other.

"Right, Will," she said, adjusting her jacket as she sat. "I want you to take me through Operation Ascott, along with the latest murder, in as much detail as you can. I've read the case notes, of course, but I'd like to know how the investigations unravelled and your thoughts on where we are now."

Jackman took a moment to cast his mind back to the cold case review, relaying each investigation in as much detail as his memory allowed. He finished with Oliver Turner's charge. He then switched to the most recent crime scene. Carmela made notes as he spoke, glancing up on occasion, asking the odd question for clarification. He examined the similarities between Eugenie Trentwood's and Jo Lamborne's attacks as he went along.

Time passed, and very soon Jackman became aware that the light had faded. He paused, momentarily distracted as he gazed around the room. The sun had disappeared, wiped out by heavy rain clouds, casting a shadow over Carmela's desk.

She guessed his thoughts, jumped up and switched on the light. "I don't know how Taylor coped in this dingy room."

She'd only just re-joined him when her phone rang. Carmela excused herself as she answered. Jackman glanced about the office. A landscape print decorated the far wall beside the bookcase. A cork board next to the door was littered with a few notices and a graph of some sort. He ran his eyes over the papers on her desk, arranged neatly in trays. It was interesting how much the absence of Taylor's family photos changed the atmosphere of the room that now seemed stark and cold, and larger somehow. It struck Jackman how little he knew about Carmela's background. She'd told him she was divorced. She'd never mentioned children, although that didn't necessarily mean she didn't have any. It seemed to him that during their fleeting friendship this past summer he hadn't learnt much about her at all. And yet, thinking back, they'd delved pretty deeply into the events of his life.

He rested his gaze on her. She was staring at the floor, her answers mostly one-worded, perfunctory, making it impossible for Jackman to second-guess the caller.

She ended the call, placed her mobile back on the table. "Sorry about that. Where were we?"

"I think you're pretty much up to date now," Jackman replied. "We're still working our way through the appeal calls."

"And we know nothing more about the attacker?" Carmela said.

"Not at the moment."

Carmela focused on her notes for a moment. "I'd like to bring in a fresh profiler. I know they've had one before, but it's different now that we've made an arrest on the Shelley Barnstaple attack. The ligature marks and bruising, age of the women and appearance, show very distinct links in the other two cases. I've a friend I met at one of the events I attended at the College of Policing. He's very good. Perhaps he'll spot something we're missing, give us a new avenue to explore, especially if we're focusing on a potential copycat." She checked her watch and stood. "Okay, leave that with me. I'll make some enquiries. I've a meeting with the assistant chief constable in twenty minutes. Be good to share some news."

CHAPTER THIRTY-FOUR

"TRUST US TO come to the busiest shopping centre in the county," Chloe huffed.

Meggy fidgeted in her pushchair as they walked into yet another clothing store. Grace had initially hesitated when Chloe phoned and invited her on a shopping trip to the Highcross Centre to find outfits for a friend's wedding. Apart from the supermarket visit, she hadn't been out since the newspaper piece. Would people recognise her? Stop, stare, talk about her behind flat hands? But Highcross was in the heart of Leicester. It would be crowded. Phil had been so pleased to hear she was going on a trip, especially with Chloe. And Chloe had graciously not mentioned the newspaper article.

They'd been at the centre almost an hour, wandering in and out of an abundance of shops. But in spite of the huge array of boutiques and chain stores with their enticing window displays, and Chloe picking, pulling and rifling through their wares, she still seemed unable to find something suitable.

The shop was rammed, the air inside stuffy. Grace could hear Katy Perry's voice in the background but couldn't make out the tune. She ran her fingers down the side of a long floral dress. "What about something like this?"

Chloe shook her head. "Too summery."

They moved further down the aisle, Chloe fingering the different dresses, trousers and tops, stopping occasionally to examine their tags. "There's not much out this season, is there?"

"I think we're stuck between summer sale stuff and the Christmas glitz," Grace said.

The pushchair rocked as Meggy wriggled again in her seat. "Want to get out."

"Not in here, honey," Chloe said. "It's far too busy."

"Want to get out now!" Meggy wailed.

Grace crouched down in front of her granddaughter. She'd pulled out her hair ribbon. Light-brown curls hung messily around her pink face. "Hey, sweetie. Would you like some cake?" Grace said, retrieving the ribbon from her lap.

The toddler tugged at the harness straps. "Want to come out," she repeated, a frown spreading across her chubby little face.

"How about we go for some cake and you can come out and sit with Granny in a big chair? Would you like that?" Meggy's face brightened. "Let's see what Mummy says."

Chloe turned. "That sounds like a lovely idea." Grace started to push the stroller towards the exit when Chloe's voice suddenly rang out. "Oh, what about this one?"

Grace stopped and looked back at a skirt and top combination in a deep red that Chloe held out at arm's length. She angled her head, nodded as Chloe moved across to a nearby mirror and pressed it against herself. "Might cover my baby bumps," Chloe said with a smile. "What do you think?"

The heat in the store was reaching nauseating levels.

"Why don't you get it?" Grace said. "You could always bring it back if it doesn't fit?"

Chloe nodded. She moved in front of the pushchair as they turned towards the till. And froze. "Grace, where's Meggy?"

Grace shot forward. The chair was empty, the harness straps strewn aside. "She was here a moment ago. I was talking to her."

Chloe dropped the clothes to the floor. "Meggy!" she called, her eyes darting about.

They moved around the area, pulling back skirts, dresses, suits. Glancing under rails. Meggy loved to play hide and seek and Grace expected to see the toddler's face suddenly poke out and say, "Boo!," followed by her infectious chuckle, as if it was some kind of game.

They widened their search, asked other customers. People joined in. It seemed almost the whole store were searching and calling for Meggy, yet there was still no sign of her.

Grace could feel the panic rising inside her. She longed to catch a glimpse of the chubby little legs, the funny upturned nose. Any minute she would. Surely? But there was nothing. She rushed to the tills, pushed past the queue to the front. The assistant, a young woman with perfect make-up raised a manicured brow. "It's my granddaughter," Grace panted. "She's disappeared."

"Grace!" Chloe was standing by the entrance, her white fingers trembling against the stroller handles. "This lady saw her. Said she left the store."

Grace looked past Chloe at the elderly woman behind her.

"She was heading to the sweet shop. I thought she was on her own, I did a double-take, but she was walking right behind a woman with a stroller so I assumed they were together." Her words trailed off as they darted out into the shopping centre towards the old fashioned sweet shop opposite with its colourful window display. The empty pushchair juddered as they weaved in and out of the shoppers. Chloe rushed to the till, her words spilling together as she asked if they'd seen her daughter.

The assistant shook her head. "I haven't seen her." She touched Chloe's arm briefly. "Don't worry, I'm sure she'll be nearby. I'll call centre security. They'll put out a tannoy message, check the cameras and ask people to look out for her."

Chloe gave her a brief description and shuddered. "Grace. We have to do something!"

"Don't panic. She's only been gone a few minutes. She can't be far away." Grace left the store, her head in a whirlwind. Just then, a hand touched her shoulder. She turned. It was the elderly woman from the other store. The woman that had seen Meggy leave. "You didn't find her?"

Grace shook her head. Quick, short bursts.

The woman's face stiffened. She looked from one to another. "I'd like to help."

"That's kind of you…"

"Pam."

"Thank you, Pam. The shop manager is alerting security. We need to split up. She has to be somewhere on this floor." Grace glanced at Chloe. She looked as though she was about to faint. "You and Chloe go left. I'll take the other side."

Without giving it another thought, Grace ran back up the shopping centre towards the exit, searching for a sign of Meggy. She stopped a woman with two small girls, a man on his own, a pair of mums with prams. The heat in her neck rose with every head shake.

Grace reached the escalator and looked up at the moving metal staircase. Meggy loved the escalator, often asked to ride on it several times. Sometimes Grace had wondered if it was the highlight of her shopping trip. Surely she hadn't travelled up there alone? For a split second she hesitated, gave another look around. Beyond the escalator was the door. The tips of her fingers just touched the rail when she heard the announcement. It was blurred, muffled by the background noise in the centre. A Queen song blared out from a shop nearby. But they definitely mentioned a small child…

Grace whisked around. She recalled seeing a sign for security near the toilets. Her blood thumped in her ears as she picked up speed, weaving in and out of people, knocking into shoulders and bags as she ran.

As soon as she turned the corner she saw the edge of Meggy's yellow jacket. The toddler was sitting on the desk, thudding her heels against it as she swung her legs. A woman was stood in front of the child with her back to Grace. She was clearly talking to Meggy because Grace could hear the toddler giggle as she approached.

Grace bypassed the woman and threw her arms around Meggy. "We've been looking everywhere for you," she said. She checked her face, her hands. Kissed her cheek.

"Hello, Granny." Meggy looked completely unfazed by the drama she'd created. She thumped her heels against the desk again.

Grace didn't hear the rush of footsteps behind her. "Oh, my darling…" She was jostled aside as Chloe grabbed hold of Meggy. "You gave me such a fright," Chloe said, hugging her tightly, stroking her hair.

Suddenly Grace remembered the other woman nearby. She looked across, and started. It was Faye, the woman she'd met briefly in Phil's shop last week. "Oh, it's you!"

Faye looked equally puzzled. "You're Meggy's grandmother?"

Grace nodded.

"I should get going," Pam said, checking her watch. "I have to pick my mother up at three."

In all the kerfuffle Grace had completely forgotten the other woman who'd helped Chloe. She shook her hand, thanked her. Chloe released herself from Meggy for a brief moment to give her thanks. As they watched her go, Chloe looked across at Grace, standing awkwardly next to Faye. "You two know each other?" she said.

"Yes." Grace could hear the squeak in her voice. She felt exhausted.

"We're old friends, well, acquaintances really. From school." Faye smiled gently as she spoke.

"Oh. Well, thanks," Chloe said. "Where did you find her?"

"Glad to be able to help," Faye said. "Her face was pressed up against the sweet shop when I saw her. She seemed to be alone, so I went over." She looked back at Grace. "She told me she came out of the shop opposite to have a look at the sweets. We went back to the clothing store and looked for you."

"We were in there, searching," Chloe said.

"I don't know how we missed you."

"It was busy," Grace said. The thought of Meggy leaving so easily, talking to strangers… It was almost too much to bear.

Meggy opened the palm of her hand to reveal a scrunched up bag of Skittles. She handed it to her mother. "Where did you get this?" Chloe asked her.

Meggy looked at Faye. "I bought them for her," Faye said. "When we couldn't find you she got a bit tearful. I picked them up from the kiosk on the way to security." Nobody spoke for a moment. "I'm sorry, did I do the wrong thing? She's not diabetic or anything, is she? She did say her mum let her have sweets."

"No. Thank you. For finding her. Keeping her safe." Tears dripped off Chloe's chin as she spoke. The toddler squirmed in an effort to get away, as she kissed her forehead again.

"Why are you crying, Mummy?" Meggy said.

At that moment a wave of exhaustion swamped Grace, sucking the very breath from her lungs. She glanced across at Chloe. Her face was blotchy, eyes swollen. "We need to get you home," she said. "I think we've had enough drama for one day."

CHAPTER THIRTY-FIVE

Terry Barnes was a tall spindly man with a head of dark, unruly hair and a warm smile. "Okay," he said to the room. "I've read through both the cases. Let's look at the information we have."

He stood at the front of the room and held up a sheet of paper in his hand, the gesture exposing a scrawny white wrist. "Don't worry about taking notes, I've made you all a copy."

Jackman smiled inwardly. No laptops, no flipchart, no PowerPoint presentation. Some of the profilers they'd used in the past were academics who seemed out of touch with the real world. Barnes was highly decorated and frequently contributed to *Policing Now* magazine. He'd assisted on major investigations all over the country, none of which he felt the need to share with the team today, which was a refreshing approach. His results would speak for him.

"The attacks are sexually motivated which generally means we are looking for an adult male," Barnes continued. "If he acted alone, which is more likely I'd say, he'd be of reasonable build. He managed to get the strapping around their neck and pulled it tight while they struggled. That indicates a level of strength. Age likely to be between 20 and 60 years old. Works alone. More than likely lives alone too. No forensics means he is meticulous, fastidious about cleanliness and systematic.

"Tall," he continued. "We know Eugenie is almost six foot. Somebody smaller would have had a problem stretching the strapping over her neck.

"He lives in the Leicestershire area. Eugenie was attacked on waste ground in Oadby. Jo was picked up somewhere near the centre of Harborough and her body was dumped in a back road leading out of the town. Whoever did this has a good knowledge of the locality, knew that these areas were relatively quiet at night, which meant he wasn't putting himself at risk of being caught.

"He had use of a vehicle. He had to manoeuvre Jo's body about, so not a three door. More likely a van I'd say. Given the way that we believe Jo was taken in the town centre he needs to be relatively unremarkable in appearance, not someone that would stand out.

"These weren't chance attacks. The methodology is the same as the first attack, but the sexual motive is different. I understand you're looking at the possibility of a copycat?"

Jackman nodded and explained the charge against Oliver Turner.

"Okay. If this is someone different, it's possible he was interrupted with Eugenie, couldn't finish what he started. But he did remove her shoes."

"That doesn't make sense," a voice piped up from the back of the room. McDonald scratched his head. "He left personal items at Jo's scene."

"But he took her clothes," Barnes said. "He likes to keep something of theirs. Maybe he went too far with the strangulation with Jo, and that's why he left items nearby to indicate her identity." He turned back to the room. "So, we are looking for a well-built male with a good knowledge of Leicestershire. He either lives here, or has lived here at some stage and still maintains a working knowledge of the area. Any questions?"

The room stayed quiet. Jackman felt breath on his neck. "You know what, sir?" Wilson whispered. "He's just described Oliver Turner."

Carmela stepped forward and thanked Barnes. "Okay, everyone. Let's re-visit the statements taken already. We can start with the ones from the nearby industrial estate. Focus on adult males with an evening job, and night workers. Ask for DNA samples to match against the blood found on the earring. Also look at ex-employees, people who deliver to the area and taxi drivers. Take another look at their alibis. Interview them again if you need to. It's just over three weeks since the murder. The public want an arrest. Let's see if we can give them one."

GRACE FROWNED AS she looked up from her dinner. The table seemed to swamp Phil and her as they sat together in the kitchen that evening. Lydia had gone to visit a friend straight from school; Lucky snored softly from her bed.

In truth Grace hadn't felt in the slightest like cooking since the event at the shopping centre the other day, but somehow it seemed important to keep going, to show Phil she could cope. She'd opted for a quick spaghetti carbonara tonight, although she'd only managed to tuck away a couple of mouthfuls. The smell of the bacon lingered, playing havoc with her queasy stomach.

"Thank you for looking after Chloe and Meggy." Phil said. "Chloe was explaining how brilliant you'd been."

Grace averted her gaze. At Chloe's insistence they'd phoned Phil at work to let him know what had happened and that they were safe. He'd called in to see his daughter, to check on them, several times since.

"I'm proud of you," he said.

Grace shook her head, as if it was nothing. Although it wasn't nothing. The scars of almost losing Meggy so closely after Jo had already penetrated deep. After leaving Faye, she'd rushed them up to the car park, bundled them all into the car. Chloe didn't argue when Grace insisted on driving her back, staying with them until Matt arrived home from work. But by the time she'd left them and driven home herself the tide of adrenalin was passing and she was reminded of the frantic terror. And guilt. Guilt that bred by the hour, festering inside her. Meggy had climbed out of the pushchair on her watch. Once again, she'd missed something.

Phil swallowed another mouthful of pasta before he spoke. "Chloe wants to do something. For Faye."

"I'm sorry?"

"That was the lady's name, wasn't it? The lady that found Meggy?"

Grace nodded.

"Chloe said you knew her?"

"It was the same lady that we bumped into at the supermarket last week."

"Thank goodness she was there," he said.

Grace rolled her fork in the pasta, over and over

again. Not for the first time, she recalled Chloe's ghostly face, the panic as she searched for Meggy, the first sighting of her sitting on the counter, chubby legs tapping against the desk as she chatted to Faye. Many a time since, she'd replayed those fraught moments. It could have all been so different.

"Do you have her contact details?" Phil continued.

Grace thought back to the meeting in the supermarket, her search for the number afterwards. For a moment she sat silently until the memorial message on Facebook prodded her. She was pretty convinced now it was the same woman. She could probably respond, send her a private message there. "I think so."

"Good. Speak to Chloe. See if you can set something up. She's torn between counselling Meggy about talking to strangers and teaching her to say thank you. Might help on both counts that you know this woman." His fork scraped across the plate as he finished the last of his food. "Might be good for you to catch up with your old friend again too."

CHAPTER THIRTY-SIX

GRACE ADJUSTED MEGGY to a more comfortable position on her lap. The café was teeming, the inclement weather forcing people off the streets, so much so, they'd had a job to find a table when they arrived. Thick raindrops and condensation shrouded the window, obscuring the view of the outside world and making it feel oppressively hot in the small area.

Chloe pushed the coats back and shifted position on the bench beside them. "Have you said thank you to Faye for the colouring book?" she asked her daughter.

The toddler was breathing heavily, head down, concentrating on keeping her red crayon inside the lines of a fairy's hat. "Thank you, Faye," she said without looking up.

Faye's face glowed. Although she'd played down her role, she'd clearly been pleased when Grace had contacted her and invited her out for a coffee. Grace stared at her now and felt a pang. At the supermarket she'd mentioned recently moving back to the area. Perhaps she hadn't built up much of a friendship group yet.

"It was my pleasure," Faye said. "I thought you looked just like the sort of little girl that would be good at colouring and I was right. You're doing a grand job there."

The toddler tossed her head to the side, exposing the corner of a wide grin.

"You really shouldn't have," Chloe said, licking her finger and wiping it across the plate to catch the last crumbs of chocolate cake. "We were supposed to be treating you. To say thanks for helping Meggy the other day."

"It was really no trouble. I'm just glad I was there." Faye adjusted the silvery scarf laced around her neck and looked across the table. "And it's nice to see Grace again after all these years."

Grace returned her smile. There was a breeziness to Faye that was refreshing.

"That's a lovely dress," Grace said, gesturing at the blue maxi dress Faye wore. She thought back to her appearance in the supermarket, the shirt hanging open over a white t-shirt and jeans. If Grace attempted that she'd have looked like she'd thrown her old clothes on to do the gardening. Yet Faye had carried it off. Just like today. She imagined Faye was one of those women who could wear almost anything, slip a necklace or a scarf around her neck and look wonderful.

Faye leant forward as if she was sharing a secret. "It's from Oxfam," she whispered. "But don't tell anyone."

"Really? I'd never have guessed."

"It really suits you," Chloe added.

"Thanks. I do most of my shopping in charity shops. There are some great bargains out there."

A loud snap interrupted their conversation, turning their attention back to Meggy who held up the red crayon. "It broke!"

"Oh dear," Faye said. "Why don't you use another colour?" She shook the box, emptying a strew of other crayons across the table.

The toddler choked out a sob and buried her head in her grandmother's chest.

"I'm sorry, Faye," Chloe said, looking up at the station clock on the wall. "She's overtired. It's past her nap time." She stood, closing the book. Faye helped her gather the crayons into their box and place them in the tray beneath the pushchair seat nearby.

"You've done this before," Chloe said, thanking her.

Meggy was rubbing her knuckles into her eyes as her mother lifted her into the stroller.

"Thanks for meeting us," Grace said, reaching for her coat.

"Oh, there's no need for you to come too," Chloe said, waving her away. "I'll take Meggy home. You stay, have another coffee. Be nice for you to catch up."

Grace couldn't help but smile at Chloe's words. She sounded just like her father.

"That would be lovely," Faye said. She tucked her hair behind her ears, uncovering a pair of silver hooped earrings. "If you've time?"

Although she would have preferred to leave the café, if nothing else for the sake of some fresh air, Grace felt a little cornered. She gave a single nod and instead pulled the rain cover down over the pushchair while Chloe heaved on her coat. They said their goodbyes. The door swung shut behind them and she turned back to Faye, smiling awkwardly. As much as she'd tried, she couldn't remember her from school. Although, her memory was so bad these days, she hadn't been able to recall the number plate of her own car when she'd been in a prang last month, and that was before losing Jo. So it wasn't too much of a surprise. It just left her feeling rather like she was sitting with a stranger now that the others had gone.

"What brought you back to Market Harborough?" Grace said after they'd ordered a fresh latte each.

"I'm sorry?"

"You said you'd been living away?"

"Oh, yes." The waitress arrived with their coffees. Faye waited for her to leave before she answered. "I've been in Manchester, must be for the best part of the last twenty years. Came back a couple of months ago. My dad was ill." She picked up a long spoon and stirred her drink, watching as the froth blended with the milky coffee.

"Oh, I'm sorry."

"It's okay." The spoon tinkled as she tapped it against the side of the glass and placed it down.

"I bet he likes having you around now though."

"Who?"

"Your dad."

Faye's eyes glazed over momentarily. "He died."

"I'm sorry."

"It's fine, really. He had cancer. It was terminal. I don't think he knew much about it at the end."

Grace thought about Jamie. Those last days and weeks of caring as he slowly faded away. "It's tough," she said knowingly.

"You've been through it too?"

Grace's own transparency shocked her. She took a moment to recover. "My first husband, Jamie. He died five years ago. Lung cancer."

"That's cruel. At least my dad was in his seventies."

Grace surprised herself by launching into the story of

Jamie's illness. How he'd attended all the tests, received the early diagnosis, and didn't share with her until he had all the details. "Sometimes he'd wake and we'd sit and chat in the darkness," she said. "The days drifted into weeks, all merging together as I fed him, changed him, administered his medicines until he was within an inch of his life." She looked away. "Later, when he slept most of the time, I'd sit beside him, finding the rise and fall of his chest comforting."

Faye gave a murmur of agreement. "I know what you mean. Dad spent his last weeks in the local hospice. He couldn't speak or feed himself. I'd sit beside him and chat, and every now and then he'd squeeze my hand." Tears pooled in her eyes. "It's strange how a simple gesture can be so comforting."

"It's hard afterwards, isn't it?" Grace said. "Even though you know what's coming, you have time to prepare, it still hits you."

Faye nodded. "People say time is a great healer. It dulls the pain a little, the shadows fade. But they never truly disappear."

Grace felt the heat rise in her face as she pictured Jo. Losing a child. Would those shadows ever disappear?

Faye seemed to guess her thoughts and pressed her hand to her chest. "I'm sorry," she said. "I don't know how we got onto this subject."

It was a moment before Grace replied. "I'm used to it," she said eventually. "People avoid what happened to Jo all the time. I see them in the street, in the supermarket, in the park with my dog. It was different with Jamie. He died of a disease so it was more acceptable to pass on their condolences. Now, they stand there with their sorry faces, can't wait to get away. They feel awkward. Don't want to say the wrong thing. Eventually they say nothing at all. Even my family don't want to talk about it."

"I'm sorry."

"Don't be. It was quite liberating to have a normal conversation for once." Grace took a deep breath. "My family want me to get therapy." The words spilled out of her mouth, almost unwittingly.

"Do you think it would help?"

"Talking to someone, reliving all those last moments… Honestly?" She shook her head. "Not this time."

"Then you have to follow your heart. You'll know what's right for you."

A chair squeaked behind her, turning Grace's head. Apart from a couple in the far corner, the café was now almost empty. Faye pulled back her sleeve. "Goodness, it's almost four," she said. "I should probably go."

"Me too." Grace grabbed her coat and bag while Faye settled the bill she'd insisted on paying.

The rain had stopped, although the early night clouds were already moving in and it was grey and bleak as they stepped outside. Faye paused, and scrabbled in her bag a moment. Grace was surprised when she produced a packet of cigarettes. She held them out, at an awkward angle. "Do you mind?"

"Of course not."

She offered her one, but Grace shook her head. The evening air held a damp freshness and she inhaled, long and deep, and watched as Faye cupped her hand around the lighter. When she emerged she took a long drag and held the cigarette up and out beside her shoulder, like a fifties film star. "Talking about my dad always makes me want a puff," she said.

Grace gave a faint smile.

"Thanks for inviting me out. It's been nice."

"It has."

Faye took another couple of drags, dropped the cigarette and crushed it beneath her foot. "Well, if you ever want to chat again, we could exchange numbers? I promise not to regale you with my dreary tales next time."

The laugh trickled out of Grace's mouth like a musical tune. It had been weeks since she'd felt anything other than sadness and, although she knew it would be short-lived, it was momentarily invigorating. Grace pulled her phone from her bag, flicked through and relayed her number.

Faye entered it into her phone. When she looked up, her face glowed. "Good, that's sorted then."

CHAPTER THIRTY-SEVEN

GRACE STOOD AT the window and watched Lydia greet her friend at the end of the driveway. The straps on her backpack flapped in the wind as she disappeared around the corner. It pained Grace that they still weren't speaking properly.

She rubbed her hands up and down her face and trudged back upstairs to bed. Her days were becoming lost in a fug, fuelled by nights of broken sleep where recollections of Jo's childhood floated in and out of her dreams. It was as if her subconscious was digging deep, trying to recall distant memories in an effort to dilute the pain. Before she woke this morning, she'd been sitting on the beach at Cromer watching her girls buy ice creams from the van nearby. Jo would have been about six at the time, yet she stood there in the queue with her younger sister huddled behind her, ordered their ice creams, handed over the money and chatted to the van driver long after Lydia came running back. Lydia mirrored Grace in every respect, even now people mistook her for her mother from behind as they shared the same shoulder length fair hair and wider build, much to the teenager's chagrin. She was meeker as well, unlike Jo who'd always appeared confident. Although Grace knew the real Jo.

She couldn't get her eldest daughter out of her head,

yet she couldn't talk about her, desperately avoiding raising the issue at home. The newspaper article had caused damage and they hadn't had time to recover. Her family coped by tiptoeing around the situation, pushing it aside and attempting to carry on as normal.

Grace pushed her head back into the pillows and glanced around the room. A yellowing patch of damp discoloured one corner of the ceiling from a dislodged roof tile that had been mended over fifteen years earlier. However many times they'd painted over the watermark, they never seemed to be able to extinguish the mark. One of Phil's suits, just back from the cleaners, hung from the edge of the wardrobe beneath it. The opposite corner, that had once housed their cribs, was dominated by a full length pine mirror that the girls had later used to admire themselves, as teenagers, all dressed up for a night out.

She smoothed the bedclothes around her. For many years she'd shared a bed in here with Jamie, the soft rumble of his snores keeping her awake into the dark hours. Later, after he became ill, the hum of his electric bed filled the room as his health slowly deteriorated. She wondered how he would cope with this cruel turn of events. The loss of his first daughter would have been near impossible to bear, but the fact that she was sexually assaulted and murdered… For the first time, she was grateful he'd died young. At least he was saved the pain.

The trill of the phone interrupted her thoughts. She glanced at the screen, her stomach dipping as she recognised the library's number. This was her boss, Julia's, weekly call, asking Grace how she was doing, politely fishing to see when she was coming back to work. She closed her eyes, silenced the ringtone. Julia had been understanding, arranging for people to cover her part time hours, saying that she could come back when she was ready on reduced hours. She couldn't have been more accommodating. But the last thing that Grace wanted to do was to discuss the trivialities of working hours. It just didn't seem important anymore.

She thought of Faye and the way that she'd confided in her the other afternoon, how good it felt to laugh. Faye had been easy company. Just the right measure of friendliness, without being intrusive.

Apart from a brief text thanking her for a lovely afternoon, Faye hadn't been in touch since. Perhaps she was busy. Perhaps she didn't want to bother her. Who'd want to become friends with a woman whose daughter had just been murdered, their killer running loose? A woman her own daughter had accused of being obsessed. But it would be so nice, refreshing even, to spend time with somebody outside of their family circle. Grace bit her lip, dithered a moment more before reaching for her mobile. It took less than ten seconds to scroll through, find the number and press call. The phone rang out: one, two, three, four. Just as she was about to hang up a voice chimed down the line.

"Hello, Grace." The warmth of Faye's tone brought an instant smile to Grace's face. "I've been meaning to call you."

"Is this a good time?"

"Yes, it's fine. I would have called you before now, but I didn't want you to think I was stalking you." She gave a short laugh. "How are you?"

"I'm okay. I was wondering if you'd like to meet up?"

"Sounds good. When are you thinking?"

"How about tomorrow. We could meet at the same café again, say about eleven thirty?"

"Great. See you there. And Grace?"

"Yes."

"Thanks for phoning."

CHAPTER THIRTY-EIGHT

JACKMAN PLACED HIS hands behind his head and stretched his elbows back. For the last couple of hours he'd pored over his policy log, picking out points of interest, scribbling notes on a pad. Officers had pulled on coats, muttered words of goodbye. The night had crept into the empty office.

He crossed the room to a notice board plastered with photos of Eugenie Trentwood, details of her attack and a map of the scene, next to Jo's murder wall, and stood back wondering what he was missing. The locations, although both in Leicestershire, didn't appear to bear any relation to each other. The girls were similar in appearance, yet didn't seem to share any interests and weren't connected as far as their enquiries showed. He checked the dates: 24th April and 29th October. Just over six months apart. They were approaching four weeks since the murder and leads were drying up, yet they were still no closer to catching the killer. He was still standing there, arms swung behind his head when he heard a voice behind him.

"You're working late, sir."

Jackman turned and smiled at Wilson who bustled into the office. "I thought you'd gone."

"Left my jacket." A button twanged against the desk as she pulled it from the back of a chair nearby. Instead of heading back out, she approached the board. "Anything I can help with?"

"We're missing something, somewhere. Can't put my finger on it."

"That statement will appear on your epitaph," she replied with a bubble of laughter. "Why not leave it for today? I'm sure it'll look clearer in the morning."

"You're probably right. See you tomorrow. Have a good evening."

She was almost at the door when a thought occurred to him. "Dee? When did your other DCI—Caldwell is it?—when did he join the homicide squad?"

"April Fool's Day. He joined us from Northamptonshire Force. I remember it clearly because we sent him an email to meet Superintendent Taylor at Charles Street Police Station. He was almost there before he realised the station had closed eleven years ago."

Jackman laughed. "I hope he took it well."

Wilson nodded, her white teeth glistening under the lights. "After a while. Anything else I can help you with?"

"No, thanks."

He turned back and noted the date on Eugenie's board. She'd been attacked shortly after Caldwell had started. He looked across at Jo's board. Her attack occurred shortly after Jackman was brought in to look at the cold cases. Was this instrumental, or a coincidence?

He switched back to his computer, worked through the old press reports. Shelley Barnstaple had never been named in the media. Early reports talked of a rape but were limited. Eugenie's attack, almost nine years later, was high profile. Two weeks after the attack, Eugenie took the unusual step of making herself known. She was interviewed in the press about her incident. He scrolled down. The person that interviewed her was Artie Black.

Artie went on to highlight the similarities with Shelley's attack. Was his memory really that good, or did he have help from the inside? Speculation spread in the media, pressuring the police to commit as to whether they were searching for a repeat offender. Taylor refused to comment, although he said that both cases were still live investigations and every lead would be thoroughly investigated.

Jackman flicked back and checked the byline on each article. All bar two were written by Artie. He went to the current news reports on Jo Lamborne. Once again, Artie covered the case, quick to point out similarities. His eyes lingered on the latest piece, a heart-wrenching interview with Jo's mother where she talked about how her family were affected by not being able to lay her daughter to rest.

Artie Black had arrived that evening at the crime scene, been in the car park at the hotel the next day. He always seemed to be around, skulking in the shadows. Were his sources that good? Was he really drawn by the attention, so astute that he was ahead of the game? Or was his involvement more of a sinister nature?

He checked his details against the profile. Artie was 44, Leicestershire born and bred. No doubt he'd have known the area well. The nature of his job meant the hours he kept were akin to shift work.

He looked back at the articles. His words were sharp, harsh in places. He'd cultivated the image of an investigative crime journalist seeking justice for victims and their families. But wading through these articles, one after another, it looked more like a personal crusade, bordering on obsession. An obsession compounded through years of reporting Leicestershire's crime? Jackman couldn't be sure.

Artie's initial refusal to put forward the witness, the last person to see Jo alive, still niggled at Jackman. It was almost like he was playing a game, showing that he wouldn't be pushed around by the police.

It was well known that some serial offenders liked to stay close to a case, so that they could check on the police investigation while planning their next move. It wasn't unusual to find reports of them visiting old crime scenes, getting to know the family afterwards. Jackman sifted back through the interviews. The journalist seemed to have all the tools at his disposal to sway public opinion and he couldn't help wondering if Artie was really on a crusade for justice, or playing a dangerous game.

CHAPTER THIRTY-NINE

GRACE EMPTIED THE bucket down the sink and placed it back in the corner of the kitchen. She'd come down early that morning to see Lydia before school and discovered a pool in the kitchen, rapidly expanding as more water dripped from the ceiling. Half a dozen phone calls later and an emergency plumber was now upstairs, working on a leaky pipe beneath the bathroom floor.

Grace cast an anxious glance at the clock. It was almost eleven. She was just thinking about postponing when her phone buzzed with a text from Faye. See you in half an hour. She grabbed her phone and selected Faye's number.

Faye answered on the second ring. "I was just leaving."

Grace explained about the burst pipe.

"What a nightmare. I hope there isn't too much mess. Do you want to leave it for today?"

"We could. Or you could come here if you want?" Grace asked tentatively. "I don't think he'll be too much longer, but you can never be sure."

"Where do you live?"

Grace relayed her address.

"Oh, that's not too far away. I'll come to you then. Give me an hour. Anything you want me to bring?"

"Just yourself."

AN HOUR LATER the plumber had left and Grace was picking at the skin around her nails. This was only the second time she'd arranged to meet Faye. If they were out somewhere, she could have made excuses, left early if things weren't going well. That wasn't going to be so easy at home. As more time passed, she felt itchy, and when the doorbell did eventually sound, she jumped.

"Sorry I'm a bit late," Faye said as Grace pulled the door open. "Stopped off to get us something nice." She held up a box of fresh cream cakes. "Hope that's okay?"

Grace felt an oozing of calm as she returned her smile. "Perfect." She stood aside and waited while Faye shrugged off her coat to reveal a pair of black jeans, a long loose jumper and a purple checked scarf.

"Another lovely scarf," Grace said.

"Heart Foundation." Faye ran the fingers of her free hand across it. "I'm always in the charity shops. I'll have to take you shopping." She bent down to stroke Lucky. "Is your leak fixed?"

Grace looked up at the ceiling as they moved into the kitchen. "He's mended the pipe. We caught it early so luckily there's not too much damage. We just have to let the ceiling dry out before we can paint it."

It wasn't long before Grace had made tea and they'd tucked into the cakes. The conversation was light and effortless. Faye talked about a man singing Irish songs on the bus on the way over. "An elderly woman joined in, and then so did the bus driver! It was hilarious."

Grace found herself giggling like a teenager. "Was he drunk?"

"I don't think so. Well, I hope the driver wasn't!" They both laughed.

Faye licked the cream off her fingers. "You have a lovely house."

"Thanks," Grace said. She gathered up the empty box and placed it in the bin. "I could show you around if you want?"

"Oh, yes please."

Grace felt a sense of pride as they moved from room to room. She'd worked hard to transform the house after Jamie died and it was lovely to show off her efforts. Faye admired her curtains and soft furnishings and talked through her own ideas for renovating her father's bungalow. Any notion of awkwardness faded as the two women wandered around chatting.

"You're very creative," Faye said as they entered the master bedroom. Grace's eyes were drawn to the watermark on the ceiling. Phil had talked about taking some advice as to how they should erase it, but she'd never really pushed the issue. Something about it was strangely comforting.

"Not really. I just read a lot of magazines and pinch the ideas."

They hovered outside Lydia's bedroom and Faye sniggered as she read the sign: *Lydia's room. You're only welcome if I say so.*

Grace rolled her eyes. "Teenagers."

"How old is she?"

"Fifteen."

"Sounds like me at that age," Faye said, a wistful look in her eyes. "I hated people wandering in and out of my room."

They were on the landing now, beside the entrance to Jo's room.

"Is this…?"

Grace nodded.

"We don't need to go in there. If you're not comfortable."

Grace hesitated. After the newspaper interview, she'd felt compelled to move back into the master bedroom and it seemed she was the only person who ever went into Jo's bedroom these days, the others seemed to make a point of avoiding it. Part of her felt it would be nice to share it with someone. "It's fine." She clicked open the door.

The room smelt fresh, thanks to a window left ajar. Grace stood aside, her eyes floating over the array of candles on the windowsill, the posters adorning the walls and books piled on top of the chest of drawers in the corner. The pause lasted several seconds as they drank in Jo's possessions.

Faye moved forward and, as she did so, her jumper brushed the windowsill. Something clinked as it dropped on the laminate flooring. She bent down and picked up a signet ring. It glinted in the light as she rose.

"Oh, thank you," Grace said as she passed it over. "This was Jo's. We gave it to her on her thirteenth birthday. I really should put it in my jewellery box for safe keeping." She slipped it on her finger.

"Must be lovely to keep a part of her with you," Faye said softly. Grace nodded. "Have the police still not found the person responsible?"

"No."

Grace bit back tears as Faye brushed her arm. "I'm so sorry."

The solemn mood continued as they moved downstairs.

"Do you mind if I smoke in your garden?" Faye asked.

"Of course not."

Grace switched on the kettle and gazed out of the window while she busied herself making drinks. She watched Faye light up, mesmerised in her own world as she pulled on her cigarette.

"I'm sorry," Grace said as Faye came back inside. "I'm gloomy company." She passed over a steaming mug.

"You've every right to be."

They sat in silence as they sipped their tea. Faye's fingers were folded around her mug, displaying nails that were painted wine red. Grace searched her mind for something to say, to break the morose atmosphere. "I never asked you where you live," she said eventually.

"Oh, Fairfax Road. Dad's old bungalow. It's a bit run down to be honest. Needs a lot of work. I just haven't felt like it since Dad passed away. But you've given me inspiration, Grace. Your house is so beautiful. I could make it really nice."

"Happy to help."

"You'll wish you hadn't said that!" Faye finished her tea and grabbed her bag. "I'd better get going."

"Are you sure you don't want me to drive you home?" Grace asked, watching Faye pull on her coat in the hall.

"No, I like the bus. Don't want to miss out on all that fun now, do I?" Grace chuckled. "Anyway, I need to get used to this area. I've a job interview nearby on Thursday."

"Oh, where?"

"On the industrial estate." She sniffed. "Admin, that

sort of thing. It'll be strange going back to work after all this time."

"Well, call in for another tea or coffee afterwards if you like. I'll provide the cakes this time."

"I might just take you up on that."

CHAPTER FORTY

JACKMAN SPOTTED DAVIES waving at him from a table beside the window as he crossed the car park of Stacks Restaurant in Leamington. By the time he'd entered and reached the table, she was holding out her glass of white wine in greeting. "You're late," she said.

He checked his watch. "It's not yet one o'clock. You're early."

Davies snorted and took a slurp of wine.

"Drinking at a meeting. I'm sure there's a rule against that," he said as he sat and ordered a mineral water.

"It's my day off."

Jackman gave her a mock look of disdain.

"John's picking me up and I have no baby. So, I'm treating myself. That all right with you?"

"As long as you can handle your drink."

Jackman smiled inwardly. He'd missed Davies' ability to see the funny side of almost any situation. They'd worked together for so many years on the homicide squad at Warwickshire that he could almost predict her answers before she gave them.

Lunch passed easily. Davies' singsong Geordie accent made him chuckle as she relayed the gossip from Warwickshire. Jackman passed on dessert, instead opting for coffee. He watched Davies place a huge spoon of cheesecake in her mouth. "Mmm," she said closing her eyes. "So, what about you?"

"Well, I'm hoping you've got some news for me."

She wiped her mouth. "I want the gossip first. What's happening in Leicestershire?"

"Not a lot. Got a new Super."

"Yes, I heard Taylor's retired. He'll be missed. Who replaced him?"

"Carmela Hanson."

Davies' mouth instantly dropped open. "Not THE Carmela, Queen of training?"

Jackman suppressed a smile. "The very one."

"And?"

"She seems okay, so far."

She pulled back, stared at him a moment. "You're shagging her."

Jackman's face crumpled. "No."

"Well, if you're not, you should be. That's some hot totty there. Anything else?"

"The reason we met—"

"You are so boring. And there was me thinking it was my delectable personality." She dropped the spoon onto an empty plate, reached down, retrieved a file from her bag and handed it over. "Right. Your support group," she said, the smile slipping from her face. "As you know, attendance averages between six and nine people, depending on the week. Only four of them came forward for interview, plus I got a statement from the group leader, Karen Wakefield. Janus gave me the whole sum of one day to travel to Leicestershire, take all the statements and write them up."

"Generous." Jackman opened the file and leafed

through the statements that had been neatly stapled together.

"Surprising. Anyway, I'm not sure they'll help you much. All have assorted mental health issues. No intelligence on file about any of them. None of them have a police record. Their statements pretty much follow the same line. Jo attended around six sessions in total. She had anxiety issues, struggled with change and yet was a regular contributor at meetings. No indication she's forged friendships with any of the members. Not surprising as we're assuming she rushed off immediately afterwards to catch her train."

"Is that it?"

"Oh, there is one other thing I'm not sure you're aware of? It's an all-women group."

Jackman turned the meeting over in his mind as he bade farewell to Davies and climbed into his car. Davies had been thorough. He'd get his team to run the group members through the Holmes computer system to check the names against statements back at the office, but he doubted they'd find anything. Everything about Barnes' profile assessment pointed to a male attacker, probably working alone. The fact that it was an all-women support group certainly didn't help matters.

IT WAS AFTER three when Faye arrived on Thursday afternoon. "How was the interview?" Grace asked as she ushered her in.

"Don't ask. The agency messed up on the dates. They tried to fit me in, but the General Manager kept calling me Marie, even though I told him twice my name was Faye, and spoke to me in engineering jargon. I'd no idea what he was talking about."

"I'm sorry. And you came all this way."

"No worries. I still get to see you, so it's not all wasted. Just need a smoke first, if you don't mind?"

"Of course not, I'll come with you."

The damp air clung to her skin as she moved outside. Grace pulled her cardigan across her chest. She watched longingly as Faye pulled a cigarette out of the packet, lit up and took a long drag.

"Want one?" Faye said holding it out.

Grace shook her head.

"How do you manage to keep your garden looking nice at this time of year?" Faye asked.

Grace followed her gaze down the lawn. It seemed an odd thing to say when the garden was hardly anything to look at. It was devoid of colour, the grass lacklustre and the trees bare. "My father was a keen gardener," Grace said. "Mum tried to carry it on after he died, hence the half-hearted attempt, until she passed away a few years ago."

"I'm sorry."

Grace gave a half smile.

"You've been here a long time then?"

"Almost twenty years. It was our first house. Jamie extended the back, gave us another bedroom and made the kitchen bigger. There didn't seem any reason to move."

"Jamie was your first husband?"

Grace nodded. "He was a nice man. You'd have liked him." Grace gave a brief overview of how she'd met and married Phil and their current family set-up. She surprised herself at how easily the words flowed. "And what about you?" she asked eventually. "Married?"

Faye shook her head. "Divorced. No kids. Left him behind in Manchester." She pulled a small tin of mints from her pocket and offered them to Grace who took one. They walked back inside and both washed their hands. "No other family?"

"No, I was an only one. Probably enough for anyone." She chuckled, wiped her hands with a towel and nodded at a photo of Jo and Lucky, heads pressed against each other, above the dog's bed. "That's nice."

"Jo insisted I put it there when she went away to university, so that Lucky didn't forget her."

"It's a lovely picture. Is there still no news?"

"Nothing."

Faye was quiet a moment. "Must be awful for you. The not knowing…" Her voice softened. "You know, if you ever need any help, someone to talk to, outside of the family, my door's always open."

"Thanks," Grace replied, and felt surprised that she meant it.

"Oh, I almost forgot," Faye said, "I got you something." She reached down for her oversized handbag and pulled out a lilac scarf. The silver thread that ran through it glinted in the light.

Grace's eyes widened. "That's for me?"

"Yes. It's not new, but you liked the one I had on the other day so much, when I saw it in the shop window, I thought of you."

"Oh, I must give you something towards it."

"Don't be silly." She waved her away. "It was pennies. Another charity shop gem."

Grace wound it around her neck and moved into the hallway, standing in front of the mirror, turning this way and that. The scarf looked a little awkward, not expertly tied like Faye's, but it instantly brightened the white jumper she was wearing.

"That colour really suits you," Faye said, ruffling it.

Grace was still wearing the scarf when Phil came home later that evening.

"There's something different about you," he said, pecking her on the cheek as she greeted him at the door. He drew back, tipped his head at the scarf. "Is that new?"

Grace beamed and nodded.

"It really suits you."

"Thanks. Faye bought it for me. A present."

"Oh, I didn't realise you were still in touch."

"She's been around a couple of times since we had coffee. We seem to have a lot in common."

Phil stood back, surveying her.

"What?"

"It's good to see you smile."

A FEW DAYS LATER, Jackman could feel his mobile buzzing as he pushed open the door to his hotel room. It was a text from Carmela: I need to talk through some issues with you. Can't do it over the phone. I'm in Warwickshire for a regional meeting all day tomorrow. Let me know if you can meet up for dinner in the evening.

Jackman re-read the message. Carmela had been out of the office the past couple of days and hadn't responded to his updates. He wondered why she needed to talk things through. He'd been planning to travel home to Stratford tomorrow and, after a couple of days away, had been looking forward to an evening in with Erik.

He ran his fingers over the screen. Could do with spending an evening at home. Welcome to join me for a takeaway.

He pressed send. For a split second, a nagging voice questioned whether inviting Carmela to dinner at his house was a good idea. Although this wasn't personal, it was work. And she'd visited his house when she'd mentored him last summer, so it's not like she hadn't been there before.

CHAPTER FORTY-ONE

GRACE PAUSED AND watched a clump of wild strawberries, swaying in the light breeze. "It's too mild for this time of year," she said.

Since the job interview, Faye had called around often and the two women had fallen into the rhythm of a friendship. Grace looked forward to Faye's visits. They were a welcome distraction, filling the void in her day when the house was empty.

Faye sneezed beside her, grappling with a tissue. "I can't wait for winter to finally arrive," she said, "to flush out all those bugs."

It was a pleasant afternoon in the local park, the sun squeezing its last rays out of the day through the branches above. The two women ambled around the perimeter while Lucky drifted off into the bushes on her extended lead.

"Still, it's nice to be out," Grace smiled. "How's your front room coming along?"

"All right." Faye stepped over a puddle. "I've painted the red feature wall. Looks really nice. You'll have to come round and see it when it's all done."

"I'd love that."

As they turned a corner, a couple approached with a Jack Russell. Lucky scooted across to meet it, yanking at the lead as it extended to its maximum.

"Hey!" A man approached, diagonally across the grass. Thick stubble poked out of his chin. Bushy grey hair dipped into his eyes. He looked like he needed a good wash. He blew out puffs of cloud as he drew close. "Faye. Faye Campbell. It is you. You look different!" He extended a hand. "You remember me, don't you? Richard. Richard Beck."

Faye froze. Nobody spoke for a moment. Grace looked from one to another.

A series of growls in the distance caught their attention. Lucky tugged at the lead pulling a reluctant Grace towards the couple. The growls descended into barks and the dogs leapt at each other.

"I'll catch you up," Faye called after Grace as she rushed forward to retrieve Lucky. By the time she'd calmed the situation, separated the dogs and made her apologies, Faye had re-joined her.

"Sorry about that," Grace said. She looked back towards the pathway. The man had gone, but something about him made her uneasy. "Who was that?"

Faye smoothed down her hair. "An old friend from college." She lowered her voice to a whisper. "To be honest, I barely remembered him. Bit embarrassing really."

Grace turned again, but the park was empty. They strolled along. A pair of blackbirds fluttered about on the grass. Grace recalled her own blank face when Faye had introduced herself in the supermarket. "I'm surprised you remembered me," she said eventually, "especially as we were in different year groups at school."

Faye smiled. "Some people stick in your mind." She kicked a stone, watched it roll to the side of the path.

"Do you remember the youth club trip to Wales?" Grace wracked her brains. Vague memories of a cold weekend of sleeping in dormitories danced into her head. "You took the top bunk next to me and we chatted the whole time. Got told off by Amy Sanders for keeping her awake. Mind you, she was a bossy cow."

Grace stared back at her blankly.

"Don't tell me you don't remember Amy Sanders? Sometimes I wonder who she married, poor sod."

"I'm sorry."

"Don't worry. Must be going through all my father's stuff, making me nostalgic."

"No, it's me. My mum and dad fostered. There were always kids coming and going at our house. I used to have people contact me after Mum and Dad died to say they lived with us for a while when I was young. Sometimes Jamie remembered them, he grew up next door, but I rarely did. I guess you can only remember so much, especially when you have children."

They moved aside to allow a jogger to pass, the lead of his headphones just visible above his sweatshirt.

"Did you ever think about having children?" Grace asked.

"I fell pregnant. Once." Faye broke off, a faraway look in her eyes. She shook her head. "I lost him."

"Oh, I'm so sorry."

"I knew he was dead, even before the midwife told me. I think you do when they're inside you, don't you? You feel everything with them. I tried to talk myself out of it on the way to the hospital that day, pretend I was imagining it, that I could still feel him moving around… They made me give birth the normal way.

Four hours I was in labour. I can still recall the pain, the agony. Only to deliver a dead baby." She looked across at Grace. They'd almost reached the road that led back to Grace's. "He was so tiny, he fitted into the palm of my hand. And so perfect. We called him Reece."

"How awful."

"It was a long time ago."

"You didn't have anymore?"

"Tried. Didn't get pregnant again. I guess it just wasn't meant to be."

Grace reeled Lucky in as they reached the curb and waited to cross. Neither spoke until they'd reached the other side. "Any news on Jo?" Faye asked.

Faye's directness was one of the qualities Grace cherished in her. She treated Jo's case respectfully, talked about it openly. She'd received numerous messages from friends and distant relatives offering her an ear, a place to stay if she wanted a break, but they all skirted around Jo's case with their awkward conversation. It was little wonder she hadn't returned their calls.

Grace shook her head. "The police haven't been in touch for a while."

"Really? What about the man they arrested for the attack on that girl years ago. What's his name?"

"Oliver Turner."

"That's it."

"They believe he's not the man who attacked Jo."

"That doesn't make sense though, does it? Both were strangled. The papers talked about the same attacker for a while."

"I don't know," Grace said wearily. "They were talking to another guy, asked me if I knew him, but that seems to have blown over too. Someone named Anthony Kendall. I looked him up on Jo's Facebook page. He was a friend of hers from Nottingham. I can't find any details on him though."

"And you're curious?"

Grace nodded. "I'm not sure why. He's obviously not a suspect otherwise the police would have been in touch, but… Oh, I don't know. She mentions him in several of her Facebook posts and he feels significant somehow. As if he was close to Jo. I know so little about her friends up there. It seems like another world."

"Why don't you visit?"

Grace flinched. "Oh, I'm not sure about that."

"I'd come with you."

"You would?"

"Of course. It's not like I have a job at the moment." Faye nudged her shoulder. "Come on. You might as well make the most of me while I'm not working."

It was tempting, Grace had to admit. Phil and Lydia wouldn't like it. They'd think she was interfering again. Not leaving the police to do their job. But she could go during the week, when they were at work and school. They'd never need to know. It was only an hour's drive.

"I suppose I've nothing to lose."

CHAPTER FORTY-TWO

CARMELA RESTED HER knife and fork together on her plate. "I needed that," she said. "Didn't know you could cook."

"It was only spaghetti bolognese."

"Still, very nice. I was expecting pizza or a bag of chips when you suggested a takeaway."

Jackman circled his plate with a spoon, scraping up the last remnants of sauce. "Do you cook?"

Erik moved forward, resting his head on Carmela's lap. She slid her chair back and stroked his ears. "Not much these days. Hardly seems worth getting the pans out for one. I've fallen into bad habits."

Jackman busied himself making coffees. When he turned around Carmela had pulled an A4 pad from her briefcase and was sitting expectantly.

"You said you wanted to discuss something?" Jackman said, carrying the coffees across.

"Yes. I've been out of the office a lot. I wanted to check how things were going with the investigation, but," her face turned grave as she crossed one leg over another and leant her elbow on the table, "something else happened this afternoon. Something that has rather changed things." Jackman sat down, placing a coffee cup in front of Carmela. "Our regional meeting was cut short by a call from Special Branch this afternoon.

There's been a terror threat in Leicestershire. Film footage was emailed to a journalist at the *Leicester Herald* this morning. It contained two masked men who said plans have been made to plant a bomb in Leicester city centre in the name of ISIS."

"And the sender?" As soon as the words dripped from his mouth, he guessed her answer.

"Anti-terrorism are still working on it. They have some ideas, but the email appears untraceable."

"Odd," Jackman said. "ISIS don't normally advertise when they are about to strike."

"That's what Special Branch said. They're working on the theory that it might be amateurs."

"Do we have any idea of when, or where?"

Carmela shook her head. "Not at the moment. The threat level has been increased to critical. This is in the strictest confidence, Will. We are only sharing with DCI level and above at present until Special Branch know what they are dealing with. But it means we need to dispatch more officers to patrol Leicester centre, certainly until we know more. Which means I'm going to have to scale down your team." She paused to sigh. "Will, you know what it's like. Threats like these are countered all the time. But we can't afford to ignore the risk right now."

"Clearly. What are we talking about in terms of numbers?"

"I can leave you with eight initially. Four detectives, four support staff. Then we'll see."

Jackman nodded. While disappointed, he couldn't argue with the requirement. "And I thought you were giving me the push."

"I'm going to be keeping hold of you for as long as I can," Carmela said with a wink. "Even if you're not technically mine. Now, why don't you let me know where we are with the investigation?"

Jackman felt a mild sense of relief as he gave her a quick update of their current position.

"No new strong leads then?"

"Not at the moment. We've put another press appeal out for the hooded witness seen across the road on the night of the murder. She was well positioned to see something, even if she wasn't involved. And we're still battling through the shift workers, hoping something might come up there." He relayed Davies' feedback on the support group. "There are some members there that haven't come forward. We could apply for a production order, force their arm?"

"I think we'll focus on the shift workers for now. Based on the profile, that's our priority."

"Okay." Jackman sat back in his chair. "Who was the journalist?"

"I'm sorry?"

"The journalist who received the email this morning."

"Oh, the *Herald*'s lead crime reporter. What's his name?"

"Artie Black."

"That's it."

"Interesting."

"Why?"

Jackman's explained his earlier concerns regarding Artie Black.

"Hmm. If he is involved, the threat would be the

perfect distraction. I take it this is speculation? There is no evidence at this stage?"

"No evidence. I can't find anything that suggests he knew either of the girls beforehand. Either he has an unnatural interest in the attacks, or he's a very diligent journalist. I can't be sure which. I can't see him manufacturing a film about a terrorist threat though. Especially if he came straight to the police with it. If he wanted to create tension, draw public attention away from the case, he'd have tried to leak something." Jackman explained about the earlier difficulties when Artie had refused to give up his source.

"Okay. We'll certainly need to tread carefully. Get everything checked and double-checked. And we'd need firm evidence before we can take any kind of action, otherwise the press will rip us apart. Find me something I can use and I'll discuss a plan of action with the assistant chief constable. In the meantime, I'll feed it back to Special Branch as intelligence."

Jackman gathered the plates and moved across to the dishwasher, battling with Erik who was trying to curl his tongue around them as he stacked them away.

Carmela carried the mugs over to the sink, grabbed a cloth and wiped the table.

"You are a bit domesticated then?" Jackman said.

"Well, I don't have an Erik to assist with the washing up in my house." They laughed as Jackman closed the dishwasher door and stood. He felt the warmth of her presence beside him. She smelt good. He turned. Too quickly. Just as she did. They bumped. Laughed again. "Why is it that in such a large room people always choose to be in the same spot?" she said. Her eyes were warm. Inviting. She pushed forward. He caught a whiff of her hair before she kissed him. Gently at first, then long and hard. Hungry.

Before he knew it she was unbuttoning her shirt, revealing the depth of her cleavage. Jackman felt a stirring in his groin, pulled her towards him. Her bra unlatched. He felt her bare breasts against him. The cutlery crashed across the tiles as he swept it off the kitchen side, hoisted her up. The urgency was overpowering, pulsing through him.

She grappled with his belt. Neither of them noticed the cafetière teetering on the edge, before falling from the kitchen side. The sound of glass smashing on the floor snapped Jackman to his senses. He drew back, blinking hard as he looked around the kitchen. Broken glass crunched under her feet as Carmela climbed down and pulled her shirt around her chest.

"I'm sorry," Jackman said. "I can't do this."

CHAPTER FORTY-THREE

"GRACE. THE LIGHTS are green."

Grace blinked, pressed her foot on the accelerator. The car moved forward.

Faye twisted in her seat to face her. "Are you sure you want to do this?"

Grace didn't answer. The closer they got to the university, the more her hands tightened on the steering wheel. Suddenly, this covert trip didn't seem such a good idea after all.

They turned left into the campus and were greeted with the sign for The University of Nottingham. The last time she'd passed that sign she'd brought Jo up for the start of her first term. The car had been brimming that day, a duvet blocking the view out of the rear window. It took several trips to empty it and carry bundles of kit across the large campus. Jo's excitement had been palpable; the thrill of the big adventure laid out in front of her. Grace recalled meeting her room-mate, Emily, a mousy-haired girl with a shy smile. Hovering awkwardly for a second as the two girls chatted, before heading off with the promise of a visit in a month or so, when Jo had discovered all the best places to visit.

"Do you want to speak to any of her tutors?" Faye's words cut through her memories as they swept into the visitors' car park.

Grace shook her head. "The police will have interviewed them. We'll try her room first."

It was just after 10.30am by the time they'd crossed the open parkland to Cripps Halls. They walked past the admin office and headed into a quadrangle block of accommodation with a square lawn in the middle. Bare tree branches swayed in the breeze. Most of the students were in morning lectures.

Grace approached the entrance to the far block and tried the door. It was locked. "Damn. I forgot about the keypad code." She looked around, working through her options and was just considering trying the admin office when the door clicked open. Two students almost fell out of the door, laughing. Lost in their joke, they barely noticed Grace and Faye exchange a quick glance and move in before the door closed again.

Grace surprised herself at how easily she found her way to Jo's room on the ground floor. She knocked on the door. The hollow sound echoed around the walls.

When there was no answer she knocked again. Nothing. Grace could feel her glimmer of hope trickling away. She glanced at the handle, just about to try it, when it jerked down and the door opened. The young woman that faced her was pale and gaunt. Her hair hung across her shoulders in a tangled mess. She was dressed in a long white t-shirt, her legs wrapped around each other as if she was trying to keep warm.

"I think we have the wrong room," Grace said. "I was looking for...err..."

"We were looking for some friends of Jo Lamborne," Faye said, stepping forward.

The woman eyed them both suspiciously. "Who are you?"

Grace peered in closer. "Emily, is that you?"

The young woman folded her arms across her chest and nodded.

"You probably don't remember me. I'm Jo's mother."

Recognition spread across the girl's face. "Oh my God." She pressed a hand to her mouth. "Sorry, do you want to come in?" She stepped back and opened the door wider for them to enter. The room was grey and smelt musty. Emily rushed forward and opened the curtains. "I work at a bar nearby. Was just catching up on some sleep," she said nervously.

Grace gave a kind smile. "Sorry to disturb you."

"It's fine, really. I thought you were another journalist at first." Grace pictured Artie Black with his affable manner and warm smile that had appeared so genuine, and cringed inwardly. The very thought of him, or another reporter, digging around Jo's room for a story appalled her. "Can I get you a drink?" Emily moved towards a kettle on the bedside table.

"No, thank you," Grace said. "We won't stay long." Her eyes spanned the room, lingering on the empty bed opposite, devoid of bedclothes.

Emily followed her gaze. "The university sent somebody to bag up Jo's things. I'm afraid there's nothing here." Somewhere in the back of Grace's mind she recalled a parcel arriving from the university, although she hadn't mustered the strength to go through Jo's personal belongings just yet. Emily scratched the back of her neck. "I'm so sorry for what happened. I wanted to write to you, but…"

"It's okay," Grace said. They stood awkwardly a moment.

"How are you bearing up?" Faye asked.

Emily shrugged. "It's been a huge shock for everyone. Jo was great." She smoothed the duvet across her bed, invited them to sit, and moved a pile of clothes off a chair in the corner, settling herself down and burying her gaze in the floor.

"Do you mind if I ask you some questions?" Grace said.

"Of course." Her eyes widened.

"Was she happy here? At the university I mean."

Emily nodded. "She settled quickly, much better than me. Seemed to make friends easily."

"Did she have any close friends, anyone in particular?"

"Not that I know of. There's a group of people from her course, they all hang around together. I was on a different course, so I don't really know them well, just in passing. The police have already interviewed them though."

"Would you write their names down for me? University was a part of Jo's life I didn't know very well. It just helps, you know, to chat to people."

Emily grabbed a pad from the side of the bed. "Sure. I don't have phone numbers for them though. You'd have to ask admin."

"That's okay." Quiet fell upon them as Emily jotted down the details. "You two must have become quite close, sharing a room together?" Grace said as she was passed the list.

Emily bit her lip. "I suppose. It wasn't for very long. And she was out a lot. But I did really like her. When we were both in we'd watch films together." She sniffed. "She was good company."

"Anyone she didn't get along with?"

Emily shook her head. "Jo liked everyone."

"What about a boyfriend?" Faye asked.

"Not that I know of."

"It must be strange to have the room to yourself now," Grace said, keen to break the awkward silence that followed.

"It is. There was talk of someone else coming in, but I don't think anyone wants to this term. Would feel a bit like taking Jo's place, I think."

"Well, I think we've taken up enough of your time. Do keep in touch. It would be lovely to hear from you."

Emily pulled her robe around her as she rose, and nodded.

They were just at the door when Grace turned. "Oh, one more thing. I wanted to have a word with Jo's friend, Anthony. You don't know which room he is in, do you?" She kept her tone casual, although inside she was battling to keep her nerves in check.

"You mean Anthony Kendall? Yes, I know him. He doesn't live here. He's got a house on Devonshire Promenade, just off the Derby Road. Number 22, I think. I've only been there once."

A TEENAGER WAS bent down, tying a shoelace as Grace turned into Devonshire Promenade and parked up opposite number 22 later that morning. They were almost within touching distance as she got out of the car and he looked up, startled.

"Anthony?"

He looked at her a moment, confusion spreading across his face, and shook his head.

"Oh, I'm sorry. I thought you were someone else." The young man moved past them.

The line of Edwardian villas that formed Devonshire Promenade faced the railings enclosing Lenton Park beyond. It was a private, unmade road and tufts of grass pushed through the gaps in the broken concrete. Leaves crunched beneath their feet in the porch area as they reached the door. Grace rang the bell.

To her surprise, a middle-aged man with bare feet answered. He was dressed in shorts, in spite of the cool weather. Grace looked past him. "I was looking for Anthony Kendall."

"And you are?"

"Grace Daniels. This is my friend, Faye."

The man switched his gaze from one to another.

"Is Mr Kendall in?" Grace asked.

"You're speaking to him."

"I meant Mr Kendall junior."

The man stood back, narrowed his eyes. "There's only one Anthony Kendall here and that's me. What can I do for you?"

Grace's breath caught in her throat. She'd expected a younger man, late teens maybe. Not somebody who looked almost old enough to be Jo's father. It took her a moment to recover herself. "My name is Grace."

"So you said."

"I'm Jo Lamborne's mother."

His smirk faded. "Oh."

A beat passed.

Faye stepped forward. "Aren't you going to ask us in?"

He looked at them a moment, as if he wasn't sure, then stood aside.

An oversized sofa covered with an Indian throw dominated the small front room and a colourful rug covered the laminate floor in front, giving it a cosy feel. Grace imagined Jo sitting there with him, chatting. The air smelt strangely sweet. Grace caught the edge of a coffee table as she sat. It wobbled slightly causing a spray of ash to skip into the air from an overflowing ashtray.

Anthony pulled up a wicker chair from the corner. "I'm sorry for your loss," he said awkwardly. "Is there any news?"

Grace shook her head. She opened her mouth to speak, but the words stuck in her throat.

"Grace just wanted to visit a few of Jo's university friends," Faye said gently. "Get a feel for her life here." He nodded, said nothing. "How long had you known Jo?" Faye continued.

"A few weeks. I met her in the student union bar."

"You're a mature student?"

"Yes."

"Were you close?"

He cleared his throat. "We got together a few times." His eyes turned sad.

"Were you her boyfriend?"

"No. We were just friends."

Grace leant forward. "The police said Jo came back

to Market Harborough for an appointment once a week," she said. "Do you know anything about that?"

"I know she went to Market Harborough. But, no, I don't know what it was for."

"Did she mention anyone that she didn't get on with, someone that she'd had an argument with maybe?"

"No." His face hardened. "Look, I'm not sure what this is all about. I've already spoken to the police."

Grace pressed on with a few more questions about Jo, and their friends, desperately trying to glean something to make her trip worthwhile. Anthony responded with short answers, his reluctance obvious.

Suddenly, the sound of excited voices outside caught her attention. They grew louder as the front door crashed open and two young men appeared. "Sorry, mate," one of them said. "Didn't realise you had company."

Anthony stood, nodded at them and held out an open hand towards Grace. "This is Jo Lamborne's mother and her friend." The two men stared at Grace. Anthony's face clouded. "I think they were just leaving."

Neither spoke as they walked back towards the car. Grace took the keys out of her bag, but turned off at the last minute and walked around the corner and into the park opposite.

"Where are you going?" Faye asked, scurrying behind her.

"I need some air."

Grace found an old bench and sat. A woman walked past, battling with a toddler in reins who wanted to walk in the opposite direction. She watched them disappear up the path. "Did you see that photo on the side of the mantel?" she asked Faye eventually.

Faye shook her head.

"It was Jo."

"Do you think they were together?"

"I don't know. I can't think straight. Why would Jo get together with a man almost old enough to be her dad?"

"Maybe they were just friends?"

"You don't usually have a photo of a friend you've only known for a few weeks on your mantelpiece."

The image of Anthony Kendall filled Grace's mind. She'd travelled to Nottingham to find out more about Jo, yet so far it had served to remind her just how little she knew about her daughter. Anthony's clear discomfort at her questions troubled her. He couldn't wait for them to leave, practically pushed them out of the door. Did he have something to hide? The wind swirled around the trees opposite, causing the bare branches to rustle against each other. It sounded like they were whispering secrets, just out of earshot.

"Come on," she said to Faye. "Let's go home."

LATER THAT EVENING, Phil let Lucky in from the garden and wandered through to the front room. "Has somebody been smoking?" he asked. "There are cigarette butts outside the back door."

Lydia looked up from her position on the sofa. "Well, they won't be Mum's. She doesn't approve."

"Oh, sorry," Grace said. "They're Faye's, I meant to pick them up."

Lydia rolled her shoulders as the television credits flashed up the screen. "I'm going up to finish my homework."

Phil waited for the sound of her bedroom door closing and scratched his head awkwardly. "There's something we need to talk about."

"Oh?" Grace could feel him on her tail as she walked through to the kitchen and placed her empty glass beside the sink, and was surprised when he took her hand and guided her to the table. "I had a phone call this evening. From Detective Parsons."

"Is there some news?"

Phil paused, a look of concern creasing his face. "I understand you've been up to Nottingham, to see a Mr Kendall?"

Her secret was out. She wasn't sure whether to be relieved or angry. She'd been bursting to share the details about Anthony Kendall with him all evening. But not like this. The very fact that the police knew made her stomach churn.

"He's made a complaint that he's being harassed. Apparently you aren't the first person to land on his doorstep."

"That's not my fault. I only went to see him because he was a friend of Jo's."

"He's not a suspect in the case, but he's apparently said he feels he's being targeted as one."

Grace scoffed.

"Look, love, I know you're hurting. But you have to accept that if he was a friend of Jo's, he might be grieving too. He's never met you, and you turn up at his home asking questions. Can you imagine what that would feel like?"

Grace pictured Anthony Kendall's face when she'd introduced herself. Over the hours that followed she'd analysed every bit of his reaction, wondering if his discomfort was due to a guilty conscience. But maybe Phil was right. His actions could have been coloured by grief.

Phil edged nearer and stroked the backs of his fingers down her cheek. "Why not think about going back to work?"

"I can't." Grace turned away before the tears swelling in her eyes spilled down her face.

"Then we need to get you back to the doctors. You'll need to get another certificate for work, and perhaps you can talk things through with them, see if there's some other way they can help. I'll come with you." He wiped away the tears with his thumbs. "I saw Beryl in the driveway earlier. She was asking after you."

Grace looked away.

"She was telling me it's the book club meet next week. Why don't you go along? I'm sure they'd love to see you."

Grace stiffened. "I can't face them."

"Maybe just see Beryl then, for a coffee? It might be good for you to get out a bit more?"

"I am getting out. I went out today. With Faye."

"Perhaps it's time to see some of your other friends."

"What do you mean?"

"Just that we don't know Faye very well."

"I know her. She understands me. She seems to be the only one who understands me at the moment."

CHAPTER FORTY-FOUR

GRACE TURNED THE box of Sertraline over in her hands. For years she'd stood by and watched Jo take antidepressants. When the doctor had offered her Citalopram that morning, she'd asked for something different, the familiarity of them too raw. But right now, these didn't hold much appeal either. "I'm not going to take them," she said.

Faye smiled comfortingly. She'd listened as Grace had relayed Phil's conversation with her the evening before. "I'm sorry," she said. "It all seems so unnecessary."

Grace rubbed her eyes. She'd omitted the part where Phil had pressed her to go out more, see other people. There was no point in upsetting Faye.

"Does make you wonder why Anthony Kendall kicked up such a fuss though. Do you think he's got something to hide?"

"I don't know. We can't visit Nottingham again to find out, that's for sure."

"Did the detective give Phil any news about Jo?"

"Nothing. I just wish I could do something," Grace said. "I feel so useless."

"I'll help you. Whatever you want to do."

"What about the other attacks? Perhaps we should look into them? We have a list of names of Jo's friends and associates. We could see if any of them feature on the other girls' Facebook pages? I'm sure the police will already have looked into this, but they won't be as familiar with some of the names, certainly the local ones, as I might be."

Faye nodded, opened the laptop and logged into Facebook. "What were their names?"

"I don't know the first one. The police never released her name. But the second girl was called Eugenie. Eugenie Trentwood." She moved across and sat beside Faye on the sofa. A list of names instantly popped up on the screen. She clicked on the first one who listed their address in Arizona, went into the second and the third. Neither showed their location or photographs. She disregarded an elderly lady, the next was around the right age, but didn't show their location. "This might be more difficult than you thought." Faye sighed.

"Wait, she did an interview for the press shortly after the attack," Grace said. "I remember it was big news at the time. I'm sure there was a photo with it."

Faye tapped away, scrolled through a couple of news reports and eventually brought up her interview, accompanied by a photo of a young woman. The sight of her curls made Grace gasp. "You sure you want me to carry on?" Faye asked.

Grace nodded. Faye brought the Facebook list up on the screen next to the article and started scrolling through. It was a tedious task. They were almost at the bottom when a photo of a girl came up. Her curls were tied back. No location was shown.

"Could be this one," Faye said. She clicked on the profile, but couldn't get any further. "You have to be friends with Eugenie to see her full profile. Not surprising really." Faye switched back to the article, browsing slowly. "Such a shame. The papers seem keen to point out the links between the attacks." She scrolled down. "I don't know… The only similarities I can see are the ages. They look different, apart from the curly hair, and don't seem to know each other." She clicked a few more keys, her eyes searching the screen. "The papers say they both had ligatures placed around their necks. Both were sexually assaulted."

Grace closed her eyes, placed a hand over her face. She'd put those details of the attack out of her mind. Hearing them again, read out loud, made her feel light-headed.

Faye looked across at her. The laptop wobbled on her knees. "I'm sorry. This must be really painful for you."

"When I think of the fear, the pain he subjected her to." Grace let her hand drop into her lap. "She must have been terrified."

Faye's eyes were set on her, examining every contour of her face. "Oh, God. It's happened to you too." A few beats passed. "You don't have to tell me," Faye said quickly.

Grace swallowed. For a moment she wasn't sure. But when she opened her mouth and started to speak, the words gushed out, almost of their own accord. She relayed the details of that awful evening, so many years earlier. An evening that had been archived in the depths of her memory until Jo's death, when it was wrenched to the forefront. Now it sat there, between them, and the thought of her daughter experiencing the same terrible pain and anguish was haunting.

The account filled her with renewed horror. She was

petrified, re-living the force of him, the menthol smell on his breath. The voice became distant, no longer hers.

Faye had taken hold of Grace's hand and didn't speak until she'd completely finished. "You poor thing." She placed the computer on the floor, stretched her arm out and hugged her friend close. Grace expected tears, but none came, her senses dazed.

She became aware of Faye moving away, leaving the room. The sound of a tap running. A glass of water was placed in front of her.

"Are you okay?" Faye asked eventually.

"I've never told anyone."

Faye widened her eyes. "What, never? What about your husband?"

"Jamie? It was before we were married. And we weren't together when it happened."

"Goodness. You did well to pick up the pieces, move forward."

"I got married soon after. Had the girls. Pushed it to the back of my mind."

"Still, an awful thing to have carried around with you."

Suddenly fear pricked the hairs on the top of Grace's arms. A nauseous sense of unease rose inside her, closely followed by surprise at how easily she'd let the secret out after all these years. She gripped Faye's hand. "You mustn't tell anyone."

Faye stroked her friend's forearm. "Of course not. I won't tell a soul."

CHAPTER FORTY-FIVE

THE PHONE WOKE Grace with a start. Somehow, sharing her secret had given her a strange sense of calm, but in spite of a full night's sleep, the first since Jo's passing, she was still tired this morning and had fallen into an exhausted slumber after Lydia had left for school. It took her a while to focus and register Faye's voice on the end of the line.

"Are you still coming over later?" she asked.

"Yes, but I wanted to speak to you about something. It's been on my mind all night. I think you should tell the police about your attack."

The words bolted Grace forward. "What?"

"It might be important."

"I'm not telling anyone, Faye, and neither are you. You promised."

"But don't you see, Grace? It could be connected to what happened to Jo."

"It was twenty years ago."

The phone line crackled. "But there may be more of a connection than you realise."

"What do you mean?"

"Is it possible your attacker could be Jo's father? What if he found out about her? Came back."

"No. No, that's not possible."

JACKMAN LOOKED UP from his notes. A deflated atmosphere pervaded the incident room. He glanced around at the handful of officers working at computer screens, pressing keys, desperately following up the last few lines of enquiry, hoping for a breakthrough that would lead them in a new direction. After working long hours these past few weeks, missing out on social events and valuable family time, they were facing the real possibility that the case they'd given all their precious hours to, was destined to be added to a long list of unsolved crimes. The pull-back on resources had left tension in its wake. But there was something else beside the strain.

As soon as desks had freed up he'd commandeered one in the corner near the window, close enough that he could hear what was going on, but far enough away that his team didn't feel as though he was breathing down their necks.

McDonald brushed past. "The Super wants to see you. Said it was urgent."

Jackman thanked him, but instead of retreating he approached Dee Wilson at the far end of the room. He gestured towards a quiet area near the filing cabinets, indicating for her to follow. "What's going on?" he said in a low voice when he was confident they were out of earshot of their colleagues.

"The chief's making changes." Wilson gave a fervent glance across the room and back at Jackman. "Parsons passed her room earlier, overheard an exchange with the assistant chief constable. Sounds like they're scaling down the investigation."

"What?"

Wilson shrugged. "That's all I know."

Jackman's mind raced as he moved away and climbed the stairs to Carmela's office. He hadn't seen or heard from Carmela since their dinner. The terrorist threat was pulling on her time. They were both tired, the accumulation of hours on the waning investigation taking its toll on him. A flashback of Carmela in the kitchen, him pressing her against the cabinets, pulling up her skirt. The thoughts made him recoil. How could he have allowed that to happen? A part of him was relieved she hadn't been in touch. Because he didn't know what to say to her.

He reached her room, gave a single knock and entered without waiting for an invitation. Carmela looked up from behind her desk. She was on the phone, her hair was pulled back into a messy pleat, her mouth tight. She nodded at a nearby chair.

Jackman took a seat and waited for her to finish. The room looked different this morning, somewhat barer, more clinical. Carmela ended the call and managed a half-smile as she faced him. They weren't moving over to the easy chairs in the corner today and her desk presented a barrier between them, reinstating their ranks, a gesture not lost on Jackman.

"Is everything okay? It's like a morgue in the incident room."

She ignored his question. "As you know, I'm under pressure with the recent terrorist threat."

"So you said."

"This is going to be a high profile investigation. We need to send more officers."

"More from my team? We're already short."

Carmela sat back in her chair. "I understand that, Will. But there are other priorities at stake here. And the chief is getting restless. We're not getting any further in the case. Maybe it's time to get a fresh pair of eyes in, to take a look at things."

"A review team, already?"

"There's something else," she said, ignoring his question. "Warwickshire want you back."

"What? I thought you said you'd keep me as long as you could?"

"And I have. But we've had you for almost five weeks. Warwickshire are short-staffed too and your own Super wants you to concentrate on your policy report." She met his gaze. "You leave today."

Jackman clenched his teeth. "Who is taking over on Operation Ascott then?"

"That's still to be decided."

Jackman scratched the back of his neck as he left her office and marched back down to the incident room. He'd tried to negotiate, appeal to Carmela's better nature, just one more week, but she was unwavering.

She hadn't mentioned their indiscretion. Hadn't spoken of their dinner together. The words were stark in their absence and soothed his conscience slightly. Perhaps she regretted it as much as he did. He hoped so.

Wilson was walking up the corridor towards the coffee machine as he made his way back to the office. He relayed his conversation with Carmela.

"When are you off?" she asked.

"Soon. You?"

"I'm one of the few staying on, picking through the embers, playing the PR game." Jackman felt a brief moment of relief that at least the case wasn't losing her. "The press are going to give us hell."

He wanted to say they wouldn't, but he knew he'd be

lying. It wouldn't be long before news of his return to Warwickshire would reach them and they would likely pounce on it, using it as an excuse to exploit the waning investigation.

"Keep in touch," Jackman said. "I'll be at the end of the phone. Any new developments, anything at all. Let me know?"

"Sure. But before that I think we need to have a few drinks. Can't let you go without a send-off." She moved into the incident room to announce the impromptu leaving drinks.

He felt his mobile vibrate in his pocket. A number he didn't recognise flashed up on the screen and he moved away to answer it, surprised to hear Grace's voice at the end of the line, and even more surprised when she asked to see him as soon as possible. By the time he walked back in he felt a buzz of excitement as people started closing down computers, putting on coats and getting themselves organised for an evening out.

"I'll meet you there," Jackman said. "There's something I need to do first."

CHAPTER FORTY-SIX

GRACE SAT FACING the detective. The camera in the corner of the room felt strangely disconcerting, eyeing her as she relayed her story.

She'd never told anyone about the attack. Ever. And now she knew why. It was impossible to keep secrets. The more people you told, the more chance there was that the sordid details would spread like a stain that could never be removed. But she hadn't anticipated for it to be made public knowledge.

A wave of nausea had hit her as she'd ended the call to Faye the other day. Would she respect her wishes, as she'd promised? Grace worked back over their conversations. Faye had confided in her over the stillbirth, been candid about her father's illness and later death. The two women had shared confidences together, as friends do, although nothing on this scale.

Her head was in a vortex. She'd phoned Faye back, cancelled her visit, feigning a headache. Problem was, with each hour that passed, Faye's words had wormed their way under Grace's skin. It wasn't difficult to work out that Jamie wasn't Jo's dad. A family photo pointed out the clear differences in their appearance.

The very notion that he might have been tracking her, watching, waiting, lurking in the background for years brought fresh bile to her throat. What she couldn't reconcile in her head was why he would attack Jo too. And why now? But if there was any chance that there might be a connection between her attack and Jo's murder, she had to do something.

She'd retreated, ignored Faye's texts as she mulled it over. When Faye eventually arrived on her doorstep, full of apologies, Grace confessed. Told Faye how she'd decided to go to the police. Faye offered to come with her and Grace agreed as long as she promised not to share the secret with another living soul. 'I don't want my family finding out,' she'd said.

By the time Grace reached the station, she was on the verge of changing her mind. The idea of going over the vile details, having them recorded on file, made her lightheaded. She'd asked for DCI Jackman, the senior detective with the green eyes who'd been kind to her. And when she finished, he'd simply said, "Thank you for bringing this to my attention. I'll have your account drawn up into a statement for you to sign." She'd gone on to repeat her fears about it being made public. "We won't do anything before speaking with you first," he'd said.

Jackman had said that there was no reason to suspect the cases were connected, but that they'd look into it. He'd checked she still had his card, asked her to call him personally if there was anything else she remembered later.

Faye was still in the waiting area as she walked back through, in spite of the hour and a half that had passed. Winter arrived as they left the station. Grace hunched her shoulders against the cold. They didn't speak of the secret cemented between them as they approached the car.

"Shall I drop you home?" Grace asked as they battled with seatbelts.

"No, I have some shopping to do. Drop me at the High Street and I'll walk back." Faye stared out of the window as the engine purred into action. "And Grace?"

"Yes?"

"Well done. I'm proud of you."

CHAPTER FORTY-SEVEN

JACKMAN ARRIVED AT the incident room early on Monday morning. He'd spent a harrowing weekend scrolling through reports of sexual attacks on women during the late 1990s. Looking for any possible similarities in the MO. Grace was at pains to say she didn't see her attacker's face and the bland description of a tall motorcyclist in leathers, of medium build with a Midlands accent, didn't give him much to go on. Part of him couldn't imagine that Jo's natural father was her attacker after all these years, but in the same breath he couldn't afford to ignore it.

Wilson crossed the threshold just as he was beside the kettle, mug in hand. "Hello," she smiled. "Wasn't expecting to see you this morning."

"There are a few more things I need to go through with you," Jackman said. He held up a spare mug. "Coffee?"

"If you're making." She shrugged off her jacket. "What happened to you on Friday then?"

By the time Jackman had finished with Grace it was late. He'd sent Wilson a text with his apologies. He didn't relish the idea of joining a bunch of cops who would have been decidedly worse for wear by then. "Got detained." He carried their coffees over to her desk, pulled up a chair and relayed Grace's account of her own attack, followed by his searches over the weekend.

Wilson didn't speak until he'd finished. "Well," she said, "looks like I missed all the action."

"You're telling me."

"Do you really think her attack, over twenty years ago, is connected with Jo's murder?"

Jackman glanced towards the window. It was a grey day, thick clouds overhead threatening rain. He looked back at Wilson. "Probably not. I've gone through all reported attacks, five years either side, put out a request for national cases with any similarities."

"Grace didn't recognise anything? Smell, voice? Nothing familiar?"

"It was a long time ago. I suppose she's blocked it out." A couple of other officers entered the room, looking a mixture of startled and pleased as they saw Jackman.

"Why didn't you call me? I could have helped."

"Grace wants to keep her attack confidential. She was quite insistent. Hasn't even told her family. She only came to me in case there was any connection to her daughter's case. I think the less people that handle this file, the better."

"You got it."

Parsons rushed in, tugging at the scarf around her neck. "Just been caught by the Super in the corridor. She wants to see you in her office," she nodded at Jackman, gave a knowing look. "Now."

Jackman sighed. "News travels fast around here, doesn't it?"

Carmela's door was open as he approached. He wandered in without speaking. She was stood at the window, looking down at the street below, hands rested loosely on her hips. She whipped around as the door clicked shut. "Will. What are you doing here?"

That weekend she'd sent a text asking to meet if he was free, no mention of his dismissal, and he'd replied to say he was busy. A couple of other texts followed but he ignored them. He'd been wrong. There was no regret about their indiscretion on her part, and he was left with an overwhelming sense of guilt.

"There's a new development."

"This had better be good."

She didn't indicate for him to sit, but he sat anyway, forcing her to take her own seat behind her desk. He explained Grace's revelation, the work he'd done over the weekend, the subsequent checks.

Carmela listened intently. "I thought I'd made it clear that you were to hand over the case?" she said when he'd finished.

"And I have. But Grace contacted me on Friday evening."

"And you didn't think to call it in?"

"This wasn't a formal interview. She contacted me in confidence. And that's the way it stays."

"Okay, thank you," Carmela said, a conciliatory note in her voice. "We'll take over from here."

"Any news on my replacement?"

She ignored his question, but her face was softening. "You didn't answer my texts."

"You were away. I was busy."

A tinge of sadness flickered across her face before it hardened once more. "Don't forget to let your own Super know where you are," she said. "And Will?" He was almost at the door when he rounded to face her. "Keep in touch."

Jackman's stomach sunk as he made his way back to the office. Carmela had been a good friend last summer, but she clearly wanted more. He couldn't deny he was drawn to her. Maybe, in different circumstances. But Alice was still here. She needed him. He turned the corner, lost in his thoughts, when he almost collided with Wilson. She stopped abruptly.

"You hanging around for a bit?" she asked.

He shook his head as a thought suddenly occurred to him. "Do me a favour, Dee. Watch that journalist."

"Artie Black? You're not serious. He's a pussycat. An annoying one, I'll give you that."

"I'm not sure."

"What are you thinking?"

"I don't know exactly." He gave a quick run through of his earlier concerns, carefully avoiding any mention of the terrorist footage. Although the work with Special Branch was ongoing, it was still bound in a thick tape of confidentiality, restricted to senior management level. "Just keep an eye on him."

Wilson gave a nod. "We're all gutted you're going. We've not even been able to have that night out, to say goodbye."

Jackman gave a short laugh. "I can always come back."

"Don't you just hate politics?"

Jackman shrugged a single shoulder. "Last week we were top of the list. Now there are new priorities. That's policing."

"I didn't mean that."

"What?"

"The superintendent board."

"I'm not with you."

"You haven't heard? A board's been announced for January. The first in six or so years. Madam Carmela is only acting. She'll have her eye firmly fixed on the goal." Jackman stood mute as the implication behind the words sunk in. "Judy, the chief con's secretary, said an email went out to top brass last week. That'll be why she's directing her resources into other areas. She won't want to be connected to a failed enquiry with bad PR like this one."

It took all of Jackman's reserves to supress his anger. He thanked Wilson, collected his jacket from the incident room, made his goodbyes and had reached the corridor before the growl of anger raged at him. How dare she? An email had gone out last week. Those words picked away at him. Carmela hadn't mentioned it. Was that why she'd kept her distance? There had been something odd about her manner, the way in which she wouldn't answer his questions about a replacement, and now he knew why.

"Is this your phone, sir?"

Jackman turned and glanced at the officer who rushed towards him, puffing like a train. "You left it on your desk." He nodded and thanked the officer. "It's rung several times. You might want to check your messages."

Jackman glanced at the phone when it rang again. He recognised Christine, Alice's carer's voice from Broom Hills, before she introduced herself. "Is everything okay?" he asked.

"I'm afraid I've some bad news for you, Will. Alice suffered a stroke this morning. The paramedics are with her now."

PART TWO

CHAPTER FORTY-EIGHT

GRACE LOOKED OUT of the window as she stirred the gravy. Another Christmas without snow. She was waiting for Phil to arrive with Matt, Chloe and Meggy in tow. Any minute now they would crash through the door, Meggy laden with her new presents to show them all, buzzing with excitement. An event like this would usually swell her heart, fill her with happiness, but today it felt as though a stone had wedged itself in her chest. And it wasn't just the thought of their first Christmas without Jo. Something had changed.

The dull sound of Lydia's music thumped the floor from above. She was still distant, spending more and more time in her room and around friends' houses of late. The supermarket had been taken over by a larger chain and Phil threw himself into his work, regularly staying late in an effort to meet the new targets and priorities that were now being introduced. Evenings were full of stilted conversation, dinner on trays in front of the television instead of around the table together, often at different times. Even Chloe and Meggy visited less frequently as Meggy started a playgroup and had a routine of her own. Jo's name was rarely mentioned, and when it was all eyes shot to Grace, almost as if it was taboo. Over the past few weeks, the distance between them had grown to such an extent that it seemed to Grace her family were becoming strangers.

The familiar sound of Faye's chuckle wafted in from the front room where Grace had left her watching a Christmas edition of *Have I Got News For You*. The two women were together almost daily now, so much so, that Grace found she missed her when she wasn't around.

The initial unease of the police interview about her own attack had passed and, when no news was forthcoming, Grace had once again buried the incident in the depths of her mind.

As the days and weeks rolled forward, Grace found that the more they dabbled in Jo's background, the more her sadness deepened. No further attacks followed and, although the shock of Anthony's middle-aged face in Nottingham that day had branded itself on her brain, she didn't want it to be her lasting reminder of Jo. Apart from occasionally discussing the case between themselves, and receiving Parsons' updates, the two women had gradually pulled back on their covert investigations.

Instead they focused on Faye's plans for refurbishing her father's bungalow and their daily routines. Faye was interested in everything, from gardening to childhood memories, and it seemed they were never at a loss for something to talk about. Sometimes Grace would even forget herself, hear the sound of her own laughter, feel a rare touch of happiness, and she was grateful to her friend for those special moments.

A robin hopped about on the lawn outside, searching for food. Grace dropped her eyes to the line of candles that ran the length of the windowsill, a legacy of the candlelit memorial service they'd held for Jo, a week earlier. Jo had always loved candles. She could still see the wonder in her daughter's eyes as she marvelled at the flickering flame.

The packed church, people jostling for spaces in the aisles, others standing along the back, filled her mind. Solemn faces singing happy tunes, holding their own young ones close. The fact that it could happen to any of them, that their child could suffer a similar fate, showed in their strained faces. Chloe wrote a poem about finding sisterhood, that Phil read for her, and Lydia read from *Peter Pan*, Jo's favourite childhood book. Afterwards everyone lit a candle in Jo's memory. The church was ablaze with tiny dancing lights. Grace couldn't leave without bringing some of it back and, at the end of the service, she'd gathered up close family's candles and brought them home.

Yesterday, she'd painstakingly dusted and vacuumed Jo's room, carefully arranging the ornaments and photos back in their usual place. To Grace, the space needed to be preserved, until the police released Jo and she could find her a special resting place of her own.

The drone of an engine was followed by the crunch of gravel outside. Doors banged shut. She looked down at the gravy, which was now bubbling in the pan, and lifted it off the heat as she felt a presence beside her.

"What's Faye doing here?" Lydia whispered, tucking her hand beneath the foil covering a dish on the side and pulling out a strip of turkey.

Grace swept her daughter's hand away from the meat. "I invited her."

"On Christmas Day?"

"She didn't have anywhere to go."

"How long is she staying?"

"For the day."

"You're joking! It's going to be hard enough as it is."

"Her dad died earlier this year. I didn't like the thought of her on her own."

"So send her to the soup kitchen, she can feed the homeless."

"That's mean, Lydia."

"No, what's mean is that we have to bear our first Christmas without Jo, and now we have to pretend, and be polite because there's a stranger here."

"Faye's not a stranger."

"She is to me."

"She's been a good friend these past weeks." She rounded on her daughter, her irritation instantly melting at the sight of the tears brimming in her eyes. At that moment the front door banged back on its hinges and Meggy ran in wearing a pair of felt reindeer antlers.

CHAPTER FORTY-NINE

JACKMAN PICKED UP a stick and hurled it into the sea, watching Erik as he splashed through the shallows to retrieve it. The beach was empty today, the wind churning up the waves.

Celia slipped her arm through his. "Mum loved it here."

Jackman gave her arm a gentle squeeze. The past weeks had been full of hospital visits and bedside vigils. The stroke had overwhelmed Alice's already weakened body. They sat and watched for what seemed like days, until doctors eventually reported that there was some brain function.

He'd never forget making that phone call to Celia. Her voice was controlled, stilted, but he knew her, could tell she was only trying for his benefit. She'd arrived early the following morning, travelled to Broom Hills and packed a bag so that her mother was dressed in her own clothes, rather than the dreary hospital attire. Later, she'd sat beside her bed, chatted away, brushed her hair. They'd had their quiet moments, where they'd shared a tear, but Celia was like her mother, practical in every sense of the word, and she dealt with the situation so much better than he did.

Celia untangled her arm and ran up the beach towards Erik who was busy digging in the sand.

Little over a month ago, he'd been sitting in the consultant's office, asking for Alice to be scheduled for more intensive tests, holding on to a ray of hope of some kind of recovery. He'd completed the forms and they were waiting for dates. Now everything was put on hold. They were told the stroke had left a shadow on Alice's brain. It was difficult to assess the extent of the damage, any usual tests for paralysis confounded by the locked-in syndrome. But what continued to haunt Jackman was that she was shut away in that shrinking body, not able to tell them if she was in pain or how she felt.

The waves folded forward. Celia was bent over a stick, writing something in the sand: *To Mum. With all our love, always.* The enlarged letters were messy and disjointed, like a child learning to write. She finished it with a big kiss at the bottom. By the time he reached her the waves were already licking the edge, ready to wash them away.

"Come on," Jackman said. "I'll race you."

"Hey, you've had a head start," Celia squealed behind him as he clambered over the sand and back towards the pathway that led to Brean Down. Erik caught them up as they passed the café, keen to be a part of the new adventure.

Christmas Day had been a sober affair. Alice loved Christmas, decorated every room in the house with fir tree branches, placed candles in the windows and always insisted on a real tree decorated with simple handmade decorations from years gone by, a throw-back from her Danish roots. Celia vowed to continue with her mother's traditions. But, after a visit to see Alice in the morning, they'd shared a quiet dinner and Celia had spent the best part of the afternoon on the phone to her boyfriend in Southampton. Erik was the only one up for a party, blissfully unaware of the sadness that encircled them both.

It took a while to make the climb. Celia was panting by the time they reached the top and stood in silence, admiring the vista over the Bristol Channel. The emptiness was calming.

"Do you remember what Mum used to say about the view here?" Celia said.

Jackman smiled. Alice loved this route. She begged him to travel across to this spot on the west coast every Boxing Day. One year it was wet, the rain coming down in sheets, yet she still insisted they make the climb. "It made her feel on top of the world!" Celia joined in the last few words and they both laughed.

"Are you going to be okay?" Celia asked as their laughter petered out. "I could stay a bit longer."

"I'll be fine. You've got finals to prepare for."

"Make sure you keep your phone on then." She moved away and ran with Erik across the grass.

Jackman tugged his phone out of his pocket. He switched it on, and waited for a sign of life, half expecting it to be dead. The battery flashed up 10 percent. He spent a few sober minutes, scrolling through personal messages of support from friends and colleagues, then switched to email and moved down the screen, hovering beside a message from Wilson. He hadn't been at work or back in touch with Leicestershire since the day he received the call about Alice's stroke.

The message was sent on the 23rd of December, just a few days earlier:

Hope you are doing okay. I've got some news. Get in touch when you are ready. No rush.

CHAPTER FIFTY

GRACE WRESTLED TO fasten the top button of her coat. It was one of those murky January days with a sprinkling of rain in the air that doesn't ever get properly light. The weather had done nothing to put off the sale shoppers though, and the centre of Market Harborough teemed with families, couples and groups of teenagers, almost as if an army of ants had invaded. She'd agreed to meet Faye in Harborough town, but was now wishing that she'd invited her around to the house as normal.

She turned up her collar, checked her phone again. No messages. She was just considering leaving when she caught sight of a red coat bustling towards her. Faye's face looked grim. "Sorry, I'm late," she said. "Boiler's broken at home. I've spent all morning trying to get hold of a plumber."

They moved into a café. "Are you sure you don't want to be home?" Grace asked. "We don't have to do this now."

"He's not coming until four o'clock. I'll be glad to warm up for an hour."

They made their way through the tables to the one beside the counter. Grace ordered drinks and cakes. It was a difficult seat, their shoulders constantly jostled by people approaching the counter to order, but there weren't any others free so they made the best of it.

"When did you find it wasn't working?" Grace said as she removed her coat and sat.

"It was cold in the house yesterday. I thought it was me and put on another jumper. But I didn't hear it this morning. The tank's quite noisy. Usually wakes me up when it kicks into action. When I got out of bed it was freezing and I realised the radiators weren't working."

"What did the plumber say?"

"Not much on the phone. He was the sixth one I called. The others were either on holiday or too busy. He says he can't do anything until he comes out and takes a look at it."

"Oh, I hope it's something small, something he can fix quickly."

"Me too, and cheaply."

JACKMAN HEAVED CELIA'S bags into the back of her car and piled the supermarket carrier bags around them. "Sure you've got enough there?"

"I'm fine, Dad. Really. They do have supermarkets in Southampton too."

He closed the boot. Celia enveloped him in a big hug. "You sure you are going to be okay?"

"I should be asking you that question. I could have driven you back."

"Dad, stop fussing. I've driven that route so many times I could do it with my eyes closed." She stuck out her elbow and he ducked back, just in time for it to miss his stomach. The action dissolved the atmosphere, restoring the jovial spirit they were both more comfortable with. "I'll call soon. Look after Mum."

Jackman's shoulders drooped as he watched her drive

down the road. Celia was returning to university and, with her finals looming, it would be several months before they would see each other again. The house was quiet as he walked back inside. Celia had barely left his side since her mother's stroke, a fact that was set to make her absence all the more difficult to bear. Even Erik seemed aware of the impending change and didn't move from his place on the sofa.

He switched on his music, waiting for the sounds of Bach to fill the room, and sat down beside the dog. Everywhere he looked there were pieces of Alice. Above the fireplace sat an oversized mirror, edged in driftwood that she'd hauled back from Portobello Market. Beside the window was an oil painting of Erik she'd commissioned on his first birthday. On the far wall hung a caricature of Alice, Celia and him on holiday in France when Celia was small. Alice hadn't lived there for over a year now, yet their home still whispered of her presence. The music crashed into a crescendo, filling the room. The house suddenly seemed overwhelming. He needed a diversion.

He re-read Dee Wilson's message and automatically pressed to call her, more in hope than expectation, and was surprised when she answered.

"Hello, sir. Good to hear from you."

He turned down the music. "You too. I hear you've got some news?"

"Ah. You got my text. Yes, it's about Grace Daniels. I think you'll be interested in the findings."

LATER THAT EVENING Grace put another log on the wood burner and snuggled on the sofa beside Lucky. The wind was picking up outside, whistling as it swished down the side of the house. Faye's boiler problem slipped into her mind. She grabbed her phone, typed out a text to her friend: All sorted?

It was a while before her phone buzzed with a reply: Afraid not. Looks like it's broken. Might need a new one.

Grace called her. "You okay?"

"Just cold."

"Why don't you come and stay here overnight? I can spare…" she hesitated a moment. The only spare room she had was Jo's and that didn't seem appropriate. "…the sofa. It's quite comfy."

"I don't know. I don't want to intrude."

"Don't be silly. It's only for one evening."

"Well, it would be nice to be warm."

"That's settled then. I'll send Phil over to pick you up."

"No, that's not necessary."

"I insist. You can't get the bus at this time of night."

Grace took down Faye's address, ended the call and wandered through to the kitchen. Phil was leant down beside the door, undoing his running shoes. A new hobby he'd only recently taken up. "Looks like we have a guest for the night," she said, grabbing the dish-cloth and wiping down the sides.

He sat back on his heels and wheezed.

"You okay?" she asked.

"Just getting my breath back. What did you say?"

"Faye's boiler's broken. She hasn't got any heating."

Phil gave a sympathetic grimace.

"Okay if you pick her up in half an hour? That'll give you a chance to get changed and her time to gather her stuff together."

"Pick who up?" Lucky rushed to greet Lydia who was now standing at the doorway.

Grace chucked the dishcloth back in the bowl. "Faye."

Lydia groaned.

"Oh, don't be like that. She's got no heating."

"Where will she sleep?"

"I'm going to make up the sofa for her."

Lydia huffed. "I'm going back upstairs."

CHAPTER FIFTY-ONE

TIME CRAWLED BY. Snow arrived, almost without warning, and disappeared the same day. Faye's boiler was a bigger problem than expected. She was told it would take a week or so to resolve, so Grace invited her to stay on a while longer. The days passed easily with Faye in the house and the two women spent many an hour walking the dog, watching television, chatting over coffee.

Lydia spent even more time in her bedroom, and it was almost a relief when the day of her school trip arrived. Perhaps the break would do them all good.

Grace knocked on the door of Lydia's bedroom, waited until she was invited in and stepped over an empty water bottle that lay just inside the door. She tried to ignore the crisp packets, books and piles of clothes on the floor that merged together to cover the carpet beneath, and watched Lydia battle with the zip on her suitcase. "Got everything?"

"Think so. I'm still not sure I should be going."

"We talked about this," Grace said. "This ski trip will do you the world of good. Give you a complete change, and you'll be with your school friends. It's the perfect time to go, before you have to knuckle down and study for those exams."

"But after everything that's happened…"

"Jo wouldn't want you to sit here and miss your trip, would she? Scotland's beautiful this time of year."

"Still doesn't seem right." She stepped back and looked her mother up and down, her face contorting. "I'm really not sure about that dress, Mum."

Grace smoothed the denim dress over her hips. "You don't like it?"

Lydia scrunched her nose. "Honestly? It looks like something Faye would wear."

Grace snorted. She'd long ago given up the possibility of seeking approval from her teenage daughter, but Lydia was right about one thing… Faye had chosen the dress. In fact, Grace had been so pleased with it, she'd bought them both one, a little treat, from one of the boutiques on Harborough's High Street.

At that moment the sound of Faye singing as she left the bathroom filled the house. They glanced at one another. Lydia pulled a face. "How much longer is she staying for?"

"Only a few more days. While her new boiler is installed."

Lydia grabbed her hairbrush and tucked it into a side pocket of the bag.

"What don't you like about her?"

"Oh, I don't know. She only talks to you. It's like you're in some kind of little club together. It's weird." She grabbed a tie from the bedside table and secured her hair in a ponytail. "And she's always here."

When she'd invited Faye to stay, Grace hadn't asked the others or given any thought as to how it might affect them. But it was their home too and suddenly she felt a sting of selfishness. Was she inadvertently contributing to the wedge that had formed between them, pushing her family aside? "She'll be gone when you get back, I promise."

Lydia grabbed hold of the bag and moved out onto the landing. "I saw her coming out of Jo's room yesterday."

"What?"

Faye's voice was louder out here, her tune filling the house.

Grace grabbed her shoulder. "Are you sure?"

Lydia nodded. "I thought maybe you were clearing it out."

"Are you sure you're not making this up?"

Lydia ignored her mother's question, instead thumping the holdall down the stairs, bumping every step, before resting it in the hallway.

Faye smiled as they both entered the kitchen. "Anyone for coffee?" she breezed.

"Why don't you ask her yourself if you don't believe me?" Lydia said.

"Is everything okay?" Faye asked.

Grace watched Lydia roll her eyes and move into the front room. "Of course. Lydia was just a bit upset. Thought she saw you coming out of Jo's room yesterday."

"Oh, I was. Phil was working on the car and you were out front talking to him. I couldn't find Lucky. So I went upstairs and checked the bedrooms. When I came down she was back in the kitchen. I'd forgotten she uses the old cat flap in the door. Sorry, I meant to mention it. Must have forgot when you came in." She pulled some mugs out of the cupboard.

"No problem. Lydia just gets a bit overprotective about Jo's room."

"Quite right too. Now, how about that coffee?"

"IT'S STRANGELY QUIET with no children in the house," Grace said later. Since Jo's death she'd been hyper-aware of her youngest daughter's movements, making sure she wasn't out alone, offering lifts when possible. She'd even taken her to the coach and waited until it left the car park for its journey to Scotland that morning, much to Lydia's annoyance. Deep down she knew that Lydia needed to go on this trip, spread her wings and breathe. Outwardly she'd encouraged it, but the prospect of losing that control over her, even for a short time, was unnerving.

Faye mustered an empathetic smile. "It's only a few days."

They were stood in Grace's back garden, coats pulled close against the sharp wind. It was a beautifully clear winter's day. Grace watched Faye take a long drag of her cigarette. She'd grown to look forward to these trips into the garden, giving her the opportunity to monitor its slow change during the winter months. A blackbird landed on the bird table and fluttered about, pecking at some crusts Grace had put out that morning.

Faye took another drag and she watched her longingly. "Want some?" Faye said.

Grace shook her head.

"You sure?"

Grace looked at the cigarette in Faye's hand. "Oh, go on then." She took it, closed her eyes and sucked, long and hard. She'd given up smoking when she was pregnant with Jo, but Jamie had been a heavy smoker all his adult life and the doctors made it quite clear that it was a contributing factor to the lung cancer that killed him. Grace responded by banning cigarettes from the house, warned her girls about the dangers associated with smoking. She blanked that out of her mind today though, and embraced the feel of the nicotine as it infused her lungs. When she opened her eyes, Faye was staring at her intently. "Mind if I finish it?" Grace said, holding it out at an angle.

"Of course not." Faye lit another and they stood there for a while. Time passed easily. By the time they had popped one of Faye's mints and gone back inside, Grace felt more relaxed than she had done in months.

CHAPTER FIFTY-TWO

WILSON GREETED JACKMAN with a wide grin as he pulled up at the curb in Arden Way and climbed out of his car. "It's good to see you," he said.

"You too. Thanks for coming over, especially while you are still on leave."

He shrugged. "Some things are important. How are things in Leicester?" he asked as they walked up the road together.

"Much the same. The incident room has wound down. The Super's swanning around on the PR train after the thwarted terrorist attack. She can barely get her head through the doorway at the moment."

Jackman gave a wry smile. When news of a house raid uncovered bomb-making equipment in Leicester City, the week before Christmas, it made national news. He'd watched Carmela on the television, making a statement to the press, thanking her officers for the work that had gone on behind the scenes to safeguard the community of Leicester once more. Her convincing smile and smooth tone reminded him of a politician.

"What about my replacement?"

"DCI Steve Morrison from West Mids is heading up the review team."

"Don't think I know him."

"Very intense. Barely talks to any of us unless he wants something. Thick as thieves with the Super though."

"Any findings on Operation Ascott?"

"Not as far as I'm aware."

"And no more attacks?"

She shook her head.

"Did you find anything on that journalist?" Jackman asked as they reached Grace's driveway.

"No. He's a slippery character, I'll give you that. Always under your feet. But I don't think he's involved."

He felt a sense of déjà vu as he stood on the doorstep and knocked. Grace opened the door almost immediately, inviting them in. She seemed brighter today, fresher. They were just settling into the sofa, Wilson retrieving her notebook when a tall woman walked through with the offer of drinks.

Wilson eyed her suspiciously and turned to Grace. "Sorry, I didn't realise you had visitors. We can always come back at a more convenient time?"

"There's no need," Grace said. She introduced Faye as a close family friend.

The detectives agreed to coffees and Jackman waited for Faye to leave the room before he sat forward. "How are you, Grace?"

"As well as can be expected."

"As you know, we've come out to see you today to give you an update on your attack, twenty years ago. Sergeant Wilson has been looking into it for you."

Wilson nodded. "We've analysed historical records. Unfortunately the computer system wasn't as sophisticated as it is now, so it's taken a while. But we have found records of three other reported incidents, two in

Derbyshire and one in Nottinghamshire, within months of yours. They were all stranger attacks, the offender wore a balaclava, made off on a motorbike and two of them report that same menthol smell, like that of a Consulate cigarette, which seems quite significant. We think it's the same man, a Martin Walker. Does that name mean anything to you?"

Grace shook her head.

"That's not surprising. He was traced after the second Derbyshire incident and charged with two offences of rape. Neither of the women claimed to know him. He served fourteen years in prison."

Fear spiked Grace's chest. "Where is he now?"

"He died in a motorcycle accident three years ago."

Grace let out a huge breath. "You really think it's the same man that attacked me?"

"Without a DNA match, we can't be completely sure, but it seems most likely. We have DNA taken from the other victims. We could see if it matched with Jo's," Wilson said. "If you want to be completely sure?"

"He wasn't involved in Jo's murder?"

"It doesn't appear so."

"Then there's no point in doing the test." Grace sat back in her chair. Deep down, she knew the answer to Jo's parentage. But seeing it confirmed in black and white would somehow soil her memory.

The door swung open and Faye entered with a tray of mugs, a plate of biscuits rattling on the side. "Do you have any news on Jo's case?" Grace asked as she set about handing the mugs around.

There was a slight pause. "We don't have anything

new, I'm afraid," Wilson said gently. "But I can tell you the case is being looked at by an external review team."

"What does that mean?" Grace winced as the coffee burnt her lip.

"A new team has come in to take a fresh look at the case."

"You won't be working on it anymore?"

"Detective Parsons will still be your contact. And I'll be assisting them with anything they need."

"But you'll be working on other cases?"

"Yes. A fresh pair of eyes will be going over all the evidence though. To make sure nothing has been missed."

"And if they don't find anything?"

"Then we will continue to appeal for new evidence."

"So, they're scaling down the investigation?"

"Not exactly. Some of us have also been allocated other cases to run alongside. But Jo's file will be kept open. And I can assure you, if anything new comes to light we'll be straight on it."

PHIL ARRIVED HOME from work that evening to find Grace and Faye ensconced in the kitchen, halfway through a bottle of Chardonnay. "Oh, hello," he said. He eyed the wine, looked quizzically from one to another. "Are we celebrating something?"

Grace and Faye exchanged a surreptitious glance. "Full moon," Faye said quickly, raising her glass. "It's supposed to bring luck this time of year."

He dropped the files he was carrying on the kitchen side. "Well, we could certainly do with some of that."

"Would you like tea, or wine?" Grace said, feeling a twinge of guilt at the flush in her cheeks.

"Nothing at the moment. I'm just going to have a lie down. It's been a heavy day. Have you heard from Lydia?"

"I had a text saying that she'd arrived and there was lots of snow. That was it."

Phil snorted. "Sounds about right."

"Maybe we shouldn't have started so early," Faye said in a low voice as his heavy footsteps took to the stairs.

Grace muffled a giggle. "Oh, don't worry about him. He's often tired when he comes in from work." But the laughter was short-lived. "I just wish there was some news on Jo's case," she said quietly. "I don't know. The longer this goes on, the more it feels like he'll never be caught. It's so cruel."

Faye rested her glass down. "I know. Perhaps the detective was right and a fresh pair of eyes will bring something new."

"I do hope so, and soon."

CHAPTER FIFTY-THREE

GRACE MISSED THE sound of the phone ringing the following afternoon. It was a couple of hours later, when she was preparing dinner, Faye sitting at the table browsing old copies of *Good Housekeeping*, that she heard it ring again.

"Grace!" Chloe sounded worried. "I wondered where you were."

"I've been here all day. Is something wrong?"

"It's Dad. He was taken ill at work. They had to send for an ambulance."

"What? How is he?"

"He's stable. In a room in A&E, while they monitor him. They think he's had a heart attack." Her voice splintered.

"Oh my God!" Grace drew a ragged breath. "Where are you now?"

"At the hospital. The shop called me when they couldn't get hold of you. I've left Meggy with our neighbour."

"I'll be there right away."

It wasn't until she ended the call that she glanced down and saw the lights flashing on the answerphone. She dashed to the kitchen, grabbed her mobile off the side. The screen was blank. She stared at it a moment, perplexed. She always left her phone on charge each night.

THE CAR PARK was full as Grace turned into the Leicester Royal Infirmary later that evening and she had to drive around the back to the overflow to find a space. Her hands trembled as she crossed the tarmac. Faye, who'd insisted on coming along to support her, guided her into the hospital.

From the moment she'd taken the phone call earlier, a million thoughts had reverberated around her head. Phil was such a strong man. So rational, ordered, fit. How could this happen? She tried to look back over the past month, searching for signs that something might be wrong. But as much as she pulled on her memories she couldn't find any. He'd been under immense stress after losing Jo. They all had been. But he was always such a calming influence. She couldn't lose him as well.

Chloe was sitting on a plastic seat just inside the entrance. She stood as they approached and hugged Grace tightly. "He's out of danger," Chloe said. "They've moved him to the coronary care unit. I thought I'd come and wait for you while they get him settled."

"What happened, Chloe? What have they said?"

"He'd been struggling to breathe all morning apparently, kept rubbing his neck, saying it was hot, but refused to admit it was anything serious. His assistant manager was making arrangements to send him home when he doubled up with chest pains. They sent for an ambulance. They'd already done an ECG when I arrived which showed signs of at least one attack. They think there's possibly been another since. The cardiac nurse said he's been very lucky. They're doing a scan, to assess the damage. I've been trying to call your mobile."

"It doesn't seem to be working." Grace covered her

face with her hands. She couldn't believe she'd missed all of this.

Chloe took a deep breath and dabbed her eyes with a tissue. "I need to get back to Meggy. Matt's working away."

"Of course."

"I'll show you to the ward." She paused, looked across at Faye. "You won't be able to come in, I'm afraid. It's family only. I can give you a lift back?"

"I'm happy to grab a seat here and wait."

"No, you go," Grace said to Faye. "I may be here a while."

Anxiety pressed on Grace as she reached the coronary care unit and they bade their goodbyes. Chloe passed over her own mobile, insisting she had a spare at home, so that they could stay in touch.

She passed the desk and made her way through to a room with glass windows that overlooked the corridor. In the short time they'd been married, Phil had always been so robust, yet today, propped up in bed, a road map of wires connected to the stickers on his chest, he looked fragile. Her stomach knotted as she plastered what she hoped would be a warm smile on her face and rushed to his side.

"How are you feeling?"

He gave a weak smile. "Been better. Any news of when they'll let me out? They're not telling me anything."

"Not just yet, love. They need to do some more tests."

"I'm sorry. This was the last thing you needed."

She took his hand. It felt alien to touch him, awkward. She suddenly became aware that they hadn't touched in a while. Those little pecks on the cheek, shoulder nudges sitting next to each other on the sofa, the softness of an embrace, they all seemed to have disappeared these past few weeks. How could that have happened?

"It's all going to be fine, darling." He patted her forearm with his free hand. "I'll be out of here in no time. You'll see."

Grace swallowed back the threatening tears, forced herself to nod.

She unpacked the clothes she'd pulled together for him, put them away neatly in the cupboard and chattered idly about home life, what Lucky did at the park that morning, anything to avoid discussing the medical details.

"Thanks for bringing this stuff in," he said.

Grace smiled. She was just about to say Faye had helped, but stopped short as she was reminded of Lydia's words. Phil had never said he didn't like Faye, but her presence in the house clearly affected Lydia. Maybe it cast a shadow over him too? She didn't want to say anything that might agitate him. Not now.

"Is there anyone you want me to call?" Grace asked.

Phil shook his head. "Chloe knows. Work are aware. Don't mention it to Lydia. I don't want her to worry while she's away. Oh, and please don't tell Ged," he continued. "She'll only fly over and make a fuss. Let's leave that for when we know what we're dealing with, eh?"

"I'll cook for you," Grace said, not wishing to dwell on the "what we're dealing with" part. "Save you having to eat the food here. What would you like?"

"Don't go to any trouble."

"I want to."

They spent the next twenty or so minutes discussing their favourite dishes that she could adapt to bring portions into the hospital. The triviality of the conversation eased the atmosphere between them and Grace sensed a closeness to him that she hadn't felt for some time.

By the time the bell sounded to announce the end of visiting time, she wrapped her arms around him, amidst the wires, and pecked him on the cheek easily.

As she wandered down the corridor, Grace made a mental list of things she could do to make life easier for Phil. He would need a period of recuperation. She'd take care of him when he came home, make sure he was happy, not stressed at all, keep him safe. It was the least she could do.

Perhaps it was now time for Faye to move back home. She hadn't mentioned her boiler over the past couple of days, but there had been so many distractions it wasn't surprising. Yes, when the time was right Phil should come home to his family. Faye would understand that.

FAYE WAS SITTING on the stairs when Grace arrived home that evening. "You startled me!" Grace said as she unbuttoned her coat and kicked off her shoes. The keys rattled as she tossed them into the dish on the hall table.

"I heard the car engine. How is he? I've been worried sick."

Grace slumped onto the step beside her. "Out of danger. But… I don't know. He looked so pale."

"His body's been through a lot. It's bound to take a while." Faye moved forward to embrace her, but Grace stood. "Tea?"

"Sure."

Grace relayed the hospital visit as she made the drinks, the words spilling out of her mouth, running into each other. "Thank God Lydia's not here to see this. I'll have to tell her when she gets home. What with losing her own dad so young, and Jo. She thinks the world of Phil."

"He's going to be okay though, isn't he?"

Grace placed the mugs on the table and eased herself into her seat. "I think so. He'll need to slow down. Take it easy for a while."

"You look worn out."

"It's just the shock." Something itched inside Grace, she couldn't sit still. Instead she pulled a couple of cookery books from the shelf, placed them on the table. The pages squeaked as she started to flick through them. "I'm going to prepare some meals to take in for him," she said. "He'll feel better if he gets something nice to eat. Something home cooked."

"Sounds like a good plan. Hospital food is the worst."

Grace leafed through a few more pages, browsing the different dishes. "Any news?" she asked without looking up.

"On what?"

"Your boiler."

"Oh, that. I spoke to the plumbers this morning. They seem to be getting on well. A bit more work to do but they're really pleased with how it's going in."

Grace lifted her eyes. "That's great."

"Yeah."

"You'll be able to move back soon then?" Faye looked momentarily taken aback. "Only I think we'll need the sofa when Phil comes home. It might be a week or so before he can climb the stairs."

"Of course. I'll get my things together."

CHAPTER FIFTY-FOUR

THE FIRST THING Grace saw when she arrived home from the hospital the following afternoon was Faye's bag in the hall. Her stomach dipped. There was talk of releasing Phil in the next few days. She so wanted the house to be ready for him.

"Hello?" she called up the stairs. There was no reply. Something didn't feel right. She peered into the front room, which was empty, and crossed through to the kitchen. Suddenly she realised what it was. Lucky wasn't in her basket. Assuming she'd gone out through the cat flap, she unlocked the back door and leant out into the garden, opening her mouth to call the dog when the sound of the gate clicked. Faye appeared with Lucky on a lead. The dog wagged her tail and jumped up at Grace.

"Hello, you!" Faye said. "I thought I'd do the dog walk. Give you one less job to do."

Grace ignored the irritation creeping under her skin, said thank you and moved aside to let her in. "I wasn't sure I'd see you."

"I haven't finished packing yet. Thought I might leave it until tomorrow, if that's okay?"

"It's not, I'm afraid. I'm sorry. I'm picking Lydia up in an hour and I wanted an evening together tonight, just the two of us, so I could go through everything with her."

"Well if it's a problem—"

"Are the plumbers not finished?"

She shifted her shoulders. "They've had a hiccup, that's all."

"Oh." For a short moment Grace was tempted to ask her to stay, just for another couple of nights. But it had already been over a week and she needed to give priority to her family right now. "I'm sorry."

Faye turned away. "It's fine. I'll get my stuff together."

HAIL CASCADED FROM the sky when Grace returned with Lydia later that evening, little needles bouncing off the bonnet of the car as they pulled into the driveway. After an initial discussion about Phil's health woes, which Grace played down, Lydia had barely drawn breath since filling the boot with her bags, regaling tales of learning to ski, midnight parties, and teachers singing at karaoke. She'd said more in that short car journey than she had in the last few weeks and it was heartening to see her so happy.

Grace cut the engine. The lights flashed as she extinguished them.

"Whoa. Now I see why you're using Phil's car." Lydia said.

"I told you, I just wanted to give it a run."

"And you pranged yours."

"What are you talking about?" Grace switched the lights back on, illuminating the driveway in front of her. The dent in the nearside rear bumper of her car was surrounded by scratches, the white primer paintwork showing through. "Someone must have hit it in the hospital car park this afternoon, you'd have thought they'd have left a note!"

Lucky scampered around their ankles as they shrugged off their coats. The house was warm and quiet.

Lydia glanced around. "No Faye?"

Grace shook her head. "She's gone home."

Earlier had been a sober affair. Faye refused to let Grace take her home, in spite of the bags she'd accumulated while she'd been staying over, insisting on calling a cab. A twinge of guilt jabbed at Grace for the relief that washed over her. She wasn't annoyed with Faye, there was no reason for them to fall out. But the focus of her attention needed to be Phil right now and she was set on restoring the house back to a family home, a place where he could walk around without his shirt on if he wished, leave his socks in front of the washing machine, watch the old war films he loved without sharing the television and feeling compelled to make polite conversation.

Lydia dumped her bags down and moved into the front room. Moments later she heard the babble of the television. "Could you close the curtains?" Grace called through from the kitchen. Perhaps she should send Faye a quick text, she thought. Something friendly. They'd grown accustomed to seeing each other daily and the dynamics had changed rather rapidly. It might be a while before they were together again. Her fingers rippled over the keys on her phone as she typed. Hope you are settling back in. See you soon xx

She was just pressing send when Lydia joined her. "Your flowers are leaking on the dresser."

"What?"

Grace grabbed a cloth and rushed into the front room. She stared at the coffee table a moment, puzzled. "Did you move them?"

"What?"

"The roses. I could have sworn they were on the coffee table this morning."

"Why would I move them? You must have put them there, not thinking."

Grace picked up the vase and immediately caught her finger on a hairline fracture in the glass. A pool of water had seeped out of it, marking the wood beneath. She wiped up the water, took the flowers back into the kitchen and was searching for another vase when the phone rang. She heard Lydia scrabble across the room to answer it and busied herself with filling the new vase, sorting out the flowers.

"Who was it?" she asked when Lydia came into the kitchen.

"No idea. They hung up." She stuck her nose in the air. "Mmm, something smells nice."

"It's lasagne. I thought we could take some in for Phil."

"How was he earlier?"

The doctors had been gathered around Phil's bedside, deep in discussion, when Grace arrived that afternoon. They'd fitted a stent to improve the blood flow through one of his arteries but were still not satisfied and talked of scheduling him in for another. It seemed his stay would be slightly longer than expected. The monitor next to him beeped and flashed. Phil's dull eyes lit up when he saw Grace, but his face seemed tinged with grey, a testament to how much he'd aged in the last few days.

"He's okay, love," she said to Lydia. "He might look a bit tired and drawn when you see him, but he's going to be fine. They've just got to fit another stent and patch him up before he can come home."

"What are you going to do about your car?" Lydia said.

"Nothing I can do now."

"The car park might have cameras there that can show who did it."

Grace thought back to the hospital car park. With the amount of vehicles shoehorned into every space during visiting hours, people attending appointments or visiting sick loved ones, not thinking straight, it wasn't really surprising that cars got bumped occasionally. "It's not worth the bother," she said. "I'll phone the insurers tomorrow, get it fixed. At least the lights are still intact." She wandered over to the fridge. "Don't tell Phil, will you? I don't want to do anything that might put him under any stress at the moment."

"Course not."

Grace's face crumpled. "That's odd."

"What?"

Grace pulled her head out of the fridge. "I thought I had another carton of milk in here."

Lydia rolled her eyes. "Oh Mum, you really are having one of those days."

CHAPTER FIFTY-FIVE

"ARE YOU SURE you don't mind watching Meggy while I go to the hospital?" Chloe said the following afternoon.

They were in Grace's kitchen, the toddler seated at the table drawing a picture of Lucky for her grandad.

"Of course not," Grace smiled. "I thought we'd go to the park when she's finished her picture."

"Yay!" The toddler squealed.

Chloe laughed. "That sounds like a plan. How was Dad last night?"

"Quite upbeat, although I suspect he was putting it on a bit for Lydia. They're talking about sending him home in a few days, as long as the next procedure goes to plan."

"That's great news."

"Isn't it?" One of Meggy's crayons fell to the floor. Grace bent down and picked it up.

"How did Lydia take the news?"

"Good, actually. She was very grown up about it."

"She is grown up, Grace. Well, almost."

"I know. I forget sometimes… I was thinking about giving her Jo's signet ring. It's a big year for her with her exams and all."

"I think that's a lovely idea. It would mean so much to her."

Grace touched her elbow. "I'll get it now, before I forget."

She raced up the stairs just as the sound of the phone trilled through the house.

"I'll get it!" Chloe called out.

Grace made for her bedroom and crossed to the jewellery box, pulling out bracelets, necklaces, rummaging through the fragments at the bottom. She moved aside the earrings Phil bought her for their first anniversary, a piece of eight coin that had belonged to her grandmother and her own mother's wedding ring. There was no sign of the signet ring. She tipped everything out, even pulled out the lining. A butterfly earring back rolled around beneath.

Chloe was in the hallway, fastening her coat when Grace reached the bottom of the stairs. "I can't find it," Grace said.

"What?"

"The ring. It's not in my jewellery box."

"Maybe you put it somewhere else for safe keeping?"

"No, I definitely put it in there. I remember."

"I'm sure it'll turn up, don't worry." Her face slackened as she watched Grace rake a hand through her hair. "What is it?"

"I don't know, there's just a few things that seem to be happening at the moment." Grace relayed her experiences yesterday: the damage to the car, the vase of flowers moved, the milk disappearing from the fridge. "Lydia thinks I'm losing my mind. Maybe I am."

"You've been under a lot pressure. It does make you do strange things. Maybe Faye popped back yesterday evening to collect some things. You gave her keys when she was here, didn't you? She might have moved a few things around, trying to be helpful. Why don't you text her?"

"I messaged her to see if she was settling back in. She hasn't replied."

"She's probably busy. There will be loads to do now the plumbers have finished. Try her again later."

Chloe was grappling with her keys as another thought occurred to Grace. "Oh, who was it on the phone?"

"Nobody. Caller hung up by the time I got there."

"Not again. That's the third time today."

GRACE WAS SITTING at her dresser getting ready to visit Phil later that evening when her eyes rested on her jewellery box. Maybe she should have another look. She applied a layer of lipstick, pulled the brush through her hair, and then shook the box upside down over the bed. The bracelets and necklaces glistened in the light. A couple of the pieces dropped off the edge of the duvet and rattled to the floor.

She was bending down to pick them up when she realised Lydia was at her door.

"You all right, Mum?"

"I can't find Jo's ring. You haven't got it, have you?"

Lydia shook her head. When Grace looked up again she'd gone. She stood and walked over to her mobile on the bedside table. Three texts to Faye had gone unanswered. It was so unlike her not to respond. She tentatively pressed call, listening to the rings before it went to voicemail. Now she really was worried. Maybe there was a problem with her mobile. She moved across to the landline, entered the numbers to Faye's mainline.

"Hello?" The voice that answered sounded full of sleep.

"Faye? Is that you?" The line went quiet. "Faye, it's Grace. I just wanted to check if you were okay?"

"I'm fine." The reply sounded cold, detached.

"Are you sure? You don't sound yourself."

"What do you want?"

Grace cleared her throat. "I just wanted to see if you were okay. And check on the keys."

"I put them in the dish in your hallway. Anything else?"

"Yes, I can't find Jo's signet ring. I—"

"Are you accusing me of something?" Her voice lowered, sending a bitter chill through Grace.

"Of course not. I just thought I must have put it somewhere. That maybe you'd seen it when you were here, only I…"

"I didn't. Goodbye Grace."

The line went dead.

Slowly, Grace replaced the phone in the cradle. She took to the stairs. Sure enough, the spare keys were in the bowl in the hallway. Grace stared at them a moment, trying to wrap her head around the bizarre way that Faye had reacted. Had she done something to upset her? Because if she had, she couldn't for the life of her think what.

CHAPTER FIFTY-SIX

GRACE CLOSED THE front door behind her. Phil's mood had been off this afternoon, the frustrations of no promise of a release date clearing scratching away at him. She called out for Lucky, but there was no response.

The house was cool today, no rush of warmth from the central heating. She made her way upstairs, checked the central heating switch. It was set to time, just the way she'd left it that morning.

After checking each bedroom, she finally stood outside Jo's. The door was still closed. She hesitated for a split second before pressing the handle, pushing it open. It was empty. Her shoulders dropped.

Grace made her way downstairs, into the front room and glanced around. The flowers sat on the dresser where she'd placed them back yesterday. She moved into the kitchen, checked the fridge. Everything looked in order. She drew a deep breath, felt the oxygen relax her as she exhaled. Maybe she'd been imagining things yesterday?

She was still looking around the kitchen when the phone rang, making her jump.

"Hello?"

The line went dead. She clenched her teeth, replaced the receiver, picked it up and dialled 1471. The number was withheld. She was just thinking about raising the issue with the phone company when it rang again. Grace snapped up the receiver, ready to give the caller a piece of her mind when Chloe's voice filled the line.

"Hi. Just thought I'd check everything was okay?"

She quickly recovered herself. "Oh, hello. It's all fine, thank you."

Grace gave her an update of the visit that afternoon and was just finishing up when she heard Meggy's voice in the background getting louder as she pleaded to speak to her grandma. Chloe refused to let go of the handset. The child started crying.

"What about you, Grace? I was worried about you after all the things that happened yesterday."

"Sounds like you've got your hands full," Grace said. "Don't worry about me, everything's good here. Thanks for phoning, darling."

"You're welcome. Ring me if you need anything." She rang off, her attention diverted.

Grace removed her coat and wandered through into the utility room to hang it up. She caught her foot on the edge of Lucky's basket, looked down to apologise and was surprised to find it empty.

"Lucky?" Once again her call was met with no answer, not even a whimper or the scuffle of paws on the kitchen tiles. Her mind raced. Occasionally Lucky climbed the stairs and, if there were any doors left open, snuck into one of the bedrooms and hauled herself onto one of the beds. But she hadn't seen her up there. Grace walked into the front room, through into the dining room and back into the kitchen, her eyes scanning every nook and cranny: sun traps, comfortable corners, regular haunts where Lucky would normally lay. Lucky was a small dog, but she couldn't disappear entirely. Perhaps she'd used the cat flap, was outside. It seemed unlikely on a dreary day like today, but worth a check.

As soon as Grace entered the garden she spotted the open side gate, hanging on its hinges.

"Lucky?"

There was no response.

The gate was always locked from the inside. Maybe she'd forgotten to lock it that morning. Maybe it hadn't caught the latch when it closed and the dog had taken herself for a walk. She raced through the gateway, down the side of the house, frantically looking around. She had no idea how long Lucky had been missing. The dog could be anywhere right now. She hovered at the end of the driveway, wondering which way to turn. They usually walked right, out to the end of the road and then left towards the park. Without giving it another thought she retraced their steps, calling out for the dog. A car raced past as she reached the main road. Lucky had no road sense. She quickened her step.

She could see the entrance to the park in the distance and picked up speed. Just as she got there she saw a ball of fur on the edge of the grass, beside a tree stump. "Lucky!" she called again, but the dog didn't move. Grace rushed to her side. "Lucky, what are you doing down here? You gave me such a…"

The dog's eyes were open, but she appeared to be in a trance-like state. Her tongue was hanging loose and she was panting heavily.

Grace saw pools of red on the grass around her. Blood. She didn't see the woman wandering out of the park with her poodle. Tears were running down her cheeks as she lifted Lucky's languid body into her arms.

"Are you okay?"

The voice behind her made her jump.

"My dog…" She looked back to the tree stump. Beside it was a pile of broken wine bottles. Scattered in between the shards of glass were small dog treats, the treats Grace bought especially for Lucky. Her favourites.

The woman gasped. "Who would do something like that?"

Grace shook her head. And the words she spoke surprised even her. "I don't know. But they don't deserve to live."

"SHE'D GONE INTO SHOCK," the vet said. "We've removed quite a bit of glass from her paws. It's left some nasty cuts on two of her pads, the front right is the worst affected. Looks like she ran right through the broken glass before she saw it was there."

Grace slowly nodded. Yesterday had been a whirlwind. The woman in the park had driven her and Lucky straight to the vet who immediately admitted the dog, stitched her wounds and kept her in overnight for observation. She'd turned the incident over and over in her mind. The side gate to their garden was always locked. She was sure she'd checked it.

"Will she be okay?"

"We've checked her heart and other organs and they seem fine. She's stable, but she has lost a lot of blood. She'll need to take it easy for a while."

Grace closed her eyes. It had been raining yesterday

morning. Lucky refused to go outside. She'd had to be coaxed. Grace had towelled her down, put her in her basket before she'd left the house for the hospital. If the gate had been open, surely Lucky would have disappeared first thing?

"Somebody's been in the house," Grace said to Chloe as they left the vets. "The side gate is always locked from the inside. There's no other access to the garden."

"Maybe you forgot to lock it, or left the gate open. You have been a bit forgetful of late, Grace."

"I didn't. I know I didn't. Those treats are unusual, we have to go to the pet shop on the other side of town to get them. Who, outside of the family, would know about them?"

"What are you saying?"

"I don't know… I just…well something has been niggling me recently. Faye has pretty much disappeared. She's ignoring my texts and then when I finally did speak to her, her voice was cold, detached."

"You surely don't think it was Faye?"

"I don't know, I can't think of any other explanation," Grace said. "I thought I was going mad, all those things moving around at home. But Lydia and I talked it through yesterday. What if she had something to do with it?"

"You can't think that."

"Can't I? Who else had keys to my house? Perhaps she copied them before she returned the originals."

"She wouldn't do that."

"Wouldn't she? There's something else. I contacted the phone company. The nuisance phone calls. It's all the same number. They asked me if I recognised it. It's Faye's mobile."

"I don't understand. Maybe she was returning your calls?"

"But some of them were in the middle of the night. She withheld her number and she didn't speak."

"Why?"

"I don't know. But she clearly feels aggrieved at something."

"Why don't you speak to her?"

"I tried again yesterday. She wouldn't answer her phone."

"It doesn't make sense. Why would she hurt Lucky?"

"I don't know that either. You know what Lucky's like, she wouldn't go anywhere with a stranger. But she adores Faye. And Faye knew that park was our usual walk. It wouldn't have been difficult to lure her down there. I can't think of any other explanation." Grace ground her teeth. "I won't have this though, I won't have her upsetting my family."

"Calm down, Grace. Think of Dad."

"I am thinking of your dad. I'm thinking of all of you. That's why Lydia and I spent the best part of yesterday evening at the police station, reporting the incident with Lucky."

CHAPTER FIFTY-SEVEN

GRACE SAT ON the bench and watched Lucky mill around in the bushes nearby. A week had passed. Lucky was making a good recovery and now able to take short walks, all be it on heavily-bandaged paws. A wave of exhaustion had swamped Grace after the incident. She'd battened down the hatches, concentrated her efforts on caring for Phil and Lucky. She began to realise how tense she'd been, overwrought after losing Jo, the police investigation and then Phil's illness. She knew she'd never rest easy until Jo's killer was caught, but the sense of calm had loosened the knot in her stomach slightly, enabling her to sleep, night after night, for the first time in months, knowing that her family were with her. Safe.

Lost in her thoughts, she didn't notice the man approach until he was almost beside her. "Penny for them," he said, giving a lopsided smile as he heaved himself down beside her. Grace looked across at him absently as recognition hit her. It was the man Faye and she had seen while walking in the park, a few weeks back. The man Faye had said was an old college friend.

"Oh, it's you," he said. "No Faye today?"

"Not today," she said, shifting up the seat, not wishing to invite conversation, especially not with anyone remotely connected to Faye.

An unpleasant odour filled her nose as he undid the

top button of his coat. She inched away further, as politely as she could. Lucky came rushing over to meet him, her extended lead winding around his ankles.

"She's a beauty," he said, fondling her head. He made a play of unravelling the lead. "What's she done to her feet?"

Grace explained how she had found Lucky.

"How awful." The dog hopped off. They sat in silence, the only sounds the hum of traffic from the nearby road and the wind rustling through the trees.

"How do you know Faye?" Grace asked.

"It's a long story," he said, eyes glazed. "Used to live near her before I moved a couple of years ago."

"In Manchester?"

He glanced across at her. "Manchester? No, Western Avenue, Market Harborough."

"Oh, I've only known her since she's lived in Fairfax Road."

She pulled her coat against her chest, made to go when he spoke again. "She ain't never lived in Fairfax Road."

Grace was on her feet now, reeling Lucky in on the lead. "What did you say?"

"I said she lives in the flats on Western Avenue. Number 32, above the shops. Always has done."

Grace adjusted her scarf, bade farewell and moved away, relieved to be away from the potent smell. He's confused, she thought to herself. Although the conversation nudged at her as she left the park and made her way through the back streets. Faye had skipped in and out of her mind this past week. A part of her felt uncomfortable about the manner in which they'd parted.

Faye had been a rock of support when it seemed she had no one else to turn to. They'd been good friends, shared confidences together. And, as her anger subsided, she couldn't help but wonder what had happened. The phone calls, the attack on Lucky didn't make sense. Maybe there was some kind of other explanation. There had to be.

Phil was sitting in his chair, watching the golf when Grace arrived back home. "Can I get you anything?" she asked.

"No thanks, love. How was your walk?"

"All right. Bleak day out. Bit of a strange question, but when you went to pick Faye up that time, it was from her home, wasn't it?"

Phil looked up, surprised in the change in conversation. "Yes, when she came to stay. Why?"

"Oh, nothing. Just thought I'd go over there. Pick some bits up. Can you remember the number?"

Phil patted his chin a moment. "Number 99, I think. Can't be sure though. She was outside, sitting on the wall when I got there. Why don't you text her?"

AN HOUR LATER, Grace pulled up outside number 99 Fairfax Road. It was a pretty white-painted bungalow, the front lawn edged with a low brick wall. She looked up at the frontage as she made her way down the driveway, catching the edge of a curtain twitch from a side window. It made her uneasy. Perhaps she should have phoned first. The front door slid open to a chain as she reached it to reveal the face of an elderly woman, the skin around her eyes creasing as she found focus.

"Sorry to bother you," Grace said. "I was looking for Faye."

"Who?"

"Faye," Grace repeated, lifting her voice slightly. "Faye Campbell."

The woman looked taken aback. "Nobody of that name here."

Grace felt her stomach tighten. "Oh, I must have the wrong house." She glanced back towards the car.

The woman watched her, said nothing.

"Sorry." Grace took a couple of steps away when she stopped, turned back. The woman was still standing at the doorway. Her face looked ghostly through the narrow crack. "I hope you don't mind me asking, but how long have you lived here?"

"Forty-three years." There was a rasp in the woman's voice as she pushed the words out. "And I've never heard of anyone by the name of Campbell."

Grace apologised again and made her way back to the car. She recalled all the conversations with Faye about renovating her father's bungalow. Faye definitely mentioned Fairfax Road. She remembered it distinctly. Maybe she'd got the number wrong.

She was just considering knocking on another door, when an address skipped into her mind. The man in the park had said the flats above the shops on Western Avenue. Number 32, wasn't it? Perhaps she was renting a place while her bungalow was being renovated. Or maybe she was looking after somebody? Grace climbed into the car and drove around the corner.

There were two stone staircases, one at either end of the bank of shops on Western Avenue, that led up to the flats above. The doors overlooked the road and the park beyond. Grace climbed the right hand staircase and made her way along to number 32. The door was chipped, the letterbox stuck open. She knocked on the door.

When there was no answer, she knocked again and peered through the frosted glass in the door. A shadow flickered in the distance. Grace knocked harder this time. Her breaths quickened. The long days they'd spent together over the past few months swam around her mind. They'd shared secrets she hadn't even shared with her family and yet it seemed the most basic fact about Faye's life, the address where she lived, was a lie.

The door jerked as it was pulled open. The face that appeared bore little resemblance to the manicured Faye that Grace had become accustomed to. Lank hair stuck out at angles; mascara smudges sat beneath dark eyes.

When she saw Grace she made to shut the door, but Grace heaved forward, catching her by surprise. She flew off balance as the door swung back. "I need to speak to you," Grace said.

She marched through a cramped hallway, past a coat rack almost hidden by an array of jackets and into a dingy kitchen. Chipped laminate cupboard doors were marked and scratched. A round table piled with post sat in the middle, four chairs tucked underneath.

"I want my keys back," Grace said.

"I left them in the dish in the hallway at your house."

"The other pair."

Faye turned away.

"Why do you keep calling the house and putting the phone down, Faye?" Grace asked.

Faye ignored her question. "How's Lucky?"

Grace stared at her a moment. She thought of the string of Lucky's favourite dog treats idly scattered over the broken glass as a fresh ball of anger rose in her chest.

Grace barely heard her words, aware of her voice rising. "It was you, wasn't it?"

The poise of Faye's icy stare was disconcerting. "You sent the police to see me."

"How could you? I took you into my home when you needed somewhere to stay. How could you hurt my dog?"

Faye said nothing.

"You've never lived in Fairfax Road, have you? Were you even at my school? Did your boiler really break? Just tell me the truth, Faye!" The questions came out like bullets, one firing after another.

The vacancy in Faye's eyes was unnerving. But what really chilled Grace was that nothing in her mannerisms betrayed the intimacy of a close friendship. It was almost as if they had never met.

Grace turned away, just as a glint of silver on the window ledge caught her eye. She moved closer. It was Jo's signet ring.

"How dare you!" Grace cried. Faye didn't flinch as she waved it front of her eyes. Grace swallowed back the tears, raised a pointed finger. "Stay away from me, and stay away from my family!"

Grace ran for the door, pounded down the concrete steps. Something about Faye's appearance, those wide eyes, the detached stance, filled her with disquiet. She'd invited Faye into her home, offered her friendship. But who was she, really? As she reached the car, she felt the signet ring in her pocket and toyed with the idea of calling the police. But right now, all she wanted was to get back to her family. And the first thing she would do is call the locksmith.

CHAPTER FIFTY-EIGHT

SUPERINTENDENT JANUS TOOK her glasses off and rested them on the desk exposing deep grooves down the sides of her nose. "I had a phone call from Carmela Hanson earlier." Jackman snapped his gaze away from the window. They were sat in her sparse office in the Leamington Headquarters, where they'd spent the last ten minutes discussing the status of the policy report on working practises he'd still not finished. "They've had a suspicious death in Market Harborough. There may be a connection with the Jo Lamborne case you helped them with last year." She glanced at her notes. "A Faye Campbell."

Jackman straightened his back. "Do we know any more details?"

"No, but she phoned to warn me. She's pulling together the same team, wants you back on loan. Thinks that, in view of your experience on the Lamborne case, your input would be valuable."

"So, I'm in?"

"Actually, I didn't get much say in the matter, she'd already taken it through management channels. Bloody annoying but," she gave an approving nod, "she'll go far, that one. Certainly knows what she wants. Anyway, I've agreed to a couple of weeks, that's all. You'll go back in as Acting Chief Inspector." She tapped her nail on the pile of paper on her desk. "And only on the basis that this report is finished and on my desk by January the 31st."

"Thanks."

She allowed herself a wry smile as she checked her watch. "Okay. Take the rest of the afternoon to hand over your current caseload to your team. You need to be at Leicestershire HQ at 8am tomorrow. I'm sure they'll fill you in then."

Jackman found a spring in his step as he took to the stairs. Unsolved cases were an uncomfortable part of working the murder squad, but the Lamborne case had been like a loose stone rattling around in his shoe. He'd found himself returning to it in quiet moments, troubled by the lack of motive or distinct pattern, something most serial offenders seemed to follow. The Leicestershire location had made it all the more difficult because he couldn't go back through the evidence, keep an eye out if anything new came to light. It would be good to take another look.

He'd reached the car park now, his feet inadvertently taking him out for some air. Davies raised her arm from where she was stood with another officer beside the bicycle shelter, stamping her feet to keep warm as she puffed on her cigarette. He returned her wave, turned the corner and leant up against the cold brick.

Faye Campbell. He didn't recognise the victim's name. If his stint with Leicestershire homicide had taught him anything though it was that they were so afraid of leaks, they didn't make links unless there was compelling evidence to do so. But the fact that they'd asked him back suggested a similar MO, or a connection to the family. He grabbed his phone, called Wilson, tapping his foot with every ring, cursing as it switched to voicemail. Instead, he punched out a text: Hope you're well. I'm joining you tomorrow morning. Can you email me everything you have on the new case so that I can hit the ground running? Thanks.

GRACE CLOSED THE door behind DC Emma Parsons. The detective's words rung out in her ears. "Faye's body was found in her flat this morning." The detective had been cagey about the details, but confirmed that the police were treating her death as suspicious. A mixture of shock, confusion and sadness hit her. Who, why?

Parsons had spoken to her gently, asked about their relationship. At first, Grace hadn't known where to start. She tried to tell the story of their short friendship. They were close, for a while, although they'd argued recently. It sounded a little like a soap opera as she spoke the words aloud and she cringed inwardly. She talked about her visit to Faye's flat the day before. Discovering she wasn't who she said she was.

Another feeling crashed in, dismissing the others. Relief. After all the bad feelings, the lies and deceit… It was a relief to think that had been dissipated. But she quickly checked herself. Although the exchange yesterday was weirdly fresh in her mind, whatever Faye was, whoever she was, whatever she'd done, they'd had some good times together. She'd been a great comfort to Grace through her grief and she didn't deserve to die.

Another death. Another murder.

A click in the distance. A door opening, measured footsteps descending the stairs. Grace raced into the downstairs washroom, pushed the door closed, splashed water on her face and looked at her reflection in the mirror. Her face was bright red.

Phil was seated at the kitchen table by the time she joined him. "Everything okay?" he asked.

Grace gave a weak smile. In spite of her best efforts, and asking the detective to speak quietly, they'd still disturbed him. For a moment she thought about keeping it from him, just like all the other bad things that had happened recently, but it was of no use. He would find out soon enough anyway. It was bound to be plastered across the local news. She sat, cleared her throat. "It was the police," she said, pressing her hand on his forearm reassuringly.

"Is there some news, about Jo?"

"No, not about Jo. It's Faye."

"Your friend, Faye?"

Grace nodded. "She's been killed."

"What?"

"The police are just looking into everything at the moment, but it seems she was killed in her flat. Her body was discovered this morning."

CHAPTER FIFTY-NINE

"FORTY-YEAR-OLD WOMAN, Faye Campbell. Killed with a single stab wound to the side of her neck. Body discovered by a parcel delivery driver, knocking the door early yesterday morning. When she didn't answer, he noticed something was awry through the frosted glass panel in her door. He looked through the letterbox and saw a pool of blood on the floor that appeared to be coming from the kitchen. That's when he called us." Jackman watched Wilson tap the pictures of the dead woman taken from a number of angles, before she turned back to the room to continue her briefing. Although he'd stayed up most of the night, poring over the case, the words, spoken aloud, cemented the facts in his mind. "No sign of a break-in," Wilson continued, "so we assume she let the killer in. Which means it's likely to be somebody she knows. No defensive wounds, she didn't put up a fight. Celeste's report is due in soon but she has put an estimated time of death within the last twelve hours of finding her body, which takes us back to ten o'clock the night before."

"The knife was left in situ?" Jackman asked.

Wilson nodded. "The carotid artery was pierced. They appeared to know exactly what they were doing."

Jackman looked from one photo to another. "Only

one stab wound. Do we know where the knife came from?"

"Forensics are checking it for fingerprints, but there is a knife missing from the block on the kitchen side."

"So, the victim might have been killed with her own knife. Are we absolutely sure she didn't do this to herself?"

"The question has already been raised. It's not impossible, but Celeste thinks it's unlikely that any victim would have the psychological strength to perform something like that, even if they were physically strong enough."

Jackman rolled his shoulders, listening to the cartilage pop and crackle. "What's the connection with the Lamborne case?"

"Faye Campbell was a close friend of Grace Daniels." Jackman could now recognise her in the photo. He had been wracking his brains all night trying to place her. She was the woman who'd brought in the drinks the last time he'd visited Grace. A very close friend then. "Is that it?"

Wilson drew a breath. "No. CSIs retrieved her phone from the scene. They've found an association with Jo Lamborne on there."

"Not unusual if she was a family friend."

"There are photos. Some of the photos are of Jo in the bridesmaid dress she wore on the day she died."

"Okay, was Faye listed as a guest at the wedding?"

Wilson shook her head.

"Anything else?"

"Her bedroom in the flat was littered with evil eyes."

"Oh?"

"Posters, charms, bracelets."

"What about an earring?"

"Nothing yet. But lots of fibres and hair samples throughout the flat, all of which need to be eliminated. We'll know more when we get the forensic report through."

"I presume someone has been out to see Grace Daniels?"

A head nodded from the side of the room. Parsons peered around the side of the officer in front of her to meet his gaze. "That was my remit, sir."

"How was she?"

"Seemed shocked. They'd been old school friends, apparently, although hadn't seen each other in years. Faye told Grace she'd moved back to the area a few months ago. They've been close since then. Faye even stayed with them for a week or so after Christmas when she had a problem with a broken boiler at home. But the two women have had a falling out."

"How much of a falling out?"

"Grace's dog was attacked and she blamed Faye. Made a formal complaint here on the 4th of January. One of the community officers went out to speak to Faye. The statement has sat on their desk since."

"Does Grace have an alibi for the night before last?"

"She was at home with her husband. He recently suffered a double heart attack and is recovering."

"Any witnesses?"

"We put out a press release for witnesses last night and have started house to house in the area," Wilson said. "Nothing yet."

"No sexual motive? Nothing missing from the house that might indicate a burglary gone wrong?"

Wilson shook her head. "Celeste examined her yesterday evening and could find no evidence of a recent sexual encounter and no defensive bruising to speak of. The television and laptop are still in place. Flat appears untouched, although to be honest there's not much of value in there."

Jackman turned back to the photos of the victim on the board, the knife still wedged in the side of her neck. Below them was a photo retrieved from her mantelpiece. The camera had caught her on centre, she was laughing, her white teeth glistening against a backdrop of blonde hair, an attractive smile. "What do we know about the victim?"

"No convictions. Looks like there might be some intelligence. The systems are down at the moment, the techies are working on it, but we'll check as soon as it's back up."

"Right, let's look into Faye Campbell's background. Who were her friends, family? Where had she been living? Who did she associate with? Make sure the search of the flat is thorough. Get them to tear the floorboards up, go through the drainage system if they have to, I don't want anything missed."

A familiar face appeared as he finished up. "Ah, DCI Jackman. Can I see you for a minute?"

He'd been relieved to find Carmela absent on his arrival that morning. The team welcomed him like an old friend, asked after the health of his wife. By the time they'd shared a round of coffee and were into briefing, it was almost like he'd never been away. Although, this was the one encounter in Leicestershire that he hadn't been looking forward to. And there was no familiarity in Carmela's face right now, no warmth.

She'd sent a couple of texts after he'd left Leicestershire. The first enquiring about his welfare, sending her regards. The second arrived a week or so later, saying she would be in Warwickshire the following day, to text if he wanted to meet up. He'd tried to phone. Several times. When she didn't answer, he'd responded to her text to say, he was sorry, but he didn't think it was a good idea right now, that he needed to focus on his family. On Alice.

He wrapped up the meeting and she said nothing, marching slightly ahead of him as they navigated the corridor and up the stairs. When they reached her office, she waited until he'd crossed the threshold and closed the door behind him. They stood in the open office.

"I was sorry to hear about Alice," Carmela said. "How is she?"

"We're not completely sure. But she is out of danger." The top button of her shirt was undone, showing a generous portion of cleavage. He snapped his gaze away.

"Are you sure you're okay?"

He gave a slightly confused nod. She'd personally requested his presence on the case. Surely she wasn't now questioning his capabilities?

"Good." Her face relaxed but her tone was still cutting. "I brought you back here for one reason only, because of your experience on the Lamborne case. With all the bad press we've had recently, I need this new case brought to a speedy conclusion. Keep me updated of any developments." She opened the door for him to leave. "Thank you."

Jackman stared at her for a split second, shook his head and wandered out. The door slammed behind him. He knew it had got out of hand that night in his kitchen, but his family were his priority right now. He'd thought he'd made that clear. The unfastened button on her shirt pressed on him as Janus' earlier comments rang in his ear, 'She certainly knows what she wants.' He trudged back down to the office. Well, people didn't always get what they wanted.

"LYDIA'LL BE DOWN in a minute," Grace said as she smiled at Meggy and placed a plate of biscuits on the coffee table.

"Party rings!" the toddler exclaimed. "My favourite."

"I remembered." Grace winked at her, and then turned to Chloe. "Lydia's got a surprise for you."

A thump of footsteps on the stairs sounded, followed by Lydia's face appearing around the doorframe.

Chloe gasped. "You had your hair cut!"

Grace had shared the same gasp when her youngest daughter had arrived home earlier that morning. No discussion, no warning. Gone were the long strands of glossy fair hair, replaced by a short spiky crop.

Lydia ran her hands through it, turned her head from one side to another. "What do you think?"

The toddler pouted. "You cut your princess hair."

"Meggy. Don't be rude. It suits you," Chloe said. "Just can't believe you didn't mention it."

Lydia shrugged. "I've been thinking about it for a while. Thought I'd surprise everybody." She squeezed into the armchair beside Chloe and fell into conversation while Meggy helped herself to another biscuit. Time passed easily. Phil joined them. Meggy climbed onto his knee and he read her a story. Grace relaxed and sipped her coffee. It was good to have her family together.

"Meggy, don't do that," Chloe said. The toddler was back on the floor and patting Lucky, a little too vigorously. Chloe leant down, held her hand and they stroked the dog gently together.

"Come on, let's go and wash your hands," Lydia said to the toddler.

Chloe watched her daughter traipse out of the room and looked up towards Grace. "Isn't it awful about Faye?"

Grace nodded. "Dreadful. I can't quite believe it."

"Do the police know what happened?"

"I don't know. They didn't say much when they came out. Only that her body had been found in her flat."

"I heard on the news she'd been stabbed," Chloe added, just as Lydia wandered back in with Meggy.

Lydia excused herself to go upstairs to do some homework.

"She's struggling with it all." Grace said to Chloe after she'd gone.

"I didn't think she liked her."

"She didn't dislike her. I think Faye was just around at the wrong time. And another death of someone close to the family… It's upsetting for all of us."

"The police came to see me," Chloe said. "I'd only met her a few times."

"We all gave statements," Grace said. "I don't think she had many friends. Sad really."

CHAPTER SIXTY

"THE PRELIMINARY FORENSICS report is through," McDonald said. "A number of hair samples that don't belong to Faye have been picked up."

It was early afternoon and Jackman had called an impromptu briefing for an update. "Anything else?"

McDonald leafed through a few more pages. "There's a DNA match on file with Faye Campbell. A match with the spot of blood on the earring, found at the Jo Lamborne murder scene."

"The evil eye. Are you sure?"

"Positive."

"Has anybody recovered the other earring?"

"It seems not."

"That's not all," Wilson said. "CSIs found a box hidden beneath the floorboards in the victim's bedroom." She clicked a button on her laptop and immediately a photo of a cardboard box, the corners of the flaps curled where they'd been folded together, filled the screen in front of them. The screen changed to another photo of a map of Leicestershire, a belt, a phallic sex toy, a pair of stilettos. Wilson listed these items as the contents of the box.

Murmurs gathered momentum as they spread around the room. Jackman squinted, trying to focus on what was beneath the objects. It looked like a blue exercise book, the sort that students used in school. He pointed at it. "What's that?"

Wilson pressed a button, starting a slide show. Photo after photo flashed up on the screen. The book contained pictures of Eugenie Trentwood and Jo Lamborne. Photos taken from various angles in shops, cafés, at bus stops. Some from a distance, some fairly close. Either the girls were ignoring the lens, or they were completely oblivious to it. As the show progressed, the photos became more sordid: Eugenie laid on the ground, unconscious, her skirt hitched up around her waist, a close-up of the bruising on her face. Jo's naked body at the murder scene, porcelain under the glistening moonlight, was the final photo.

Parsons closed her dropped jaw. "She kept a picture diary?"

"Somebody did," Jackman said. "Any news on that intelligence?"

"No criminal record, but a string of complaints about Faye Campbell on file," Parsons said. "In 2002 there was a complaint made about her taking money from an elderly lady. No action taken as the complaint was initiated by the victim's family. The alleged victim refused to press charges. Two harassment warnings, one in 2005 and another in 2010. The first, a man. The second, a woman."

"What happened?"

"Details were logged on the system, but no other action taken, apart from the warnings. There's not much on there, to be honest. Names, dates. That's about it."

"See if you can trace the complainants, will you? Find out more details. And check with other forces to see if they have anything? We'll need to trace her NHS number too. Grace implied Faye was delusional, she'd apparently pretended to live at another address, on Fairfax Road. Does she have a medical history of psychiatric problems? And get a production order on the support group that Jo attended in Market Harborough. Some of those members still haven't come forward."

Jackman turned back to the room. "What else do we know?"

"Faye's phone was cell sited in Harborough town the night Jo Lamborne was murdered," Wilson said. "The number matches texts found on Jo's phone, but we hadn't been able to trace it earlier because it was unregistered."

Jackman looked back at the last photo on the screen. Was it Faye that Jo approached on the other side of the road the night she was killed? Her height and build certainly matched the description, although a black hoody wasn't listed in the inventory of materials recorded at the flat. "Check the transactions on Faye Campbell's credit card, will you? Does she have any insurance? We know she doesn't own a car, but she'd have needed a vehicle to transport the body."

Wilson echoed the room's thoughts. "Why would Faye Campbell kill Grace Daniels' daughter, and in such a horrific way?"

"That's what we need to find out," Jackman said. "But one thing's for sure. It gives Grace the perfect motive."

"CAN YOU TELL me where you were on the night of Monday the 11th of January?"

Grace had been in the kitchen kneading bread when

the detectives arrived that evening, and let Phil answer the door while she washed her hands. Parsons had crossed the threshold accompanied by another detective Grace didn't recognise. There were no smiles today, no reassurance as Parsons arrested her on suspicion of Faye's murder. Grace's mind had gone blank. She could barely even remember the drive to the police station. It wasn't until she was standing in the custody suite, asked to relay her name, address and advised of her right to legal representation, that the true extent of the situation hit her. She hadn't stopped shaking since.

"I've already answered these questions."

"For the tape, please?" Jackman continued.

"I was at home with Phil, all evening."

"Ah, yes. We've interviewed Mr Daniels. He admitted he went to bed early."

"He's getting used to some new medication. He gets tired easily."

"For his heart condition?"

"Yes."

Jackman nodded. "But he can't confirm you were there."

"I was there."

"Are you sure there isn't anybody else that can vouch for you?"

"No."

"Have you ever visited Faye's home on Western Avenue?"

"Yes, on Monday afternoon. I already told the other detective—"

"Monday the 11th of January?"

"Yes."

"How many times?"

"Just the once."

"What time did you arrive? And what time did you leave?"

Grace thought hard. "I didn't check the clock, but it must have been about 1 o'clock when I arrived. I only stayed a few minutes."

"And you had an argument?"

Grace gave a small nod.

"Tell me, what that was about?"

Grace relayed the details of her visit to Faye that afternoon. As she spoke the words, Faye's menacing glare crept into her mind.

"How would you describe your feelings at the time?"

"I was angry, of course. But not enough to kill her. I'd never do anything like that."

Jackman retrieved a clear plastic wallet from the file on the table in front of him. "I'm showing Grace Daniels Exhibit BRO123A. This is a statement from Faye Campbell's neighbour in which she states she saw a woman of your description visit Faye's home at approximately 22.30 on the evening of—"

"It wasn't me," Grace interrupted. "She must be mistaken."

Jackman pulled out a bundle of photographs. "I'm showing Grace Daniels Exhibit BRO125A and 130A." The photographs were of the items in the box found in Faye's flat.

Grace cringed, turned away. The revelations disorientated her. "I don't understand, have you got some news on Jo?"

"Are you sure there isn't anything else you'd like to tell us?" Jackman said.

"What?" Grace glanced at her solicitor.

"If you've some new evidence, Chief Inspector, I think you need to share it with us," her solicitor said.

"These items," he pointed at the photographs, one by one, "were found in Faye Campbell's house."

Grace's heart skipped a beat. "I'm not with you."

"We believe Faye was an associate of Jo's. We believe she was in Market Harborough town centre the night Jo died."

"What?"

"We have reason to believe that Faye Campbell was involved in the death of your daughter."

Grace stared at the photos in front of her. Beads of sweat merged together on her forehead, trickling to her brow line. She tasted bile but sat there frozen, unable to move or fight it. Instead she turned, opened her mouth and watched as the vomit splashed across the floor.

CHAPTER SIXTY-ONE

LATER THAT EVENING, Wilson stooped to switch off the footage after the team had re-watched Grace's interview together.

McDonald was the first to break the silence. "She didn't know," he said.

Carmela raised her eyes from the desk in front of her. "That's a bold statement."

"You saw the look of horror on her face."

"Maybe she's playing us?"

"If she didn't know, she didn't have a motive."

"She was spotted in the vicinity that evening."

Jackman turned back to the board. He'd barely spoken to Carmela since their meeting on his first morning back, but her growing presence at briefings was starting to grate.

"Let's go back to the beginning," he said, cutting through their argument. "We need to understand Faye's relationship with Jo and Grace, her motivation for being involved with Jo's death. What do we know about Faye's background?"

"Very little," Parsons said. "Neighbours say she kept herself to herself. Parents died when she was young, no siblings and no other family to speak of. Her movements for the last few weeks don't tell us much either. She stayed with Grace for a while after Christmas be-

cause she was having some work done at home to replace a broken boiler."

"And was it really broken?"

"The flat has a very old boiler. There are no signs
of any recent work. Since moving back from Grace's,
she's barely left her flat according to the neighbours.
The only contacts on her mobile are a few texts and
a call from Grace, and several very short phone calls
she's made back."

"What about the intelligence?"

"McDonald and I have spoken to the complainants."
Parsons rested her notebook on the table, licked her
thumb and forefinger and leafed through the pages until
she found what she was looking for. "The first complaint related to an elderly lady named Caroline Welsh
in 2002. Caroline passed away in 2004, but I did manage to speak to her daughter who lives in France. She
said Faye befriended her mother, carried out chores,
did her shopping. The family thought Faye was helping
until they came over from France to visit and discovered that the elderly woman's savings, almost £5,000,
had disappeared. They blamed Faye, ended her contact with their mother and reported it to the police, although her mother refused to press charges, claiming
they were friends and she had gifted the money to Faye
to buy some furniture she needed for her own home.
No action was taken."

Parsons turned a page and continued. "In 2005, we
received a complaint from a man she had been dating.
He'd broken off their relationship after a four month affair and claimed she was obsessed. She'd moved herself
in, was using his credit cards. When he finally kicked

her out she kept ringing him, putting messages through his door, turning up at his work."

"Unusual for a man to complain of harassment," Wilson said.

"Apparently it went on for quite some time. He worked in a travel agency in Leicester, she'd visit and make a scene. He was concerned about his job." She scratched at her temple. "He did say she made threats, but he withdrew his statement almost as soon as he'd placed it, said he felt sorry for her. She was visited by an officer on the 22nd of September 2005 at Western Avenue and given a harassment warning. Case closed.

"The last complaint was in 2010," Parsons said. "A Samantha Meadows. Wealthy middle-aged woman. Met Faye in a dentist surgery waiting room after she'd split from her husband. The two women got talking, arranged to meet and became friends. Over almost a year she took Faye on various holidays to Portugal, Italy, Turkey and allegedly became concerned when Faye started helping herself to her wardrobe, dressing like her, contacting her friends directly. When she found Faye looking through her personal effects at home, she ended the friendship. She complained to the police when Faye persistently phoned and turned up on her doorstep and Faye was given another harassment warning. The complainant lives in Australia with her daughter now."

"Interesting," Wilson said. "All quite a few years apart…"

"These were the people that took the trouble to complain," Jackman said. "There could have been others that didn't. What about Faye's work?"

"According to her national insurance record, she

drops in and out of the system. Last place was a laun-
derette in 2014. Doesn't look like she's stayed anywhere
for long."

"How did she meet Jo?" Jackman asked.

"The techies are still going through her internet history. They've retrieved loads of searches from her hard
drive on strangulation, links to news reports on the rape
of Shelley Barnstaple. They're cataloguing them with
dates and times as they go along. Looks like it started
a month or two before Eugenie Trentwood's attack."

"So, if we assume Faye planned this and was our
copycat attacker on Operation Ascott, why did she attack Eugenie Trentwood? There's no connection there."
His question was met with blank faces. "And, why did
she kill Jo?"

"To get close to Grace?" Wilson said. "They didn't
meet up again until after Jo died."

"But why befriend Grace afterwards?"

"It's not unusual for a killer to stay close to a case."

"No, there's something else," Jackman replied. "Get
the hair samples at the murder scene pushed through.
Let's see if anyone else visited Faye that evening. And
chase that production order for the support group that
Jo attended. If Faye had a history of mental health problems, it's possible they could have met through those
channels."

"I'll check on it," Wilson said.

"The intelligence indicates that Faye has befriended
people in the past for personal gain, but murder seems
a stretch. Why change tactic? Was somebody else involved?" He turned to Carmela who'd stood in the background, watching the briefing unfold. "Your friend at

the College of Policing, the profiler. Do you think we can get him back in to look over the case?"

She nodded.

"Right." Jackman looked back at the room. "Any news on school records, medical records, where she has worked?"

"We're working on it," Wilson said.

"We need to find out more about Faye's history."

"We're struggling with that one, sir," McDonald said. "We know her mother died when she was young, but there's a huge gap in between that and her working life."

"No luck with social services?"

He shook his head. "They can't find her records."

Jackman surveyed his team. They looked tired, weary. And there was still a wealth of enquiries to follow up on. "Okay, I'll pick that one up. We need to move fast on this now. We're close, we're just missing something."

GRACE STAGGERED INTO the custody cell. She didn't hear the door bang shut, the lock click, the yell of a fellow prisoner as he called for his brief. All she could hear right now was the blood pulsing in her ears.

Faye was involved in Jo's murder? An image filled her mind. The two women laughing together, Faye tucking a strand of hair behind her ear. It morphed into her placing a strap around Jo's neck and yanking every breath from her body. Grace wrapped her arms around herself. Jo had been undressed. Sexually assaulted. Her body left exposed to the elements.

Grace's mind reeled. How did they know each other? How did they meet?

She thought of her first meeting with Faye in the supermarket. The shopping centre when they lost Meggy. The thought of Faye watching and waiting for an opportunity to get close sickened her.

The woman she'd spent time with, shared confidences with, invited into her home. All those conversations and questions about Jo's case. She'd been grateful to have someone to talk to, to confide in. Taking her into Jo's room, her comments over their visit to Nottingham. Yet all the time Faye was trying to wheedle her way closer into their lives and destroy everything in sight. Faye had even pressured her to report her own attack to the police, all the time knowing it wasn't relevant.

She'd been so thrilled with the scarf Faye had bought her, had even worn it when the police had arrested her. Grace placed a hand to her neck. The custody sergeant had removed it to be kept with her personal items. She wanted to rip it to shreds.

Disbelief gave way to anger. How could she have forged a friendship with a woman involved in her daughter's murder, invited her into her home, into her confidence and not suspected anything? How could she not have seen through all those lies right in front of her? A ball of rage rose inside, gathering momentum. Grace didn't know who had killed Faye, but of one thing she was completely sure. They'd done her a favour. Because if Faye wasn't already dead, she would kill her herself.

CHAPTER SIXTY-TWO

RURAL LEICESTERSHIRE WAS quiet the following morning. Bach filled the void in the car, the ebb and flow of the music once again easing Jackman's mind. He glanced at the clock on the dashboard. It was 10.30am. They could only keep Grace for another eight hours under her current custody conditions before they had to apply for an extension. Something about her interview, her relationship with Faye, didn't ring true.

Faye's motivation itched away at him. The earring, the items found at her house, her phone, all pointed to her involvement in Jo's case, but they were lacking a motive. Was there somebody else involved in the case, somebody Faye was harbouring? A male partner perhaps?

The rain had ceased, although a blanket of cloud still covered the sky leaving a grey January day in its midst. He wound down the window, inviting the damp air to seep into the car. A frustrating hour had been spent that morning, making call after call, being passed from one office to another, in an effort to track down somebody that was working in Leicestershire Social Services who might have a recollection of Faye's early life. Turning back the clock to the eighties had proved tricky. Many of the officers he spoke to hadn't worked there at the time, he suspected some of them hadn't even been born then. Eventually he'd been emailed a list of retired officers and worked through them, one by one. Two of them had passed away, another was on a cruise. Finally somebody recognised Faye Campbell's name and gave him the details of someone they believed had worked her case in the 1980s: Meredith Atkinson, retired in 2006. It had only taken him a few minutes to trace her address and phone number, but when he'd tried to call there was no response, so he'd driven out there anyway in the hope that he might catch someone at home.

Jackman arrived at a detached house with a large oak door. As he approached he was surprised to find it open. An elderly lady looked out. She was leaning on a wooden stick. "Can I help you?" she asked.

Jackman introduced himself, held up his badge. "I'm looking for Meredith Atkinson."

The woman peered in closer at his badge before she met his gaze. "I'm Meredith Atkinson. What can I do for you?"

"I'm working on a case you might be able to help me with, from your social services days. A Faye Campbell."

Meredith rocked on her stick. "You'd better come in."

Her stick tapped the parquet flooring as she guided Jackman through to the front room. He turned down her offer of refreshments. He didn't want to see her struggle with a tray, and she struck him as the sort of woman that wouldn't likely accept assistance.

"What can you tell me about Faye Campbell?" he asked, when they'd settled themselves into the two armchairs.

"What do you want to know?"

"As much as you can tell me really." He gave a scant

overview of Faye's body being found. "I'm working on the murder investigation. We've been struggling to put together Faye's background."

"I was allocated her case when her mother died of a drugs overdose in the early 1980s." Creases folded around her eyes as she narrowed them. "She must have been about four."

"I'm having difficulty tracking down the records."

"I'm not at all surprised. It was before computer systems existed in the way they do now. Everything was recorded in paper files. The offices I worked from had a fire in the early nineties. Loads of files were destroyed at the time, Faye's being one of them, no doubt."

"Do you have any recollection of your cases? I appreciate it's a long time ago."

"Not all of them. Just the significant ones." Meredith pushed a wisp of grey hair out of her face. "Behavioural problems are expected in a case like Faye's. She hadn't bonded during her younger years. Foster parents are trained, supported on how to deal with children that have experienced this kind of trauma. But Faye was an exceptional case.

"We tried several homes. It was all fine at first and then problems would creep in. She seemed to delight in telling lies, upsetting people. When she was six she ran away. The police found her on a station platform, begging."

"What happened?"

"She was moved to a children's home. Given counselling. Dropped out of the system ten years later. I always wondered what happened to her."

"Do you recall what schools she attended?"

Meredith thought for a moment. "They'll have been the local ones in Market Harborough, I suppose."

"Can I ask, have you ever heard of Grace Daniels?"

"Daniels? Isn't that the woman whose daughter was murdered last year? I read about it in the local newspaper."

Jackman nodded.

"Awful affair. Faye wasn't involved in that, was she?"

Jackman didn't answer. Grace wouldn't have been Daniels back in the eighties. He worked through the file in his mind, finally recalling Grace's maiden name.

"She would have been known as Grace Norton," he said. "Do you know if Faye had an association with her, growing up?"

"Is that the same woman? Goodness, I never made the connection. Well, yes. I remember the Norton family very well indeed. In fact, Faye even stayed with them for a while when she was young."

JACKMAN PULLED OVER and answered the phone on his way back to the station that afternoon.

"Hello, stranger." Davies' rich Geordie accent filled the car.

"Hey you. How's things?"

"Pretty good. Got a phone call last night, asking me to hotfoot it over to interview another five witnesses from the support group first thing this morning."

"Ah, sorry about that."

"Don't be. Most exciting thing to happen to me in a while."

"How did you get on?"

"Five ladies all together. Not a particularly chatty

bunch, I have to say. But one of them had coffee with Jo Lamborne a couple of times before the sessions. She says they talked about Jo's life in Nottingham, her family mostly. Jo had a rough time before she left for university, called at drop-in centres occasionally for some help. She was texting a woman she'd met at one of them called Faye."

Jackman felt a frisson of excitement. "Did your interviewee ever meet Faye?"

"She says not. And Jo never mentioned her again."

CHAPTER SIXTY-THREE

"THE STATEMENTS, THE previous reports, her medical records and her background all indicate a pattern of behaviour. Faye Campbell was a high functioning sociopath. Charming, charismatic even, but manipulative." The usual feet shuffling and paper turning quietened at this point as everyone's attention was on the profiler, Terry Barnes.

"Her mother died of an overdose when she four and it seems that she was passed from one foster home to another. Nobody could cope with her," Jackman added.

"How did we not know this?" Wilson asked.

"There are no records. Apparently the social worker's office to which she was allocated had a fire in the early nineties. All Faye's records were destroyed. According to her medical records, Faye was diagnosed with conduct disorder at aged twelve, received treatment for around four years, when she dropped out of the system."

"Conduct disorder?" Wilson asked.

"They don't diagnose sociopathy until adulthood," Barnes said. "Many sociopaths exist in society. Raised in a secure environment they can cope with their condition, have jobs, families. You would probably never notice anything different about them. But Faye was unusual. She didn't bond during her childhood, failed to accept the normal rules of society. Her pattern of behaviour suggests when she was on a high, she was logical, decisive, charming. When she was on a low, she was completely destructive to herself and those around her. It's the most dangerous combination."

"There's more," Jackman said. "The social worker told me that Faye lived with Grace's parents for a while when she was nine years old."

"What?" Wilson looked shocked. "Surely Grace would remember that?"

"Not necessarily. Grace's parents couldn't have children of their own, so they adopted her."

"We already know that."

"But they also fostered. They'd have taken in hundreds of children while Grace was growing up. Some stayed a few weeks, others months, the longest was just over a year. Faye attended Grace's school for a while."

"Why did she leave the family?"

"Apparently she'd developed an obsession with the boy next door. Followed him everywhere. When he didn't return her affections she stole things from him, and eventually tried to set fire to his bedroom. The story was hushed up at the time. He was a close friend of Grace's, so much so, that he became her first husband."

Wilson's eyes widened. "Jamie Lamborne? He was Jo and Lydia's father. Died of cancer five years ago."

"That's the one," Jackman said. "It's possible she met Jo, recognised the name and discovered the connection. Perhaps she became jealous of Grace's stable home, the fact that Grace married Jamie and had a family of her own. Faye never had any of those things."

"But why murder her daughter?"

"The intelligence reports suggest Faye befriended

vulnerable people, latching onto them for financial and personal gain," Barnes said. "When she had bled them dry she moved to the next victim. People are easier to manipulate when they are vulnerable. Faye came along at the right time. Well, no, that's not strictly true. She manufactured the whole thing, chose her moment carefully, would have planned meticulously, hence the sexual motive. It was the perfect mask. The police would be sent in a different direction, immediately thinking they were looking for a man. She'd read about Shelley Barnstaple's attack, copied the details as much as possible, manipulated the evidence to suit her own needs. Eugenie Trentwood was her practice, her run-up to the main event."

"Grace mentioned Faye was interested in Jo's case," Wilson said. "She took that as friendship, an offer to assist her in finding the truth."

Jackman nodded. "If she could find out about the police investigation, she could help to steer the attention away from her. Hence the visit to Anthony Kendall in Nottingham. I'd bet it was Faye who encouraged Grace to take that trip." He thought about Grace's confession of her own attack. Once again attention had been pushed elsewhere.

"She lied about where she lived, her backstory was so contrived, so practised that she probably deluded herself into believing it," Barnes added. "She even lived with Grace for a while, enjoying the lifestyle, the close friendship while it suited her."

"So what changed?" Wilson asked.

"Seemingly there are no constants in Faye's life," Barnes said. "No siblings, parents, family or friends to speak of. Every relationship she has is short lived. She might have set out to harm Grace and her family, but she's unbalanced. She plays with her victims. Watches them, gets close. The same scenario was playing out over again. Only this time, she took it further than she'd ever done before."

"So she told Grace she'd murdered her daughter?"

"I doubt she admitted it. Grace certainly hasn't said anything to support that. We are dealing with a highly manipulative woman here. Maybe she scattered clues, left Grace to discover the truth for herself."

The door snapped open. McDonald entered, closely followed by Carmela. "Remember Faye's neighbour said she saw the person who'd visited Faye that evening?" McDonald said. "We've just had the results of her ID. She picked out Grace."

Jackman nodded. "Okay."

"There's something else." He waved a piece of paper in his hand. "Faye's credit card bill show she hired a white escort van for two days from the 29th of October."

"The day Jo died," Jackman said. "Contact the hire company. We'll need to seize the vehicle, get it examined by CSI."

Carmela looked at Jackman. "A word, please?"

Her face was frosty as Jackman stepped into the corridor. "We have Grace's DNA at the scene plus hairs from her dog, probably fallen from her clothing," she said. "We have a witness placing her there that night. She had motive, means and opportunity."

Jackman shook his head. "Something doesn't feel right."

"What? A gut feeling?" she scoffed. "We don't work

on feelings here, Will. We work on evidence. The CPS are going to charge Grace with murder pending further enquiries. Your work is done here." And with that she turned and walked away.

CHAPTER SIXTY-FOUR

GRACE SAT, STARING into the shadows of the corridor beyond, separated from her by a line of solid steel bars. It was cold down there. Sporadic memories of the morning's events washed through her.

She'd woken with a start. Raised voices, banging; fists on metal. Her neck still ached from the hard pillow in the police cell.

Breakfast had been a cup of weak tea and two slices of buttered toast, brought in by a jaded custody officer who looked like he was approaching the end of a heavy shift. He'd placed it down on the edge of her bed and retreated.

Later, a female detention officer had guided her down the corridor, past the other cells, into a shower area. The backs of the officer's boots were visible through the gap at the bottom of the cubicle door as Grace rubbed the tiny slab of white soap over her body. The towel was threadbare at one end, its harsh bristles dragged across her skin. She'd had to borrow a hairbrush, leave her hair to dry naturally. No hairdryers and cosmetics here. Her family had brought in her black trouser suit and white shirt, the one Grace kept aside for funerals and important school meetings, in an Asda carrier bag, along with clean underwear. She thought about the police checking through the contents and recoiled. She'd been charged with murder. This was her life now. Nothing was private.

Grace ran her fingers around her right wrist, gently massaging the skin. A female security officer arrived almost as soon as she was dressed and handcuffed her own wrist to Grace's. She was then led through the car park and into an internal cell within a police van, and asked to sit on a plastic bench, her handcuffs removed before the door was banged shut. The journey to the court seemed like hours. But they'd arrived early, beating the local press, which was something to be thankful for.

Grace picked a stray thread from her trousers. She'd sat in the same cell that morning, waiting to be called into court. Her solicitor, Jane Barrington, had come to see her, briefed her on what to expect, although Grace didn't recall the conversation. She just kept thinking, hoping, that suddenly the police would find something, realise their mistake and let her out of the cell so that she could go back home with Phil and Lydia. Leave this nightmare behind her.

Anxiety rose as she'd sat there waiting for the court hearing. Her solicitor had said it was a formality, but how could it be? Why was she there if there wasn't an element of hope?

She could hear the guards in their offices nearby, talking amongst themselves, making phone calls. She heard Peterborough mentioned, and somewhere called Foston Hall was talked about time and time again. It wasn't until they mentioned Holloway that she realised they were calling prisons. Making arrangements. Surely not for her? Holloway was for serious offenders.

People like Myra Hindley and Rose West. Surely they
wouldn't send somebody like her there? She blanked
out the voices, thought about her family. She longed to
see them, feel a little of their support.

Finally an officer had arrived, unlocked the door,
re-cuffed her and led her up the metal staircase. The
courtroom was austere and imposing and not unlike
those Grace had seen on the television in crime dramas.
What she hadn't realised was how terrifying it was.
She'd caught sight of the three magistrates at the front
of the room, two men and one woman, watching her as
she walked in. It wasn't until she was in the dock, the
handcuffs removed, that she saw the public gallery. Phil
was there. He'd offered her a gentle smile, although his
face was creased in concern. He was flanked by Lydia
and Chloe who both looked pale. Beside them she recognised the police sergeant from Jo's case, Dee Wilson.

A man had stood, asked her to confirm her name.
Her voice croaked as she did so. The magistrates barely
looked at her as the prosecutor, a grey-haired man in a
similar grey suit had then stood and read out the charge
of murder, asking for the matter to be sent to the Crown
Court. His passing shot, "Bail is not applicable in this
case," knocked her sideways.

Grace had glanced across at Phil. The courtroom
swayed around her. Was this really it? The moment that
she would be sent away, interned? She'd been raised to
think that prisons were for bad people, criminals that
had committed heinous acts. Stone walls, barred windows. People transported with blankets over their heads.
Not innocent everyday folk, wrongly accused.

And what about her family? How were they to cope

with this? She was innocent. She'd wanted to scream and shout, to bang on the screen in front of her. How could this happen? Instead she'd felt a tugging at her arm. The officer wrestled with her wrist as she replaced the handcuff. In less than two minutes it was all over. She'd managed one more look back at her family, their terror-filled faces the last thing she saw before she was led away, back down to the cell.

Her solicitor had barely spoken a word. Grace hadn't been invited to defend herself. She'd been told that the hearing was a formality, a part of the process to give the state continued powers for detention. But it was pointless. She was going to prison and there was nothing her or anyone else could do about it.

Grace sat back on the bench and pressed her back into the cold wall. A raised voice in the distance caught her attention. "Holloway it is then. I suppose I'd better go and give her the good news."

HOURS LATER, JACKMAN joined the group of officers standing around the computer screen as they watched the press conference. Carmela was sat beside the chief constable as he announced the results. A female murderer was big news. The chief constable had taken it upon himself to face the public, in full uniform, ready to squeeze every bit of PR out of the result. The police had been heavily criticised for not catching the offender earlier and he was finally able to assure them that the serial attacker was off the streets. Grace's charge was mentioned briefly, but played down. Nobody was going to allow her involvement in Faye's murder to spoil the PR bubble.

Carmela praised her officers for their commitment and tenacity, working around the clock to solve the case, hailing it as a result for the whole of Leicestershire in the fight against serious crime. A stepping-stone closer to a safer community.

Artie Black opened the questioning, chewing on the end of his pen as Carmela promised him an interview in the *Herald* the following day. It wasn't long ago that they'd speculated over his possible involvement, and now he was interviewing the Super. Jackman thought about their dealings together: the witness he'd refused to give up early in the case, the terrorist film footage with which he'd followed protocol. He was a slippery character, one of the trickiest journalists he'd crossed paths with, but not a killer.

At the end of the conference, Carmela flashed a warm smile.

Cameras clicked as they took their leave.

"She certainly knows how to play the press," Wilson whispered in Jackman's ear as somebody flicked the screen off.

McDonald gathered his coat. "Right, who's up for the pub?"

A low-bellied roar went up around the room. She turned to Jackman. "You're not escaping this time."

ON THE ROAD back to Stratford, Jackman's mind was on the case. He couldn't argue with the witness statements, the hair fibres found in Faye's house. With no suggestion of any other suspects, everything pointed to Faye killing Grace's daughter and worming her way into her friendship afterwards. It was almost reasonable to accept that Grace, having discovered this, would feel betrayed and want to avenge her daughter's attacker. But Grace's face in that interview room… Every time the image entered into his mind, Jackman winced. He'd interviewed hundreds of people over the years, but something about her involvement in Faye's murder didn't ring true.

PART THREE

CHAPTER SIXTY-FIVE

GRACE GLANCED OUT of the window. The sun was rising. Beautiful swirls of yellow and orange peering over the rooftops, decorating London's skyline. This was the fourth cell she'd been moved to since her time in Holloway and she was grateful for the view it offered over the walls and into the world beyond. Many a time she'd stood there, watching vehicles crawl down the nearby roads, pedestrians dancing around them like little ants in the distance, dreaming about what the people of London were getting up to. Her eyes dropped to the coiled barbed wire that topped the prison walls.

Almost eight months had passed since she'd been swept through the prison gates, only to face the humiliation of being searched by the guards, and later examined, internally and externally, by a doctor. She'd been issued a bag of basics which included a bar of carbolic soap, a towel that felt more like a wire brush and a pair of starched cotton pyjamas that scratched at her skin.

It wasn't until Grace reached Holloway that she realised her story had made national news. She was surprised how many of the inmates knew who she was and were surprisingly sympathetic to her plight. Many of them were mothers themselves. Women had sauntered in and out of her cell all afternoon on that first day. Some just wanted to take a look at her, others sat on her lumpy mattress and asked questions; some even patted her on the back, showing their approval as if she was already convicted.

But there were others who took an instant dislike to her, their disapproval fuelled by her notoriety. She learned to be mindful of their watchful gazes, the warm breath on the back of her neck as she used the communal telephone to call home. But the remand wings were transitional places, people constantly coming and going, prisoners being moved cells to avoid them forming close associations, and no two days were the same.

She quickly grew accustomed to the constant jangle of keys, the clang of metal, the banging of doors. Holloway ran on a strict routine. Doors were unlocked at 8am, when they were allowed a short interval to shower and breakfast before they were expected to either head for work or the education block. No prisoner was allowed to be idle. Within days the education officer had looked at her file and placed her in the library, indexing their historical collection. A job which eventually earnt her credits towards a television in her cell, a grateful addition to pass the boredom during lockdown.

Grace moved away from the window and smoothed the dark suit Phil had sent in for her. She'd had to breathe in to fasten the trouser zip when she bought it for Meggy's christening, almost two years earlier. Today it hung off her bony frame. For the next few days she would be in limbo, held between two worlds, while the courtroom picked at the bones of her previous life, scrutinising every aspect, every relationship, as twelve people decided her fate.

The remand cells were different to the rest of the

prison. These inmates weren't convicted criminals and were offered more privileges like wearing their own clothes, receiving food parcels from home, and regular visitors. Leicestershire's close proximity to London had been a blessing, enabling Phil to hop on the train twice a week, dedicating both his days off to making the hour and a half's journey for a short visit. During his last visit he'd told her there had been an announcement in the press. The government were closing the Victorian prisons, replacing them with modern new-builds. Whatever happened, it was unlikely she'd return here. Phil's days off were always separate. The supermarket insisted on it. Which meant, if she wasn't placed close enough for him to be able to travel down and return in the same day, his visits would be restricted to monthly, or even less. The very thought filled her with horror.

She picked up a pile of letters, bound together with an elastic band, and ran her index finger over the biro scrawl. Phil. In addition to his visits, he'd written two or three times a week. Sometimes just a few lines, sometimes several pages. Everyday news about the family: what Meggy was doing, how his work was, updates about Lydia and Chloe, Ged's life in Spain, their friends, their neighbours. Sometimes they took a while to reach her and were superseded by his visit. They had to be passed through the prison censorship, especially if they were accompanied by a photograph, but she still devoured them afterwards, fixed the photos to the board next to her bed, and they became her most treasured possessions.

The last photos brushed together as she plucked them from the board. Her gaze lingered over one of Lydia, standing beside her sixteenth birthday cake, holding her thumbs up, smiling for the camera. Her hair had grown into a short bob and was tucked behind her ears.

Grace stroked the photo. On the few occasions Lydia had visited her mother in Holloway, she'd been tense and barely spoken. Her eyes bulged and her skin was sallow. Phil said she'd shut herself away, under the pretence of studying for her GCSEs. But Grace could clearly see the signs of a struggle. And no wonder. She'd lost her father, her sister and now faced the threat of losing her mother. This was around the age that Jo had displayed signs of depression and the thought of losing another daughter, especially when she couldn't be there to help her, was agonising.

Eventually Grace had written to Ged, asking her to invite Lydia to Spain for the summer, take her away from the mounting press speculation, the comments and whispers. She flew out as soon as her exams were finished, not even returning to receive the results, which Phil collected and read to her over the phone. She'd scraped through the most important ones, but, as feared, the grades weren't good.

Lydia had written, less than Phil, but an email arrived every few weeks. They were always upbeat, as if she was trying her hardest to cheer her mother up. Ged wrote occasionally too, mostly to reassure her that Lydia was eating, going out, socialising. They'd both flown home yesterday, and would be in court to support her. Apprehension and excitement at the thought of seeing them filled Grace in equal measure.

Grace placed both piles of letters into her prison-issue bag and checked her bedside cupboard one last time. She'd been told to be up early. Be packed and ready to go through the release procedure in readiness for her transportation to Leicester Crown Court. Her solicitor had told her that the next few nights would be spent in a holding cell at Peterborough Prison because it was nearer the court. The thought of going to another prison was terrifying, but she couldn't think about that. Right now she needed to be strong, truthful, confident, so that she could convince the court of her innocence.

She sat on the edge of the bed, churning over possible questions she might face. At their meeting yesterday, her solicitor, Jane Barrington, had encouraged her to write out her account of the case again, to make sure it was fresh in her mind. They discussed possible awkward questions, apparent inconsistencies within her account. Answers to those questions whirled around her head until they made no sense at all. She took a deep breath, sat tall. Calm. Keep calm.

A single bang at the door interrupted her thoughts. The sound of a key being inserted into a lock followed. The door was wrenched open to show a guard with a grim expression on his face. "Ready?"

CHAPTER SIXTY-SIX

LESS THAN THREE hours later Grace was standing in the dock, staring through the safety glass that separated her from the courtroom. The drive down from London that morning, sitting in the back of a security van with only a small side window, had felt like they were cruising over a constant line of potholes. The holding cell, beneath the courts, was cold and stark. The endless walk up the stairs, handcuffed to an officer with a train of keys strapped to her belt, had blurred into the background, overtaken by the humiliation as she entered the small room at the back of the courtroom and felt a sea of eyes rest upon her.

James Sheldon, the prosecution barrister, had completed his opening speech. The court hushed as the first officer on scene took to the witness stand and described finding Faye's body in a pool of blood when he arrived at Western Avenue on the morning of the 12th of January.

Statements were read out about hair samples showing Grace's presence in the house, her saliva on Faye's dead body. Expert witnesses on blood spatter and crime scene investigation were called and dispensed with, sometimes with undue haste. Sheldon was setting the crime scene, creating a vivid image in the minds of those present.

Grace had heard all this before, been privy to these details during the long conferences with her legal team in prison. Judge Browning had his head down and was tapping the keys of his computer. Every now and then he'd raise his head, peer over his glasses, before returning to his keyboard. Earlier she'd been surprised by the patience and generosity he'd displayed with the jury, how he'd been at pains to explain the nature of the case along with their duties, almost as if their jury service was doing him a personal favour.

She tried to get a better view of the public gallery that ran down the right-hand side of the courtroom, directly opposite the jury and separated by the barristers and the legal teams in the middle. Her family were on the back row, closest to her. In front of them were a group of strangers. She wondered what their interest was in the case. Detective Wilson sat on the front row, beside two women. As she looked on, the older of the two women gave a supportive sideways glance to the other. Her mother maybe? There was something familiar about the younger woman. Grace scrunched her eyes to focus, just as the woman looked around at the press seating behind. It was Eugenie Trentwood. The brown corkscrew curls, so similar to Jo's, were tied back. She looked small, a shadow of her former self. Grace's heart ached. She wasn't quite sure why she was there today, but her heart tore in two when she considered how much that girl had been through. And now her case seemed to have been pushed aside to make room for the events that followed.

The rise and fall of Sheldon's voice filled the courtroom. He was clearly a man who enjoyed an audience.

He paused at intervals to look at the jury. He wasn't handsome, but there was something welcoming about his manner. She could imagine him sitting around a table, hosting a dinner party, his guests chuckling at his anecdotes.

Eleanor, her defence barrister, had been conspicuous in her silence all morning. Apart from a few whispers with the junior beside her, a man with dark features who didn't look long out of law school, and her solicitor behind, no cross examination followed. The defence weren't contesting the crime scene or Grace's presence in Faye's flat because she had visited earlier that afternoon. "No point in arguing with the evidence," Eleanor had said. "Every word counts. Better to concentrate the jury's minds on the areas that matter."

By the time the home office pathologist took to the stand, her French accent echoing through the court as she answered her questions, it was late afternoon. Celeste was describing the knife wound as a "deliberate violent blow to the neck which pierced the right external carotid artery." Faye would have lost consciousness almost immediately, bled out in less than a minute.

Grace shut the words out of her mind, focused on the crest on the wall behind the judge. The court wasn't at all what she'd expected. On television dramas they were high ceilinged, wood panelling cladding the walls. This was modern, perfunctory almost, with the magnolia walls and blue carpet, but there was still an air of austerity about it.

Eleanor rose slowly, taking her time to survey the pathologist before she started her questioning. The heads of the jury turned, riveted at this new addition to their stage.

Eleanor's ginger hair was fastened securely into a hair net, just visible beneath her wig. "Can you confirm how many knife wounds Ms Campbell suffered from?" she asked.

"One."

"And what happened to the knife?"

"It was still in situ."

"Have you had any other cases of fatal knife wounds where the victim dies of one wound, the knife still in situ?"

"No, but every case is different. And every case is considered on its own merit." The pathologist returned her hard stare.

"Quite." A single glance at the jury. "Is it not possible that Ms Campbell inflicted the wound on herself?"

Celeste paused before she answered. "The angle of the wound makes it unlikely."

"Unlikely. I see." Eleanor looked towards the judge. "No further questions, Your Honour."

Grace watched her sit down and turn a page in her book. The show was over before it started. Her intention was clear: to cast some doubt over who was responsible for the death. But the manner in which the jury shifted in their seats and checked their watches showed that they weren't convinced.

Disappointment clutched at her.

She could still remember the official letter she'd received at Holloway during her third week on remand. The guard had passed it to her while they were on recreation. It of course had already been opened and checked, but he'd had the decency to fold it over, keeping the contents private from curious fellow inmates nearby. Grace had pocketed it, waited until she was safely tucked away in her cell before she opened it. As soon as her eyes skimmed the words, shock pulsed through her body. She'd been turned down for legal aid.

Grace was stunned. This was England. She'd assumed everybody was entitled to legal representation here. But the law said otherwise. A combination of their joint salaries and savings pushed them over the threshold.

They'd used the balance of their savings to pay for Grace's representation. Phil was resolved, insisting it was a short-term problem and that when she was acquitted the money would be refunded. But what would happen if she wasn't? Her family would not only have to bear the public humiliation, but also the financial impact.

CHAPTER SIXTY-SEVEN

IT WAS WITH increasing trepidation that Grace entered the dock after lunch on the second day. It was a strange experience, sitting behind that glass screen, on show like a prize exhibit in a zoo. People glared, pointed at times, scrutinised her every move and yet she wasn't permitted to respond. Not yet.

She turned away, stifled a yawn. The remand wing at Peterborough was noisier than she had been accustomed to at Holloway. Prisoners shouted, thumped the metal doors to attract attention, called out to each other. It made for a turbulent night and, as she lay on her thin mattress, the bony hand of loneliness rested on her shoulder. These were holding cells, kept aside especially for short term visitors, prisoners attending court. Her letters and photographs had been taken, locked away in the prison property store, and without them she was bereft.

Sheldon had completed the forensics before they'd adjourned and a stream of witnesses would now move through the witness stand. Everyone rose for the judge to enter. His wig was slightly lopsided, as if he'd put it on in a hurry, but he seemed oblivious as he took his position at the front of the room.

The sound of a walking stick creaking with every step hushed the courtroom. Heads turned towards the entrance, fixed faces filling Grace with a renewed sense of fear. The woman that appeared walked slowly, resting her free arm on an usher who guided her to the witness stand. Her scalp was visible through thinning hair and her hands shook, but something about her countenance was hard, resolved. She read her oath clearly and loudly. She'd been there before.

"Would you please confirm your name for the court?" Sheldon asked.

"Meredith Elizabeth Atkinson."

"Could you tell us your connection to the deceased, Faye Campbell?"

"I was the social worker, assigned to her case when her mother died."

Grace sat forward.

"How old was Faye Campbell when she was taken into care?"

"Four years old."

"And can you explain to the court the circumstances around her parents' death?"

"Her mother died of a heroin overdose. As far as I'm aware, she never knew her father."

A paper rustled in the public gallery.

"I see you have made a statement to the police. Why is there no public record of your responsibility in this case?"

"The offices I worked at on Welford Road, Leicester, had a fire in October 1992. We were just in the process of transferring paper records to computer. Faye's records were destroyed, along with lots of others at that time."

"So, it would it be fair to say you took over Faye's case about thirty-six years ago?"

"Yes. About that."

"Did you have a big caseload?"

She nodded. "Reasonable for the time."

"And may I ask, Ms Atkinson, do you remember intimate details of other cases?"

"Not all of them, no. But Faye's case was remarkable."

"In what respect?"

"She was passed through four foster homes in the first three years she was under my remit. Nobody could cope with her."

"And why was that?"

"She lied, ran away, seemed to delight in upsetting people."

"Upsetting people. Can you elaborate on that?"

"I distinctly remember one family reporting she'd drowned their own child's hamster. They said that she'd dropped it into an aquarium and watched as it struggled for its life. Faye must have been around five at the time. Even from a young age, she didn't express any remorse."

Grace gripped the rail in front and fought to keep her face impassive.

"What happened to Faye?" Sheldon continued.

"She was later diagnosed with conduct disorder. Spent some time in a children's home where she was offered therapy. When she was sixteen she became responsible for her own care."

Sheldon looked down at his notes. "Can you give the court an account of what happened during the summer of 1987?"

"The children's home where she was living was being renovated. We had to place all the children in alternative care until the house was finished. I arranged for her to be placed with a family, just a short-term measure, although it turned out to be much shorter than I'd anticipated."

"Was that a wise decision, considering her history?"

"Her mental state was assessed. She appeared to be responding to the therapy."

Grace tensed as Meredith went on to describe the time Faye spent with Grace's family when she was young. She looked across at Lydia. The stretch of neck visible between Lydia's hairline and her collar turned red and blotchy as the social worker's account progressed. Through conferences with her legal team, Grace had discovered Faye's early association with her family, her infatuation with Jamie, how she had stolen things, tried to set fire to his room. She'd had no idea at the time and, bizarrely, Jamie had never mentioned it. But now, she'd had time to process it, adjust. She'd written to Lydia, tried to relay the details and remove the shock of the revelation in court. But Jamie was Lydia's father. And hearing the sordid details in an open courtroom made them all the more real.

Sheldon explained to the jury how Jamie Lamborne was Grace's first husband. At that moment Meredith looked directly at Grace, the first time since she'd entered the courtroom. Her face was devoid of emotion, but there was something in her eyes. Some kind of compassion there.

This was a woman who'd been close to Faye in her

younger years, watched her grow up, develop into the monster she became.

Eleanor stood briefly. "No questions, Your Honour."

Faye's background wasn't an issue, but it still left Grace uncomfortable.

She'd been told the courtroom wasn't about emotions, it was about fact. Proving the truth. But they were wrong. It was a game. And Sheldon had taken an early lead.

CHAPTER SIXTY-EIGHT

JACKMAN LOWERED HIS statement and scanned the courtroom. His eyes briefly met Wilson's in the public
gallery, washed over Grace's family, resting on the defendant sat in the dock at the rear. It had been almost
eight months since he'd left Leicestershire, numerous
Warwickshire files taking his attention in the interim,
yet Grace Daniels' case had wriggled its way back into
his mind during quiet moments. For some reason, he
couldn't let it lie. The expression on her face that day
in the interview room still bothered him and the more
he thought about it, the more he was convinced she
hadn't known it was Faye that killed her daughter until
he'd told her. If it had been a Warwickshire case he'd
have trudged down to the exhibits store to take another look, gone over the evidence again as the file was
put together for the Crown Prosecution Service. But it
wasn't a home fixture and Carmela had made it quite
clear that his work at the Leicestershire Serious Crime
Unit was finished.

He raised his gaze to meet the prosecution barrister,
answered the inevitable questions about what action was
taken and why during the early stages of the investigation. Court didn't make Jackman nervous. He'd attended
enough hearings over the years to watch out for the
snide little questions the barristers snuck in, and took

his time to respond, giving measured answers backed up by the evidence gathered. Even the most ruthless killer was entitled to legal representation.

The barrister paused to look down at his notes and Jackman glanced at the public gallery. Dee Wilson had kept him updated as the trial approached, but the scarcity of her texts made it obvious that she'd been moved elsewhere too. As far as Leicestershire were concerned, this case was closed.

"Thank you, Inspector. May I draw your attention to the statement from a Detective Constable Parsons in which she states that Grace was given an informal warning about her conduct in Jo Lamborne's case." Jackman was handed a copy of the statement, despite being already quite familiar with the contents. "Can you tell me more about that?"

"We interviewed a friend of Jo Lamborne's from Nottingham, an Anthony Kendall, in the early stages of the investigation and eliminated him from our enquiries," Jackman said. "Grace and Faye also went to visit him and he later complained of harassment."

"May I ask what gave Mr Kendall cause for complaint?"

"He said they were asking lots of searching questions about Jo. He felt he was being treated like a suspect."

"So they were carrying out their own little investigation?"

"I couldn't say. I'm just aware that they visited him, and of what he said."

"And what made you aware of their visit?"

"He made an informal complaint."

"Informal?"

"He acknowledged that Mrs Daniels was going through a difficult time, didn't want to take any formal action. Just asked that he be left alone to grieve."

"And how was this informal complaint dealt with?"

"I instructed the family liaison officer, DC Parsons, to have a quiet word with the family."

Sheldon paused. "Is this a normal course of action in such a case?"

Jackman knew Sheldon was telling a story, building up to his crescendo. Motive was his biggest ally right now and he wanted to show how the women had become close enough to share confidences, support each other.

"Grace had recently lost her daughter so I would say that yes, it seemed the most appropriate course of action under the circumstances."

"Have there been any further complaints made about either of these two women?"

"Not Grace, no." Jackman proceeded to explain the historic complaints of harassment the police had received about Faye.

"Thank you. I'm showing Inspector exhibits BRO125A and 130A. Can you please explain to the court what the items are in this box?"

Jackman tensed as the television screens on each side of the courtroom mirrored each other, showing pictures of the evidence they'd found in the box beneath the floorboards of Faye's bedroom. He could see Grace's youngest daughter's flushed face in the public gallery and shifted uncomfortably. This evidence had been discussed at the coroner's hearing, when it was established that Faye was in fact responsible for Jo's death, but seeing it displayed here in open court was clearly shattering for the family. Sheldon was pushing the point. By the time they'd worked through the exercise book with the array of photos of both Eugenie and Jo, taken from a variety of angles, a stony silence filled the room.

He went on to explain how a small spot of blood on the earring found at the scene matched with Faye's DNA, how her phone showed an association with Jo.

"Thank you. It is a matter of public record, is it not Inspector Jackman, that on the 19th of May 2016 Leicester City Coroner's Court determined that Jo Lamborne had been unlawfully killed by Faye Campbell?"

"That's correct, yes."

"Did you ever interview Faye in the course of the murder investigation?"

"No."

"Did you ever meet Faye Campbell?"

"She was at Grace's house when I visited once. We were briefly introduced."

"And when was this?"

"Tuesday the 29th of December."

"And how did Grace introduce Faye to you on that day?"

"Grace referred to Faye as a close family friend."

"A close family friend that sought out her daughter, murdered her in cold blood." Sheldon paused a moment. "Did Grace ever make you aware of any concerns about Faye, that their relationship had changed perhaps?"

GRACE LISTENED AS Sheldon moved on to explore her complaint about the injuries to Lucky, the phone calls, but the words petered into the distance. There was a shift in the atmosphere. The jurors turned to Grace, some with pity on their face, others with sadness. They were seeing her as a girl, mother, wife. Someone like them who'd been wronged in the worst possible manner. Their faces relaxed, their minds posing the question: What would they do in those circumstances?

At that moment, Grace broke all the rules. 'Don't react, don't engage, don't show emotion.' All the advice she'd been given fell foul as she closed her eyes, dropped her head and blocked out the courtroom. Sheldon had just presented evidence that gave her the strongest possible motive for murder.

AFTER LUNCH IT was time for the cross-examination. "I understand that forensics examined the knife that killed Faye Campbell?" Eleanor asked Jackman.

"Yes."

"And on behalf of the police, can you tell me how many sets of fingerprints they found on that knife?"

"One," Jackman replied.

"You are absolutely sure?"

"Yes."

"Can you tell the court who those fingerprints belonged to?"

"Faye Campbell."

Grace sighed inwardly. They'd already established the knife had been removed from Faye's own collection that were situated in a knife block on the kitchen side. Of course her prints would have been present. And wouldn't the killer have worn gloves? The frustration was beginning to eat away at her.

"I understand your enquiries into Faye identified a

number of previous allegations where, as a consequence of her actions, several complaints were made about her behaviour?"

"That's correct."

"Would you say you've had extensive dealings with Grace during the course of this enquiry?"

"I would."

"And has her behaviour to yourself or your fellow officers ever been aggressive or violent?"

"No, never. Grace was always polite, courteous and pleasant to deal with. We have no previous record of any dealings with her in the past either."

"Did she ever express vengeful intent towards her daughter's killer?"

"Not that I'm aware of."

"Thank you. We've heard how a complaint was made about her by Mr Anthony Kendall. Did he make any allegations about violent, aggressive or threatening behaviour?"

"Not at all. He was merely concerned that he'd been asked uncomfortable questions."

Eleanor let his answer hang in the air a moment. "Inspector, may I ask why you were brought to Leicestershire?"

"I was brought in as a regional lead on adult sexual offences, tasked with reviewing old cases and looking at working practises with a view to streamlining them."

"A lead? So you have some expertise in this area?"

"I've worked homicide and major crime for almost eighteen years. I suppose that gives me some level of expertise."

"May I ask, how many fatal knife injuries have you attended over the course of your career?"

He paused for a moment. "I couldn't say exactly."

"An estimation then? Would you say it's more than twenty?"

"Yes, I'd estimate that."

"Thank you. Was there anything about this particular injury that struck you as different from the others?"

Sheldon rose. "Objection. Your Honour, the method of killing isn't in question here."

The judge gave Sheldon a hard stare. "Overruled. The witness is a highly experienced officer. His experience on this point is relevant for the court."

Jackman knew exactly where this was leading. "There was only one wound," he said, "the knife was still in situ. Most stabbing victims have a number of wounds."

"Was this not questioned?"

"It was. And we relied upon the expertise of our pathologist."

CHAPTER SIXTY-NINE

By DAY FOUR, the lack of sleep was starting to take its toll. The night before, a new prisoner had spent almost half the night intermittently banging the door of her cell, demanding to see the governor. Grace's head had ached from the minute she'd landed in the courtroom, only to find that the trial had been delayed, the first hour taken up with a legal argument. During these moments the court was emptied, leaving only the legal teams, the clerk and the judge present. Jane Barrington later advised her that the discussions were to do with the admissibility of evidence regarding the knife wound, but the extra hour in her cell did nothing to calm her frayed nerves.

By the time they were all back and ready to begin, it was almost midday.

Sheldon lingered over Barnes' credentials as he introduced himself and shared them with the courtroom. He was making a point that he was a highly decorated and respected expert in his field of criminal profiling, with a special interest in personality disorders, and the court couldn't have failed to note the significance.

"I understand you have studied Faye Campbell's medical records, the statements in the case?" Sheldon said. "What did you deduce?"

"A pattern of behaviour indicating that Faye Campbell was a high functioning sociopath. Considering her background and the police intelligence, my theory is that she met Jo, made the connection with Grace's family, decided to seek her out, befriend her and subsequently harm her."

"Why murder her daughter?"

"Grief makes people vulnerable. They are much easier to manipulate when they are vulnerable."

"In your experience, what would be the expected reaction of a rational person, somebody like Grace for instance, when they discovered a close friend killed their daughter?"

"Anger. Frustration. Naturally she'd feel betrayed."

"Enough to motivate her to kill?"

"In the right circumstances, possibly enough to motivate anyone to kill."

"No further questions, Your Honour."

ELEANOR WAITED FOR the shuffles of the court to settle before she opened her line of questioning.

"Mr Barnes, did you meet Ms Campbell?"

"Not in person, no."

"But you've examined the statements in the case, her medical records?"

"Yes."

"And you've examined the circumstances of the case, are familiar with how she died?"

"Yes."

"Is it possible, therefore, that she could have inflicted the wound on herself?"

"Cases of suicide by stabbing are incredibly rare," Barnes said. "The person would need to be strong, not only physically but also mentally to carry out something like that."

"Thank you. You wrote a profile for Operation Ascott and Jo Lamborne's murderer, did you not, in November of last year?"

"I did."

"In your profile, you clearly suggested that Jo Lamborne's offender was male. Directed police to look for men that fit into certain categories. Why is that?"

"The sexual motive in the case, the way that the women were attacked, suggested a male offender. But people with Faye's condition usually have an exceptionally high IQ. She was single-minded, meticulous in her planning and this was the perfect foil to send the police in a different direction. We now know she'd read about the Oliver Turner case, copied the details as much as possible. Eugenie Trentwood was her practise run, before the main event."

"Objection, Your Honour," Sheldon stood as he spoke. "Faye Campbell is not on trial here."

"Sustained." The judge turned to Eleanor. "Keep to the current case, please."

"Of course, Your Honour." She turned back to the witness. "Mr Barnes, in your report you described Faye Campbell as single-minded, somebody who would perhaps stop at nothing to achieve her goals. In your opinion, would she be capable of killing herself in this manner?"

"I can only speak for her mental state. Her personality disorder makes her extraordinary in that respect. She was ruthless. And if her goal was to make Grace suffer, put her behind bars, away from the family she lived for, then it's possible that she may have been psychologically capable of that."

"No further questions, Your Honour."

THE AFTERNOON OPENED with renewed vigour. Sheldon read out the statement made by the woman who'd helped Grace in the park when Lucky was injured. It was short, to the point. She mentioned how she'd remarked on what sort of person would injure a dog in that manner, and Grace's response, 'They don't deserve to live.' Grace blanched. It was a passing comment, fuelled by anger.

Sheldon followed with the introduction of another witness to the stand. Grace squinted as a young woman in tight denims strolled into the courtroom. She didn't recognise her.

"For the purposes of the court," Sheldon gestured towards the jury, as if only he and they were present. "Can you identify yourself?"

"My name is Rose Hunter. I live in the flat next door to Faye Campbell's."

"Thank you. And how long have you been Ms Campbell's neighbour?"

"Almost two and a half years."

"How would you describe your relationship?"

"Faye kept herself to herself. I saw her on the balcony a few times, we nodded, said hello."

"Had you ever been in her flat?"

"No."

"Could you explain to the court what you saw on the evening of the 11th of January."

"I was watching the end of the news in my front room, just thinking about going to bed when a figure walked past. She turned and looked in. Gave me quite a fright to be honest." She turned to the judge briefly. "I don't tend to draw my curtains because we are on the first floor, and overlook the park.

"I heard the knocker on Faye's door immediately afterwards and closed my curtains, in case her visitor made the same route back. A few minutes later there were raised voices. I couldn't make out the words but somebody was clearly agitated. Then it all went quiet. The front door banged shut soon afterwards."

"Could you tell if those arguing were male or female by their voices?"

"It sounded like they were both female."

"What time did the figure walk past your window?"

"The news was just finishing, so I guess it was around 10.30pm."

"And what time did they leave."

"Around ten minutes later."

"Around?"

"I didn't look at the clock. But enough time for me to go into the bedroom and get changed for bed."

"Did you see or hear anyone else visit the flat that evening, or earlier perhaps?"

"No. I was out shopping in the daytime though. I returned home just after 6pm."

"One final question, if I may? Did you undertake the police formal identification process in order to pick out the person you saw attending Faye's flat that night?"

"I did."

"Thank you. My learned friend may have some questions for you now." Sheldon looked pleased as he excused himself and sat.

It was a moment before Eleanor rose. "Miss Hunter," she finally said. "Can you explain the layout of your flats?"

"Yes. We are a row above a bank of shops on Western Avenue."

"And the access points?"

"There are two stone staircases, one at either end."

"Two? So, if somebody had approached Faye Campbell's flat from the staircase at the opposite side to your flat, they wouldn't have to pass your window?"

The witness shifted position. "No. But I only heard one knock, followed by raised voices. And they were female voices."

"If you could just answer the questions you are asked, thank you. So, it's conceivable the person you thought was Grace could have walked past the entrance to Faye's flat and down the other staircase, and somebody else knocked and entered?"

"No, I heard her voice."

"Did you actually see the women arguing?"

"No."

"Have you heard the defendant speak before?"

"No."

"Then how do you know whose voice you heard?"

The witness cleared her throat.

"Had you ever met Grace Daniels before you saw her that evening?"

"No, never."

"You'd never seen her before?"

A head shake. The judge leant forward. "Could you voice your answer for the court, please?"

"No."

"Thank you. Can I draw the witness's attention to Exhibit BRO138A, a newspaper article written about Grace losing her daughter, featuring a family photograph. According to the *Leicester Herald*, this article received over 42,000 hits online, was printed in their weekly newspaper and circulated to around 10,000 homes. Are you telling me that you didn't see it?"

The court clerk passed the article to the witness. She gave a fleeting glance. "No."

"I put it to you that the person you saw that evening wasn't in fact the defendant. That you saw someone who fitted Grace's description, had seen the photo in the newspaper and thought it was her."

Grace's cheeks burned as Rose Hunter's eyes bore into her. "It was her. I'm sure of it."

AFTER THE WITNESS was released, Detective Jackman was called back to the dock and asked to read a transcript of Grace's police interview. Grace sat uncomfortably as the interview was read verbatim, the detective reading his parts and Sheldon, hers. It was Friday afternoon. The jury were waning. The questions and answers were wooden. This was the interview that led to Grace's charge and Sheldon clearly wanted to leave them with a powerful message for the weekend.

As soon as they finished the judge checked his watch. It was 3.10pm. He told the jury they were free to go until Monday morning when they would resume. Reminded them that they should discuss the case with no one.

Grace watched their faces relax. It had been a heavy week. They were ready to go home and rest into the cushions on their sofas. Maybe they'd watch television tonight, moan at the adverts between the programmes, or maybe their partner would cook them a meal and they'd share a bottle of wine. She watched them longingly as they filed out of the court.

CHAPTER SEVENTY

"ALL RISE FOR the judge."

Grace stood and watched as Judge Browning entered the court with the weariness of a Monday morning. Without looking up, he thanked everyone, sat and opened his laptop while they settled into their seats. His face was slightly tanned and Grace wondered what sort of weekend he'd had. Perhaps he'd been to a garden party, or had a round of golf.

It had been a long, hot August. Grace could only imagine the array of colours decorating the gardens across the country. The cold brick buildings of Holloway were surrounded by concrete recreational areas, covered in wire mesh to stop prisoners throwing packages to those below, the view out of her cell window providing her only fix of greenery. At Peterborough, her window faced a brick wall.

Back in prison, the suspicious stares and whispers on Saturday followed Grace. There was none of the camaraderie of Holloway, none of the kindness of women. She ignored the wary glances, sat alone for dinner, spent recreation time in her cell. It was almost a relief when a disturbance on the remand wing put them in lockdown on Sunday. The heat levels were suffocating in the enclosed area and without her possessions, no books or magazines to read, the boredom had given way to anxiety. The case rolled around in her head. More than anything, she wanted it over, decided. Some sort of end to this hell.

It seemed to take forever for the court to proceed that morning. Eleanor was consulting her junior and the whispers between them were starting to grate. This wasn't a tennis match, where the coach discussed the tactics with his team while the match was ongoing. This was her life, and the fact that she wasn't party to their little discussions galled Grace. Eleanor had come on high recommendation. Phil said they needed an experienced barrister, someone with a track record of results in serious crime cases. Eleanor was a senior barrister, her solicitor referred to her as Queen's Counsel, and she came with a hefty price tag. A price tag that was slowly draining them as the days went by. Grace sincerely hoped she was up to the job.

The defence opened with a string of character witnesses.

Julia Declan, Grace's manager from the library, stood at the witness stand in her best olive suit and crisp white open-collared shirt, and talked about Grace's diligence and reliability during their fourteen year working relationship. Grace's eyes brimmed as she recalled ignoring her calls, deleting her messages after Jo had died. Julia answered the questions confidently. Eleanor was attempting to strengthen the ropes of her case through Grace's support network, to show that Grace had a comfortable life, was a good mother, surrounded by people that cared about her, in order to discredit the notion that she would jeopardise it all by killing Faye, and Julia was a good witness.

"Mrs Declan, can you tell the court the date Grace last came into work?" Sheldon said as he began his cross-examination.

"It was Wednesday the 28th of October. The day before…" She hesitated a moment. "The day before her daughter, Jo, died."

"And was that her last shift that week?"

"She works part time. Monday, Wednesday and Friday. But obviously she couldn't work the Friday that week."

"Obviously," he said, letting the word hover in the air. "And when did she return to work after that date?"

"She didn't. She was on compassionate leave, followed by sick leave."

He cast a glance at the jury before he turned back to the witness. "So she didn't return to work?"

"Not as such. But we kept in contact. I phoned her weekly to see how she was." She looked towards the judge imploringly. "We were all very much looking forward to her coming back to work. She was a popular member of the team."

The judge gave a gentle smile.

"When was the last time you actually spoke to Grace?"

"The week before Christmas."

"December, not January? I thought you called her weekly?"

"Grace's doctor's certificates stated that she was suffering from anxiety and depression. It was felt…" She coughed. "I felt that she needed some time. I didn't want to pressure her."

"I see. Did you meet up with Grace at all, visit her after her daughter died?"

"I didn't visit. The family were in mourning. It didn't seem appropriate at the time." Another glance at the judge, almost for reassurance. "But I did see her at the memorial service."

"And when was that?"

"Two weeks before Christmas."

"And how did Grace seem that day?"

"As well as can be expected. It was her daughter's memorial service. She was grateful for people coming, thanked me on the way out."

"Did you speak to her?"

"Only to offer my condolences. It was busy."

Sheldon gave a brisk nod and looked at the judge. "I've nothing further, Your Honour."

BERYL KNIGHTON WAS next up. Warmth filled Grace's chest as she watched her friend and neighbour take her oath. They'd moved into Arden Way within months of each other. Beryl was older than she, her own family grown up, and she'd babysat Grace's girls in their early years. Even last year the two couples shared BBQs together. Grace noticed her freshly washed hair, the smart shift dress she'd bought for her cousin's wedding a year earlier, no inkling of the gardening clothes she normally wore, and listened as she talked about Grace's reliability, kindness, grounded personality, how she'd supported Beryl following the death of her mother last year.

By the time Sheldon stood to cross-examine, Beryl had restored some of Grace's belief in the kindness of humanity. She promised herself that if she got out of there, she would make more time for her friends, cherish them.

"Mrs Knighton, would you remind the court how long you have known the defendant?" Sheldon asked.

"Almost twenty years."

"Right. And would I be right in thinking you have a close friendship with her?"

"Yes, I'd like to think so."

"Thank you. May I ask when you last saw the defendant?"

Beryl blinked. "The day she was arrested. I saw her in the driveway as she was led to the police car."

"I mean to speak to. You've said you were close friends, you spent time together."

"I think it would be at Jo's memorial service last December."

"You think? Can you be sure?"

Beryl blushed. "Yes, I'm sure of it."

"And what did you talk about?"

"I offered my help with the family. I used to babysit the girls when they were younger."

"Thank you. And before that?"

"I'm not sure exactly."

"Not sure. I see. And, may I ask, how many times in the normal course of a week, would you say you saw the defendant?"

"It depended on the time of year. If it was summer, we'd see each other out in the garden almost daily, chat over the fence. In the winter less often, maybe just passing on the driveway. We went to a book club once a month together in Great Bowden."

"Okay. And how often did you see the defendant after her daughter died?"

Quiet fell upon the court. It was a moment before she spoke. "Once or twice."

"Once or twice? This was a good friend of yours, was it not? By your own admission you shared confidences, supported each other. You'd spent time together, yet you only saw her once or twice?"

"I called around several times, phoned her."

"But Grace didn't wish to see you."

"Grace withdrew after Jo died. From everybody. She was grieving."

"So, for the two months leading up to her arrest, it's fair to say you barely saw or heard from her?"

The witness opened her mouth and closed it again.

The judge leant forward. "Could you answer the question, please?" he said to Beryl.

She glanced at Grace, her face full of sorrow. "Yes, that's fair. But she knew I was there if she needed me."

Grace cowered inwardly as Beryl left the witness box. She'd closed her doors when Jo died, shut the world out, pushed her friends aside. The only person she'd allowed in, invested her time with, was Faye.

CHAPTER SEVENTY-ONE

AFTER BERYL'S QUESTIONING, the judge adjourned for lunch. Grace sat in her cell and imagined him in his chambers, enjoying a light salad, perhaps a glass of spring water or a green tea. He looked like the type of person who would drink green tea. The jury would slope off to the canteen, sampling food chosen off a menu, cooked by chefs, chatting with each other about their weekends. Back in her cell, Grace's lunch was brought in by a security guard on a plastic tray. She poked the omelette around the plate, counting down the minutes until she heard the familiar jangling of keys outside her door. Court was characterised by late starts, long lunches and early finishes. The practical side of Grace understood why. The jury not only had to travel in from far and wide, but proceedings in the courtroom were draining. Every piece of evidence had to be examined, every comment scrutinised. They needed time to process the information. But for Grace, every minute, every second that passed was torture.

Grace was finally led back up to the dock and waited as Eleanor called her next witness to the stand.

The court lighting glinted off the bald head of the short stocky man who made his way down to the witness stand with a slight limp.

"Doctor Reid, can you identify yourself for the

court?" Eleanor asked, after formalities were completed.

"Doctor Jacob Reid. Senior pathologist at the Royal Free, London, based at Barnet."

"Thank you. I understand you specialise in knife wounds?"

"I've examined hundreds of cases of victims who've suffered knife wounds, and written papers on the most regular and dangerous areas for major medical journals. The dissertation paper for my doctorate concentrated on this area."

The judge sat forward. "Ms Talbot-Deane. Has this line of questioning been agreed with the prosecution?"

"It has, Your Honour."

He sat back, steepled his fingers as Eleanor continued. "I understand you've examined the forensic material available in this case?"

"I have."

"Can you tell us, in your expert opinion, what are your findings?"

"Most people that are attacked with a knife, even if they don't die, have multiple wounds. Panic sets in. The killer goes into a frenzy, keeps going even after the victim is dead, afraid they might rise up and try to defend themselves. Here, the deceased has one stab wound and the knife wasn't removed."

"Thank you. So, in your opinion, it was unusual to have one wound?"

"Yes. I've only had four cases in my entire career where the victims have died from a single knife wound. And none of these were murders."

"We've heard from the pathologist that the direction

of the wound would make it difficult for the deceased to stab herself. What do you make of that?"

"Difficult, but not impossible if she was minded to kill herself and knew where the main arteries lay."

"Would such knowledge be freely available?"

"It wouldn't be difficult to research where the main arteries are positioned. Hit them and you bleed out quick. A search on the internet would provide that information. The difficulty lies in whether she'd have the mental and physical strength to carry out such an act."

"Have you ever considered a case where the victim has stabbed themself in this manner?"

"I have. Four months ago a man in Chiswick died of a single stab wound to the neck. He had a history of mental illness and the circumstances around his death gave no suspicion that any other party was involved."

"And the knife was lodged, not removed, in the same manner?"

"It was."

"Was there a coroner's finding in this case?"

"Yes. The coroner reached a decision of suicide."

"This is inconsistent with the police pathologist's report in Faye Campbell's case."

"It is."

"Can you reconcile this inconsistency?"

"Merely that I have more experience of knife wounds."

Eleanor bowed to the judge. "No further questions, Your Honour."

Sheldon moved his robe back and rested his fist on his hip as he stood. "Doctor Reid, you've given us an account of a similar case of death by a single stab wound to the neck."

The pathologist pushed his glasses up his nose. "Yes."

"Of all of the substantial cases of fatal stabbings you have considered nonetheless, it is right, isn't it, that instances of self-stabbing are very rare?"

"It is."

"Thank you. May I ask you to remind the court, if you would, if the victim in the second case was male or female?"

"Male."

"You clearly stated earlier for the court that a victim of a suicide in such a manner would have to be strong, both mentally and physically, to carry out such a crime."

"Yes."

"As prosecution counsel, I've also seen the papers on this other victim. Wasn't it the case that he was over 6ft tall and 18 stone, a former boxer I believe?"

"Yes, but—"

"Thank you, Doctor. No further questions, Your Honour."

Grace watched as Eleanor dispensed with her prized witness. When her solicitor had said they were bringing in an expert on knife wounds, she'd been impressed with Eleanor's sharp efficiency. This was her trump card. But once again, Sheldon shot them down in flames.

LATER THAT AFTERNOON, Grace heard the key turn in the lock of her holding cell. Before adjournment, another expert witness had taken to the stand, this time a Doctor of Psychology who confirmed Faye's personality disorder, said she was obsessive, vindictive, remorse-less in pursuit of her goal, even if it meant killing her-self. Once again, Sheldon had argued against his theory based on her physical strength.

Grace stood, preparing to be taken back to Peterbor-ough for the night, and was surprised to find Eleanor Talbot-Deane and Jane Barrington enter. They looked oddly out of place in the small area with their dark suits and coiffured hair.

Eleanor's wig and gown were absent, showing a pe-tite frame with ginger hair smoothed back from her face. She wasn't concerned about the prosecution's questions to her expert witnesses. It was all about plant-ing the element of doubt, she said. Moreover she was keen to check that Grace was ready to take the witness stand in the morning, prepared for examination. She had none of Sheldon's warmth and despite being on her side, her confidence was intimidating. Even Jane Barrington, who wasn't usually stuck for words, was conspicuous in her silence.

"My counterpart, Mr Sheldon, will provoke you," she said. "The prosecution's case is based around you having a temper and losing it, so don't. Be prepared for leading questions. Make sure you direct the answers to the jury and don't let him wear you down. As long as you stick to the facts and keep emotions out of it, you'll be fine." She gave a smile as she left, the first touch of warmth Grace had seen since the trial began, and the rarity of it made it feel all the more comforting.

CHAPTER SEVENTY-TWO

IT WAS A Tuesday morning when Grace took the long walk to the witness stand. After almost a week in the dock, she should have been used to the heat of eyes poring over her, but today their gaze was different. More intense. Scrutinising her every move. She read out the oath, desperately trying to ignore the croak that splintered her voice.

Eleanor stood and confirmed Grace's name, address and date of birth before kicking off with some basic questions. Grace felt herself relax slightly.

"So, it's fair to say you've lived in Market Harborough all of your life?" Eleanor continued.

"Yes."

Eleanor took her through the loss of Jo, how it made her feel and how her life had changed. "It's a matter of agreement that your daughter, Jo, was murdered at the hands of Faye Campbell," Eleanor said as she finished. "When did you discover this fact?"

"The police told me when I was interviewed on the 13th of January."

"Not before?"

"No. I had no idea."

"Grace, can you explain to the court the circumstances in which you first met Faye Campbell?"

Grace slowly relayed the details of their meeting

in the supermarket, the incident at the shopping centre, the coffee she shared with Chloe and Meggy that sparked off a friendship culminating in a series of visits to Grace's home.

The words dripped out of her mouth, almost of their own volition, as she talked about their ensuing friendship. Faye became her rock of support after losing Jo, somebody she could talk to without the fear of upsetting them, someone she could confide in. Grace felt the desperate need for the court to understand, to comprehend the spell that beset her to unknowingly befriend the woman that killed her daughter.

Eleanor didn't interrupt, allowing Grace's words to fill the courtroom, the only other sound the soft tapping of the court clerk's keys on her keyboard as she made her notes. As her words eventually dried up, Grace became aware of a tear rolling down her cheek. She swiped it away.

"Thank you," Eleanor said gently. "I realise this must be hard for you." A slight pause. "Did you ever visit Faye's home during your friendship?"

"No. Never. She told me her father had died recently. She said she was living in his bungalow on Fairfax Road while renovating it. There was a lot of work to do. It wasn't a good time to visit, but she did say I would be invited round when she'd finished."

"The court has heard that Faye also lived with your family for a short while in 1987. Can you tell us any more about that?"

"I'm afraid not. I don't remember."

"Not at all?"

"I was only nine years old. My parents fostered a

lot of children. There were always people coming and going."

"Interesting. How did Faye introduce herself when you first met?"

"As an old friend."

"And you accepted that?"

"I looked her up on Facebook." Grace felt her cheeks redden. "Her page said she'd attended Welland Park School, so I assumed she must have been a school friend that I didn't remember. It was a long time ago."

"Did you know of Faye's infatuation with your next door neighbour, the man who later became your husband?"

Grace shook her head. "No, I didn't know about that."

"Did Faye ever stay with your family in Arden Way?"

Grace explained about Faye's broken boiler after Christmas, how she'd slept on their sofa until Phil's heart attack, the strange circumstances that occurred after she'd left, culminating in the attack on Lucky. Even now, the words she'd rehearsed on numerous occasions over the past months seemed foreign.

"Let's talk about Monday the 11th of January. The day Faye Campbell died. Can you give the court an account of your movements that day?"

Grace explained how she'd woken early, as usual, done some housework, prepared Phil's breakfast. Later she moved on to her walk with Lucky in the park and was just relaying her conversation with the man she'd met that knew Faye when the judge cut in.

"Has this man given a statement to the police, Ms Talbot-Deane?"

"Yes, Your Honour. My learned friend, Mr Sheldon, is in receipt of his statement. He lived in Western Avenue for over twenty-three years, used the laundrette beneath Faye Campbell's home. Was a distant acquaintance until he moved a couple of years ago."

The judge clicked a few more buttons on his laptop until he found what he was looking for, nodded and eased back into his chair. Grace waited until Eleanor prompted her to continue and went on to describe her visit to Fairfax Road, and later to Western Avenue. By the time she'd finished she felt like a wilted balloon.

"Thank you," Eleanor said. "What time did you visit Faye's home in Western Avenue that day?"

"It was around one o'clock when I arrived."

"And how long did you stay?"

"Only a few minutes." Grace explained the ensuing argument, Faye's reaction, how she'd driven home in shock.

"What time did you arrive home?" Eleanor asked.

"About one-twenty."

"Did you go out again later that day?"

"No."

"Thank you. No further questions, Your Honour."

"Mrs Daniels, are you in the habit of making friends with somebody you've met once in a supermarket?" Sheldon was leaning his elbow on his lectern as if he had all the time in the world. His questions since he'd taken over cross-examination had been mild. He'd checked her movements, the facts. His tone was easy, almost friendly.

"She said she was an old friend."

Sheldon looked down at his notes. "An old school friend you said you don't remember?"

"That's right. But she seemed genuine. It was a difficult time."

"Of course. The court has heard that Faye Campbell murdered your daughter, Jo Lamborne, last October." He enunciated every syllable, paused after each word. He wanted the jury to know this was significant. "When did you find out that she was responsible for Jo's death?"

"As I said earlier, when I was interviewed by the police."

"Oh, come now, Mrs Daniels. You've already told the court about the change in your relationship with Faye Campbell, how you believe she injured your dog. You even shared your argument with us that you had with Faye when you visited her on the day she died."

The air in the courtroom thickened. Tiny spikes prickled the back of Grace's neck.

Sheldon stood tall, but didn't adjust his tone as the questions grew more hostile. There was no reason to raise his voice. He wanted the jury to empathise with Grace, to understand why she would plan the murder of her daughter's killer. Because that made her guilt the more likely option.

"I put it to you that you argued with Faye that afternoon and you discovered something, the truth about your daughter's death."

Grace's throat constricted. The courtroom blurred in front of her.

"Would you like a glass of water?" the judge asked Grace.

The kindness of his words induced the rush of tears

that she'd kept so deftly at bay. Grace cleared her throat, shook her head. "No, thank you."

Sheldon gave her a moment before he continued. "It played on your mind as it would any mother. Perhaps she revealed something, a secret that only you and Jo would know. You couldn't let it lie."

"No."

"You went back that evening to have it out with Faye, lost your temper and stabbed her in cold blood."

Grace shook her head, tears rolling down her cheeks now. "I was at home."

"Mrs Daniels, we have a witness that places you in the location, hair samples that showed your presence in the flat. You had means, motive and opportunity."

"I didn't do it."

CHAPTER SEVENTY-THREE

GRACE WATCHED THE jury trail back into the courtroom, one behind the other. Her knees started shaking. She pressed her heels to the floor.

It was late morning and already the temperature in the enclosed area was reaching unbearable heights, exacerbated by the growing number of bodies filling the public gallery, all here to witness her fate. Grace could see Ged beside Phil, Lydia at the end. The journalist who'd interviewed her after Jo died was in the row behind, pen poised.

Fatigue pulled Grace in all directions. After days of questioning witnesses, different faces filling the box, the barristers had each taken the floor and delivered their closing speeches to the jury.

Sheldon opened for the prosecution, using sweeping hand gestures as he painted a picture of Grace, the grief-stricken mother, welcoming Faye's friendship, inviting her into her home, being duped with false kindness, until she found out that Faye murdered her daughter and set out to avenge Jo's death. Even now, as she recalled his speech, Grace shrank into herself, willing the world to swallow her up as the eyes of the court flashed back and forth between Sheldon and herself.

It took almost two hours for him to complete his

speech and afterwards, even Grace had to admit his argument was compelling.

The jury sat back wearily as Eleanor Talbot-Deane took over after lunch. The rise and fall of Sheldon's speech had been exhausting, but Eleanor was more measured. She didn't deny the two women had forged a friendship, argued, fallen out. The base of her argument was that Grace couldn't have killed Faye because she had no motive. Grace didn't know who had killed her daughter until after Faye had died.

She picked holes in witness statements, talked about tenuous links with evidence, encouraged people to listen to the experts when they considered who was responsible for Faye's death.

"If, in fact, you do think she was murdered, consider this… We've heard how Faye Campbell lived a volatile lifestyle," Eleanor had said. "She forged love/hate relationships with people and exploited them for her own ends. In such cases a whole stream of people would have been lining up to kill her, all with firm motives intact."

The courtroom hushed as Eleanor sat. Was it enough?

After two days of deliberations the judge had called the jury back in yesterday afternoon. Grace sat with bated breath while the elected foreman stood.

"Do you have a verdict upon which you are all agreed?" the judge had asked.

He looked slightly sheepish as he answered. "No, Your Honour."

The judge had sent them away again for further deliberation, giving them the option of a majority verdict of 11:1 or 10:2. Anxiety clawed at Grace. Her solicitor told her that if the jury couldn't agree on a majority verdict, the case would be adjourned and scheduled for re-trial. The thought of going through another trial, the same evidence unfolding again, was incomprehensible. She couldn't even contemplate returning to prison, back to another cell, her fate left hanging in the balance.

After almost another's day's deliberation the jury was back in court. Would she return home to her family? Sleep beside Phil under their soft duvet tonight? Or would she be sent to a cold cell, in yet another strange prison, with a lumpy mattress, a foam pillow and graffiti scratched into the walls?

The judge folded his hands together and sat forward. "Members of the jury, have you reached a verdict on which the majority of you are agreed?"

The lead juror stood. "Yes, we have."

"And is your verdict, 10:2 or 11:1?"

"10:2"

"On the matter of the murder of Faye Campbell, do you find the defendant, Grace Daniels, guilty or not guilty?"

A brief hesitation. A pin drop could be heard throughout the courtroom. He looked at Grace. "Not guilty."

The room began to sway, slowly at first, then with growing momentum. Grace was aware of the rumble of voices but they sounded far away. A sea of faces swam across her view, superimposing themselves on top of each other. The voices merged together. Heat rose and her head spiralled. Then it all went black.

"How's Alice doing?" Wilson said to Jackman.

After the drama of Grace fainting at the verdict, they'd stayed in the courtroom while one of the jury members, a self-confessed first aider, had attended her. When she came around, surrounded by her family, they left and were now in the foyer, along with the press who'd been ushered out earlier.

"Not bad," Jackman said. Although there was still no concrete evidence of any improvement, his wife had slowly gained weight these past few months and seemed brighter somehow. "The doctors are pleased, talking of scheduling her in for more tests to monitor her progress."

"That's great news."

"Thanks."

Wilson nodded and cast a glance towards the entrance. "Somebody's stalking you," she said, her words accompanied by a gurgle of a laugh.

Jackman could see Carmela beside the entrance, talking to Sheldon. His robes flapped in the breeze that seeped in through the open doors as he waved his arms about animatedly. It seemed his gestures were just as affected outside the courtroom.

Jackman had noticed Carmela arrive that morning. She'd snuck in on the last day of the trial to sit at the back, just before the jury's verdict. Hoping to capture some last minute PR at a positive verdict, no doubt. But any political capital she'd hoped to gain had been dashed and now she would face the inevitable awkward questions from the press that followed an unfavourable result.

Warwickshire had demanded his presence after he'd given evidence during the first week of the trial and he'd had to rely on Wilson for daily updates. But he'd insisted on making the journey these last few days.

"How are things at Leicester?" Jackman said, keen to change the subject.

"Busy. She certainly knows how to play the game," she replied, gesturing to Carmela. "Isn't winning any popularity contests with the team though."

Jackman sighed. "I fear this result won't help you there." They watched as more people streamed out of the room, gathering in the foyer. Grace joined them, surrounded by the bubble of her family. A few members of the press flew to her side, accompanied by camera flashes. Jackman bade his farewell to Wilson and approached Grace, sidestepping her family, excusing himself through to Grace.

She looked up to meet his gaze, clearly unsure of how to react. "This has been a terrible ordeal for you," he said. Voices hushed around him. "I hope you and your family can put this behind you and find some happiness going forward." He extended his hand. She looked at it, hesitated a split second before she grabbed it and thanked him.

More cameras flashed and clicked as he made his way towards the exit. Grace's family had formed a wall around a bewildered Grace who stood beside her solicitor while she prepared to make a speech on behalf of her client.

Carmela was still beside the door. Jackman weaved through the bodies. He was almost at the exit when someone moved in front, blocking his passage. He saw Carmela excuse herself, step towards him. He braced himself for contact. At the last minute, somebody caught her elbow, forcing her to turn back. She rounded to see Artie Black, the journalist. She switched her gaze between Artie and Jackman, barely hiding the irritation in her face. A flood of other reporters surrounded her, blocking her in. She gave Jackman an imploring glance before she turned to the crowd and gave them her attention.

The air was balmy as Jackman stepped out of the court. He slipped off his jacket, loosened his collar as he descended the steps, pausing at the bottom to answer his ringing mobile.

"Hi, Dad!" The buzz of excitement in his daughter's voice caught his attention.

"Hey, Celia. What's up?"

"That job. The research assistant at Swansea University. I got it!"

"That's brilliant!"

"I know. The letter arrived today. I can't believe it!"

It had been lovely to have Celia move back home after she'd graduated earlier this year, but he'd always known it was only temporary. As soon as she'd passed over the threshold she was filling out job applications. But her field of marine biology was niche and, as the months passed and nothing was forthcoming, he could see an air of despondency beginning to settle. The news warmed his insides.

"This calls for a celebration," Jackman said. "Book a table, wherever you want to go. I'll be home in a couple of hours."

"No need, I'm cooking. I've started already. Better make it an hour and a half."

"I'll do my best."

Jackman quickened his step as he ended the call and made his way back to the car. For once, he was really looking forward to the drive back to Stratford.

EPILOGUE

THERE WAS A sense of peace as Grace walked back through her front door later that afternoon. Chloe had shot off straight from the court to pick up Meggy, accompanied by Ged and Lydia. They'd all arranged to meet back at the house later. But, for now, it was just Phil and her. Lucky rushed out to meet them and Grace scooped her up, smothering her with kisses and cuddles. "I've missed you so much!" The dog wriggled as she nuzzled into her fur.

She placed Lucky down and shrugged off her coat, inhaling deeply. There it was, a mixture of fabric softener, air freshener and scented candles. The smell of home. She smiled as she moved into the front room, and jumped. The cheer that greeted her was deafening. Smiling faces popped up from every corner, balloons hung from the ceiling in a myriad of colours, their strings trailing across shoulders, much to Meggy's delight who jumped up and down, clapping her hands. In truth, Grace was craving a quiet cup of tea on the sofa with Phil, Lucky curled around her feet, something she'd dreamed about during those long evenings locked up in her cell. But there were friends here she hadn't seen since Jo's memorial service, old colleagues from the library. They'd gone to so much trouble that she forced on her best smile and circulated, politely thanking everyone for their support. There'd be plenty of time to reacquaint herself with the old place later.

Chloe disappeared and returned to the room offering visitors cake. Meggy traipsed behind her, lifting the edge of her Cinderella dress with her podgy hand. Phil, Ged and Lydia bustled in and out of the kitchen serving drinks and making tea. An hour passed easily, and another. Grace could feel her energy starting to wane, the life trickling out of her smile as fatigue set in, and was relieved when people started to say their goodbyes and the room began to thin.

Grace was just closing the front door to her old work colleagues when she caught a familiar smell. She followed it into the kitchen. Ged looked up from where she was wiping a cloth across the kitchen work surface. "Dropped a glass of red wine," she said. "Can't get rid of the smell." Her face creased into a grimace.

The potent aroma of bleach whisked Grace back to prison where the smell of cheap watery bleach pervaded the floors and landings. She swallowed, forcing herself back to the present, wondering how often over the forthcoming days and weeks certain sounds and smells would transport her back to the regime she was so relieved to leave behind.

"There, I think that's better." Ged moved to the sink and rinsed her cloth. "How are you doing?" she asked. The material squeaked between her fingers as she squeezed it out.

Grace walked around the edge of the kitchen, dragging her fingers across the top of the work surface, the hob, the fridge, soaking it all up. At first glance, nothing had been changed. Nothing moved. The kettle still sat in the corner beside the hob, the microwave on the far wall, flanked by the coffee machine and the food mixer. This was her haven and suddenly she felt a shot of adrenaline pump through her veins, crushing the weariness in its wake. She looked across at Ged and smiled. "It's so good to be home."

"I bet."

She looked at the back door and frowned. The old wooden door with the cat flap had been replaced with a white plastic one, half-glazed. "What happened there?" she asked.

"Phil arranged it, not long after you left," Ged said. "I think he thought it would make you feel more at ease, knowing that Lucky was safe. I'm surprised he didn't mention it?"

Grace thought back to their long discussions during prison visits. Time was precious. Long after he'd left and she'd been escorted back to her cell, she'd lay on her bed and replay their conversation in her mind, holding onto every word, every little reminder of home. She wracked her brains. Maybe he did and she'd pushed it to the corner of her mind with everything else going on. "Where is Lucky?" she asked, her eyes darting around the room. "I had such a lovely welcome from her when I came home. Haven't seen her since."

"No idea. She's probably hiding upstairs, away from the crowds."

Grace peered briefly into the dining room and took to the stairs, relishing the feel of the soft carpet under her feet, taking time to absorb every photo, every memory as she climbed. She hovered beside a photo of Lydia cradling a lemur in a zoo in Spain. This is what she'd missed. Home. Her family. Those little reminders of her memories that clung to the walls. The feeble attempt with the notice board in her cell at Holloway didn't even come close.

Clothes tumbled out of the washing basket as she reached the landing, a pair of trainers were scattered to the side. There was a time when this idle mess would have bothered her. Not anymore. No longer would she moan at Lydia for not changing her bed sheets every Saturday, Phil for leaving his used coffee mugs on the floor beside the sofa. Now these little habits seemed so trivial.

She called out for the dog. When there was no answer she absently wandered into her bedroom and looked around. Her perfumes still lined the dressing table, her hairdryer and brushes beside. The full length mirror dominated the corner of the room. The figures on the digital alarm winked at her as time rolled forward. Sometimes in the cell, she'd close her eyes, do a tour of home in her mind, reminding herself of what it was like, what she would hopefully be returning to one day. She'd followed every photo, every ornament in the downstairs rooms, the landing, the bathroom door with the loose lock that had to be lifted to work properly, her bedroom with the watermark on the ceiling. Her little piece of reality. She sat on the edge of the bed and laid back, her legs dangling over the side, sinking into the duvet, inhaling the smell of the freshly washed linen.

Grace wasn't sure how long she laid there, enjoying the moment, until a faint whimper caught her attention. She hauled herself up, followed it to Jo's old room, pushed open the door and was just about to enter when it came again. It was coming from Lydia's room. She walked back on herself and opened the door.

Lucky gave another whimper as she entered, wagging her tail. "There you are," Grace said. The dog was curled in a tight ball, in no hurry to move. She'd scrunched up the duvet to form a little bed and was nestled inside. Grace sat beside her and stroked her head, absently looking around the room. It hadn't changed much.

A photo on the top of Lydia's dressing table caught her eye. She stood, peered in closer. It was of Jo and Lydia, taken the Christmas before Jo died, sitting at the kitchen table. Grace reached for the frame to take a closer look when she felt something, a small figurine, slip behind the dressing table. Lydia didn't welcome uninvited visitors into her room. Everyone, apart from Lucky, it seemed, respected that. Even on a day like today, she could imagine the scowl on Lydia's face if she found her mother there.

Grace stuck her hand down the back, scrabbling behind the dresser. She reached down, as far as she could. Her fingertips brushed the edge of something, but couldn't quite grasp it. She lifted the pile of clothes off Lydia's chair and pulled it over, climbed up and reached further, pulling out a plastic carrier bag. As she did so, the ornament slipped down further. She couldn't even see it now. She was just wondering whether to push the bag back down and hope that Lydia didn't notice her ornament was missing when she noticed the weight of the bag in her other hand. Inside was a grey jersey top with white lace around the cuffs. She lifted it out. It seemed stuck together. She pulled at the material and gasped. It was encrusted with smears of blood. A leather glove slipped out of the bag and fell onto the carpet, followed by another. Grace's chest tightened. She'd seen that grey top before.

Grace didn't hear the footsteps on the stairs. Didn't notice the face that appeared around the doorframe. She lifted her gaze to face her youngest daughter.

Lydia's eyes ran over the bag, the top, the gloves. She froze. Neither of them spoke.

"It's not what you think," Lydia said eventually.

Grace didn't answer straight away. She stumbled as she climbed off the chair, her mind reeling. "This was Faye's top. She wore it once when she came over. I remember commenting on it, the unusual lace around the cuff."

Lydia looked as though she was deflating in front of her. The anger that she had stored over the months, trickled away. "I didn't think they'd send you away. I thought you'd be allowed to come home until the trial. If I'd known—"

"What? Lydia, what are you talking about?"

"I kept it, brought it back and hid it here after the police had finished the house search. If they convicted you, I knew I'd hand it in. It's bound to have my DNA on it, show that it's me that's responsible. Not you." A strangled sob caught in Lydia's voice. "I'd never have let you go to prison, Mum. You have to believe me. I never meant for any of this…"

Grace's mind raced. Murder. This was murder they were talking about. A cold, calculated act. Surely her own daughter couldn't be capable of that? It couldn't be true.

"I was so angry after what happened with Lucky. And when you came home that day after you'd been to Faye's, I overheard you telling Phil about the signet ring. She didn't even live in Fairfax Road. There were so many lies. I always knew there was something odd about her. I wanted to know why."

Grace frowned. "But you were at Sally's that night." She recalled an argument they'd had about the sleepover. Sally's parents were away; Grace wasn't sure they should be left alone at fifteen. Phil had stepped in and said she should go, it would do her good.

"Sally went to sleep early," Lydia continued. "I slipped out. She only lives a few streets from Western Avenue. I just wanted to see her, to try to understand. I entered from the back, behind the pub." She cleared her throat. "She sneered at me when she answered the door. As if it was all some kind of joke. I followed her into the kitchen, tried to reason with her, asked her why she kept lying. I told her she couldn't do this to our family, especially after everything we'd been through. To stay away from you, from us. Suddenly her face changed. Her eyes were weird. And then…and then she said, 'She barely made a sound when she died. Just a little squeak as the last breath of air squeezed out.' I watched her as she threw her head back and cackled. Don't you see? She was talking about Jo, Mum. I could barely believe it. I was so angry. She killed Jo. She was evil. I just grabbed the knife out of the block on the side, lunged at her. She didn't move, didn't even attempt to fight back. The last thing I remember is her eyes. Those horrible dark eyes, glaring at me as she fell to the floor." Lydia stopped. She drew short, ragged breaths. "I panicked. Grabbed something to wipe my hands. The blood was all over me. I couldn't get it off. Please, Mum, you have to believe me." She was crying now, tear drops spotting the carpet as they dropped off her chin. "I didn't mean for her to die."

Grace was struggling to comprehend her daughter's story. To take it all in. She thought of the witness, saying she had seen someone matching Grace's description visiting the house that evening. It was one of the pieces of evidence in the prosecution case, not significant on its own, but grouped together with others it built to make a convincing case. Another image floated into her mind. Lydia's surprise haircut the day after Faye died. Grace grappled with her thoughts. Before the haircut, Lydia and she had looked alike, with their long fair hair. People had commented on it many a time. She placed her hands over her face.

"Mum. Say something. Please?"

Grace tried. But her mouth was dry.

Shuffles on the landing outside were swiftly followed by a voice. "Granny! I was looking for you." Lydia turned away, wiping the tears from her cheeks as Meggy ran into the room.

It was a moment before Grace recovered herself. She scrambled to put the items back into the bag, push it back behind the dresser, move the chair back into place.

"We were just looking for Lucky," Grace said. Her voice sounded small, alien. "Shall we take her downstairs?"

Grace scooped up the dog and followed Meggy and a silent Lydia downstairs. Ged was in the hallway when they reached the bottom. She stroked Lydia's arm. "You okay? You look tired."

Lydia turned away. "I'm fine."

"It's been a long day," Grace said. "For all of us."

Chloe was stood beside the fireplace. "There you are.

I've got an announcement to make." She waited until they were all in the room. "I'm eight weeks pregnant!"

Grace stared at her aghast. Phil hugged Chloe, shook Matt's hand. Ged was holding Meggy by the waist, swinging her around. Grace stood there. Watching them all. The moment was surreal, almost as if it was happening to someone else. Finally, Grace blinked. "That's wonderful news," she heard herself say to Chloe. "Wonderful."

"Thanks. I've known for almost four weeks. It's been awful not saying anything. But I wanted to wait until today to tell everyone. When we could put all of this behind us and look forward to something. Together."

"More babysitting duties," Ged winked at Grace.

Grace battled to keep her nerves at bay. She dare not look at Lydia who was stood beside her, mute. "This calls for a drink," she said.

As soon as she reached the kitchen, Grace closed the door and rested against it. Thoughts swirled around her head. Her daughter had taken a life. Killers went to prison.

The room started to spin. She grabbed the back of a chair. Gulped slow breaths, in and out.

Phil's face flashed up in her mind. For the first time since his heart attack, she'd seen fresh colour in his face, a renewed vigour in his step this evening. The joy of his family reunited. The bright eyes and smiles around her.

How could she go to the police now, subject her family to more heartache, just when they were putting the nightmare of the last twelve months behind them?

And what about Lydia? She could only begin to imagine the pain, the panic. All that blood. A scene that would haunt her for the rest of her life. Perhaps that was penance enough.

Faye had murdered Jo. Their beautiful Jo.

Grace bent down, retrieved a tray from the cupboard and began loading it with glasses. Slowly, the kernel of an idea began to form in her mind. Tomorrow they'd clear out Jo's room, burn some of her stuff, the clothes that Grace couldn't bear to recycle, in the garden. Jo loved flames, it would be their last tribute to her. The plastic bag would be lost, and everything in it turned to ash.

The door snapped open. Ged's face was full of smiles. "You're taking your time, Grace. Are you sure you haven't forgotten where the glasses are kept?"

The tray of drinks rattled as Grace followed Ged back into the front room and handed them out. Almost immediately, Phil held up his glass, was just about to speak when Grace stepped forward. "Darling, if I may?" she said. Phil stepped back as Grace looked around at the room. "I can't tell you what these last months have been like. Well, I'm sure you know. This nightmare began when Jo was taken from us. She'll never be forgotten. Never be replaced. But I'm hoping that now, together, we can now move forward. Taking the memory of Jo with us. You're my family. I love you all and I'll do anything to protect you." She glanced at Lydia as her tearful eyes raised to meet hers. "I'll be damned if anyone tries to hurt my family again. What's happened has happened. There's nothing we can do to change it. And so, now, with this wonderful news of a little one joining us, I'd like to propose a toast… To new beginnings."

They all raised their glasses. "To new beginnings!"

* * * * *

ACKNOWLEDGEMENTS

I FIND WRITING novel acknowledgements incredibly difficult. Many people are involved in writing a book and I'm always worried I'll miss somebody out. So, if I don't mention your name here, know that I AM heartily grateful for your support. I just have a very poor memory!

My thanks go to the people of Market Harborough for their assistance with location ideas for this novel, most particularly Mike Nichols and Louise Tester. Your knowledge (both historical and present) was extremely useful.

Dennis Hines gave me great insight into prison life and a fabulous tour of the real thing which was invaluable and much appreciated.

I'm grateful to all the staff of Criminal Court Number 6 at Leicester Crown Court, including the judge, court clerk, barristers and ushers who allowed me to sit in on their hearings and who answered my constant questions. It was fascinating to find out how the court system worked and, as usual, any deviations from reality or errors in the book are purely my own.

I was very lucky to have Clare Read, psychologist and dear friend, kindly look over the profile for my antagonist in this novel and provide much needed feedback. I'll always be grateful for your input and reassurance, Clare.

I'd also like to thank all the detectives and retired detectives who've helped with procedural research, most notably Ian Patrick and Rebecca Bradley who are not only fabulous beta readers, but great writers themselves, and wonderful friends.

I spent a memorable day with fellow writer, Elaine Aldred, researching areas in Nottingham and looking at the university parklands. Thanks so much to Elaine for such a wonderful day and for introducing me to Bromley House Library—a truly magical place.

Gratitude goes to Tom Chalmers, Lauren Parsons, Lucy Chamberlain, Allison Zink and Robert Harries at Legend Press for continuing to have faith in my work and believing in the DI Jackman series.

One of the loveliest things about the world of publishing is the support you receive from other authors who become firm friends. I'd like to thank all my fellow writers, especially those who keep me sane—you know who you are!

Since I started my writing journey I have also received wonderful support from book clubs including Anne Cater and all at Book Connectors; Shell Baker and Llainy Swanson at Crime Book Club; Tracy Fenton, Helen Boyce, Sumaira Wilson and Teresa Nikolic at The Book Club (TBC); David Gilchrist at UK Crime Book Club; and Lizzie Hayes at Mystery People. I'm hugely grateful to you all.

Also, to the wonderful book bloggers, without whom the word about new books would never get out. I'd need another book to mention you all individually here, but I'm in awe of your relentless reading and reviewing. You make the book world such a lovely place to be a part of.

I am blessed with support from family and friends who have helped and supported me along the way including David and Lynne Anderson, Derek and Sarah Archer, Colin Williams, Emma Thompson, Stephanie Daniels, Philip Bouch and far too many more to mention—you know who you are.

And, as always, David and Ella, my nearest and dearest, who live with my characters daily and make it possible for me to write. I really appreciate you guys.

Get 4 FREE REWARDS!

We'll send you 2 FREE Books plus 2 FREE Mystery Gifts.

Harlequin Intrigue books are action-packed stories that will keep you on the edge of your seat. Solve the crime and deliver justice at all costs.

FREE Value Over $20

YES! Please send me 2 FREE Harlequin Intrigue novels and my 2 FREE gifts (gifts are worth about $10 retail). After receiving them, if I don't wish to receive any more books, I can return the shipping statement marked "cancel." If I don't cancel, I will receive 6 brand-new novels every month and be billed just $4.99 each for the regular-print edition or $5.99 each for the larger-print edition in the U.S., or $5.74 each for the regular-print edition or $6.49 each for the larger-print edition in Canada. That's a savings of at least 12% off the cover price! It's quite a bargain! Shipping and handling is just 50¢ per book in the U.S. and $1.25 per book in Canada.* I understand that accepting the 2 free books and gifts places me under no obligation to buy anything. I can always return a shipment and cancel at any time. The free books and gifts are mine to keep no matter what I decide.

Choose one: ☐ **Harlequin Intrigue Regular-Print** (182/382 HDN GNXC) ☐ **Harlequin Intrigue Larger-Print** (199/399 HDN GNXC)

Name (please print)

Address   Apt. #

City   State/Province   Zip/Postal Code

Email: Please check this box ☐ if you would like to receive newsletters and promotional emails from Harlequin Enterprises ULC and its affiliates. You can unsubscribe anytime.

Mail to the **Harlequin Reader Service:**
IN U.S.A.: P.O. Box 1341, Buffalo, NY 14240-8531
IN CANADA: P.O. Box 603, Fort Erie, Ontario L2A 5X3

Want to try 2 free books from another series! Call 1-800-873-8635 or visit www.ReaderService.com.

Get 4 FREE REWARDS!

We'll send you 2 FREE Books plus 2 FREE Mystery Gifts.

Love Inspired Suspense books showcase how courage and optimism unite in stories of faith and love in the face of danger.

FREE Value Over **$20**

YES! Please send me 2 FREE Love Inspired Suspense novels and my 2 FREE mystery gifts (gifts are worth about $10 retail). After receiving them, if I don't wish to receive any more books, I can return the shipping statement marked "cancel." If I don't cancel, I will receive 6 brand-new novels every month and be billed just $5.24 each for the regular-print edition or $5.99 each for the larger-print edition in the U.S., or $5.74 each for the regular-print edition or $6.24 each for the larger-print edition in Canada. That's a savings of at least 13% off the cover price. It's quite a bargain! Shipping and handling is just 50¢ per book in the U.S. and $1.25 per book in Canada.* I understand that accepting the 2 free books and gifts places me under no obligation to buy anything. I can always return a shipment and cancel at any time. The free books and gifts are mine to keep no matter what I decide.

Choose one:
☐ **Love Inspired Suspense Regular-Print** (153/353 IDN GNWN)

☐ **Love Inspired Suspense Larger-Print** (107/307 IDN GNWN)

Name (please print)

Address   Apt. #

City   State/Province   Zip/Postal Code

Email: Please check this box ☐ if you would like to receive newsletters and promotional emails from Harlequin Enterprises ULC and its affiliates. You can unsubscribe anytime.

Mail to the Harlequin Reader Service:
IN U.S.A.: P.O. Box 1341, Buffalo, NY 14240-8531
IN CANADA: P.O. Box 603, Fort Erie, Ontario L2A 5X3

Want to try 2 free books from another series? Call 1-800-873-8635 or visit www.ReaderService.com.

LIS21R

Visit
ReaderService.com
Today!

As a valued member of the Harlequin Reader Service, you'll find these benefits and more at ReaderService.com:

- Try 2 free books from any series
- Access risk-free special offers
- View your account history & manage payments
- Browse the latest Bonus Bucks catalog